Dracula and the Eastern Question

Dracula and the Eastern Question

British and French Vampire Narratives of the Nineteenth-Century Near East

Matthew Gibson

First published 2006 by
PALGRAVE MACMILLAN
Houndmills, Basingstoke, Hampshire RG21 6XS and
175 Fifth Avenue, New York, N.Y. 10010
Companies and representatives throughout the world.

PALGRAVE MACMILLAN is the global academic imprint of the Palgrave
Macmillan division of St. Martin's Press, LLC and of Palgrave Macmillan Ltd.
Macmillan® is a registered trademark in the United States, United Kingdom
and other countries. Palgrave is a registered trademark in the European
Union and other countries.

ISBN-13: 978–1–4039–9477–6 hardback
ISBN-10: 1–4039–9477–3 hardback

This book is printed on paper suitable for recycling and made from fully
managed and sustained forest sources.

A catalogue record for this book is available from the British Library.

A catalog record for this book is available from the Library of Congress.

10 9 8 7 6 5 4 3 2 1
15 14 13 12 11 10 09 08 07 06

Printed and bound in Great Britain by
Antony Rowe Ltd, Chippenham and Eastbourne

Contents

List of Maps

Acknowledgements

I would like to extend my thanks to Dr Terry Hale of Hull University and Dr Diane Mason of Bath Spa University College for their willingness to share vital information with me, and would also like to express my gratitude to the University of Surrey for having provided research money which allowed me to undertake valuable trips to the Public Records Office of Northern Ireland in Belfast and to the Bibliothèque Nationale de France (François Mitterand) in Paris. In particular, I would like to thank the staff at the Public Records Office of Northern Ireland, Leeds University Library and Mrs Virginia Murray, curator of the John Murray Archive, for their generous help while conducting my research. I should also like to extend a very warm thank-you to my patient map-maker, Vaughan Allen.

The book is dedicated to the memory of my parents Hugh Ian and Sheila June Gibson.

The author and publisher would like to thank the following for permission to reproduce copyrighted material.

An extract of a letter by Jules Verne to his father. 'La Correspondance Familiale de Jules Verne', Lettre 159 de Jules Verne à son père, le 'lundi [novembre (?)] 1870', in *Jules Verne* (Lyons: La Manufacture, 1988), p. 454 is reproduced by permission of Olivier Dumas.

An extract from John Polidori's letter to Lord Byron, 11 January 1817 by permission of John Murray Archive.

An extract from John Polidori's letter to Gaetano Polidori, Dec 1813 (Angeli-Dennis collection, box 31, folder 5) by permission of University of British Columbia Library, Rare Books and Special Collections.

Extracts from letters by Anthony Hope Hawkins to Bram Stoker (13 June 1897; 27 Jan 1898; 28 May 1901) by permission of A.P. Watt Ltd on behalf of John Hope Hawkins.

Every effort has been made to trace all the copyright holders, but if any have been inadvertently overlooked the publishers will be pleased to make the necessary arrangement at the first opportunity.

Note on Translations

All translations from French and Italian are by the author. The attempt has been in most cases to prioritise exactitude over stylistic felicity. In nearly all cases (except where it would prove too cumbersome or obvious) I have provided notes reproducing the original text or have placed the original French beneath the English text.

Introduction

In his amusing travel book of 1875, the mysteriously initialled R.H.R describes how he decided to relax after what he considered to have been one of the best meals of his life at the Russian consulate in Cattaro, Dalmatia: 'I got another chair, and stretched my legs on it; the natives stared – no Oriental ever thinks of stretching his legs – the acme of comfort for him is to tuck them under him.'[1] This distinction between an 'Oriental' and a Western custom is designed to show the exotic nature of his location – what can be more exotic than a difference of custom in a function which for most of us seems natural, not cultural? – but also to define the area in which the traveller finds himself: it is a part of the Orient, and he is amongst Orientals. Few people today would define the Dalmatian coast (now southern Croatia and Montenegro) as 'Oriental', although they would not hesitate, I should think, to describe it as 'Balkan', and a part of 'Eastern Europe'.

However, the idea of the South Eastern European countries of the Balkans as being not merely Eastern (in the sense of a Slavic Eastern Europe to which, as Larry Wolff has shown,[2] they have also variously been perceived as belonging since Venetian times) but 'Oriental' (i.e., part of the East that not does include North Eastern Europe and Russia, and is mainly non-Christian) is a common one throughout the nineteenth century and up until the first Balkan war. In *Eothen* (1835), Alexander Kinglake declared that having left Austro-Hungarian Semlin for Turkish-occupied Belgrade 'I had come, as it were, to the end of this wheel-going Europe, and now my eyes would see the splendour and Havoc of the East.'[3] Europe ends at Belgrade for Kinglake, although in his travels to Constantinople he is almost oblivious of the Christian Slavs and interested only in the Turks, even though he would have travelled through Southern Serbia, an area by then independent of Ottoman rule. H. Charles Woods,

1

in his long and ominous warning *The Danger Zone of Europe: Changes and Problems in the Near East* (1911), defines the Near East as the Balkan Peninsular and Asia Minor, and justifies a decision to include chapters on the history of Turkey itself only because 'as Asia Minor is ruled by and is dependent upon the Government of Constantinople, the conditions actually prevailing in this part of the Ottoman Empire actually influence the fate of European Turkey, and thus affect the question as to whether or not the Balkan Peninsula is "the Danger Zone of Europe" '.[4] Most strikingly, the important London monthly magazine, *The Near East* included articles on Bosnia (at the time under Austrian rule, but titularly part of the Ottoman Empire), Montenegro and Serbia along with reports from Yemen and Morocco. Thus, although classifactions of the Orient always appear to have been nebulous, and the identity of South Eastern Europe – including on occasions some parts of what we might now term 'Middle Europe', like Hungary – was somewhat 'overdetermined' in Western eyes (as 'Eastern Europe', 'the Balkans', 'the East', 'not Europe' and 'le Monde Slave'), the area was nevertheless characterised as belonging to an 'Oriental' East and 'The Near East' up until the first Balkan War of 1912. In the nineteenth century these particular regions of the Near East form the area around which politicians framed 'the Eastern Question': namely, the problem of how to resolve what to do with them once, as appeared inevitable, the Ottoman Empire would fall.[5] Thanks to British interference, as we shall see, this inevitability was postponed for a very long time. We shall also see that the British and French vampire story is a fertile means of political commentary upon the Eastern Question.

Maria Todorova has classified this area as being a separate one to the Oriental East in the minds and vision of eighteenth- and nineteenth-century Western Europeans and Americans, called either 'the Balkans' or 'Haemus'.[6] Unlike the 'Orientalism' of Said, she understands the concept of 'Balkanism' as 'being a discourse about an imputed ambiguity' (Todorova, p. 16). Her understanding of Balkanism as being a Western means of representing South Eastern Europe results from both her objection to the simplistic and ideally reconstituted binary of Edward Said's concept of 'Orientalism', and from her own detailed study of the writings about the region by travellers and diplomats from many different countries over five centuries. She observes that Said has allowed the Ottoman Orient to be confused with the Arab Orient (p. 12), and furthermore that his acceptance of the Foucauldian idea of 'discourse' over and above examining the history of representations more rigorously (p. 9), has meant that there is no space for other contradictory discourses within this Gramscian 'hegemony' – a hegemony which Said has perhaps invented more than he has described.

Although I accept that Todorova's understanding of the Balkans as 'an imputed ambiguity' of Eastern and Western traditions over what is an 'Ottomanised' region of Europe is true, I do not accept that we cannot in some ways see the region as being part of the Old Near East, and thus as 'Oriental'. This is because it strikes me that the Near East, as both a cultural and a political concept (i.e., the area which had been or was still under Ottoman power) does not negate the narrower cultural construct of the Balkans. For a nineteenth-century Englishman the Levant and the Gulf are distinct parts of the Near East, just as is French North Africa: all were, in different ways and to varying degrees, engaged with an Islamic system of government, past or still current, and were crucially either involved in trade routes with India, or else with preventing Russia or Austria-Hungary from spreading their wings and destroying those trade routes. They are all separate regions and yet are joined by history, geographical proximity and social organisation, and are also, in a political sense, an important factor in the perpetuation of Britain's and France's economic health. All are therefore capable at different times and by different factions as being seen as part of 'The Near East', something which cannot be said of the Balkan nations *after* 1912, when Turks left the region *en masse*, and the different peoples tried to solidify themselves as European nation states, away from the aegis of either Austria or the Ottoman Empire.

Where I thoroughly agree with Todorova is that Said has been woefully lacking in attempting to define 'Orientalism' without looking at British and French attitudes to the Turks: the people whom, as she is quick to point out, did control most of what the British and French considered to be the Near East for some six centuries ([Todorova, p. 12] up until the twentieth, in many areas), as opposed to the few decades in which Britain controlled her old Near Eastern (modern Middle Eastern) colonies. Following from Todorova's own critique of Said's omissions and inability to align ideological positions with factual reality, three major objections to Said's ideas must be addressed before we can begin to observe political attitudes to the Eastern Question in a more objective and plural light, and as they are represented in the vampire narrative.

The first is that Orientalism was a hegemonic discourse, which, in Said's view, perfused all areas of British and French attitudes to the Orient, and created the boundaries for knowledge about an area that contained a complexity ignored by the Europeans.[7] Maria Todorova's own examinations of the accounts of British travellers like David Urquhart and Jonathan Morritt demonstrate that attitudes towards

Ottoman rulers, and indeed Ottoman customs, were often favourable in contrast to the contempt felt for the Greek or Slavic peasants under their control.[8] Thus the idea of a hegemonic discourse seeing 'Orientals' as 'irrational, depraved (fallen), childlike "different"' as opposed to the European who is 'rational, virtuous, mature, "normal"' (p. 40), which Said discerns everywhere in the discourse he understands as 'Orientalism', (Said, p. 51), in all its areas of knowledge, is grossly simplistic since English aristocrats who discerned the nobility of Turks on their travels through Roumelia invert this binary entirely.[9]

A second contention of Said is that this discourse was a justification for rule and imperialism. 'To say simply that Orientalism was a rational-isation of colonial rule', he writes, 'is to ignore the extent to which colonial rule was justified in advance by Orientalism.' (Said, p. 39). As well as arguing that Orientalism was an inclusive discourse which equated knowledge with power and created both the object of knowledge and the method of knowing, Said argued that it was a means of justifying control: by defining Orientals as irrational and childlike, Orientalist scholars were constructing an object of knowledge which justified the actions of colonisers from Napoleon to Lord Balfour with the right to impose their rule. This movement from the ideal to the real, from discourse to actuality, is characterised as follows:

> at the outset one can say that so far as the West was concerned during the nineteenth century and twentieth centuries, an assumption had been made that the Orient and everything in it was, if not patently inferior to, then in need of corrective study by the West. The Orient was viewed as if framed by the classroom, the criminal court, the prison, the illustrated manual. Orientalism, then, is knowledge of the Orient that places things Oriental in class, court, prison, or manual for scrutiny, study, judgement, discipline, or governing. (pp. 40–1)

The body of knowledge, Orientalism, seeps to the justification of rule and rule itself, further reinforcing Said idea that the discourse was hegemenonic and transcended civil societies (schools, families, clubs, newspapers etc, which disseminate ideology) and political societies (law courts, governments, police forces, think-tanks etc, which make and implement policies).

However, such a claim needs a wider proof. If Orientalism is a hegemonic discourse held by the British and French about the Orient in relation to Europe, and if it justifies and helps to enforce power over it, then that should be manifest throughout its history. What one finds puzzling on leaving *Orientalism* is that at no point in the book does Edward Said mention Sir Stratford Canning. Canning was Britain's intermittent ambassador to the Ottoman Empire from 1809–61, and a Turcophile,[10] who saved the Turks from extinction in 1812 when he helped them broke the Treaty of Bucharest against the advancing Russians,[11] and who was an instrumental support to Turkish concerns during the Crimean war. Even at the time of the Russo-Turkish war (1876–78) he was arguing that the Turks, despite the misrule in their region, should be supported by Britain in the continued possession of their Balkan and Central Asian provinces as a bulwark against Russia. Nor do we find any reference in *Orientalism* to the Treaty of Berlin (1878), in which Disraeli, with French support, ensured that large parts of the Balkans were returned to the Ottoman Sultan, Abdul Hamid II, in order to make sure that the Russians could not nestle in Roumelia and threaten the Mediterranean. Just as British aristocrats like Morritt and Urquhart saw the nobility of the Turks as being traduced by the barbarism of their European subjects, and found much to admire in Turkish rulers (Todorova, p. 94), so also politicians supported an Islamic oriental state against the interests of Christian Europeans, when they saw that it was in their own interests to do so.

A final objection is to Said's use of this Gramscian idea of hegemony between civil and political societies: that all areas of society, whilst appearing to be independent and autonomous, are in fact complicit in the same hegemony, and that the political societies of imperial nations 'impart to their civil societies a sense of urgency' which interferes with the civil societies and circumscribes their knowledge (p. 11). While I do not wish to attack Gramsci's excellent and useful distinctions per se, I believe that we can see a very real fissure between different ideas about Orientals (which as Todorova has shown are in any case extremely varied) and the crudely self-interested decisions made at treaties by politicians and the justifications that they give. While there may, I do not deny, be relations between the ideas prevalent in a 'free' society and the secret wishes of a government, at moments of crisis political societies may verge very widely from the ideas of civil societies. This is no more true than in Disraeli's open support for Turkey at the Treaty of Berlin, justified by his famous 'Peace with Honour' speech, which led to the British electorate punishing him in 1880: areas of the civil society clearly differed with him as regards the British government's behaviour in the Near East, as the marvellous Tenniel cartoons of the time also demonstrate. Similarly, his own absorption in the civil societies (which, as we can see in the accounts of men like George Stoker, Urquhart and Morrit, were not part of a 'hegemony' at all), that he reflects to some extent in his novel *Tancred* (where Orientals are indeed portrayed in keeping with certain negative stereotypes) clearly did not affect his policy-making at the Treaty of Berlin: pure commercial self-interest did instead. As Linda Colley has shown, while Said may be justified in 'investigating the minds and myths of empire makers, and not just their weaponry and economic muscle', nevertheless 'material factors did matter, and were bound to matter' (Colley, p. 132). This is an extremely important point since, as shall be shown with regard to *Dracula*, the vampire narrative with Near Eastern setting can encode 'Orientalist' assumptions about a society while also suggesting a political solution which refutes entirely the idea that Oriental power should be diminished; the cultural and political meanings diverging from each other widely.

In post-Napoleonic Europe, British and French policy towards the Near East and attitudes to the Eastern Question, are in constant flux. At a representational level this also has an effect, as Ottoman and Balkan peoples are frequently recast according to different stereotypes in different media. Thus one must observe Britain's and France's relations with the Near East in terms of their material and wider economic interest, rather than fall into the trap of hegemony, to understand that representations of Orientals in Britain and France are plural, varied, and reactive to real situations involving other imperial powers like Russia and Germany, rather than being a simplistic, self-perpetuating binary.

In dealing with how vampire stories set in the old Near East actually confront the Eastern Question, the intention here is to look at literature in the light of genuine political events, balancing sections of literary analysis, biography, and detailed historical context. The assumption in each case is that the story is connected to a referential context upon which the author is either commenting codedly, or is discussing in ways which his unconscious prejudices determine. While in certain cases stock stereotypes about the Orient are used for political reasons (as is the case in the work of Le Fanu), other contradictory stereotypes (e.g., the Turks as noble and civilised rulers; the Venetians as despotic and medieval) also raise their head, making absolute patterns of consistency hard to discern. It is thus only through analysing the concrete political circumstances against which they were written that we can be confident of why particular representations arise.

Interpretations of the vampire

The vampire, as literary phenomenon, has its origins in Near Eastern traditions, and its fame in the West is almost entirely attributable to the

collection of accounts made by Dom Calmet for his *Treatise on R(*
(1746). Hence it has a local habitation and a name, although it
formations into the literary vampire depend upon attitudes in th
rather than in the region from which the superstition itself hails.

To begin with, the vampire as a *literary* theme has its precursor in the
Graveyard Poetry which induced both terror and horror in the hearts of
readers more used to (and bored by) the rationalism of Augustan literature. It is one of several Gothic and Romantic themes that caused the
terror mingled with delight that Burke, in his famous philosophical
essay, considered the essence of the sublime in taste.[12] David Punter sees
the vampire as being, like the undead Wanderer, a specific Romantic
Gothic type in its literary manifestation, and understands it politically
as being a bourgeois anxiety about the resurgence of the old aristocratic
class which the newly dominant would like to suppress.[13] Similarly,
Judith Barbour understands the vampire story as being the 'aerial battle
of locked divinities'[14] between the old master and his suffering servant,
and the result of a moment when the old regime returned after the
restoration of the Bourbon dynasty in 1815.

Perhaps in keeping with this notion of struggle with the past, many
critics have seen the original vampire stories as proof of the primal
horde theory of Freud, in which the father harasses the sons and the
sons have to combine in order finally to overcome the father. James
Twitchell records how in Calmet vampires are portrayed as preying
upon their own, and how the 'dhampire', who eventually stakes the
vampire through the heart, is often a younger, sonlike figure.[15] In later
literary adaptations of the vampire, as Leatherdale notes, the vampires'
sucking blood from their own may be seen as the sublimation of an
incest anxiety (a potential in both *Carmilla* and *Dracula*) as well as a
possible sublimation of homosexual anxieties.[16] The female vampire can
also be seen as representing male fears about the new woman
(Leatherdale, pp. 145–8). Thus the superstition of the vampire along
with its sucking blood, constant resurgence as living dead and nocturnal
life-style, presents a plethora of political and sexual meanings.

More recently, the concept of vampirism has been understood as
signifying degeneration from the unknown, in particular from the racial
'other' of Eastern Europe.[17] Indeed, the vampire has been seen as the
metaphoric representation of Eastern Europe's unresolved racial mixture.
Stephen D. Arata has discerned in it the British public's fear of reverse
colonisation, thus constituting an anxiety caused by guilt at their
own colonialism.[18] However, as William Hughes has pointed out, the
post-colonial Gothic with regard to Eastern Europe must be treated with

some caution, given that the British possessed no colonies there,[19] the closest they came to this being in the novels of Anthony Hope!

I would agree that the Eastern European setting for the vampire is important, but not in the way that Arata believes. To see *Dracula* as a representation of the racial other, a repository of anxieties by a colonial elite who harbour a reverse Orientalism, or Occidentalism, about the West which he invades (*Victorian Studies*, 33: 621–45, at 634), is too imprecise. Less than simply a fear of reverse colonialism from an all purpose Oriental 'Other', it is in fact a very detailed and complex reaction to a recent set of events in the Balkans, in particular the Treaty of Berlin and Russian interference. In fact all of the writers to be discussed – Polidori, Le Fanu, Stoker, Nodier, Mérimée and Verne – were dependent upon scholarship and research into the politics of the region: all were reacting against recent events as opposed to general, over-arching discourses, and in several cases were trying to capitalise upon topicality. Furthermore, in Le Fanu's and Stoker's case that topicality is less to do with their Irishness, as many recent critics have believed, than it is with a more wholly British attitude to the area in which their tales are set – although this is not to deny that the Irish political situation could not in addition affect their attitude towards it.

Thus the time is ripe for reconsidering vampire narratives set in the Balkans and Near East as being discussions of the region itself.

Political allegory

A question arises as to how these works are capable of 'encoding' political attitudes to the Near East in relation to their authors' home countries. Whether the attitudes are unconscious or intended is a question that will immediately strike the reader. My contention is that in the majority of cases, the vampire narrative set in the Near East is a deliberate and coded practice, which makes use of either careful dating, or else literary and contemporary allusion, to embed certain political ideas. If one takes into account that the very first of these narratives, John Polidori's *The Vampire*, was written as a careful indication of Polidori's own relation with Lord Byron, and that he takes Lord Byron's own rhetoric and inverts its meaning (he was, after all, rewriting Byron's *Fragment*, but adding his own emphasis), then it does not seem too fanciful to see later aristocratic vampire stories as using both the myth and the symbolism to suggest other topical ideas not present at a literal level.

Furthermore, in Polidori's case the rejection was political as well as personal, expressing ideas that would not have been fashionable at the time amongst circles in which he moved (particularly the philhellene aristocrats who would have read his story). Likewise Le Fanu's *Carmilla* also presents quite extreme attitudes to topical politics in Austria-Hungary, using vampirism as symbolism. For Mérimée too the vampire is used in various ways both to condemn the earlier colonisations of Dalmatia, but also to praise the Napoleonic project, while the work of Verne uses literary allusion to create metaphorical resonance beyond the literal meaning of the work in a comment upon the political situation in Transylvania. In all cases the vampire has an allegorical, political meaning that is created either through intertext (as in the case of Polidori and Verne), or else through relation to recent events (as in Le Fanu's, Stoker's and Mérimée's work), and in each case it represents an extreme or marginal position that was more comfortably suggested than openly avowed.

The way in which such allegory works can best be explained through reference to the work of two literary theorists who have looked at the novel, Paul de Man and Fredric Jameson. de Man understood the figures of literary works as frequently imposing 'allegories of reading' upon the reader by using metaphor in order to prioritise certain passages, and thus certain readings, over others. Hence he saw the interpretation of texts as dependent upon certain strategies understood by the reader and facilitated by the text itself. These strategies depended upon the notion that reading was a kind of 'getting inside' the text, which 'unite[s] outer meaning with inner understanding, action with reflection, into one single totality',[20] as opposed to the more 'external' mode of reading the text by its literal relation to a concept. Our reading is organised by assumptions (de Man, p. 15), which prioritise rhetoric over grammar, and metaphor over metonymy, allowing the reader to think that they are unravelling the mystery of the text at certain key points. Thus metaphorical passages were themselves metaphors of the process of reading, involving, as they do, a privileged sense of moving within.

Such priority, often accepted by semioticians without question, involves the assumption of a controlling, metaphysical presence to the text, whose removal allows immediate conflicts here. By using deconstructive techniques, de Man shows that this allegory of reading can easily be inverted, and the text can become a site of contradiction. In particular, he shows how a passage from Proust's *A la Recherche du Temps Perdu* presents Swann's act of reading as a cool antidote to the heat of the exterior, but most importantly uses metaphor to express its superiority through the figure 'torrent d'activité' (p. 66) as though reading replaces the motion of heat with the fast motion of cool water, and also invites us to prioritise the passage. However, as de Man explains, the phrase 'torrent d'activité' has become a dead metaphor, to the extent that it is more like a literal figure for physical exertion which causes heat, thus implying, through a more deconstructive reading, that there has been no replacement of heat with coolness at all, nor any figural superiority of one activity over another. An interpretation which divorces self-presence from the text, and exposes 'reading' to a plethora of new figural interpretations, presents such contradictions as being a central element of the text itself.

In the following analyses there are, needless to say, fundamental differences to de Man's study. To begin with, all of these readings attempt to locate the political symbolism either within the intention or, at the very least, within the latent and historically demonstrable prejudices of the author, rather than to see the text purely as an autotelic but self-contradictory plane. The lesson of de Man is nevertheless a useful one, not least because he shows how figures can be simultaneously metonymical and metaphorical, and also contradict each other in a way designed to refute the 'organic' theory implicit to much humanist and common sense criticsm. However, where he invariably sees metonymy as undercutting metaphor, in the vampire novel set in the Near East we shall see the opposite: implicit metaphor, constructed through intertext or allusion, undercutting the literal naming of the narrator, and allowing reactionary or extreme views to refute the surface meaning. Whereas de Man sees the text as deconstructing itself through this ludic combat between two modes of representation, the present study discerns instead a combat between acceptable expression and implicit feeling, or on occasions conscious intention and subconscious anxieties which are located both within history and the personal predilections of the authors.

This brings us to Jameson's understanding of allegory (not of reading, but of allegory itself) as an element in the developmental stages of fiction, and as thus being an important aspect of Third World literature. According to Jameson, in contradistinction to the literature of the high capitalist West, literature of the Third World is inescapably public, and thus national allegory rather than a literal exploration of individual character.[21] For him, this means that stories in the Third World are 'figural' rather than 'literal' (Jameson, p. 321), and that their characters take on the identities of entire communities. He recognises this process as being 'tribal' rather than individual, and formed by the peculiar sense of class and national identity which is entirely at odds with the construction of identity among the liberal bourgeoisie of the West:

> Third-world texts, even those which are seemingly private and invested with a properly libidinal dynamic – necessarily project a

political dimension in the form of national allegory: *the story of the private individual destiny is always an allegory of the embattled situation of the public third-world culture and society.* (p. 320)

He further insists that, unlike in Western conceptions of allegory, meaning can shift in a way that does not adhere to the classical unities expected by pedantic critics of the developed nations (p. 324), and that a work can have more than one allegorical meaning.

Jameson's theory of national allegory finds its absolute inverse in the vampire tale with Near Eastern setting. To understand this one must first take into account that allegory, a form which he says was discredited in the Romantic era in the West (p. 324), is initially a result of popular myths and superstitions becoming more philosophically understood once a belief in their literal reality begins to wane (as in Spenser's *Fairie Queene* or *The Romance of the Rose*: works which take once literal beliefs like the existence of monsters or a material paradise and convert them into the representation of metaphysical or abstract ideas). The accounts originally collected by Calmet and adapted by Byron, Polidori, Le Fanu, Mérimée and others are themselves examples of a set of tribal beliefs (although filtered entirely through Western media) which are ripe for a political or social explanation once the superstition fades (or rather, when exposed to the West, where they are purely superstitions). At that point the superstition can become either a metaphor for the primitiveness of the society or else an allegory of a political situation.

In this sense the vampire novel represents the conversion of an East European or Near Eastern superstition to a West European political comment about East European society. The superstition is filtered through Western ideas – and also the forms of literary representation, namely the bourgeois novel – to create Gothic: a genre which already depends upon a tension between naturalism and the supernatural, and reason and terror, and so involves a contradiciton of modes of representation. Thus, whereas in Jameson's understanding of Third World narrative the literal and the allegorical are seamlessly combined in the same story, in the Western vampire novel there is normally a contradiction between the open narration (which is usually naturalistic in the initial expectations it provokes), and the political opinions presented by its embedded allegory once the shock of the supernatural has been accepted, in keeping with the collision between two types of literature (naturalism and allegory) and two political opinions (open liberalism and embedded conservatism). In this way the national allegory of the tribe's folk beliefs and continuing superstitions have become part of the Western observer's rhetoric of either denunciation or of sympathy.

It is partly for this reason that I have chosen to steer from attributing recent post-colonial theory to these works. Not only are the political opinions towards the Balkans of these works for the most part far from colonial in aspiration, but the two main strands of post-colonial criticism – the binarism of Said which observes Western texts discerning the Orient as racial other, and the more complex Bhabba notion of the 'hybrid', in which the narrative work of the Third World culture adopts the language of the aggressor in order to articulate its local content,[22] – simply do not apply. The first method has been rejected for reasons already given, namely the need to observe the real circumstances against which texts are written and understand its complexities. The reason for rejecting the second is also obvious, since the text envelops Near Eastern superstitions into a Western articulation that gives the Near Eastern myth no true voice of its own, and whose 'otherness' is in fact controlled by already existent Gothic traditions. There is no space for hybridity of any kind (with the exception of Mérimée, whose *La Guzla* is a more complex work entirely, as shall be shown), especially since the texts which informed the writers of the superstition (whether Fortis, Calmet, Wagener or Emily Gerard) were all Western, and for the most part were not actually reliable.

Thus in the Near Eastern vampire story the Western novel envelops the already modified superstition with its own narrative techniques for presenting character and material realism, and in doing so exploits the superstition for psychological terror while allowing its supernatural elements to become allegory. The allegory or metaphor to which it turns the vampire, in its relation to the culture it either threatens or is threatened by (which has the dominant voice), is also rarely one which argues for British or French colonialism: the political purpose of the vampire figure, while always directed towards the culture from which it is presumed to have come, and which is presumed to have originally articulated it, is too varied to admit of a simple political relation from West to East. As was said above, in relation to the ideas of Edward Said, in each case its meaning can only be understood by research into the exact historical context alone.

Paul Féval

One obvious omission from this work is the early vampire stories of Paul Féval, the Feuilletonier who wrote three vampire novels with an Near Eastern basis, *La Vampire* (1856), *Les Chevaliers Ténèbreux* (1860), and *La Ville-Vampire* (1875), which, like the historical novel, weave in private events around known public figures. The reason for this exclusion is that they relate vampirism to the political history of France as a means of commenting upon France's domestic problems rather than upon the Near East itself. Nevertheless, they deserve to be mentioned briefly, not simply due to their merits, but because explaining why they have been excluded will also define the scope of this project, and the similarities between the texts to be considered.

The first novel relates the story of a beautiful Hungarian, female vampire, Addhéma, who has been causing bodies to be thrown down the river Seine in the Spring of 1804, just before the first consul declares himself Emperor and as the Breton, Georges Cadoudal, is plotting to assasinate him.[23] The second, set some years later during the Bourbon dynasty, deals with two Hungarian vampires (really East End villains), who journey round Europe robbing and pillaging the aristocracy before turning up at the palace of the Archbishop of Paris. In both novels the vampire has a Near Eastern origin, and a partial Near Eastern setting. In the first, Addhéma has her tomb in an islet in the Save in Southern Hungary (now Northern Serbia) near to Semlin and Szeged. She is really a Bulgarian who came and settled in the region, indicating an even closer relation to the Ottomans ([Féval, *La Vampire*, 101] at the time of the 1804 setting, this bordered upon what was simply European Turkey-land, as Southern Serbia was a full part of the Ottoman Empire until 1814). Her origins are thus on the edge of the Ottoman Orient, and the history and geography of that region is described as faithfully as is the history of revolutionary France. In *Le Chevalier Ténèbre*, the tomb of the chevaliers is also described as being near Szeged in Southern Hungary, and is within sights of Belgrade.[24] The exotic location, in these political and historical vampire novels, would seem to be important.

However, what is most striking in both cases is that the political allegory of vampirism, whilst taken from the Near East, applies entirely to domestic French situations. In both cases there are two offered resolutions, one naturalistic, one supernatural: one related to brigandry the other to vampirism proper, making the allegory very obvious, and drawing upon Voltaire's joke in *Dictionnaire philosophique* that although Paris and London did not appear to have vampires like the Serbs, the Hungarians and the Poles, they in fact did in the form of bankers and businessmen.[25] In both cases the vampire is related to corruption and greed resurging in French society, with the Near Eastern origin being a convenient smokescreen for an author writing during a time of intense censorship, the Second Empire of Napoleon III (1851–70), nephew of Napoleon I.[26] In relating vampirism to brigandage in *La Vampire*, Féval is commenting on the bourgeois greed that was to plague France from the first Empire on, resurfacing after the 1830 revolution and the accession of King Louis-Phillipe (Orléans) and the bourgeois constitution. In *Le Chevalier Ténèbre*, Féval shows class warfare, and the resurgence of greed and kleptocracy during the restoration era, since the vampires, whose multiplicity of ethnic origins only serves to negate their importance as specific national types, represent the danger the aristocracy faced from the lower orders.[27]

Thus, regardless of his actual political position, Féval uses the vampire story of the Near East as an allegory of political corruption in the context of genuine history, weaving the Gothic elements in and around real events and people in France, and furthermore to symbolise domestic situations (the rising bourgeoisie under Napoleon; the reemergence of class war under the Bourbons), so that allegorically the vampires constitute subversive comments about the realities of the past, and of the present under Napoleon III's dictatorship. Here, therefore, the vampire superstition is not only used to create a submerged national allegory, but is also disguised as a comment on the East itself, in an attempt to obfuscate the internal as external and avoid the attentions of the authorities. The concealment is, in other words, affected by external censorship.

The same cannot be said of Polidori, Le Fanu, Stoker, Verne, and even Mérimée. Their use of a Near Eastern superstition is a comment upon the Near East in relation to their own countries, and one concealed by self-censorship rather than the curtailment of the state. The vampire is thus a national allegory of the 'other', but one which is against the attitudes of the time, or the personae which the authors would otherwise like to promote. However, in keeping with the complexity and variety of the representations of the Near East, that national allegory is continually changing, continually reappropriating both praise and blame, as the following chapters shall show.

1
Polidori's *The Vampyre* and the Dangers of Philhellenism to Italian Liberation

It has been argued that Polidori's *The Vampyre* is something of a short story 'à-clef'. Lighting on the similarities between Ruthven's character and that of Lord Byron, and the clash of personalities between the two which erupted while Polidori was staying with Byron as his physician, critics have understandably regarded Aubrey, the young accomplice of Ruthven on his disgraceful travels through Belgium, Italy and Greece, as a projection of Polidori's own suffering self, and Ruthven as his famous patient: an idea supported by the fact that Ruthven was the name Lady Caroline Lamb had already awarded the Byron figure in her own very obvious roman-à-clef, *Glenarvon*.[1] It is also clearly an interesting hypothesis that the first aristocratic vampire in literature was really a means of poking fun at the dual nature of a famous poet and public personality. The Greek setting for the tale has been considered by one critic in particular as simply an example of the extent to which Polidori was influenced by his benefactor-cum-rival.[2]

More recent criticism of the work has turned towards investigating the relevance of this Greek setting. Ken Gelder points out that the story iro- nises Byron's *The Giaour* and later *Fragment* and argues that in it high society preys upon the Greek peasants, in what Gelder suggests is an attack on the upper classes rather than a bold comment on the politics of Greece per se: 'Polidori's story seems to suggest that "society" itself is vampirish; its aristocratic representatives prey upon the people wherever they go.'[3]

Despite this, Gelder shows that the tale deals with the reality of Greece in a way which Byron himself did not, since while declaiming its degen- eracy, Byron did not attempt to draw realistic portrayals of contemporary Greek society. What makes Polidori's work so different from previous vampire stories, claims Gelder, is not only that he gives his vampire the attributes of the aristocrat when poking fun at Byron, but also that he couches the myth of the vampire very much in terms of the superstitions of the country folk of Greece. Defending Polidori against Skarda's view that the tale is inferior to Byron's, Gelder argues that Polidori writes a story which is aimed more at the general public, but which also draws attention to the legitimacy of this literature by insisting on the greater beauty of popular myth over classical art, through a passage which acts almost as a metafictional motif. When examining the passage in which Ianthe tells Aubrey stories of vampires which distract him from the lettering on old tombs (partly quoted below, p. 24), Gelder observes:

> The word 'excite' is repeated several times: these animated stories in turn animate Aubrey. The distinction is drawn between classical texts – which require contemplation and 'proper interpretation' – and what we might see here as popular fiction, which immediately realises its content through direct stimulation of the reader's imagination. The former are dead texts, while the latter are very much alive – and seductive, too, for Aubrey's 'excitement' as he listens to Ianthe is surely also sexual. (Gelder, p. 34)

Gelder argues that in keeping to the popular traditions of Greece, Polidori not only writes a work more suitable for 'popular' fiction, but also examines the contentions and threats to Greek national identity in a much more realistic way, since his 'arrangement in "The Vampyre" would seem to be close to the truth here: the "folk" seem oblivious to the classical antiquities around them – the latter being of interest only to foreigners like Aubrey' (p. 38).

However, the fact that Polidori places the vampire in contemporary Greece and its popular superstitions, is not necessarily, as Gelder maintains, a reflection of the rise of interest in folklore during the nineteenth century (pp. 38–41), nor necessarily due to a greater sense of realism about Greece than Byron possessed. The contention of this chapter is that Polidori in fact raises the ordinary Greek life over the tombs of its past and turns Byron himself into the vampire figure in order to argue against philhellenism, and present a view that it preys on and disturbs the very people whom it professes to save.

The reasons for this, beyond personal resentment of Byron himself, are not easy to discern, however, oblique references in his correspondence and journal demonstrate that it is probably resentment of philhellenism for obsessing the British Whigs at the expense of Italian independence. While Polidori harboured virtually no interest in Greek independence, he believed most profoundly in the rights of his fellow Italians to self-determination, unity and the overthrow of Austrian rule. It is possible that he understood – unlike even the later Byron, who was only to be awakened to Italian nationalism after living in Ravenna (1820–21)[4] before moving to Genoa and then Greece – that this would have entailed a necessary sacrifice of Greek independence, since weakening Ottoman rule near Dalmatia would only have strengthened the Austrians' hand in the region (the Ottomans were excluded from the Treaty of Vienna which determined the post-Napoleonic carve-up,[5] and lost absolute rule of Serbia in 1814). More probably, however, the overwhelming interest shown in the Greek cause by British Liberals like Frederick North and William Eton eclipsed the cause of Italy, and thus irritated Polidori: an irritation which appears to surface in a letter to Lord Byron. It is for these reasons, therefore, that he writes a work based on Byron's own original *Fragment* that argues surreptitiously for the continuation of the status quo in Greece, and which stands Byron's own use of the vampire theme on its head.

Byron and Greek vampires

Philhellenism was a popular creed in the early nineteenth century. It combined an interest in studying and reviving the classical remains of Greece with the desire to evoke the spirit of liberty, and thus of renewal, in its by now 'degenerate' peasant inhabitants. During the renaissance the interest in observing the classical past had centred upon Rome and its remains, which were seen as a window to the whole classical world. However, according to Terence Spencer the discovery of the Doric column in the mid-1700s turned attention upon Greece itself. Le Roy's *Ruines des Plus Beaux Monuments de Grèce* (1758) inspired architects like Stuart and Revett of the Society of Dilletanti to write a long study of Greek, but in particular Doric buildings, so that by 1794 the emphasis for studying architecture had shifted more from Rome to Greece, and a visit to the peninsula had become essential for young British architects.[6]

Other sciences also found their way to Greece. Young graduates like John Tweddell and Sir William Gell (whose *Intinerary of Ithaca and Greece* Byron reviewed in *The Monthly Review* in 1811 [Spencer, pp. 208–9]) arrived to make descriptions and topographies of the rediscovered land. Coupled with this was an awakening of political goodwill towards its inhabitants, and a growing desire to promote Greek liberty. William Eton's important work, *Survey of the Turkish Lands* (1798), inspired many young men to espouse the cause of Greece, since it argued that the

Greeks were a noble people traduced by Turkish rule (pp. 234–5). This, of course, was hotly disputed by others like Jonathan Morritt and David Urquhart,[7] but the idea of Greece as 'Fair Greece, sad relic' presented by Byron in Canto Two of *Childe Harolde*, was widely accepted: that of a once noble, heroic and sophisticated people brought low to peasantry and brigandage, but still capable of greatness, was a familiar theme in the philhellene agenda.

Where Byron was particularly effective as a promoter of Greek nationalism was in his ability to characterise the reemergence of a classical civilisation in wholly Romantic terms, stressing the renewal not of reason, order and metropolitan culture – the very values which the Augustans (whose work he personally admired more than that of his contemporaries) had discerned in first century Rome – but imagination, sublime landscape and a local folk-spirit. His giaour and corsairs are condemned to wild imagination and extreme emotions in a primitivism which he at once condemns and admires, allowing a taste for the sublime to enthuse the language and emotions of his Greek heroes: a feature which was to appeal to the Italian nationalist and Romantic, Ludovico di Breme, who similarly wished to build a love of nature, primitivism and racial bonding over the classical past of Italy in a bid to unite the peoples of the many republics and kingdoms of his own peninsula.[8]

However, Byron's taste for the sublime and Romantic in the Greek situation extended on certain occasions towards the terror and horror of the Gothic, as a means of simultaneously exciting the reader and condemning the Turkish presence, achieved most effectively in his long poem *The Giaour* (1812). Not lost on Byron was the reputation for superstition and irrationalism of the modern day peasants of Greece, as witnessed by the reports in Dom Calmet's *Revenans et Vampires* (1746), and repeated in Southey's long note to the story of the vampire Oneiza in *Thalaba*,[9] which Byron used when writing his poem.[10] Translating Calmet, Southey presented many reports describing the 'vroucolacas' of Greece, one of which, from the Island of Milo, reports a vampire that emits a stream of blood after being unearthed and decapitated after 40 years. Byron also takes these superstitions and legends and fashions them into a Gothic tale.

While Byron was not the first to write a vampire story set in Greece, he was the first to do so with an explicitly political motive. Although in *The Bride of Corinth* (1797), Goethe tells the story of the young man of Athens who, still following the old religion, is victimised by his degenerate Christian bride, the purpose of this poem is to present the subversion of culture due to the Christianisation of Greece. The difference between the Christian God and the gods of the classical past is continually stressed to express the exciting idea that the bride has been betrayed by the mother's conversion since 'the old gods' joyous congregation' has left the house and 'The Sacrifices here/Are neither lamb nor steer,/ Human victims suffer heretofore unknown.'[11] For Byron the motive is more to point out Greece's degradation in Ottoman hands: illustrating, through vampirism, the idea of 'Fair Greece, sad relic'.

In writing *The Vampyre*, Polidori was certainly borrowing more than just a few ideas from his former patron. The work was first published under Byron's name in the April 1819 edition of *The New Monthly Magazine* by Henry Colburn, who had been sent the manuscript by a lady residing in Italy. Polidori had to write to Colburn in order to reclaim his authorship, before publishing it with a new, learned introduction which again talked up the Byron connection for commercial reasons. In the letter in which he declared his rights to Colburn, he nevertheless admitted that Byron had been very much in his mind when he wrote it:

> I received a copy of the magazine of last April (the present month), and am sorry to find that your Genevan correspondent has led you into a mistake with regard to the tale of *The Vampyre* – which is *not* Lord Byron's, but was written *entirely* by me at the request of a lady, who (upon my mentioning that his Lordship had said that it was his intention of writing a ghost story, depending for interest upon the circumstances of two friends leaving England, and one dying in Greece, the other finding him alive, upon his return, and making love to his sister) saying that she thought it impossible to work up such materials, desired I would write it for her, which I did in two idle mornings by her side. These circumstances above mentioned, and the one of the dying man having obtained an oath that the survivor should not in any way disclose his decease, are the only parts of the tale belonging to his Lordship.[12]

The circumstances in which he wrote the tale explain in detail not only why Polidori may be excused the charge of plagiarism or fabrication, but also why the Byronic element is so evident in it: rather than simply recreating the story with a malevolent twist against the original creator, Polidori engages with Byron's actual ideas.

William Rossetti believes the lady for whom Polidori performed the exercise to have been the Countess of Breuss, and the occasion just after Polidori had left Byron's house but was still in 'that neighbourhood' (*Polidori, Diary*, pp. 12–3). However, Lorne Macdonald declares that we cannot be sure for whom Polidori specifically performed this task, and does not instance the time.[13] Still, the tone of the work, which bitterly turns the themes of Byron's previous vampire tales against Byron himself, indicates that just before (when relations were already strained) or just after the break (September 1816) was the most likely time. Indeed, the very fact that Polidori answered the challenge set him in such a frankly ironic and self-conscious way, means that he took on not just Byron but also the terms of Byron's previous work, making a study of the *Fragment* (which he may not have actually read, but would probably have heard read out loud after the ghost stories were finished at the Villa Diodati) and *The Giaour* (which he surely had read since it also influenced his much earlier work *Ximenes*) a crucial stage in understanding the full meaning of Polidori's own piece.

In Byron's *Fragment*, the narrator is travelling to Ephesus with Augustus Darvell, a superior aristocrat who is about to die. They stop off at a Moslem burial ground when Darvell, foretelling his own imminent demise, demands an oath of secrecy from his companion. After the companion has sworn, there occurs the curious detail of the stork with a serpent writhing in its beak perching on a tombstone. Darvell insists that he be buried where the stork is sitting. Then he asks his friend:

–You perceive that bird?
– Certainly–
–And the serpent writhing in her beak?
–Doubtless: there is nothing uncommon in it; it is her natural prey. But it is odd that she does not devour it.–
He smiled in a ghastly manner, and said, faintly, – It is not yet time ![14]

He dies, leaving his mortified companion to carry out the funeral plans.

Although the story does not continue, the image clearly portends the future of the vampire. What is left ambiguous is who will devour whom. The irony may be that the caring stork will in fact be devoured by the serpent it has failed to kill: a portent of the end in which Darvell was to return to London and hold his young companion to the oath not to tell of the death while courting his sister.

Byron's earlier work, *The Giaour*, also used the vampire motif in a Greek setting. The tale is told in fragmented form, once again utilising the Gothic tradition of the discovered manuscript. It tells the story of how the giaour, or wandering Christian renegade, steals into the Haram of the Pasha Hassan, where he is having an affair with the female slave Leila. Once the affair is discovered, Leila is thrown into the Aegean to her death, and Hassan and his men follow the giaour with the intention of dispatching him. Instead, the giaour kills Hassan in combat. Through some supernatural force the brigand is punished:

> thou, false Infidel! shalt writhe
> Beneath avenging Monkir's scythe;
> And from its torments 'scape alone
> To wander round lost Eblis' throne;
> ... on earth as Vampire sent,
> Thy corse shall from its tomb be rent:
> Then ghastly haunt thy native place,
> And suck the blood of all thy race.
>   (Byron, p. 259, ll. 747–50; 755–8)

The last part of the poem deals with the vampire confessing his sins in a monastery before finally being released from his curse to die. The fragmented form of the poem ensures that we never see the vampirism itself, and centre mainly on the relation between the earlier loss of his beloved and his later, guilt-ridden sojourn in the monastery.

In both works the use of vampirism has a clear political motive: to represent the heinous effects of the Ottoman occupation of Greece. In the *Fragment* the vampire, Augustus Darvell, is related to the Ottomans themselves. He dies in a Moslem cemetery travelling to the ruins of Ephesus, and his ring bears Arabic inscriptions; the narrator recalls how they were upon 'a wild and tenantless track through marshes and defiles which lead to the few huts yet lingering over the broken columns of Diana, the roofless walls of expelled Christianity, and the still more recent but complete desolation of abandoned mosques' (Byron, *Fragment*, p. 229). The barrenness of the landscape thus bears witness to three phases in history: the ruin of the Greek culture, the expulsion of Christians by Moslems and the final desertion of Moslems themselves. All point to a society that has decayed due to the Turkish influence, which is related to the vampirism of Darvell himself, who is a mahometan disguised as an English gentleman. *The Giaour* also presents the idea of degeneration, although this time the oppressed native is the vampire, degenerated by an Ottoman curse. In one the vampire is the Turkish predator upon Greece, in the other the vampire is the result of Ottoman occupation degrading the region.

In both cases, however, we are invited as readers to find delight in either the terror of the diabolical persona, or in the moral complexity of the protagonist. In the *Fragment* we have a sublimity of the Burkean kind, in which our terror at the evil protagonist causes delight and even attraction from an aesthetic distance,[15] while in the latter we have the failure to reconcile contradictions in emotional, and thus moral, responses, which causes the free play of images and associations in our attempt to understand the effect: an example of the more complex Kantian sublime, which is similar to Byron's own notion of 'mobility'(and which McGann has related to a flexible class position).[16] Despite the contradictions in both poems, the complex emotions which they seek to provoke are drawn for political reasons, and to lead the reader to a condemnation of Turkish rule.

Polidori and Byron

Following the lines of Byron's *Fragment*, Polidori also kept to the familiar Greek setting, and indeed appears initially to maintain its political line by criticising the Ottoman rule obliquely when describing the state of Greek ruins. When Aubrey arrived in Greece

> He then fixed his residence in the house of a Greek; and soon occupied himself in tracing the faded records of ancient glory upon monuments that apparently, ashamed of chronicling the deeds of freemen only before slaves, had hidden themselves beneath the sheltering soil or many coloured lichen. Under the same roof as himself, existed a being, so beautiful and delicate, that she might have formed the model for a painter wishing to pourtray on canvass the promised hope of the faithful in Mahomet's paradise, save that her eyes spoke too much mind for anyone to think she could belong to those who had no souls. (Polidori, pp. 39–40)

Here Polidori's narrator both suggests the degeneration of the Greeks under Ottoman rule, and seemingly attacks the Islamic religion which the Ottoman system used in order to organise its government and tax system. The decayed writing on their neglected monuments symbolises the extent to which the Greeks of modern days are distant from the achievements of their forefathers, but the reason for the decay is expressed, in ironic terms, as being a result of shame – transferring the shame which contemporary Europeans feel for their betrayal to the monuments themselves in an eloquent pathetic fallacy. The beauty of Ianthe as the paradigm of the beauty virtuous Moslems are supposed to meet in heaven, is used to represent the brute colonising of the Ottomans, and is ultimately presented as an excuse for damning their religion as godless, since in fact 'her eyes spoke too much for anyone to think she could belong to those who had no souls' (p. 40). This image is doubly damning, since Polidori was no doubt not only aware that seven virgins await the faithful in paradise, but also that Islamic art forbids the depiction of the human form, making the example even more ironic than its surface flippancy suggests: the idea that Moslem men themselves have no souls may be implied in the obvious irony that they are not allowed to appreciate what Westerners would consider to be good art. Therefore, while in both statements the effect is, initially at least, a denigration of the values of the Ottoman presence, in both statements the performative irony overlies any serious discussion of the Ottomans in Greece themselves, and presents the narrator as a haughty, disdainful philhellene, offsetting his own superciliousness through oblique wit.

However, the following iterative description of Ianthe on her trips with Aubrey to the ruins, presents a very different view of the Greek peasantry to that painted by Goethe or Byron:

As she danced upon the plain, or tripped along the mountain's side, one would have thought the gazelle a poor type of her beauties; for who would have exchanged her eye, apparently the eye of animated nature, for that sleepy luxurious look of the animal suited but to the taste of an epicure. The light step of Ianthe often accompanied Aubrey in his search after antiquities, and often would the unconscious girl, engaged in the pursuit of a Kashmere butterfly, show the whole beauty of her form, floating as it were upon the wind, to the eager gaze of him, who forgot the letters he had just decyphered upon an almost effaced tablet, in the contemplation of her sylph-like figure. Often would her tresses falling, as she flitted around, exhibit in the sun's ray such delicately brilliant and swiftly fading hues, as might well excuse the forgetfulness of the antiquary, who let escape from his mind the very object he had before thought of vital importance to the proper interpretation of a passage in Pausanias. But why attempt to describe charms which all feel, but none can appreciate? – It was innocence, youth, and beauty, unaffected by crowded drawing-rooms and stifling balls. (pp. 40–1)

The image of a beautiful, 'unconscious' girl, at one with nature, draws the antiquary away from the writing of ancient Greece. The living world of modern Greece is far stronger than the civilised Greece of writing, making the antiquary turn from his object of study: a fact that shows Polidori had understood Rousseau's ideas on the noble savage and the corrupting effect of civilisation, an effect which Rousseau had also famously ascribed to writing.[17] The natural charm of the young girl dancing in nature is reminiscent of other female naturals like Wordsworth's Lucy or Coleridge's Lewti, and is contrasted quite self-consciously to the women of refinement with whom Aubrey has already consorted, and who up until now have been Ruthven's normal prey. In short, the neat contrast between herself and the effaced tombs of her forefathers serves to make Ianthe more than a simple metonymy, but a metaphor of an innocent, pastoral culture, that is alive, unsophisticated and in danger of destruction. Her 'innocence, youth and beauty' are implicitly compared with a dead, artficial and bookish culture: not the culture of ancient Greece itself, so much as its present use in the hands of antiquarians and philhellenes. The fact that she has a metaphoric meaning (as the soul of Greece herself) further enhances her superiority over the rest of the contrast, since the ancient Greek tombs only ever retain a metonymic meaning: the effect of a decayed civilisation. The present-day 'sylph-like' soul of Greece, which Ianthe represents, is not degenerate, but prelapsarian. The embedded textual allegory restores the allegory of reading which de Man exposed so ruthlessly, as the implicit metaphor of modern Greece triumphs over the metonymical representation of a self-conscious fad for the past. Thus, through this contrast Polidori surreptitiously attacks the notion that modern Greece has degenerated and is in need of a regeneration of its classical past.

However, together with this love of primitivism, there is an acknowledgement of the more corrupt elements of Greek life, once Ianthe describes the ever-present reality of the vampire, who may prey upon young maidens. Here too, the main effect would appear to be a denigration of the civilised beneath the primitive:

> Ianthe cited to him the names of old men, who had at last detected one living among themselves, after several of their near relatives and children had been found marked with the stamp of the fiend's appetite; and when she found him so incredulous, she begged of him to believe her, for it had been remarked, that those who had dared to question their existence, always had some proof given, which obliged them, with grief and heartbreaking, to confess it was true. She detailed to him the traditional appearance of these monsters, and his horror was increased, by hearing a pretty accurate description of Lord Ruthven. (Polidori, p. 42)

The tradition of the vampire would appear to be local, since the old men 'at last detected one living among themselves' who happened to be a vampire – although there is no indication that one has ever been caught.

There is also a 'traditional appearance' which corresponds to that of Lord Ruthven, which may mean simply that he is one of a brood, or else that the vampires, having never actually been decapitated, are in fact all one man, Lord Ruthven: a man whose exterior is entirely civilised.

These two elements of Polidori's narrative, the superiority of peasant Greece over its civilised antecedents, and the presentation of the local vampire as being a civilised invader, whose real-life basis on Lord Byron we may take as being an integral part of the story, point to a very different political view to that openly, if ironically, expressed at the beginning of the passage by the narrator: namely, that *The Vampyre* constitutes an attack on philhellenism, with Polidori understanding that the modern Greek peasant culture is perfectly adequate and sufficient to itself under Ottoman rule, and that the philhellene is the potential ruiner of calm, who, with his misguided attempts at resurrecting the classical Greek culture, will destroy the edenic soul of modern peasant Greece (the initial attentions of Aubrey the philhellene which lead Ruthven to Ianthe). Thus the Near Eastern superstition has been transformed into a national allegory of the 'other' through its enclosure within the West European naturalistic and contemporary narrative – in this case, however, it argues that vampirism is a result of Western meddling rather than Ottoman misrule: quite the opposite of the *Fragment* upon which it is based.

That Polidori was attacking philhellenism, and in particular the philhellenism of his patient and patron, can be demonstrated by the fact that the description of Ianthe dancing includes images which act as a riposte to specific figures already used by Byron in *The Giaour*. Patricia Skarda has noticed that Polidori's description of Ianthe as being like a gazelle in her light tripping form rather than in her eyes, 'since who would have exchanged her eye, apparently the eye of animated nature, for that sleepy luxurious look of the animal suited but to the taste of an epicure', is a conscious attack on Byron for his use of imagery, since Byron had used the image of a gazelle's eyes in both the dedication to his own Ianthe in *Childe Harolde*, and in *The Giaour* when describing the beauty of Leila. Skarda also interprets it as an attack upon Byron's own jaded morality for assigning the image to the hedonist's taste (*Studies in Romanticism*, 28:2 254–5). She acknowledges that Polidori applies the image 'more sensibly' to the girl's body, but still sees the attack on Byron as 'clumsy' (254). Skarda notices other images from *The Giaour* in the above passages of *The Vampyre*, namely the image of 'eyes' when referring to the Islamic doctrine on women's souls, and the 'Kashmere butterfly' (255),[18] which in her view have been plagiarised and turned into 'merely decorative' features in Polidori's tale.

However, if we take into account the circumstances in which *The Vampyre* was written (the reproduction of the *Fragment* after the spat with Byron) and analyse the borrowings properly, we see that nothing could be further from the truth. These images in fact constitute forms of metalepsis that transcend elements taken from the *Fragment* and demonstrate that Polidori was alluding to the political ideas of Byron's earlier work in order to subvert them. They form a powerful intertext that helps to enhance the metaphorical meaning of Ianthe in her opposition to the tombs, and thus demand a thorough re-examination of them in the light of their Byronic origins.

The narrator of *The Giaour* initially places himself in the position of someone approaching the Greek coast and, curiously, uses a metaphor which anticipates the concept of vampirism, or living death:

> He who hath bent him o'er the dead
> Ere the first day of death is fled,
> The first dark day of nothingness,
> The last of danger and distress,
> (Before Decay's effacing fingers
> Have swept the lines where beauty lingers,)
> And mark'd the mild angelic air,
> The rapture of repose that's there,
> And fix'd yet tender traits that streak
> The languor of the placid cheek,
> And – but for that sad shrouded eye,
> That fires not, wins not, weeps not, now,
> And but for that chill, changeless brow,
> Where cold Obstruction's apathy
> Appals the gazing mourner's heart,
> As if to him it could impart
> The doom he dreads, yet dwells upon;
> Yes, but for these and these alone,
> Some moments, ay, one treacherous hour,
> He still might doubt the tyrant's power;
> So fair, so calm, so softly sealed,
> Such is the aspect of this shore;
> Tis Greece, but living Greece no more!
> So coldly sweet, So deadly fair,
> We start, for soul is wanting there.
> (Byron, p. 253, ll. 68–93)

This passage has several functions. The first is to use the idea of the calm but recently dead body to represent the current condition of

Greece. It is still healthy upon a first impression, but, as with a dead body, later 'We start, for soul is wanting there'. In terms more Romantic than Classical, the serenity of Greece 'So fair, so calm ... So deadly fair' is its very death, arguing by contrast, that if it were alive there would be a more rugged, sublime landscape than one so serene. In this way, Byron surreptitiously injects a Romantic and sublime aesthetic into his philhellenism and understanding of pre-Ottoman (which for him is classical) Greece. A second function concerns the feminisation, which serves, as Nigel Leask has pointed out, to invite a comparison with the dead Leila,[19] who, as Ken Gelder has also noted, 'is made to stand for Greece itself' (Gelder, p. 27). The way in which we treat Leila as a metaphor for the state of Greece has much to do with the fact that the language in this passage could interchangeably refer to the land itself and the 'softly sealed' concubine who has been drowned off the shore in a sack.

A third and more subtle function, however, is to portend vampirism – not just that of the giaour, but of the whole country (of which Leila and the shore are emblematic). For if the recently dead body represents Greece under the 'tyrant', there is an anomaly in its symbolism, since Greece has not simply been colonised recently, but has been under Ottoman rule for some time (the poem is set in the 1770s, during the rule of Ali Hazan [Gelder, p. 29]). The idea of presenting Greece under Ottoman tyrany as like a newly dead body leads us inevitably to the further shock of vampirism: the only way a dead body can retain its beauty so long is if it is one of the undead. The only way the Greek people may keep the semblance of beauty and vigour is if they resort to the sort of parasitical and ultimately futile acts of rebellion which the giaour (a Christian of mixed racial origins rather than a pure ethnic Greek) commits and to which the Ottomans later curse him.

This image finds a fitting response, however, in Polidori's portrayal of Ianthe, whom he also turns into a symbol of modern Greece herself through juxtaposition with the tombs of classical Greece. It will be recalled that Polidori's narrator first describes her as an image of the 'Mahometan paradise, save that her eyes spoke too much for anyone to think she could belong to those who had no souls' (Polidori, p. 40). This image picks up a comment actually made by Byron's narrator on the death of Leila:

> 'Oh! who young Leila's glance could read
> And keep that portion of his creed
> Which saith that woman is but dust,
> A soulless toy for tyrant's lust?

> On her might Muftis gaze and own
> That through her eye the Immortal shone;
> (Byron, *Works*, 257, ll. 487–92)

The Moslem religious leaders would have been able to see that through the eyes of Leila the divine shone to reveal paradise, if they had looked at her. Thus the spiritual nature of Leila's beauty is used to attack Islamic attitudes towards women. In Polidori's work, however, the trope is used to turn the situation round: Ianthe represents paradise, and it is the Moslem masters who do not have souls. Soullessness is attributed to the Ottoman invaders (with the implicit joke that she could never embody their paradise, since Mahometans do not permit figural painting), while she is presented by contrast as being very much in possession of her soul thanks to the 'speaking'['spoke'] of her 'eyes' (Polidori, p. 40). Furthermore, she is presented as being free, rather than a slave, completely inverting the relationship which Leila suffered with her Moslem masters, as though she is in fact superior to them, morally and spiritually, and above all unaffected by their presence. Presented as a direct contrast to the ancient Greek surroundings, Ianthe is more than simply a symbol of womanhood (as Leila also is in Byron's poem), but is symbolic of a 'sylph-like' modern Greece that Byron describes so differently in *The Giaour* through the landscape. By responding to Byron's two images of Leila and the coast of Greece under Ottoman occupation, Polidori turns Ianthe into an image of freedom and spiritual triumph, superior to and unmolested by her occupiers, while the remains left by classical Greece are really dead, since the dancing form 'let escape from his [Aubrey's] mind the very object he had before thought of vital importance to the proper interpretation of a passage in Pausanias' (p. 41) – vital of course being an ambiguous word.

This same passage which extols Ianthe's beauty also refers to another image from *The Giaour*, where we are told that often would 'the unconscious girl, engaged in the pursuit of a Kashmere butterfly, show the whole beauty of her form, floating as it were upon the wind, to the eager gaze of him, who forgot the letters he had just decyphered upon an almost, effaced tablet, in the contemplation of her sylph-like figure' (Polidori, p. 41). The image of the Kashmere butterfly was first employed to present the dangers of beauty to its possessor:

> As rising on its purple wing
> The insect queen of eastern spring,
> O'er emerald meadows of Kashmeer

> Invites the young pursuer near,
> And leads him on from flower to flower
> A weary chase and wasted hour,
> Then leaves him as it soars on high,
> With panting heart and tearful eye:
> So beauty lures the full-grown child,
> With hue as bright, and wing as wild;
> A chase of idle hopes and fears,
> Begun in folly, closed in tears.
> If won, to equal ills betray'd,
> Woe waits the insect and the maid;
> A life of pain, the loss of peace
> From infant's play, and man's caprice.
> (Byron, *Works* p. 256, ll. 388–403)

This metaphor is originally used to turn round neatly the suffering of pursuer and pursued; while Byron initially spends time exploring the frustration caused by the pursuit of beauty, he switches quite suddenly to describing the misery of the beautiful object – butterfly or woman – once captured by the pursuer turned captor. Just as the 'insect queen' is finally the object of an 'infant's play', so too the beautiful woman, once caught, is subject to the whim of the pursuer. It is interesting that he should spend so long describing the pursuer's frustration and pain, when it is ultimately the pain of the pursued that the image is being used to represent in the actual poem (namely the suffering of Leila, thrown into the Aegean in a sack). This is due to Byron's insightful understanding of the double-sided nature of romantic liaisons, in which the initial suffering of the pursuer is a double-spur to the strict confinement he then imposes on the object of his desire, once she is caught, so that almost imperceptibly the pursuer's original frustration and tears are transferred to the maid's 'loss of peace'. The image is also interesting from an Orientalist perspective, since through the metaphor (a butterfly 'of Kashmeer') it presents the love of the Oriental as being an infantile emotion.

The ambiguous quality of the image – that is, the transposing of the pain of the pursuer Hassan onto the pursued Leila – is, I would argue, noticed by Polidori. He makes Ianthe, Aubrey's object of pursuit, into the pursuer of a literal butterfly of Kashmere. Here, however, there is no sense of frustration on the object's part, nor is there any 'loss of peace' attributed to the pursuer. Nevertheless, as in the original there is a transferral of epithets from one to the other, although this time from pursued to pursuer, from the butterfly to the girl herself, since she is also 'floating as it were upon the wind' and 'sylphlike', as though pursuer and her object are simultaneously of one and the same kind (rather than reversing roles, as in Byron's original metaphor). Furthermore, the quality is not frustration and tension, but lightness and thoughtlessness, and is also suggested through concrete metaphor (Ianthe becomes like a butterfly), rather than the direct naming of the emotions, inviting the reader to see the two as being materially similar before then inferring the emotional quality. The butterfly, as in Byron's original, is also an oriental image, and thus suggests an 'Oriental' emotion, but one very different to the infantile sadism that Byron discerns. Thus the shifting of epithets from one to the other suggests, in contrast to the haughty islamophobia of the narrator, that the Orient is in harmony with the local Greek culture, and not opposed to it, both being essentially the same.

It also constitutes a displaced symbol of the real love pursuit here: namely Aubrey's for the Greek girl, implied by his 'gaze' on Ianthe. This is a technique used by Byron himself throughout *The Giaour*, as he allows images to symbolise more than one character (the shore of Greece representing both Leila and her lover; the qualities of Hassan and the giaour being interchangeable as an illustration of degeneration). So too the quiet gaze of the motionless Aubrey over Ianthe chasing the butterfly suggests the chase could also be a symbol for his own pursuit of Ianthe herself, and thus transfers these qualities of harmony and homogeneity to himself and his beloved. Here the love pursuit is without the frustration and tension as the two belong to each other and are of the same kind in this edenic world. Thus the image of the perils and frustration of sexual love in the Orient is turned into an image which represents harmony, innocence, perfect beauty, and reality transfomed by imagination. Not only does Polidori take images and use them more appropriately, but he also turns the ideological content around.

This interpretation of the work sees it as a specific attack on both Byron's poetic practice and his political views, rather than the unaknowledged plagiarism which Patricia Skarda has observed in the reproduction of the tropes (Studies in Romanticism, 28:2 255). Instead, Polidori has responded to images in Byron's work by creating metalepses which contribute to the metaphorical meaning of Ianthe as modern Greece, and thus subverts the original sense. In doing so his story prioritises the anti-philhellene message of the work over the more open islamophobia through an embedded national allegory. Polidori is denouncing the philhellene project, and with it the idea that Greece has degenerated under Ottoman rule and is in need of both regeneration from its classical past and renewed liberty.

What must now be taken into account are the reasons why Polidori should have attacked the philhellene position. It was not merely the result of a disaffection with the most famous philhellene of the time, namely Lord Byron, whom Polidori had attempted to upstage at Geneva and with whom he had thus come into conflict. Nor was it due to any true conviction in the nobleness of an uneducated Greek woman over her classical antecedents: Polidori had never been to Greece, and was himself passionately interested in both the classics, and in the monuments of another past ancient culture with which he identified, that of Rome, and so it is hardly likely that he would present ancient civilisation as being genuinely inferior to the modern world. It is more likely that he was using the girl as a rhetorical motif with which to attack philhellenism for ulterior motives.

Ximenes

To attain a better understanding of why Polidori ironises tropes from Byron's *The Giaour*, it is worth examining the earlier, equally 'Byronic' drama, *Ximenes* (1813), penned when the author was only 18, and set on a Greek island. The plot is as follows. Ximenes, once Orlando, has returned to avenge himself on his former friend Francesco, now living under the name Gustavus.[20] Years earlier in Florence, Orlando had wooed the beautiful Eliza, and entrusted her care to Francesco, who had in turn simply turned her against him. While eloping with Eliza, Francesco also killed Orlando's father (Polidori *Ximenes*, pp. 18–9). Orlando has thus now disguised himself as the priest Ximenes, and come to the island to hatch his plot.

Francesco's (i.e., Gustavus's) son Anselmo wishes to marry Euphemia, the daughter of the local pasha, Almoraddin, but Ximenes has other ideas. While Almoraddin is prepared to accept the marriage if Anselmo converts to Islam (p. 31), Gustavus is worried, since he fears that if his son marries a Moslem the two of them, father and son, will be damned all the more, a thought which the 'priest' Ximenes drives home to him by inventing the fact that Orlando (i.e. himself) has died in Jerusalem (pp. 48–51). He also projects his voice in Gustavus's hearing, pretending that it is the damning judgement of God which tells the father to kill the son (pp. 73–4). Ximenes spurs on Gustavus to kill his own son (p. 77), but he eventually only stabs him (p. 95). Almorradin arrives to uncover the plot, and Ximenes is imprisoned. The play ends with Ximenes in the condemned cell, not regretting his behaviour, and finally killing himself (p. 103).

While noting the Byronic influence in the play (as well as that of Wieland and Shakespeare), Lorne Macdonald sees in it an inversion of

Polidori's oedipal relation with (and murderous intentions on) his father, since Gaetano Polidori, like Anselmo, had embarked on a mixed marriage, and had never quite reconciled himself to this. He also understands Ximenes's eventual suicide as constituting an introversion of the character's former murderous intentions against Gustavus, and thus as a sublimation of John Polidori's own suicidal tendencies as a result of introverting his patricidal feelings (Macdonald, pp. 28–9).

Macdonald's brilliant Freudian interpretation of an otherwise mediocre play should not detract from its possible political meanings. For one thing, the play shows much Byronic influence, in particular from *The Giaour*, which had been published the year before. In uncovering his true identity to Rinaldo, a Venetian whom he enlists in his plan of vengeance, Ximenes declares:

> I will lay by him, and here
> Will live a vampire on his son and him,
> Sucking in living drops his very blood.
>   (Polidori, *Ximenes*, p. 20)

The reference is metaphorical, but the situation similar to that of the politically motivated vampirism of *The Giaour*: Ximenes will now prey upon his victim like a vampire, in revenge for the losses he has suffered. However, there are differences between the two scenarios, since Ximenes will avenge himself on Gustavus not for having killed his beloved but for having stolen her with her own consent, and then killing his father in the process.

The political context of his revenge is also different, since its enactment is more within an Italian Catholic than a truly Greek context. Although the environment is a Greek island, presumably Cyprus or another island which the Ottomans had wrested from Venetian hands during the reign of Soliman the Magnificent (hence the coexistence of a Venetian, like Rinaldo, with Euphemia and Almoraddin), Ximenes is a native of Florence, as is Gustavus, although both have inexplicably lived on the island before. As a monk he now wears a 'cowl' (p. 23), as Dominic describes his dress, in keeping with Catholic orders. A central motif of the work is Catholic confession, since the one true priest on the island, Dominic, gives Ximenes his ideas for vengeance by stating that Gustavus is too scared to take on the 'duty of confession' (p. 26). Ximenes realises the power he could hold over Gustavus if he could get into the position of confessor, and so suggests relieving Dominic of some of his duties (pp. 27–8).

There is nothing in the description of the religion of the island to distinguish it from Catholicism, and the sense throughout is that Polidori understands the religion of the island to be Catholicism and not Greek Orthodoxy (what Orthodox priest would be called Dominic?). Therefore, far from being a work truly Greek in political context, *Ximenes* is a play addressing issues that relate to the Italians. The Catholic faith, its ability to instill fear of damnation through confession, and in particular the role of the priest/confessor in stoking rather than assuaging fears of damnation, is the major political theme of the work. Ximenes is capable of preying upon Gustavus's fears with tales of a dream in which he paints a picture of Gustavus in heaven and then in hell with his son:

> – With hellish joy,
> With thongs of lead, he smote thy naked back,
> Where loathing worms suckt up the dropping blood –
> Anselmo cried, as each hard blow he dealt,
> 'Why let me wed that Moslam infidel?
> Why not, as heav'n ordain'd, not take my life?'
>
> (p. 77)

Through such scenes of hellfire he goads Gustavus on to attempt the deed of filicide. Although antiCatholicism is a familiar feature of the English Gothic, Polidori's attack on Catholicism is far more considered than the highly prejudiced portrayal of claustrophobia or sexual perversion that one finds in the works of Lewis or Mathurin: he is attacking the psychological stranglehold which the Catholic confessor may hold over his communicant, and is doing so from the perspective of a lapsed Catholic who had undergone confession regularly at Ampleforth School.[21]

However, his further inclusion of Italian characters and features to this early play points to an already enlarged sense of the importance of Italy, which was to grow in him over the coming years after the crumbling of Napoleon's Kingdom of Italy in 1814 and his journey through a newly Austrianised peninsula in 1816. Indeed, *The Vampyre* itself has an Italian episode, one of some political importance if we consider the biographical implications of the short story. Aubrey and Darvell initially part company in Rome because the former is enlightened there, by a letter from his guardian, as to the true nature of his travelling companion. Upon asking Darvell his stealthy intentions towards a young girl who is always intensely chaperoned due to the customs of the country, he ascertains their impurity and decides upon a new course of action:

> immediately writing a note, to say, that from that moment he must
> decline accompanying his Lordship in the remainder of their
> proposed tour, he ordered his servants to seek other apartments, and
> calling upon the mother of the lady, informed her of all he knew, not
> only with regard to her daughter, but also concerning the character of
> his Lordship. The assignation was prevented. Lord Ruthven next day
> merely sent his servant to notify his complete assent to a separation;
> but did not hint any suspicion of his plans having been foiled by
> Aubrey's interposition. (Polidori, pp. 38–9)

Here Polidori/Aubrey preserves the Italian girl from the rapaciousness of
the Byron figure. The desire to preserve an Italian woman from rape, in
what is a far less symbolic passage than that on the Greek remains, suggest
a resentment of his master over political differences, and places Polidori
in the role of saviour and champion of his beloved land against the
English libertine Byron.

While in *Ximenes* a Greek setting is exploited to illustrate Italian issues,
in *The Vampyre* the relations between Greece and Italy are more subtly
explored, but also related more to the topical situation. Nevertheless, it is
arguable that the same interest in a united Italy and Italian nationalism
spurred Polidori's reason for abjuring the philhellene in *The Vampyre*, one
year after the fall of Napoleonic Italy and the return of the Austrians to
the peninsula: two power-blocks Polidori had consistently opposed.

Polidori and Italy

The story of Napoleonic Italy is one of frustrated hopes. Initially many
Italian Jacobins (extreme Republicans and Libertarians) had been optimistic at the prospect of free republics fostered by France when the young
General Bonaparte had invaded Italy in 1796, and pushed aside many of
the local, Hapsburg-supported Princes.[22] However, after the Treaty of
Campo Formio in 1797, when the dismayed Venetian Republicans were
handed over to the Austrian Emperor (Woolf, p. 165), Bonaparte had
sought first to combine the northern and central republics under one central Italian Republic, the Cisalpine Republic (1797–1800 [p. 164]), later
renamed the Italian Republic (1800–1805 [p. 198]) and had then refashioned the Republic as the Kingdom of Italy (1805–14 [p. 191]) once he was
proclaimed Emperor. Naples was placed under the rule of his brother-in-
law, and best cavalry officer, Joachim Murad, while Etruria was put under
the rule of his Hapsburg wife, Maria Luisa (p. 206 [see Map 1]).

Map 1 South Eastern Europe in 1812

Despite promises, throughout both kingdoms the gap between rich and poor increased during the Napoleonic order, and Bonaparte himself came to rely more and more upon local aristocrats to enforce his civil service (p. 212). Conscription into Italian legions was heavy, but Napoleon always dispersed them among several fronts since his generals feared the possibility of pro-Italian unity (p. 205). Towards the end of his rule in Italy Napoleon was facing revolt from patriots (usually from the land-owning class), Catholics (dismayed at the curbing of papal power) and disgruntled Jacobins (usually the middle class [Woolf, pp. 218–21]).

However heavy the burdens of the Great Empire upon the Italian peasantry, the levying of some 360,000 troops from all over Italy into a mixed Italian legion under Murad, helped to foster an Italian nationalist movement.[23] This was further spurred by the fact that after the fall of Napoleon's Kingdom of Italy, Murad broke treaties with the Austrians and attempted to raise a united rebellion against the Hapsburg Emperor, leaving a powerful pro-Italian rather than pro-Napoleonic legacy behind him (Nicolson, pp. 185–6). A further spur was Napoleon's contemptuous treatment of the Pope, who became a servant of L'Empereur rather than the other way round. W.R. Thayer was right when he assumed that Italian nationalists, although opposed to Napoleon's rule, had been galvanised into unity by his presence.[24]

By 1816, however, Italy was firmly under Austrian power. Lombardy-Venetia was a direct principality of the Hapsburg Emperor, while other regions were ruled by his cousins and children, with the exception of Victor Emmanuel I in Sardinia, the Bourbon Ferdinand in Sicily and the Pope. After Napoleon's first abdication in 1814, Austria had swept over the Alps to claim lands that had first been ceded to France and Italian Jacobins in 1796. The various Republicans and Patriots in Lombardy, Piedmont, Genoa, Tuscany and others had looked to England for the setting up of liberal constitutions as an antidote to the increasingly autocratic rule of Napoleon's Kingdom of Italy (which comprised most of the northern and central Republics). This was a hope which had been encouraged by the English governor of Sicily, Lord Bentinck, on his arrival in Genoa in April 1814, and which had originally been ratified at the Treaty of Paris, on May 30th of that year, after the Italian Kingdom had fallen (Nicolson, pp. 185–6). These promises were effectively dropped after Napoleon's return to France in March 1815, and full British approval was given to both the reincorporation of Lombardy into the Austrian Empire, along with Venice, and the reinstatement of Hapsburg princes on the thrones of minor Italian Kingdoms (Woolf, pp. 222–6). Furthermore, the six provinces of Napoleon's Illyrian

Republic, which he had wrested from Austrian rule by 1809 and had actually incorporated into the French Empire, had been won back by Austria (with much Russian support)[25] and were ratified as part of the Hapsburg Empire during the Congress of Vienna (1815), giving the Austrians a renewed bridgehead over Dalmatia and into the Balkans against Ottoman possessions. When John Polidori was to visit Italy in 1816, he was to arrive in a peninsula firmly under Austrian rule, and which saw England as the betrayer.

This betrayal was all the more painful given that an Italian language journal published in London, called *L'Italico*, had recently been railing against Napoleon and calling for Italian unity and independence with the British government's full support. The journal (published every month from May 1813–May 1814) was divided into the sections 'Literature', 'Politics' and 'Miscellany', and included reviews of plays and recently published poems. It also contained many translations into Italian of letters and proclamations by the leading political and military figures of the day, including Castlereagh, Pitt, Wellington, Viceroy Eugene[26] and others. One subscriber was a 'Mr Polidori'[27] who is noted as demanding 'two copies'. Since Gaetano was a translator of Italian literature and ex-secretary to Alfieri, it is hardly surprising that he should have ordered the only work in England that kept abreast of new publications at home. His son John, however, appears to have been infected more with its patriotism.

The journal describes the momentous events of 1813, as the allied forces prepared to roll back Napoleon's 'Grande Empire', and optimistically appeals to the English to assist their friends. One piece, dated 30th October 1813, and entitled 'An Address to the English', calls on them to invade as the time is now ripe:

> The Italian Nation is ready to receive and make use of your help; may bands of Anglian heroes disembark on the unprotected shores of Tuscany or Liguria; may they bring us thousands of arms, and you will then see if the Italians also know how to follow the example of every other nation, to run beneath the common standard of national liberty, and even lend them a hand in giving the final blow to the usurping collosus who is already crumbling.
>
> [l'itala nazione e pronto a ricevere e far uso de vostro soccorsi; – che delle bande di Anglici Eroi sbarchino sulle non prottette coste della Toscana o della Liguria;– che vi portino migliaja d'arme, e vedrete allora se sanno anche gli Italiani seguire d'ogni altra nazione l'esempio, correre sotto il commune stendardo della libertà nazionale, e prestar

anch'essi una mano per dar l'ultima pugnalata al colosso usurpatore che gia sta crollando]. (*L'Italico*, II. 10 204–6 at 206; 30. Oct. Milano)

The article is polite towards Russia and Austria, but sees them as being without the 'means' which Britain possesses.

We know that Polidori wanted to see Italy free and united from his undergraduate days, when it was still part of the Napoleonic empire, from a letter he wrote his father on the subject in December 1813 (just before Lord Bentinck's arrival to Italy and when insurrection in the Kingdom of Italy was imminent), which ends: 'I hope therefore that you will not hesitate in allowing me to respond to the cry of my country, which now calls me to arms.' It may well have been the very 'Address to the English' from Milan in the December 1813 edition of *L'Italico* which inspired Polidori to such passion. It should also be noted that he took these political views not from his father (who was entirely blasé towards his country of origin) but from his own intellectual endeavour, and sense of difference from the English with whom he grew up and with whom he lived – a sense which *L'Italico's* rhetoric probably did much to inflame.[28] His illustrious patient Lord Byron, however, did not share Polidori's anti-Napoleonic views when they first crossed the continent to Geneva in 1816 (he was to be converted later [MacCarthy, p. 471]), although they were both agreed that the current Austrian occupation was insupportable.

Polidori's nationalist views were confirmed on his visit first to Lake Geneva as Byron' s private physician, and then later during his visit to Italy itself, even if they were now directed against Austria rather than France. While staying with Byron he met a character, at Mme de Stael's villa, whom Lorne MacDonald suggests 'rekindled his enthusiasm for Italy' (Macdonald, p. 79) 'Monsignor Brema, friend of Ugo Foscolo, enthusiastic for Italy, encomiast in all, Grand almoner of Italy, hater of Austrians' (*Diary*, p. 147; 5 Sept. 1816).[29] Later, he was to meet di Brema again in Milan and learn more about the suffering of the Milanese under Austrian rule. It is between these two meetings that Polidori most likely wrote *The Vampyre*. While in Milan that October he was imprisoned and then expelled for making fun of an Austrian soldier at the opera house, a probable reaction to another, earlier event concerning a man who had been accosted by the Austrian governor Suvorov ('Swarrow' as Polidori writes it [p. 183; 8 Dec 1819]) for not doffing his hat to the Emperor when in the same opera house [pp. 183–9; 8 Dec. 1819]). In Milan he also wrote several poems in which he extolled Italian independence, and condemned the treachery of Bonaparte for having promised freedom only to betray the Italian people: this was felt especially acutely since, in Polidori's view, Bonaparte was really an Italian.[30]

It thus seems that although Polidori was exposed to philhellenism while travelling with Lord Byron (and also later when with Lady Guilford [Macdonald, p. 139]), it never consumed him in the same way as did Italian nationalism. He does, however, seem to have understood that there was a comparison to be drawn between his desire to see Italy independent and the philhellene project. This becomes most apparent in a letter he sent to Byron while in Italy, after he had been expelled from Lombardy-Venetia:

> The scenery of Lombardy to Bologna is plain fruitfull but not beautifull but from Bologna (see there by all means the ruin from the Madonna di San Luca) to Florence + Aruzzo the scenery improves at every step The Cypress is common + tho the olives are not beautifull yet even they cannot destroy the effect of the 'colline' covered with Villas. I think that in this scenery you would often find what would recall Greece to your mind if altogether I have understood your descriptions – perhaps even if you read Pignotti Storia della Toscana you would not find it less devoid of recollections attached to caracters worthy to be rivals of those that even your imagination has painted. Indeed the more I read the Italian historians and the more I think upon the caracters of those around me the more nature I find in your pictures. (11 Jan. 1817)

The letter was ostensibly an attempt to re-ingratiate himself with Byron, however it can also be read as a form of gentle arrogance towards a man whom he secretly loathed. The subtext was that Italy affords as much of a heroic past, and also as many rebellious, nationalist characters as the giaour and corsair of Byron's poems: philhellene works with a political bent. The characters he reads of in Pignotti are 'worthy to be rivals' of those in Byron's work. This term is in fact quite hostile, since it implies that Italians are not only as worthy of attention as Greeks, but that they can also compete for attention with them. In such a manner Polidori excitedly transposes the philhellene project of Byron onto his own beloved Italy, and indirectly suggests that it become a subject for Byron's own pen. The comparison is especially pointed given that Pignotti's *Storia* paints a very precise and unromanticised account of the wranglings between various factions in Tuscany, rather than providing glamourous figures like *The Giaour*.[31] He describes political turbulence, but not banditry.

However, while Polidori was prepared to compare Italy to Greece when addressing Byron directly, the rivalry had been far less equal when he attacked Byron surreptitiously in *The Vampyre* to deliver an anti-philhellene message. The aristocratic outsider, a representative of Byron himself, is the real predator rather than the Ottoman presence to which the narrator refers, in a neat turnaround from the politics of Byron's *Fragment*. This again forms a stark contrast with Polidori's presentation of the Italian situation, since in both poems and letters he refers to the invidious nature of the Austrian presence.

Thus Polidori's execration of the philhellene Byron, and presentation of modern Greece as edenic and better left unroused by the memories of its heroic past, may be a begrudging denigration of a cause which in his view had led to people ignoring the claims on independence of a country with a similarly heroic, classical past. The very self-conscious comparison which Polidori makes between Greece and Italy in his letter to Byron supports this view, as does the fact that, despite his exposure to philhellenism through Byron and his coterie, and later through Lady Guilford, Polidori never expresses any support for the Greek cause in any of his letters home.

However, a more pragmatic reason for maligning philhellenism would have been the relationship between the Ottomans and the Austrians over the Adriatic. After the fall of Napoleon's Illyrian Republic in 1813, the area was given to the Austrians through Russian and British pressure.[32] This meant that Austria bordered the Ottomans both in Albania and Bosnia, not to mention other areas. Ottoman power was thus depleted, since Wallachia and Moldavia and rump Serbia were now out of Turkish control.[33] Furthermore, Tsar Alexander was now keen to pursue his own claims against the Ottomans, including areas around the Black and Caspian seas, and the right to spiritual dominion over all the Sultan's Christian subjects, rectifying concessions he had made to Turkey at the Treaty of Bucharest in 1812 (Nicolson, pp. 245–6). Both Russia and Austria-Hungary were now part of the 'Holy Alliance' of Christian Emperors, and were committed allies. Given the fact that Austrian influence was growing at the expense of Ottoman, it is not too much to suggest that Polidori's maligning of the philhellene cause was also motivated by pure pragmatism, since the further increase of Austrian domination made the possibility of independence for Italy even slighter, as their frontiers crept along the Adriatic coast.

In summation, intertextual allusions and the use of metaphor in Polidori's *The Vampyre* facilitate an embedded allegory which, contrary to some of the oblique references of the surface discourse, presents a view of Greece under the Ottomans as being sufficient to itself and as merely disturbed by the meddling of philhellenism. It also inverts some of the Orientalist assumptions about Ottoman rule present in the work of Lord Byron by adapting many of his own figures and imagery. This practice is spurred by Polidori's resentment at the way in which Whigs in England had ignored the cause of Italy, and his belief that it was 'worthy to be rival [s]' as a cause with Greece. It is also possibly a result of his realisation that Greek independence might well simply strengthen the Austro-Russian position in Southern Europe at that time.

2
J. Sheridan Le Fanu's *Carmilla* and the Austro-Hungarian *Ausgleich* (1867)

There is little surviving documentary evidence that J.S. Le Fanu showed any enthusiasm for the Eastern Question. While articles from the era of his tenancy as owner and editor of *Dublin University Magazine* (1861–69), show that he may have harboured an interest in Irish politics, particularly from July 1867 onwards,[1] no references to Hungary, the Austrian Empire or the Ottomans survive which might provide us with an insight into his views on events in Eastern Europe and beyond. The Austro-Hungarian setting for his vampire story *Carmilla* can, therefore, easily be dismissed as no more than a convenient one for a supernatural tale exploring lesbian sexuality (made necessary by the increasing redundancy of Catholic Italy and Spain as sites for the marvellous and superstitious), or else as a projection of his enduring interest with his own Irish situation. Certainly few scholars have paid attention to the geography or contemporary politics of the region in which the story is set (Styria), not even the group of Slovenian scholars like Dolar and Copjec who themselves hail from close to the unfortunate Laura's castle.[2]

Le Fanu's choice is, however, at the very least influenced by established lore on the residence of vampires, a tradition established by Dom Augustin Calmet's famous work of 1746, which had recently been translated by Henry Christmas (1850). The fact that the majority of 'oupires'[3] or vampires described by the *Lettres Juives* from which Calmet quotes are Hungarian, may have been enough motivation for making Carmilla a Magyar (i.e., ethnic Hungarian) as well.[4] Placing a vampire story in Styria – an area not specifically mentioned in Calmet, but bordering upon Hungary – is thus in keeping with his attempt to inject the story with historical verisimilitude and thus plausibility (an important aspect of the Gothic).

While the scholarship of Calmet at least explains Le Fanu's choice of a Middle and East European setting for a lesbian vampire story, most political discussions of *Carmilla* have centred around the Irish situation in the nineteenth century in Le Fanu's lifetime. Alok Bhalla, for example, sees a criticism of the brutality of the Anglo-Irish aristocracy towards the Catholic peasantry in the behaviour of the house of Karnstein, and a belated recognition of this fact in Laura's father.[5] Although Bhalla does not make the connection (being too early), we might now see this in relation to Roy Foster's 'protestant magic' argument, in which the failing fortunes and insecurities of the Anglo-Irish after Catholic emancipation in 1829 combine with their neurotic guilt to create a literary Fantastic. While Foster does not illustrate the thesis with Le Fanu's work, his name is included alongside Stoker, Mathurin and Bowen: 'marginalised Irish protestants all, often living in England but regretting Ireland, whose occult preoccupations surely mirror a sense of displacement, a loss of social and psychological integration.'[6] McCormack makes a similar argument in relation to *Uncle Silas*, in which Maud's life with her uncle represents a kind of unravelling of the inner man of her father, like the stripping away of the fake gentility of a class whose power had depended upon rapine, and which now seeks to prevent a feminine (implied Catholic) successor from taking power.[7] The work could also be read as a displaced allegory of the corrupt years of the Williamite succession after 1690, since Carmilla's family disappeared around 1698. Victor Sage harps on this date to argue that 'Le Fanu's earlier social allegory of the corrupt legacy of the Williamite period peeps out' in the story,[8] although since Carmilla is the displaced rather than the triumphant (who would more properly be Laura and her wise-seeming father, who fought for the Austrian army), this seems a rather inconsistent interpretation of such a possible allegory.

To see an expression of Irish politics within a tale set in an area of Europe with similar problems to Ireland is legitimate given Le Fanu's past. Le Fanu had always been associated with the Conservative cause in Ireland, although he had supported repeal of the union in 1847 thanks to his friendship with Thomas Davis and Isaac Butt (McCormack, pp. 100–3). Although not politically active by the 1860s, and in fact something of a recluse, he was nevertheless a part-owner, with Henry Maunsell, of the *Dublin Evening Mail* during this era (p. 209). While he may not have written this newspaper's harsh critiques of Nationalist activity, they certainly would have passed through his hands.

It is therefore tempting to see the politics of Unionist Ireland in Le Fanu's tale set in mid-century Austria, whether as justification for the ascendancy or sublimated guilt for its atrocities over the Catholic aristocracy, since the date of one of Carmilla's final portraits before committing suicide is 1698. However, this date also points to the possibility of an interest on Le Fanu's part in the politics of Austria and Hungary throughout the period, since it corresponds to the time in which the Austrian Emperor 'regained' his Hungarian lands. Other features of the tale also indicate a possible comment on Austrian politics, both past and contemporary.

The contention of this chapter is that *Carmilla* is heavily influenced by the politics of Middle Europe, and that Le Fanu, rather than taking Styria simply as a fashionable location for a modern vampire story or as a mask for Ireland, is commenting upon recent politics in the region itself, and the dangers of the Ausgleich of 1867. He is warning that the Emperor's creation of the Dual Nation, and the granting of autonomy and separate citizenship to Hungarians, is a danger to the stability of Central Europe, for reasons that shall become clear. The vices of vampirism are thus a veiled symbol for a new political instability to Austria of which the Hungarians are the certain harbingers. That said, Le Fanu's reactionary attitude to Austria-Hungary appears nevertheless to have been influenced by a similar problem at home, the Fenian rising, an event exactly contemporary to the Ausgleich. The story does not constitute a displaced allegory of the Irish situation, as Sage and Bhalla believe, so much as betray the political influence of similar situations closer to Le Fanu's home which, through parallel, determine his attitude to Austria. The embedded national allegory represented by the vampire is of a brutal Hungarian past set to destroy an orderly present.

Hungary 1526–1867

Carmilla's compatriots had enjoyed a rather inglorious history over the three and a half centuries before Le Fanu invented her unique life. After the Battle of Mohacs in 1526, much of central Hungary and Croatia was ceded by King Louis II to the Turks, although Transylvania remained under the rule of John Szapolyai,[9] despite his being temporarily ousted by Ferdinand of Austria (Ferdinand had right of kingship due to the fact that he had married King Louis's sister Anna in 1521, and was recognized as heir [Leger, p. 256]). Through a pact with the Turkish Sultan, John regained his kingdom in 1529, but at the price of huge concessions to Soliman the Magnificent (p. 316). In subsequent years the Szapolyais had to grant ever greater concessions to Soliman and later Sultans in order to keep the semblance of Hungarian autonomy in Transylvania.

The reality of Ottoman rule became so obvious that by 1566 Sigismond Szapolyai demoted himself to 'most serene prince' in order to appease Soliman (p. 321). After his death the Bathory family took over in Transylvania, and asserted more independence. During this period historical Hungary was ruled by the Austrians just north of the Danube and in Croatia, by Turkey south of the Danube as far as Voivodina, and by a Hungarian himself in Transylvania, whose sovereignty was recognised (and in truth largely controlled) by the Ottomans but not by the Hapsburgs. The area bordering Styria was under Ottoman rule throughout the sixteenth and seventeenth centuries.

The year 1599 changed all this with the invasion of Transylvania by the Austrian General Basta (p. 326), and the attempt by Emperor Maximilian II to take over the land originally promised to his father Ferdinand by Louis II of Hungary. The Austrians were eventually driven out, in 1606, and successive Hungarian monarchs managed to rule the region largely independently. In the 1680s the Protestant Prince Tököli pushed the Austrians out of Upper Hungary, before going into league with the Ottoman Sultan.[10] Transylvanian autonomy was to continue until 1699, when the region was eventually annexed by a strong Austria, the final result of a long campaign from the raising of the Siege of Vienna in 1683.

The Siege of Vienna is a curious event, not least because what should have been the crowning achievement of Ottoman military success in Europe turned into its singularly most disastrous move. Fearful of any encroachment upon his dominion, the Pope Innocent XI entreated the Polish king Jan Sobieski to come to the relief of the Austrians, and he did so, inflicting spectacular casualties upon the Turks (Leger, p. 269). The deathwound on the army of Soliman II paved the way for the revanchement upon what Emperor Leopold I considered to be his ancestral lands. In 1699 the Treaty of Karlowicz was signed, in which the Turks accepted the victories of his son Prince Eugene, and by Leopold's death all of Hungary, including Transylvania and Voivodina, had come into the Austrian Empire (nominally at least), except a tiny territory to the East between the Theiss and the Maros rivers (p. 337), which was still Ottoman.

There were frequent insurrections by Hungarian malcontents. In 1703 Ferenc Rackoczy II, stepson of Tököli, returned to his native country and proclaimed Hungarian independence and the beginning of a civil war against the Austrians (Szabad, p. 153). Eventually shaken by his defeat, the Hungarian Diet accepted the olive branch offered in the Peace of Szathmar (1711), which included a general amnesty and recognition of Hungarian rights (Leger, p. 341).

Throughout the eighteenth century there were continued concessions to Hungarian autonomy. Indeed, under Marie Therese and Josef II all of the Austro-Hungarian Empire benefited from the relaxation of serfdom and of tithes in an attempt to break the tyranny of local aristocracies.[11] In 1787 a Hungary that included Croatia and Transylvania was divided into ten regions, but with a centralised system in Budapest. After Josef's death in 1790, Leopold II came to power and, with what Barbara Jelavich understands as a 'greater sense of political realism' (Jelavich, p. 27) abolished the regions and reinstituted the Hungarian Diet.

During the middle of the nineteenth century there was increased Hungarian nationalism. In 1843 the Hungarian Diet proclaimed Hungarian the main language of their province, replacing as an official language the Latin used there formerly, much to the chagrin of the other peoples in the country (p. 40). In 1848 the uprising under Kossuth was so successful as to secure virtual independence for Hungary, and a liberal constitution of its own devising, only to be brutally crushed by the Russian army in August of the following year (pp. 47–8).

The new, 19-year-old Austrian Emperor, Franz-Josef, abolished autonomy and asserted direct rule over all of his Empire: neoabsolutism replaced the local constitutions allowed by his predecessors as all was brought under a Viennese bureaucracy in which he had the right to appoint the main ministers but not the parliament. However, this proved untenable, and by 1865 the Emperor was bowing to the pressure for appeasing the Hungarians (pp. 62–3). Deak's proposition that the Empire be drawn up along dualist grounds eventually led to the Ausgleich of 1867, in which Franz-Josef refashioned the Empire into two, allowing the Hungarians separate citizenship, their own power of taxation, and the withdrawal of the imperial patent over conscription. The newly enfranchised parliament had the rule of Transylvania and Croatia, although no separate army and no separate currency. Furthermore, Franz-Josef directly appointed the ministries of defence, finance and foreign affairs for the whole nation (pp. 65–7). Despite this, the Hungarians had the ability to block reforms in the entire Dual Nation, and frequently asserted this power (p. 73). It was against these immediate events that Le Fanu published *Carmilla* in the 1871–72 editions of *The Dark Blue*.

The British attitude to the Austro-Hungarians, and its likely impact upon Le Fanu, is complex. Le Fanu's political hero, Lord Palmerston (McCormack, p. 220), had taken a slightly anti-Austrian position throughout his tenure as Foreign Secretary before the 1848 election, disagreeing with the Austrian foreign minister, Metternich (whom he hated), over democratic government for Switzerland and the freedom of

Italy in 1851. Similarly, there was perplexity over Austrian refusal to take part in the Crimean War against Russia, even though this would have been an impossible commitment for Metternich, given the debt he owed the Russians after the suppression of the Hungarian uprising: an uprising which had been popular amongst ordinary Britons.[12]

However, while Palmerston himself had condemned Austria for its treatment of Hungarians when he was foreign minister in the Liberal government in 1848, he had nevertheless regretted the uprising since he saw no real reason for Hungarian independence and a weakening of Austrian power north of the Alps.[13] As Pribram writes: 'He certainly sympathized with the Magyars' desire to maintain their constitutional rights, but he did not want Hungary to become independent of Austria, because he feared she might then be sacrificed to Russian expansionist policy' (Pribram 1951, p. 41). Since Le Fanu's decision to write a short-lived political column in 1865 for the *Dublin University Magazine* was prompted, according to McCormack, by Palmerston's death and a need to fill a political vacuum, one might expect an observation of Palmerston's opinions to serve as a close barometer of Le Fanu's own (McCormack, p. 220). Generally speaking, the position of a Palmerstonian Conservative at this time would have been to favour the continuation of Austrian rule in Middle Europe as a bulwark against further Russian advances into Central Europe, but to be exasperated at the lack of commitment shown by the Austrians over other issues like Russia, Italy and Poland.

Carmilla's specific setting is, of course, in Styria, near the town of Gratz, which had in fact never been part of Hungary. For this reason the inclusion of a Hungarian dynasty like Carmilla's in a Styrian village in the late 1690s is frankly unlikely. Both Upper and Lower Styria, which held both German and Slavic language communities, had been Austrian possessions since the time of the division of Hapsburg lands between the two brothers Charles and Ferdinand in 1519. After Ferdinand I's death in 1571, Styria was still not to be part of a united Austrian Empire until Leopold I's accumulation of all ancestral lands in 1665, since Ferdinand divided his provinces between all three of his sons (Leger, p. 259). Today Lower Styria, or at least part of it, helps to form Slovenia (the bulk of which is the old Austrian province of Carniola), although the area around Gratz in Upper Styria is still a part of Austria. Whether Laura's Schloss and the village of Karnstein are in Austria or Slovenia today is a difficult, and frankly meaningless task, to decode, although being south of Gratz, both are clearly on the border between Upper and Lower (we are told that Mircalla's lover was a native of Upper Styria, hence his closeness to Karnstein).[14]

Despite this minor error on Le Fanu's part – which may have been as a result of reading a certain travelogue from the 1830s (see below p.58) – the intention was still to illustrate Hungarian-Austrian relations at his own time, for his further knowledge of the region's history – not to mention details of Austro-Hungarian life – is impeccable. Indeed the details of both the setting, and the plot of *Carmilla*, demonstrate considerable research on his part.

The politics of *Carmilla*

The story of 'Carmilla' is that of a coming of age for a young Austrian lady called Laura, brought up in a deserted Schloss bought by her father after his retiring from a career in the Austrian army. Her mother was of part Hungarian heritage, descended from the old Karnstein family whose ruined village is situated nearby, her father an Englishman of more lowly origin whose services to the Austrian Empire have permitted him to live in grander style than he would expect at home (Le Fanu, p. 244). She has two 'governantes', a Swiss lady called Madame Perrodon and a younger French lady called Mademoiselle De Lafontaine (p. 245), who has the gift of second sight.

As a child she experienced a strange visitation from a young woman who hugged her and bit her breast, which she still remembers (pp. 246–7). Now as a young woman she is lonely and needs company, and desperately desires the presence of the niece of her father's friend, General Spielsdorf. Sadly, it soon transpires that General Spielsdorf's niece has died (p. 249). A carriage breaks down outside her Schloss, in which there are two women, an older and a younger. Laura's father offers to take in the younger who is unwell, and the offer is accepted (pp. 253–4). Later, Mlle de Lafontaine tells Laura that she saw a black, turbaned woman inside the carriage who was gnashing her teeth with anger (p. 257).

During her visit the young woman, Carmilla, is continually unwell and only ever arises at sunset. A strange disease, called the 'oupire', in which young girls waste away to death, breaks out amongst the local people and Laura herself starts to feel feebler. The doctor Spielsberg tells Laura's father that the explanation may be supernatural, but he refuses to believe it (p. 271). They unearth a portrait of a lady who looks entirely like Carmilla, dated 1698, whose name turns out to be Mircalla, but as yet none make the connection that their guest may be one of the undead (pp. 272–3). Eventually, Laura's mysterious dreams of visitation, coupled with the discovery that Carmilla is absent from her room during the night, lead the father to accept that the doctor's reasoning may be right, and he organises a trip to Karnstein, the town holding Carmilla's tomb, to meet a local priest.

On the way they meet his old friend General Spielsdorf, who is on a similar visit, but to get at the tomb of Carmilla itself (p. 292). He tells the story of how, at a masked ball, he met two ladies, one younger, one older, the latter of whom secured his hospitality for the younger (p. 301). His niece, like Laura, had been happy to have a companion, but sadly died as a result of the bloodsucking which took place (p. 305). He now wishes to find the tomb and behead the vampire (p. 306).

Neither the priest nor the local people can find it, but fortunately a Moravian baron Vordenburgh, who has details of her whereabouts from a manuscript made by Carmilla's former lover, can trace it for them (p. 313). When Carmilla returns, she initially escapes their grasp, but eventually has to return to her crypt to sleep, and is beheaded (pp. 310–11). To help her recover from both the illness, and presumably the death of her lover, Laura's father takes her on a tour.

The influence of Austro-Hungarian history on the tale is apparent from the dating. The last known picture of Carmilla, from 1698, is from one year before the Treaty of Karlowicz when the Sultan conceded the Hungarian territories to Leopold I of Austria. Since she looks exactly as she does in the painting, we may assume that it was painted very close to the date of her suicide, which turned her into a vampire (p. 318). When the picture is uncovered, Carmilla tries to affect a blasé attitude to the resemblance, by declaring that she, like Laura, may be related to the Karnsteins. 'Are there any Karnsteins living now?' she asks with faux naïveté. Laura replies:

> None who bear the name, I believe. The family were ruined, I believe, in some civil wars long ago, but the ruins of the castle are only about three miles away.
>
> How interesting! she said languidly. (p. 273)

Although Victor Sage declares that the civil wars refer to the Williamite wars, and thus that Carmilla is a symbolic legacy of the original Williamite ascendancy (Sage, p. 199), this seems unlikely due to the fact that she would have been one of those swept away by the change rather than the ascending. However, if we treat the location of the tale less metaphorically, the civil wars can easily be seen as referring to the uprisings of disaffected Hungarian nobles under Ferenc Rakoczy II against their new Austrian masters, which did not end until 1711. Since Laura identifies with Austria, from her point of view these insurrections would have been civil wars. Perhaps Carmilla's languid understatement at that moment is a means not only of masking her true identity, but also of concealing a smouldering difference of opinion as to how the wars should in fact be labelled.

The date of Carmilla's exhumation is also given obliquely, since Laura informs us, when the coffin is opened, that 'The features, though a hundred and fifty years had passed since her funeral, were tinted with the warmth of life' (p. 315). Since Carmilla was probably buried in 1698–99, this puts the date of both her disinterment and of the events in the story at around 1848, the year of the Hungarian uprising, or its suppression in 1849.

The significance of this timing from a historical point of view is quite obvious, given that the Karnstein family is Hungarian. The Hungarian aristocracy fell with the capitulation of the Turks to the Austrians – not only in autonomous Transylvania but in other areas under Ottoman rule, to be replaced by a 'superior' civilization which left Hungary to the mercy of Leopold's Catholic fanaticism (Prince Tököli of Transylvania was a fervent Protestant, although his stepson, Ferenc Rakoczy II, was in fact Catholic). The association of Carmilla with the turbaned black woman also highlights the sense that the Hungarians rode on the fortunes of an Oriental power. Thus for Le Fanu the Hungarian uprising of 1848 represents the resurgence of an older, and more primitive order which is associated with Ottoman rule.

Although fanciful by the standards of the 1840s and 1860s, this interpretation of Hungaro-Ottoman relations is accurate by the standards of the later seventeenth and early eighteenth century. Hungarian rulers, including Tököli, had always tended to side with the Ottomans rather than the Austrians,[15] since the Sultan at least recognised the legitimacy of their crown in Transylvania, while the Austrians did not. In the only English language book on Hungarian history to be published in Le Fanu's own lifetime, Emeric Szabad reports how the rebel Ferenc Rakoczy II had declared, on returning to Hungary in 1703:

> Who does not know that the days of the rule of the Crescent are now looked back upon as moments of happiness? And who is not aware, from the accounts lately made public, that the sums, extorted by the Austrians in a single year, exceeded the tribute the Turks used for half a century? (Szabad, pp. 154–5)

The Hapsburgs of this era also refused to tolerate Protestantism, being heavily influenced by the Jesuits, while the Ottomans did not repress the faith of almost half the Magyar population in those dominions that they possessed outright.

In Jamesonian fashion (see Introduction, pp. 25–7) the 'appalling superstition' of a native people becomes a national allegory when presented as a Gothic tale which casts this superstition about revenants from the dead, who suck the blood of the young and spread sexual perversity, as symbolic of a political threat. It thus constitutes a negative judgement of the 1848 uprising against the Austrian Empire's superior order: one which will weaken the body politic of the future – metaphorically bleed it. Kossuth's rebellion represents less the establishment of a more just and enlightened society than the return to a more brutal past: a feature supported on a less metaphorical level by Carmilla's expression of a preference for mediaeval justice when, reacting to the insolence of a pedlar, she suggests to Laura that her own father 'would have had the wretch tied up to the pump, and flogged with a cart-whip, and burnt to the bones with the castle brand' (Le Fanu, p. 269). Given the time it was written (1870), the tale further works as a warning about the recent Ausgleich (1867). The Dual Nation could undermine Austrian power further and degrade the whole society, particularly if Carmilla is suggesting there should be such retributive forms of local justice.

That Laura's father is an Englishman rightly reflects the fact that many of the Austro-Hungarian officers were foreign recruits, but helps to give her an even stronger association with the forward-looking and democratic West, just as the black woman in a turban gives Carmilla an association with a despotic and chaotic East, regardless of the specific relation to Turkish rule. However, despite this seeming juxtaposition, that Laura's mother should have been a descendant of the Karnstein family and thus Laura herself be a blood relative of Carmilla, suggests that the young lady is mixed, in both a political and a rational sense: she is partly western and partly oriental; partly rational and partly governed by the same Dionysian urges that rage through the vampiric visitor.

This itself might serve to confuse us: why should the invader of Laura's calm also be part of her nature? Copjec's answer has been to argue that the story illustrates the uncanny, or unheimlich: the persistence of the familiar in the foreign in which the repressed dream comes to the surface.[16] However, from a political point of view this serves to confuse the polarity between East and West, unreason and reason, which the tale sets up. An answer to this problem arises from analysing the sources themselves in greater detail.

Sources

The major vampire sources for the story are the tales of Dom Augustin Calmet. These had been translated into English by the Reverend Henry Christmas and published in 1850, and were clearly of use to Le Fanu. Robert Tracy, in his notes to *In a Glass Darkly*, shows how the story of the Moravian enticing the vampire up Karnstein church steeple before beheading him, is taken wholesale from one of Calmet's accounts (Le Fanu, p. 346).[17] There are many other correspondences as well, such as the passage in which Carmilla is finally defined as a vampire, near the end of the tale, along with an explanation of the superstition:

> The disappearance of Carmilla was followed by the discontinuance of my nightly sufferings.
>
> You have heard, no doubt, of the appalling superstition that prevails in Upper and Lower Styria, in Moravia, Silesia, in Turkish Servia, in Poland, even in Russia; the superstition, so we must call it, of the vampire. (Le Fanu, p. 315)

This listing of East European regions, including many of the above places, is a feature originally repeated throughout Calmet's own commentary over his sources, although unlike here Hungary, the country from which there are most accounts of vampires, is always included. For example, at the beginning of Calmet's book (in Christmas's translation) we are told how: 'In this age, a new scene presents itself to our eyes, and has done for about sixty years in Hungary, Moravia, Silesia and Poland; men, it is said, who have been dead for several months, come back to earth' (Calmet, 1850, 112). Later in the introduction he tells us 'I undertake to treat here on the matter of the vampires of Hungary, Moravia, Silesia, and Poland' (II 4), and we are even informed that 'Turkish Servia' (II 38) is also a country in which vampires are common. At no point, however, does Calmet mention Styria, and in this we can see the depth of Le Fanu's research into the region (see below p.58), and also the extent to which he wished to juxtapose Austria with Hungary by choosing an area of one that borders the other.

Le Fanu's direct reading of Calmet also influences the exact physical descriptions of the vampire, adding to the 'scientific' proof of its reality. When Carmilla's sleeping body is uncovered in the crypt of Karnstein, we are told that:

> The limbs were perfectly flexible, the flesh elastic; and the leaden coffin floated with blood, in which to a depth of seven inches, the body lay

immersed. Here then, were all the admitted signs and proofs of vampirism. (Le Fanu, p. 315)

The depiction of her flesh as containing life, her limbs as still being movable and her whole body as being covered in blood, probably derives from another story in the *Lettres Juives* quoted by Calmet, and in Christmas's translation. The body of Heyducq Millo, the Hungarian vampire who had been infected in 'Turkish Servia', is described as follows: 'His body was red, his hair, nails and beard had all grown again, and his veins were replete with fluid blood, which flowed from all parts of his body upon the winding sheet which encompassed him' (Calmet 1850, II 38). As well as being drenched in blood and still elastic, we are told of Carmilla that 'there was a faint but appreciable respiration, and a corresponding action of the heart' (Le Fanu, p. 315). Calmet's old man of 'Graditz', who was exhumed in 1738, is found in his grave: 'with his eyes open, having a fine colour, with natural respiration, nevertheless motionless as the dead' (Calmet 1850, II 36). One can see, therefore, that there are strong verbal and physical similarities between Le Fanu's description of Carmilla's exhumation, and those provided in Christmas's translation of Calmet.

All of these details pertaining to Carmilla's body are called 'the admitted signs and proofs of vampirism,'(Le Fanu, p. 315) and Laura appears to be keen to show the proof of something her sceptical father had so long doubted. From the author's point of view the evidence would have been best gleaned from a 'scientific' and empirical work on the revenant, since the events of the tale are supposed to suspend our disbelief as they do Laura's and her father's. Thus the intended science of Dom Calmet facilitates the 'scientific' nature of Le Fanu's descriptions.

A more politically motivating source for Carmilla is the account of the crimes of Erzsebet Bathory, who was imprisoned for life by the Austrians on account of her terrible cruelty to young peasant women – a source mentioned, although not explicated, by Jean Marigny.[18] The story was first dredged up from Viennese court archives of 1611 by Michael Wagener for his book *Beitrage zur Philosophischen Anthropologie* (1796), but was translated for an English audience first in 1863, by William Sabine Baring-Gould.

Baring-Gould quotes Wagener's description of how a certain 'Elisabeth—' was awakened to the joys of cruelty when she corrected a servant-maid by boxing her on the ears so that her blood gushed onto her mistress's face. He recounts how: 'When the blood drops were washed off her face, her skin appeared much more beautiful – whiter and more transparent on the spots where the blood had been.'[19] Thus she resolved to bathe her whole body in human blood, so frequently, that she bathed every morning (Baring-Gould, p. 140).

Elizabeth lured girls to the castle and then beat them till their bodies were swollen, and ready to be used for blood, but appears in the process to have become interested not just in the rejuvenating liquid, but in the cruelties themselves, committing torture. Baring-Gould relates how on one occasion she stripped a servant girl naked and smothered her with honey, casting her out (presumably to a death by bee stings), and how she stuck needles in those that sat next to her 'especially if they were of her own sex' (p. 140). This mixture of sadism with female homoeroticism can be read as implicit to Wagener's account in Baring-Gould's translation, and thus may have inspired Le Fanu's decision to write the first story about a lesbian vampire. The Hungarian nationality of Erzsebet Bathory also may have helped influence Le Fanu to make Carmilla a Hungarian as well – and possibly, since she was against the Austrians, led him to investigate the dynamic of Austro-Hungarian relations.

Cruelty combined with lesbian sexuality brings us to another source of *Carmilla*, namely 'Christabel'. Arthur H. Nethercott and Giovanna Silvani have already explored this relation,[20] but a reexamination of its significance in the light of Austro-Hungarian politics produces startling results. In the poem Christabel goes out late at night to seek a phantom lover, only to meet instead Geraldine, a beautiful lady dressed in white silk and gems who has been kidnapped and left in the forest by a group of knights. Christabel feels pity for her and so takes her back to her chamber, and allows Geraldine to lie with her. Geraldine is not telling the truth, of course, and 'In the touch of this bosom there worketh a spell'[21] – through her breast she induces a trance in the unsuspecting Christabel.

The next morning Christabel is conscious of having sinned, although why, she does not know. She takes Geraldine to see her father Sir Leoline, who immediately becomes enraptured with the beautiful Geraldine, especially when he hears she is the daughter of his old friend Sir Roland. He asks Bracy the bard to go and visit Sir Roland, but the bard tells him first that he has just experienced the most bizarre vision of a snake killing a dove. At this point the jealous Christabel sees Geraldine look at her like a snake – 'the lady's eyes they shrunk in her head, / Each shrunk up to a serpent's eye' (Coleridge, p. 233, ll. 584–5) – and finally breaks the silence on her jealousy, asking her father to send Geraldine away. He refuses, ashamed that his only child should dishonour him so.

The two parts of the poem are very different, having been written at a distance in time (1797 and 1800). However, the overall poem deals with the relation between sexual awakening and moral corruption. A particularly unusual feature is the relationship between Geraldine and Christabel's dead mother. The theological background to the poem is Catholic, with various references to the Virgin Mary, whom Christabel actually thanks for having saved Geraldine. However, the history of Christabel's own mother is equally significant to the visitor. Once in the chamber she asks:

> And will your mother pity me,
> Who am a maiden most forlorn?
> Christabel answered – woe is me!
> She died the very hour that I was born.
> I have heard the grey-haired friar tell
> How on her death bed she did say,
> That she should hear the castle-bell
> Strike twelve upon my wedding-day.
> O mother dear! That thou wert here!
> I would, said Geraldine, she were!
>
> But soon with altered voice, said she –
> 'Off wandering mother! Peak and pine!
> I have power to bid thee flee.'
> Alas! What ails poor Geraldine?
> Why stares she with unsettled eye?
> Can she the bodiless dead espy?
> And why with hollow voice cries she,
> 'Off, woman off! this hour is mine –
> Though thou her guardian spirit be
> Off, woman, off! 'tis given to me.'

(pp. 222–3, ll.194–213)

Geraldine competes with the mother for possession of the daughter. However, she also resembles the mother in that she too wears a shroud (p. 216; l. 13), being dressed in a 'silken robe of white' (p. 217; l. 59); moreover, she imparts her spell through her breast in an imitation of maternal suckling (p. 224; l. 267). The implication is that the mother figure is both the protector of virginity and the imparter of sexual knowledge: that Geraldine is both sexual and chastising. The moral ambivalence in the poem has been seen as a result of the Unitarian Coleridge's unusual views on emotional education.[22]

There are, nevertheless, subtle changes from the relation between Geraldine and Christabel's mother, to that between Carmilla and Laura's mother, which have a profound effect upon the political meaning of Le Fanu's tale. While the guardian spirit of Christabel's mother does not interfere, the same is not true concerning that of Laura's mother. During a visitation, Laura describes how:

> One night, instead of the voice I was accustomed to hear in the dark, I heard one, sweet and tender, and at the same time terrible, which said, 'Your mother warns you to beware of the assassin.' At the same time a light unexpectedly sprang up, and I saw Carmilla, standing, near the foot of my bed, in her white nightdress, bathed, from her chin to her feet, in one great stain of blood.
>
> I awakened with a shriek, possessed with the one idea that Carmilla was being murdered. (Le Fanu, p. 283)

Here the spirit of the mother warns Laura against the invader (unsuccessfully, since Laura's immediate impression is that it is Carmilla herself who is in danger), rather than the invader warning off the mother as in the poem, and the mother's spirit presumably provides the spurt of light which illuminates the form of Carmilla drenched in blood – in the original poem the chamber keeps out the light of the moon, presumably a symbol of virginity (Coleridge, p. 222; l. 176). The mother's moral link with Geraldine is severed entirely in this work, and the ambivalence of maternal protectress and initiator into sexual life is divided, so that the dead mother, whose only link with Carmilla is the more real one of genealogy, is not associated with the sexual and certainly not with unorthodox sexuality.

The ambivalence of the mother figure as both protectress and beloved is not, however, entirely lost in Le Fanu's story, but is loaded entirely onto Carmilla's side of the family. The woman who accompanies Carmilla in the carriage, and Millarca to the ball, identifies herself as her mother when she calls Carmilla 'My daughter' (Le Fanu, p. 253). Carmilla also confirms this. When she 'comes to' in the Schloss after her accident, Carmilla asks for 'Mamma', and then further asks: ' "Where am I? What is this place? ... I don't see the carriage; and Matska, where is she?" ' (p. 255).

The word 'Matska' would appear to be a corruption of the word for 'mother' in certain slavonic languages (notably Polish), 'Matka':[23] the diminutive, with the 's', is a way of signifying affection (although rather imperfectly since Matka, already ending 'ka', unlike other words cannot really be diminuised in this way).[24] Indeed, any reader who read this word, even if they knew no Slavonic languages, would probably assume it to signify the mother due to the fact that it begins with M, and because Carmilla has already called for 'Mamma' (p. 255). Since Le Fanu probably never went further than Paris, and might well assume that his audience itself did not know the difference between Slavonic languages and Hungarian (which would have been Carmilla's first language), it would hardly be surprising if he put East European words in the mouth of a vague 'East European' vampire without checking for accuracy. Since many of the local people in Styria (although not all) would have spoken Slovenian, or even Serbo-Croatian, it would not be such a grave error – although the word for mother in Slovenian is in fact 'mati' or 'matica', and in Serbo-Croatian is 'maika'. A Polish word in the mouth of a Hungarian aristocrat would, nevertheless, not be so obvious an error for the nineteenth-century British reader.

However, the word 'mátka' is also to be found in the Hungarian tongue, and means 'betrothed' or 'fiancée'. Hence, it would appear that Le Fanu is punning, imperfectly, on the similarity between the Polish word for 'mother' and the Hungarian word for 'betrothed', disguising both in a faulty form of Slavonic diminution. The ambivalence between the two meanings of the word, the woman as beloved and mother, recalls the relationship of Geraldine to Christabel, but is now entirely centred through the introduction of this third female onto the Geraldine figure, Carmilla, and not on to Laura. Laura's own mother, although a descendant of Carmilla, firmly rebels against family history from the grave in wanting to save her daughter from both death and perversion. Thus the ambivalent mixture in mother--daughter relations of virtuous protector and lesbian attachment, which are present in Coleridge's poem, are now completely divided upon family lines. Lesbianity and incest, while part of the Hungarian Karnstein family, are elements that its present and most recent incarnations are determined to cast out. Contrary to the arguments of the recent school of Slovene *Carmilla* critics, the potential subliminal meanings of motherhood relating to breast-feeding and the other concepts are ironed out in what is effectively an untangling of the moral equivocation of 'Christabel' in order to illustrate a political division. Indeed it is possible that the double meaning of 'Matska' points to the fact that the lady is not really her mother at all, but an older lover in a convenient façade.

Thus the sources for *Carmilla* which deal with Hungary point to a likely interest in the region which colours the portrayal of the vampire as Hungarian, blood-thirsty and a lesbian. The treatment of 'Christabel' and its symbolic paralleling of lesbian love object and maternal figure is treated to a bifurcation which indicates that, while the heroine may have such perversity in her family history, still latent in her own desires, it is something which nevertheless belongs to her family at a different time and must now be purged through removing the 'assassin'. This separation helps to illustrate the divide between the morality of an Austro-Hungarian family under Austrian rule now, as opposed to its antecedents of a Hungarian family under Ottoman rule.

Despite the obvious political convenience of Styria, it is still slightly surprising that Le Fanu should light upon it and describe it so intimately, when Calmet did not even mention it. The answer to this perhaps lies in Le Fanu reading one of the few recent English language travel books devoted entirely to Styria, namely Captain Basil Hall's *Schloss Hainfeld; or, a Winter in Lower Styria* (1836).

Basil Hall and his family are staying in Naples when the Polish countess Rzewuska informs them that she is to pass on an invitation from Countess Purgstall of Styria to come and stay with her in her Schloss Hainfeld, south of Gratz, on account of an earlier friendship with his father, Sir James Hall, during her youth in Edinburgh.[25] Hall's account constitutes one of few at that time to describe the remote province of Lower Styria, and does so with regard to its lonely castles and decaying aristocratic families.

The countess has not changed anything in the castle since her husband's death during the Napoleonic wars, and even stays in the bed where her only son died (pp. 36–8). She is now so ill as to be constantly bedridden, but well read due to a literary youth when she was friends with Sir Walter Scott, and so generally very good company for the Halls. In an episode worthy of someone who is described as physically in 'bodily decay' (p. 38), she shows Captain Hall her iron coffin when explaining to him how she, a Protestant, can be buried in her dead husband's family vault without touching Catholic earth (pp. 59–60).

Her macabre aspect and sense of humour may have interested Le Fanu, but it is a verbal similarity which indicates that this travel book probably inspired Le Fanu to set his vampire story in the desolate and wooded Styria described by Hall: 'Miss Jane Anne Cranstoun was born in Scotland about the year 1760, of a noble family, both by the mother's and father's side' (Hall, p. 35). This may explain why Le Fanu gives a Hungarian vampire a German name. The teutonic basis of the name

'Cranstoun' makes it far easier to convert to a German language 'Karnstein' than to anything Hungarian. The fact that Countess Purgstall turns out to have been the first person to publish Scott's first poem, a translation of Buerger's Gothic ballad *Leonora* (pp. 331–4), suggests why he wished to refer to her obliquely in the form of Carmilla Karnstein (whether Countess Purgstall would have appreciated such a coded homage is perhaps open to question).

From a political point of view Hall's book may also have presented Styria as a likely site of political tension. Hall describes how Schloss Riegersburg, a now desolate former castle of the Purgstalls, had been under constant attack from the Ottomans in previous years:

> In old times it had proved a fortress of such strength, that the Turks, when they conquered and overran the greater part of the country which now forms the Austrian dominions, never made any impression upon it; and it is said, they never dared to attempt its capture. (p. 52)

Further to the Ottoman connection, Hall also stresses the barbaric and primitive nature of the Hungarian aristocracy when describing one of his excursions over the border (p. 70). The eccentricity of Jane Cranstoun, and lonely grandeur of Styria and its Schlosses as described by Hall, may have combined with Le Fanu's interest in Hungarian threats to Austria to become an inspiration for the Hungarian Vampiric invader, who attempts to usher in a final, Ottoman revenge. While a few other travel books from the era describe Styria,[26] only Hall describes it as a desolate area of ruined castles and impoverished aristocrats, he alone having had such unique access to them, making his work another possible source for *Carmilla*.

The Ottoman past to the region is symbolised in the story by the black woman gnashing her teeth in the carriage. As a motif she is literally concealed, since only Mademoiselle De Lafontaine, who has the gift of second sight, is able to see her:

> 'Did you remark a woman in the carriage, after it was set up again, who did not get out,' inquired Mademoiselle, 'but only looked from the window?
>
> No, we had not seen her.
>
> Then she described a hideous black woman, with a sort of coloured turban on her head, who was gazing all the time from the carriage window, nodding and grinning derisively towards the ladies, with gleaming eyes and large white eye-balls, and her teeth set as if in fury. (pp. 256–7)

The turban denotes the woman as being Oriental, and perhaps represents, in rather Swedenborgian fashion, the inner woman of the vampire unveiled. Carmilla is externally pale, and confirms that she comes from a castle to the West of Laura's own (p. 263). The real Carmilla is an emissary of a collapsing civilization to the East, bent upon revenge against the modern day Austrian commoners who now inhabit the grand Schlosses of Styria, and is either black-hearted, or else more lecherous than her virginal demeanour portrays.

That the woman should be described as 'black', and not simply of darker skin, may be due to the distinctions of the time, since Gypsies were often described as 'black' – although this is unlikely given the fact that she is also described as having 'large white eyeballs', in keeping with a black African stereotype. Politically it presents us with something of an anomaly if the woman is of southern African descent. While her turban definitely marks her out as symbolically Oriental, her blackness does not make her obviously Oriental in any given symbolic structure, since Sub-Saharan Africa was never under Ottoman rule, merely a source of slaves for the Empire.

A major reason for making the hidden anima of Carmilla a turbaned black woman rather than a turbaned Turkish or Arab woman, is probably, as Diane Mason has noted, the recent stir created by Manet's portrait 'Olympia',[27] exhibited in Paris in 1865. The picture showed a beautiful naked white courtesan on a divan, facing the spectator as though he or she were a client entering the room. Behind her is a cowed-looking black woman with a multicoloured scarf wrapped round her head (almost like a turban), holding red and white roses – presumably sent as a gift by the client in the position of the spectator. On the couch next to Olympia is a black cat.

Following the original art criticism of Sander Gilman,[28] Mason relates how the black woman in the painting has been considered a symbol of the degenerate 'animal' sexuality governing Olympia, somehow degrading her (Mason, p. 128),[29] as well as a coded reference to lesbianity (since black was a colour related to lesbian desire in gynaecological books of the time), and hence its re-emergence in Le Fanu's tale. It could also be an ironic comment on normative Western values, as it inverts the relation of white and black to good and evil: a wicked white prostitute served by a kind-looking black servant, the portrayal of the latter obviously increasing the shock caused by the painting. The representation of a black woman next to a prostitute, holding red and white flowers (symbols of the holy virgin), recalls the images used for confusing the sacred with the profane in Baudelaire's poems, in which sexual images of creole women symbolise correspondences to both angels and demons. In Le Fanu's work the sexuality is of a lesbian vampiric type, and the derisive grinning of the furious, black, turbaned woman from behind Carmilla as she is carried out prostrate, represents this sexuality as far more vicious and rapacious than in Manet's painting. Furthermore, rather than her forming a contrast to the pale woman, the black woman is now related to her entirely due to the theme of revelation through second sight: she is not her complement, but her inner soul. Thus the sense of moral equivocation suggested by the flowers and the pale skin of the prostitute is entirely lost in translation, just as the moral equivocation of 'Christabel' is also lost in the story. The cat, an image of the predatory sexual soul, is also a Baudelairean image (Mauner, p. 94), and although it is unlikely that Le Fanu would have read any of Baudelaire's poems, its status as a sexual predator in the painting would not have been lost on him, perhaps explaining why Carmilla's transmogrified form is a black cat.[30]

Thus Le Fanu found the details about Hungarian vampires through his reading of Calmet and of Baring-Gould, seeing their domain as the most likely area for vampirism mixed with sexual perversity (the Baring-Gould book, in particular, was still much in vogue). His use of Calmet allowed him to ground the events of the story not only in 'accurately' recounted detail, but also to copy the style of scientific appraisal apparent in Calmet's accounts and thus give a semblance of empiricism in Laura's history, helping the reader to suspend disbelief. The Austro-Hungarian setting further gives political prominence to the fantastical vampire, allowing Le Fanu to use a symbolic figure, the bloodsucking parasite, and thus suggest rather than express overtly a highly reactionary political position towards Hungary which, as we shall see, would otherwise have been considered extreme in Victorian Britain. The anomaly of his siting a Hungarian aristocratic dynasty in obscure Styria may owe much to the inspiration of Captain Hall's travel book, and the description of Countess Purgstall, whose maiden surname of Cranstoun probably inspired the name Karnstein.

The treatment of 'Christabel', which in the original possesses an ambivalent relation between Geraldine and the mother figure, and an uncanny presentation of virtue as being mixed with sin, involves a bifurcation of the morally dubious symbolism which presents Laura as far more virtuous than Christabel, and Carmilla as far more purely corrupting than Geraldine, allowing the degenerate elements of Laura's psyche to appear less necessary than simply parts of a lingering history, with the mother figure completely divorced from the sexual connotations of the predator. The same is true in Le Fanu's use of the Manet painting

'Olympia' with the morally dubious image of the black, turbaned woman, who represents Carmilla's real self as now wholly evil, and separated from the virginal flowers of the painting. Austria is a force for order and good, Hungary a site for evil, perversion and the reemergence of the Orient in Europe – not the Russian expansionism which Palmerston had feared, but Ottoman aggression. The allegory of *Carmilla* is not only a surreptitious warning of the Hungarian threat to Austria after the Ausgleich, but also one which fictively purges present-day Austria of its Hungarian past.

The political context: Fenians and Magyars

Although allegorically Carmilla's vampirism relates to Hungarian history rather than to Ireland, there is nevertheless an Irish political parallel to the Austrian situation, which may have governed Le Fanu's attitude to the Austro-Hungarian Ausgleich, that can be gleaned from the reactions of the paper he co-owned at the time, the *Dublin Evening Mail* (*DEM*). Despite the fact that his political position became softer at this time, and that he contemplated the virtues of disestablishing the Church of Ireland which Gladstone put into effect after his own electoral victory of May 1867, the *Dublin Evening Mail*, for which he occasionally wrote, still took a very harsh and unsympathetic line towards both Irish Nationalists and the Catholic church generally. A perusal of its columns also gives us a good idea of how the local concerns of unlicensed arms among Fenians in Ireland would have influenced Le Fanu's attitudes towards a similar threat in Hungary.

The steps that led to the Ausgleich are for the most part well documented in the paper, usually under the section 'News of this Day'. This section details how the Hungarian Diet, on 12th January 1867, rejected the Imperial patent as regards reorganising the army, and that Deak's suggestions for reforming it were unanimously accepted by the House ([*DEM*, 12th Jan. 1867] in other words they were attempting to release Hungarians from direct conscription into the Emperor's army, which the Imperial government still insisted upon). On 17th January, the *Dublin Evening Mail* reports the Diet's adoption of the new draft constitution proposed by Deak (the Hungarian parliamentary leader), together with the proposal of another more extreme parliamentarian (Madorancz), that the Imperial patent should be rejected. On 24th January we are told that Count Andrassay, the Austrian foreign minister, had agreed to negotiate with Deak for the creation of a Hungarian Ministry, and that he 'will press for withdrawal of imperial patent over reorganization of the army' (*DEM* 24th Jan. 1867).

Some days later we are informed that there is 'Difference of opinion reported between Deak and Andrassay on uniform monetary unity and railway systems for Hungary and the rest of the Empire' (29th Jan. 1867). In a later article of the 11th February the Prime Minister Count Beust is singled out for praise by the commentary section of the *Dublin Evening Mail*, indicating that the newspaper is largely supportive of the reforms in Hungary (*DEM*, 11th Jan. 1867).

On 12th February it is reported that there has been further wrangling over whether the Austrian Ministry should have its own 'Minister of War', an issue over which Count Andrassay concedes, while on 14th February reports of Hungarian demonstrations against Deak's party for being too conciliatory are also mentioned, although the Left in the Hungarian Diet professes to oppose such manifestations. On 20th February it is announced that Andrassay has left Pesth for Vienna to put the results of his negotiations before the Emperor. Finally we are told, on 21st of February, that:

A great demonstration took place yesterday evening at the National Theatre. Shouts were raised of 'Long Live the King'. From all parts of Hungary accounts continue to be received of enthusiastic festivities held in honour of the restoration of the Hungarian constitution. In the military provinces public opinion is in favour of the union of Croatia with Hungary. (*DEM*, 21st Feb. 1867)

The Emperor did not in fact arrive for his coronation as King of Hungary over a new Hungarian constitution until much later, in mid-March. Although more is reported concerning the settlement of the new Hungarian constitution within the new 'Dual Nation', the *Dublin Evening Mail* does not mention the event of the coronation, because from then on paper space is dominated by recent telegraphs about the Fenian uprising.

Despite the fact that the editors of the *Dublin Evening Mail* tend to report the Ausgleich in laudatory terms, there is still the whiff of possible discord. In several articles the potential problems of Croatian objection are noted as well as the fact that the Transylvanian Diet was against compromise.

The most serious problem, however, which the rejection of the Imperial patent did not effectively change, continued to be reported: namely the army question. It was the rejection of the Austrian Emperor's right to allow army reforms from Hungarians that had initially caused the parliamentary revolt and had led to the creation of a separate

Hungarian ministry. A Hungarian Ministry with its own minister of war in a separate constitution had appeared to be the main target and victory of negotiations (fiscally the two nations were still one, although the Hungarian diet now had the right to levy its own taxes), and the results were duly applauded by the *Dublin Evening Mail*. However, on March 5th, the day of the armed Fenian rising, the newspaper had the following to report:

> News of this Day
> Levy of Troops in Austria:
> Pesth, March 4th – The lower House of the Hungarian Diet has been appointed to consider the government bill proposing the levy of 48,000 troops in the Hungarian provinces. The report announces that, in consequence of the explanation which the committee received from the President of the Ministry, they felt bound to press their conviction that, in view of the great decrease which had taken place in the effectiveness of the army, the contingent of forty-eight thousand men demanded from Hungary and Transylvania was not too considerable. (*DEM*, 5th March 1867)

The Emperor and his ministers were still determined to maintain power over a combined army, regardless of the official withdrawal of the Imperial patent, and were simply using the Hungarian Ministry to put this into effect. All-in-all, during this period the *Dublin Evening Mail* had faithfully reported the Austrian withdrawal of patent over conscription, the right of the Hungarian Diet to levy taxes, the rejection of fiscal independence, and had approved the Austrian ministers' actions.

A situation in which provinces of a union refuse to accept the rule of its Emperor and reject his right of conscription may well have had a parallel significance for Le Fanu, an Anglo-Irish Conservative and Unionist, since over the next few weeks the reports in his own paper were mainly about the Fenian uprisings at Drogheda, Tallaght, Cork and Limerick. Each day new telegrams were posted in the *Dublin Evening Mail*, articulating both the fear and scorn of Le Fanu's class. From January onwards there had been stories of possible Fenian risings, with isolated reports of men being arrested in Dublin and Belfast, often without any clear warrant on the part of the authorities. On 6th March however, the announcement of armed columns rising at Drogheda and at the foot of Dublin Mountain, in Tallaght, burst onto the front page. By 8th March the newspaper, while still continuing to report the isolated incidents of Fenian arrests and ambushes in all parts of the country, was confident that the uprising had been quashed.

Right from the start the *Dublin Evening Mail* assured its readership that the constabulary and the army had County Dublin well under control, and poured nothing but derision upon the Fenians themselves:

> this grand demonstration of the military aptitudes and prowess of fenianism has been conducted, from first to last, with the caution of runaway schoolboys, the dodges of pickpockets, and the timidity of men-milliners. The conspiracy broke down everywhere from the sheerest want of average pluck. The sight of a red coat, except on a deserter's back, was enough to rout a fenian column. (8th March 1867)

This contempt was clearly bravado masking a justified fear, since the Fenians, in taking up arms against the British Empire at its height on borrowed American money, were anything but cowardly. The numbers involved – seven hundred at Tallaght and one thousand at Drogheda – were also substantial.

The sudden and sporadic nature of the risings, which, in keeping with the laws of guerrilla warfare, seemed to come suddenly and from nowhere, was also deeply unsettling for Unionists. As McCormack writes 'Fenianism appeared to come from without, utterly alien and inexplicable' and 'impressed the Irish middle classes with the intangible and ever-present character of their enemies' (McCormack, p. 240). Fenianism, unlike the tithe wars, was a conspiracy from outside: its manifestations were occasional and brief, but very violent when they occurred. It was also, crucially, based upon an ideal mythology, that of the tales of Finn and the Fianna, a heroic band of warriors who had sought adventures rather than stay at home and serve their king. O' Mahony's choice of the name was not only a reflection of his aspirations for restoration of a Gaelic Ireland with no British presence, but clearly intimated the type of violence that would best suit an insurrection: roving and unexpected.

The fear of Fenianism and its sudden emergence at the time of the Ausgleich partly explains why Le Fanu chose to write a vampire novel in the Austro-Hungarian hinterland which spans the time of the Hungarian uprising and effectively denigrates its cause, especially since the rejection of the Imperial patent over conscription into a united Austro-Hungarian army threatened the renewed problem of an alternative fighting force, and thus insurrection of a vampiric nature. The two situations had obvious parallels for the Irish Unionist and a decided opinion upon one of them would lead to a similar reaction to the other, as well as to a sympathy for those who had most to fear from the success of insurgency.

However, the fact that Carmilla is linked to the Oriental past of the Balkans signifies that there is a cultural threat in the story that cannot be seen as pertaining to Ireland. However much Anglo-Irish and English writers have denigrated Ireland's Gaelic and Catholic culture as mad, wild and primitive, the Oriental connection is not one that can be applied to the Irish situation. Furthermore, as an editor of a newspaper and as someone who had already written stories set on continental Europe, it is not too much to assume that Le Fanu took an interest in continental politics for their own sake. It is hardly surprising that he should do so given that the question of Italian unification and liberation from Austria-Hungary had been an important issue from 1859–60. Thus the external Irish situation should be seen more as an influence on the Austro-Hungarian politics of the work, rather than as an inherent part of it.

Furthermore, Le Fanu was dependent in this era upon his English readership (McCormack, p. 238), and directed his stories to suit their interests more than those of his fellow Anglo-Irish at home. *The Dark Blue*, in which Le Fanu first published *Carmilla*, stressed in an 'Address to the Public' that it wished to 'combine the salient points of existing monthly periodicals, and so appeal to a larger class than any of its competitors'.[31] The periodical appears to have been broad in its interests and outlook, since it includes many articles on contemporary European politics, and reviews of continental literature, making it seem highly cosmopolitan by the standards of the 'splendid isolationism' which prevailed at the time, with series like Professor Blackie's 'Sketches of Travel in Germany' (Sept 1871 to Feb 1872), 'Women in France' by 'A.P.'., and 'Russia and Pan-Sclavism' by J.W. Tipping. In the very edition in which the last installment of *Carmilla* appears, March 1872, there is an article called 'The Present Condition of Austria' condemning the instability of a country with 'A minority dominant, but incapable of maintaining its domination' (*The Dark Blue* (*TDB*), III (March – August 1872), 15–23 at 23). Thus a vampire tale which dealt with an obscure part of the Austro-Hungarian empire, but which also loosely alluded to the political problems of that region, would not have been unappreciated by *The Dark Blue*'s readership.

Therefore, in the light of the external political problems in Austria at the time, and the readership to which Le Fanu was appealing, the embedded national allegory of *Carmilla* is almost certainly a surreptitious comment on the region in which it is actually set, although its slant was influenced by a parallel situation in his own country.

As stated earlier, Le Fanu's political beliefs were on most issues akin to the views of his great hero Lord Palmerston. Like Le Fanu, Palmerston was a middle of the road Conservative, who had crossed the floor to become first foreign minister, and then Prime minister, in different Liberal governments. His politics on Ireland could be summed up as a combination of pragmatism, humanitarianism and conservatism. In this Le Fanu was similar to him, being liberal towards middle-class Catholics, but firmly behind the Union.[32]

Palmerston's position on Austria-Hungary had likewise always been mixed. When foreign minister during the Hungarian uprising, he condemned atrocities against the Hungarian people, but regretted that the revolt had in any way been necessary (Judd, p. 89). Nevertheless, after the revolt had been crushed and some of the rebels had come to Britain, Palmerston was accused of setting spies on them to see if they were in league with British arms manufacturers (Judd, p. 109). Although from 1859–60, when prime minister, he gave verbal aid to the Italians seeking unification and pressurised the Austrians to give up the Venetian republic and other Italian possessions, he also admitted in private that he was 'very Austrian north of the Alps, but very anti-Austrian south of the Alps' (p. 140). Like his political hero, Le Fanu was someone who supported the status quo, and while capable of being fair-minded in his later years, he basically did not believe that the map of Europe should be changed substantially either at home or abroad.

Palmerston died two years before the Fenian uprising and the Ausgleich. Like Le Fanu, he would have certainly condemned the Fenians. However, it is unlikely that Palmerston, despite his hounding of Hungarian refugees with spies, would have taken a completely negative view of the Ausgleich. Nevertheless, his disciple Le Fanu, because of the terror of a similar threat in a broken United Kingdom, and an unfounded hatred of the Orient, seems to react to Hungarian politics in a way that condemns any loosening of the Austrian grip. It is an opinion formed by both experience in Ireland, a faith in the powers that be and a general disregard for the new nationalisms that had surfaced in the glorious – although not for him – year of 1848. Thus these views – in contrast to the open approval expressed in his newspaper – are concealed, embedded, in what is more metonymically simply a lesbian vampire story.

In summation, we can see that *Carmilla* represents a negative evaluation of the recent Ausgleich between Austria and Hungary, and of the earlier Hungarian uprising, due to both the dates of Carmilla's death and resurrection, and the way in which Le Fanu manipulates his various sources to rid Gothic works of their ambiguity and politicise the relation between Austrian and Hungarian oppositions. The position that Le Fanu takes is a reactionary one which he suggests, rather than expresses openly, through the vampire theme's correspondence to historical dates. He understands Hungarian resurgence, wrongly, as constituting the potential harbinger of Ottoman power in the region, which is probably due to his knowledge of earlier Hungaro-Ottoman alliances in the face of Austria, but his major reason for condemning concessions to Hungary outright are probably the coincidence of similar problems in Ireland at the time of the Ausgleich, in the form of the Fenian crisis. His position is more reactionary than that of Lord Palmerston, although broadly in line with his hero's desire to see the maintenance of Austrian political power north of the Alps. It is also entirely unacceptable from the perspective of a Liberal in his own day.

3
Bram Stoker's *Dracula* and the Treaty of Berlin (1878)

In recent years there has been a marked rise in the interest in Bram Stoker's status as an Irish writer, and in particular with regard to seeing *Dracula* as referring to the Irish Land League crisis. Terry Eagleton has seen in Dracula himself a personification of the bad conscience of the Anglo-Irish[1], while Michael Moses has discerned in him the veiled form of Charles Stewart Parnell, a traitor to the Unionist cause.[2] Bruce Stewart has more recently attempted to portray the novel as presenting the full gamut of Stoker's objections to the Irish Land League, with Dracula probably representing the 'gombeen man' or Catholic landlord, and the Slovaks and Gypsies who help him to cart his earth, peasant-farmers. For Stewart this implies not so much anti-liberal tendencies as despair at the backwardness of all sections of Irish society exposed by the agitation.[3] There has even been a full-scale study of the Irish Gothic centring on *Dracula* which argues that his Transylvanian castle and its blood-thirsty women represent, in a twist on the 'protestant magic' argument of Roy Foster,[4] a sublimation of the concealed perversities of the Anglo-Irish nuclear family.[5] It appears, therefore, that *Dracula*'s Transylvania is for a large number of critics merely a masked Ireland, although Nationalists and Revisionists will no doubt continue to debate Stoker's true political attitude to his mother country for some time to come.

Far fewer critics, however, have looked at the politics of the novel in terms of the Eastern Question, a political issue which was important to Bram Stoker not simply as a possible topical selling-point, but because his own brother, George Stoker, had spent time in the Balkan region. Indeed, although Stoker's portrayal of Transylvanian history is famously garbled, his interest in Balkan, Ottoman and Austro-Hungarian politics ran deep. Vesna Goldsworthy has argued that *Dracula*, and other vampire novels set in the Balkans, represent the fear of 'reverse colonisation', and the reassuring contrasts in identity between a stable Britain and an unstable East European hinterland.[6] William Hughes, noting the problems of seeing Stoker's Eastern Europe as sublimating anxieties about colonialism when Britain had no colonies there, argues that Transylvania must, for the post-colonial critic, represent the 'undefined' 'Racial other', in which the novel is read as 'an abstracted conflict of Orient against Occident',[7] rather than a more defined threat like the Indian mutiny. He then further argues that *Dracula* could just as easily be read as a critique of the colonial predator: the 'Rhodesean colossus' who does as he pleases (Hughes, pp. 100–1). As he notes, the necessary obliqueness of Eastern Europe's relation to British colonialism makes such vague motifs inevitable given the lack of a hard basis in historical fact.

So far the only critic to observe *Dracula* seriously in relation to the Eastern Question is Eleni Coundouriotis. Understanding Dracula to be the 'Ottomanised European',[8] she argues that Stoker was following a Gladstonian position in fearing a Turkified Balkans which could not be absorbed into his idea of European states, and that the novel is an attempt at a 'deligitimation of history' (*Connotations*, 9:2 144) or an attempt to repress it. The Ottoman Empire having failed to Europeanise itself leaves the peoples it once oppressed in a position that cannot be absorbed into Europe and thus, in an obvious symbiosis, its European residue is a threat to Britain's own understanding of itself as a European state:

> Dracula represents the irreconcileable aspects of history that do not fall neatly into a European narrative of progress and cannot be accommodated without forcing a significant change in that Western identity. British policy indicated a preference for a Europeanized Ottoman state over the ressurection of a pre-Ottoman, Christian Eastern Europe that would ally itself to Russia. Yet the Europeanized Ottoman state had proven to be impossible to realize; hence, Britain's burden as the hegemonic force behind the Concert of Europe was to create a new Europe by destroying what remained of the sick man of Europe and his antithesis, the powerful belief in the existence of a 'pure' Christian Europe. The destruction of Dracula fantastically enacts the destruction of these historical resonances. (*Connotations*, 9:2 154)

Thus for Coundouriotis *Dracula* acts as a form of textual repression of history in relation to contemporary reality, due to Britain's need to secure a sense of national selfhood in the face of reform, so that Dracula becomes symbolic not simply of the Balkans, but of its unassimilable Turkish past.

In the following chapter it will be shown that the opposite is true. That rather than delegitimating and repressing history, *Dracula* is an attempt to justify it; and furthermore that Dracula himself is not treated as a part of Ottomanised Europe, but as Turkey's less worthy opponent. Above all it shall be shown how a concrete event, the Treaty of Berlin in 1878 (the year Stoker moved from Dublin to London), coloured Stoker's attitude to Balkan politics in 1897 (the publication of *Dracula*).

The Treaty of Berlin

At the Congress of Berlin in June 1878, the fate of the Balkans was sealed for the next forty years in a way which dismayed many of the Balkan peoples, Liberals in England, and even the Ottoman Sultan Abdul Hamid II, in whose favour it mainly went. Earlier that year the Russian advance had halted at San Stefano, some three miles from Constantinople itself, where a treaty had been signed on 3rd March. This treaty ratified the complete independence of Rumania, Serbia and Montenegro, the return of Bessarabia to Russia (including part of the coast of the Black Sea north of Moldavia) and autonomy to a new Bulgaria, which incorporated land from Thessaly, all of Macedonia, and even part of Albania. The Turks kept Bosnia and Hercegovina, to the chagrin of the Serbs, and a curtailed Albania, but the Sandjak of Novipazar was divided between Montenegro and Serbia (see Map 2). Despite face-saving over titular rule in Bulgaria, the Sultan had lost most of his European possessions by this treaty.[9]

The Treaty of San Stefano was allowed to pass by the major powers because the Austro-Hungarian First Minister, Andrassay, had failed to realise the threat a Russian presence would have in these new 'Slavo-phil' and Orthodox states. Only Britain, from amongst the major powers, recognised the threat, and so tried to shore up a bloc for maintaining the Ottoman presence in Europe as a counterbalance to Russia (a possible threat to Britain's control of India – a fear Stoker himself may well have shared [see note 16]). Listening to British and Austrian grievances, Bismarck called for a new treaty in his capital, Berlin. Disraeli came to a pre-summit agreement with the Austrians that he would support their annexation of Bosnia, Hercegovina and the Sandjak of Novipazar if Austria-Hungary would support Britain's own pitch to gain occupation of Ottoman Cyprus.[10] A fleet with some 7000 British soldiers on board was sent from India to Malta, and the Russians, taking the hint, were ready to honour the Anglo-Austrian position in return for unhindered passage through the Bosphorus and the continued possession of Bessarabia (Pribram, 1951, p. 53).

Map 2 The Balkans after the Treaty of Berlin

The result was that no sooner had Bulgaria celebrated the prospect of becoming a new Balkan superpower, than she was split into three again with Northern Bulgaria maintaining its autonomy within Ottoman sovereignty. Eastern Roumelia (mainly southern Bulgaria) was reoccupied by a garrison of janissaries (Watson, p. 461), although with curbs imposed. Macedonia, however (at that time part of Bulgaria), was restored to full and absolute Ottoman rule. The Austro-Hungarians took full possession of Bosnia, but lost patience in pursuing sovereignty from the Sultan over the other two southern Slav possessions, Hercegovina and the Sandjak of Novipazar (Pribram, 1951, p. 54), and so settled for occupation of them – for the moment at least. The now fully recognised Kingdoms of Serbia and Montenegro savoured their freedom, as did Northern Bulgaria, and expressed their gratitude to the Tsar, although as Slavo-phil countries they effectively counted as Russian possessions in the Great Power ratio. Disraeli, needless to say, was cock-a-hoop about gaining Cyprus, the last piece in the jigsaw of Mediterranean dominance, and returned to London from Berlin to make his famous 'Peace with Honour' Speech, which critics, including Gladstone, called the 'Peace that passeth all understanding, and the Honour that is common among thieves'.[11]

Despite a return in 1880 to Liberal government, which was anti-Austrian, anti-Ottoman, and mildly pro-Russian, the status quo did not change materially for many years: Liberals derided the Ottoman and Austro-Hungarian presence, but the signing of a triple pact between Russia, Austria-Hungary and Germany in 1882 (the *Dreikaiserbund*) effectively limited British influence in the years around the turn of the century, and verbal deterioration in the relationship with both Germany and Austria-Hungary could not be effected with action.[12] The Bulgarian unification with Eastern Roumelia by Crown Prince Alexander Battenberg in 1885 reversed the Great Power interests spectacularly, as Tsar Alexander III, dismayed to see that a puppet prince was capable of shaking off his strings, had him kidnapped and deposed the following year. Britain's new Conservative Prime Minister Lord Salisbury, however, used the opportunity to promote a new buffer state to Russian expansionism. As G.D. Clayton writes:

> Both Britain and Russia, therefore, had swung round to adopt, on the Bulgarian issue, attitudes entirely opposite to the ones they had pressed in 1878. Salisbury, in encouraging a big Bulgaria, was actually undoing what had seemed his and Disraeli's major achievement at the Berlin Congress.[13]

Salisbury's change of opinion on Bulgaria shows the extent to which Conservatives as well as Liberals had abandoned Turkey, regardless of whether Britain was attempting to side with members of the *Dreikaiserbund* or not. In the 1890s there were further rebellions of Christians in Macedonia (Pribram, 1931, p. 57), and Lord Salisbury considered Turkish partition to endear himself to the other major powers. In 1896, Salisbury sided with the Greeks and Cretans against the Turks, mainly it would seem to drive a wedge between Russia and Germany, since Germany and Austria-Hungary were now firmly behind Turkey, and both Britain and Russia were alarmed at the degree of cooperation between Berlin, Vienna and Constantinople. Furthermore, massacres of Armenians in 1894 and 1896 (the year before *Dracula* was published) galvanised British public opinion firmly against the Ottomans and the Sultan Abdul Hamid II (Clayton, p. 184). The Ottomans and the Greeks went to war in April 1897 over Cretan sovereignty (it was still not part of Greece), resulting in a crushing defeat for the Greek army of King Constantine – who was supported by Britain – on 19th May 1897.[14] This was the day before Bram Stoker signed the contract for *Dracula* with Constable and Company.

Stoker was a personal friend of William Gladstone, a Liberal in politics and a tacit supporter of independence for Ireland. He was someone whom one could expect to feel sceptical towards high imperialism and to favour the more moral and humanitarian line in foreign policy favoured by a man like Viscount Strangford. Although David Glover has argued that *Dracula* represents his desire, chiefly in relation to Ireland but also elsewhere, to resolve liberal notions of independence for small nations and anxiety about the threats posed them by potential racial degeneracy,[15] it appears to me that Stoker's political position as regards the Balkans and the so-called Eastern Question was decidedly Conservative, more so in fact than that of Lord Salisbury, and in keeping with the legacy created by Disraeli, Layard and Salisbury himself at the Treaty of Berlin in 1878, which was 12 years old when he began his research into *Dracula*, and 19 years old when he completed it in 1897. Stoker's views are also in accord with those of his younger brother George, who, while working as an army surgeon for the Ottomans, became unashamedly pro-Turkish in his sympathies. The impact of the Treaty of Berlin can be discerned in both *Dracula* and Stoker's later novel *The Lady of the Shroud*, and it would appear that, at an immediate political level, it is in this context that Stoker's greatest work should really be read. *Dracula* does not represent a condemnation of Turkish influence upon areas that have fallen under its sway so much as a complaint that the natural degeneracy of Balkan Christians requires their Ottoman rulers, an idea prevalent in the Turcophile writings of pre-nineteenth century writers like Henry Blount (1636) and Jonathan Morritt (1796), and more recently David Urquhart (1838), and in the caustic irony of Disraeli himself, who had expressed delight in meeting brutal Pashas during his own grand tour as a young man.[16]

Turcophilia

Stoker's major sources for the progeny, superstitions and ethnographic descriptions of Eastern Europe were, as Clive Leatherdale has shown, William Wilkinson's *An Account of the Principalities of Wallachia and Moldavia* (1820), Emily Gerard's essay *Transylvanian Superstitions* (1885) and Major E. C. Johnson's *On the Track of the Crescent* (1885), whose works he blended into an interesting falsehood.[17] If we examine the lecture on Transylvanian history Dracula gives Jonathan, in which he delineates the history of his race, we see that Dracula is a 'Szekely', whose people apparently came down from Iceland to settle in the Carpathian basin to mix with the Huns. Once there they met 'the Magyar, the Lombard, the Avar, the Bulgar and the Turk', each of which the Szekelys drove back, before Arpad the Magyar came in the ninth century and befriended them, trusting them with the guardianship of the frontier against 'Turkeyland'.[18]

Stoker's ethnography here derives entirely from passages in Johnson's *On the Track of the Crescent*. In a passage which Leatherdale strangely omits from his otherwise comprehensive *The Origins of Dracula*, Major Johnson exploits the event of his arrival at Buda-Pesth to describe the history of the Carpathian basin, which is a series of invasions: after the arrival of Huns there followed the Avars, who drove the Lombards into Italy before the Magyars came to join their relatives the Huns in the ninth century under Arpad.[19] Johnson later describes the Szekelys (also called Szecklers) as a people who 'claim to be descended from Attila and the Huns' and 'were found settled on the eastern frontier when the country was conquered by the Magyars' (p. 205). Stoker took these details, but manipulated them to allow the Szekelys to be the earliest group, who pushed out all the others (except the Huns) before the Magyars arrived.

In this Stoker is doubly wrong, although guiltlessly so on the second count. The origin of the Szekelys as a people is still uncertain, but it is likely that they were either a Hungarian tribe that was lured into the Carpathian basin by the Avars before the Hungarian conquest, or that they were a group of Turkic tribesmen who assimilated with the Hungarians, and then came with them, choosing to settle on the borders of the basin in Transylvania.[20] As such, they became famous for their clashes with the Turks and other enemies of Hungary (Makkai, p. 519). In saying that the Szekelys were met by the Magyars and befriended by them when Arpad the Magyar came, his source Johnson was simply repeating the eleventh-century *Chronicle*, which stated that they were the descendants of Attila the Hun, a belief which archaeologists declare cannot be true (p. 520).

Stoker's further history of the Dracula clan was suggested by *all* three sources in conjunction:

When was redeemed that great shame of my nation, the shame of Cassova, when the flags of the Wallach and the Magyar went down beneath the Crescent; who was it but one of my own race who as Voivode crossed the Danube and beat the Turk on his own ground! This was a Dracula indeed. Who was it that his own unworthy brother, when he had fallen, sold his people to the Turk and brought the shame of slavery upon them! Was it not this Dracula, indeed, who inspired that other of his race who in a later age again and again brought his forces over the great river into Turkeyland; who, when he was beaten back, came again, and again, and again, though he had to come alone from the bloody field where his troops were being slaugh-tered, since he knew that he alone could ultimately triumph? They said that he thought only of himself. Bah! What good are peasants without a leader? Where ends the war without a brain and heart to conduct it? Again, when, after the battle of Mohacs, we threw off the Hungarian yoke, we of the Dracula blood were amongst their leaders, for our spirit would not brook that we were not free. Ah, young sir, the Szekeleys – and the Dracula as their heart's blood, their brains, and their swords – can boast a record that mushroom growths like the Hapsburgs and the Romanoffs can never reach. (Stoker, *Dracula*, p. 29)

Here we can see Wilkinson's notes on Wallachia and Moldavia influencing Stoker's grasp of history. Wilkinson describes in his rather imprecise chronology how a Wallachian Voivode Dracula was defeated along with the Hungarians at 'Cossovo' battle in 1448, but was avenged by another Dracula (presumably his son) in a rather unwise skirmish across the Danube after 1460 (exact date not given). The Sultan Mahomet pushed this Dracula into hiding in Hungary and placed his brother Bladus on the Wallachian throne.[21] This is what, according to Wilkinson, 'laid the foundations of that slavery' (Wilkinson, p. 19) which the Wallachia of his day knew as its constitution.

These elements crystallise in the speech Stoker's Dracula gives to Jonathan and, as Leatherdale notes, explains why the Vlad the impaler myths never surface in the novel – the author was unaware of them.[22] Wilkinson explains in a footnote how Dracula can mean 'evil' in the Vlach language (Wilkinson, p. 19n), and thus Stoker links the mysterious attributions of Wilkinson with the exciting Transylvanian nosferatu described by Emily Gerard in her article on the superstitions of that region.[23] Since from Johnson, Stoker learnt that the Szekelys were one of the major groups in Transylvania, Wilkinson's Vlach (or Wallach) has simply moved westward in the novel, changing nationality at the same time. Stoker's subsequent comment that the Szekelys 'threw off the Hungarian yoke' at the Battle of Mohacs is a further misappropriation of enemies, since Johnson, his source for this detail, describes the battle (1526 AD) as being the point at which Hungarian independence fell into the hands of 'the unspeakable' – meaning the Turks.

However, another reason for making Dracula a Szekely, or Szeckler, is more political. The Nosferatu or vampire was a Transylvanian figure, but known amongst Rumanian rather than Hungarian speakers, who provide the majority of the superstitions in Emily Gerard's article. The Szekelys, according to Johnson, 'received certain privileges' from the Magyars 'for having guarded the frontier toward Moldavia and Turkey-land' (Johnson, p. 234). The mixture of Wilkinson's Turk-hating Dracula with the Szekely people described by Johnson reinforces his identity as a guardian against the Turks. Indeed the most important aspect of Dracula's lecture to Jonathan Harker on Transylvanian history appears to be this enduring conflict against them, as he describes how 'again and again' he went over the Danube: he pits the Crescent against the Cross, even though the latter has by now forsaken him. If we take into account that the Kossovo Battle of the Wallachs and Magyars against the Turks in 1448 described by Wilkinson is relatively minor compared with the famous battle of Kossovo Polje in 1389,[24] when King Lazar's brother-in-law, Vuk Brankovic, performed the act of treachery which facilitated the Turks' victory,[25] the fact that Stoker emphasises this location and the subsequent betrayal by a brother from Wilkinson's account may mean that he has confused the two battles (he may again have heard legends of the former from his brother, who worked very close to Kossovo when helping Lady Strangford at her hospitals in Batak, Carlovo and Panagurista).[26] Thus he cements the anti-Turkish element in Dracula's history all the more pointedly, linking Wallachs and Magyars with Serbs.

Throughout the novel, despite all the parodying of the British upper class and lambasting of the new woman which critics have found in the work, the Turkish connection is never too far away. When Jonathan crosses the Danube in Buda-Pesth, he finds that 'the most Western of splendid Bridges over the Danube, which is here of noble width and depth, took us among the traditions of Turkish rule' (Stoker, *Dracula*, p. 1). This tells us immediately we move from 'West' to 'East' in the book that we are entering a land once occupied by the Ottomans. Before they set out in search of Dracula, Van Helsing warns his younger accomplices that 'he was no common man' since he was the same 'Voivode Dracula who won his name against the Turk, over the great river on the very frontier of Turkey-land' (p. 240). As Coundouriotis has also noted, Dracula's motivation for infesting London with vampirism appears to be a sense of having been betrayed by West Europeans for his valiant frontier work (*Connotations*, 9:2 149). He mentions this euphemistically to Mina Harker in the only scene when he is allowed to speak for himself while in England. Castigating Mina for working with the others to stop him, he sneers:

> They should have kept their energies for use closer to home. Whilst they played wits against me – against me who commanded nations, and intrigued for them, and fought for them, hundreds of years before they were born – I was countermining them. (Stoker, *Dracula* p. 288)

If we take the continued 'them' to mean the 'they' rather than the 'nations' (which is also semantically possible, but unlikely given the repetitions of 'they' and 'them'), then Dracula's meaning is that he is being attacked by the very people whom he has helped to protect by fighting the Turks in previous years.

If this is the meaning, then Stoker is accurately reflecting the feelings of many Middle and East European people as regards the lack of gratitude shown them by Western Christians for fighting the Islamic hordes, a feeling still prevalent among Serbs and Macedonians today. His brother George had served as a doctor during the Russo-Turkish war which led to the Treaties of San Stefano and Berlin, and Stoker may have heard from a reliable firsthand witness about this attitude. If, however, George Stoker's *With 'The Unspeakables'* reflects conversations which the younger brother had with the older (George lived with Bram and his wife for ten years after this war, at Cheyne Walk, London[27]), Bram Stoker would have heard mainly positive information about the Turks, and negative views about their enemies the Greeks and Bulgarians. The political slant of

With 'the Unspeakables' may account for why *Dracula* as a book defies the Liberal line on the Eastern Question.

Throughout his travels in Roumelia, George Stoker is keen to emphasise the distinction between the character of the Turkish people and that of the Turkish government itself. At the very start of his travelogue, he declares:

> The character of the latter is sufficiently well known not to necessitate any criticism on my part. We must, however, in common justice, allow that it was rather hard, when it had established a constitution and begun to try to reform, that Russia should pounce down on the country and prevent even an attempt to mature the scheme of reformation. (G. Stoker, p. 3)

This sets the tone for the rest of the book and basically for George's rather young and naïve political assessment of the Balkan situation. He does understand – and he is liberal enough to do so – that the Ottoman Empire is a hopelessly backward and negative force in Europe and that, objectively perceived, the Serbs, Greeks, Bulgarians and Macedonians still under Ottoman rule deserve their freedom and self-determination in the name of democracy and progress (very much the Gladstonian line). However, his personal fondness for the honesty and charity of the Turks and loathing of the selfishness and arrogance of Greeks and Bulgarians sways his political judgement against this Liberal position (implictly towards the Disraeli and Canning line). He reports, for example, how a Bulgarian sneers at financial donations from British charities, since 'the English know very well that the money they are subscribing now they will soon recover by means of their commerce with us' (p. 7). While describing his experiences George provides many examples of the generosity of Turks as opposed to the shiftlessness and cunning of Bulgarians and Greeks (pp. 4 and 6–7), one such example being that when a certain Captain Layard lay dying a Greek boy refused to give up his blanket to ease his suffering while a Turk did (p. 76).

He also spends much time assessing the culprits of famous atrocities like the Batak massacre, for which he blames Pomacs ([p. 40] ethnic Bulgarian Moslems) rather than the regular Turkish soldiers themselves. He describes how the brother of Suleiman Pasha, Ibrahim, is administrating Phillipopolis badly when he first arrives there, but that by the time he returns the Porte has replaced him, illustrating the Ottomans' will to reform (p. 90). The book concludes by condemning the reprisal massacres of Christians on Moslems, asking how, in all conscience, Western Europeans can allow them to go on (pp. 112–15).

It appears, therefore, that George's division between the character of the Ottoman government and that of the Turkish people was not enough to prevent him from actually feeling some sympathy for the government whose soldiers he tended over two years. His turcophile sentiments are hardly unique, and are if anything in keeping with a long tradition. Maria Todorova writes that during the nineteenth century the British attitude towards the Balkans was divided between aristocratic Turcophiles, and liberal pro-Christians (Todorova, p. 97). The liberal interest in Slavic as opposed to Greek Christians was a relatively new development in the 1870s, championed first by Irby and Mackenzie,[28] and ultimately Viscountess Strangford (whose reports in the British Press George does much to try to refute), and of course the American journalist Januarius MacGahan (whose vivid reports of atrocities in the *Daily News* did much to stir British sympathies against the Turks).

Todorova recounts how in earlier times the refined manners of Ottomans and degeneracy of Greek peasants had swayed the sympathies of English travellers. One traveller in particular, David Urquhart, a disillusioned philhellene, described in 1838 how the servility of Greeks in fact corrupted virtuous Turks (Todorova, p. 94).[29] Class affinities and disillusionment with the Greek peasantry had swung the sympathies of eighteenth-century British travellers towards the Ottomans as surely as classical education and disillusionment with Britain's own imperial barbarities had swayed Byron and Shelley towards supporting the Greeks. Turcophile sympathies were still prevalent among the ruling class in the 1870s, and were certainly powerful when determining policy over the Eastern Question. By the time of the Treaty of Berlin philhellenism was for the most part an anachronism (most of Greece was by now free), and an intellectual like Viscount Strangford, scornful of the idealism of the philhellenes, had turned his attention to the Bulgarian, Macedonian and Serbian causes (Todorova, p. 101). In this new, more pro-Slavic phase of liberal anti-imperialism, George Stoker was siding with the traditionally turcophile aristocracy for similar reasons to their own: repugnance at the poor manners of the Christian peasantry and a recognition of British self-interest. While David Glover notes how Stoker compares the dancing of Bulgarian peasants to the jigs of peasants in his native Ireland in his attempt to show that '[t]he reach of the imperial guilty conscience seems to be virtually limitless'[30] and Haining and Tremayne have considered whether, through his travels, George might have come close enough to Rumania to obtain access to the Vlad the Impaler myths (Haining, p. 122), the more obvious political significance of George Stoker's views on his brother's book is yet to be taken seriously in discussions of *Dracula*.

Turcophilia in the novel seems to go beyond simple vilification of Balkan Christians to an implicit comparison between British Victorians and the Turks, as well as a bizarre exemption of the Turks from the West/East divide which otherwise is so important in the novel. The speech in which Dracula tells Jonathan Harker of his lineage is ultimately a useful clue for Van Helsing in predicting Dracula's movements, but is also important for denigrating Eastern Christians. When the group are in Varna considering where Dracula will go next, Van Helsing points to that passage in Jonathan's diary, quoted above, where Dracula declares how when his 'predecessor' had gone, 'again and again' over the Danube into Ottoman rule, 'when he was beaten back, came again, and again, and again, though he had to come alone from the bloody field where his troops were being slaughtered, since he knew that he alone could ultimately triumph' (Stoker, *Dracula*, pp. 340–1). Van Helsing uses this to show that Dracula 'has not full man-brain. He is clever and cunning and resourceful; but he be not of man-stature as to brain' (p. 341). This is because he is a creature of habit who simply repeats his previous behaviour, and is incapable of learning from experience. Van Helsing couches this in the terms of one of the popular psychological theories of the day:

> The count is a criminal and of criminal type. Nordau and Lombroso would so classify him, and *qua* criminal he is of imperfectly formed mind. Thus, in a difficulty he has to seek resource in habit. His past is a clue, and the one page of it that we know – and that from his own lips – tells that once before, when in what Mr Morris would call a 'tight place', he went back to his own country from the land he had tried to invade, and thence, without losing purpose, prepared himself for a new effort. He came again, better equipped for his work; and won. So he came to London to invade a new land. He was beaten, and when all hope of success was lost, and his existence in danger, he fled back over the sea to his home; just as formerly he had fled back over the Danube from Turkey land. (p. 342)

This reading of Dracula's self-eulogy has surprising consequences when applied to the contemporary political situation. First, Van Helsing is looking for patterns of criminal behaviour in what Dracula himself understood as the exploits of heroism dosed with pragmatism. Dracula always returned to his castle, because he had to preserve himself to fight for his people another day and was clearly successful enough to do this many times ('again and again'). For Van Helsing to look for patterns of criminal behaviour in Dracula's motives for retreat denigrates his declaration of heroism beyond the more plausible charge of prosaic pragmatism, unconsciously casting a great general as being engaged in nefarious activity. This correspondingly casts the Turks in the role of policemen and keepers of the peace, rather than occupiers and torturers, the view of them held by Byron, Shelley, Gladstone, Strangford and most men who believed in the right to independence of either the Greeks, or other Balkan nations. Second, in looking for patterns of behaviour in Dracula's past and comparing the present situation with his previous fights against the Turks, Van Helsing is surreptitiously identifying himself, Seward, Mina Harker and the others with the Turks, as being the containers of criminals, and London as having been 'invaded' in the same way that Turkey was repeatedly 'invaded' by the monster (conveniently ignoring the fact that Turkey was the aggressor at that time).

In contrast to Coundouriotis's belief that *Dracula* echoes Gladstone's fear that the Balkans represents a hybrid society which, thanks to its Ottoman past, cannot be incorporated within Europe (*Connotations*, 9:2 153), and whose history must thus be repressed, we can see instead that latent Turcophilia suffuses the book, and is used to justify indirectly Turkish rule of the Balkans, both past and present, and also to justify the Treaty of Berlin which has left so many of the Balkan Christians whom George Stoker despised under Ottoman rule. Although in his following book, *Miss Betty* (1898), the heroine's rascally fiancé Rafe Otwell redeems a life of crime by fighting to free himself from a Turkish galley 'for Faith and Freedom',[31] this work is set in the early Georgian era and is a highly stylised piece of historical fiction, which draws from memories of Cromwell's and Queen Anne's time, fashioning the fiction into a Romance which clearly aims to emulate the values, and also the scenario, of Restoration drama. *Dracula*, although a Gothic novel which includes the marvellous or supernatural, is placed entirely within the political and technological realities of his own time, and hence addresses the political relation to Turkey in a much more urgent – and positive – way.

When the gang all chase Dracula's coffin at the end of the book they pointedly miss out Turkey. On arrival at the port of Varna, Jonathan Harker notes in his diary that 'this is the country where bribery can do anything, and we are well supplied with money' (Stoker, *Dracula*, p. 334) concerning their intention to rumble Dracula's coffin when it arrives. He is referring to the Turkish tradition of Baksheesh, but does not actually mention it in relation to the Turks themselves at all. The 'country' should in fact be Bulgaria, although throughout the novel it is easy to assume that Varna is in Rumania, since the country he intends is never made clear. The journey they make after they hear that Dracula is already at Galatz ([p. 337] in Rumania), is along the Danube, then up into the Bistritza river and into the Sereth. Thus they go from Varna, through Veresti, Galatz, Fundu and up the Borgo pass near Bistritz in Transylvania – a journey probably measured by Stoker himself on Johnson's map, tucked at the back of the Major's book.

All-in-all, while we can see that Stoker does not praise the Turks outright, there is much evidence to show that he takes a pro-Ottoman position on the question of Balkan independence, presenting the Christians they have fought as being irrational, and dangerous to Western society. In particular while Buda-Pesth and Transylvania are defined as Oriental and as showing 'the traditions of Turkish rule' (Stoker, *Dracula*, p. 1), the Turks are themselves exempted from the chaos and danger of the Orient, while the Balkan Christians are heavily representative of it. This was not a liberal position, and more in keeping with the views of eighteenth-century travel writers like Jonathan Morritt and the turcophile aristocrats of his own day.

Austrophilia

Another interesting feature of the gang's chase is that there is no mention of the fact that they leave Rumania for Transylvania; furthermore, at no point in the book is it made clear that Transylvania was currently part of the Austro-Hungarian Empire. It is as though Stoker does not want to remind us that these evil and supernatural events are happening inside the Hapsburgs' domain. Another poignant element, from a political point of view, is Harker's description of the region the count lives in compared with other parts of the Austro-Hungarian Empire. At the time of writing, Austria and Hungary were the major components of the Austro-Hungarian Empire, which had been remodelled as the 'Dual Nation' in 1867 as a means of appeasing Hungarian Nationalist sentiment, with the ethnically mixed Transylvania being put under Hungarian control. While Jonathan Harker moves far into Hungary and then Transylvania he sees the initial movement from the Austrian capital to Buda-Pesth as like 'leaving the West and entering the East' (Stoker *Dracula*, p. 1). The movement from Buda-Pesth to Klausenburgh, and then to Bistritz in Transylvania, constitutes an even greater shift eastwards and into disorder. As Jonathan states 'It seems to me that the further East you go the more unpunctual are the trains.What ought they to be in China?' (p. 2). It is interesting that in condemning the 'East', he avoids condemning the real Eastern influence, namely Turkey, in keeping with his somewhat self-contradictory desire to suggest that the Turks are rightful policemen of the Balkans, while the East itself is shambolic and primitive.

When Jonathan escapes from the count's castle, he finds salvation first in Klausenburgh (a Hungarian town with a German name), from where he is sent back to Buda-Pesth, but to reside in the safe Catholic Hospital of St Joseph and Ste Mary. It is as though he there escapes the evil eye and the irrationalism of the Eastern world (p. 99). The orderly environment of a convent under Hapsburg rule, whose name significantly recalls the two great Austrian rulers of the late eighteenth century, is at odds with the Liberal's contempt for that dynasty, but helps to cast Dracula himself as being not quite of Christendom, despite his impeccable military record in fighting Christ's enemies, as though Buda-Pesth is more Western than Transylvania, Vienna more Western than Buda-Pesth, on a sliding scale of order and chaos.

Pro-Austrian sympathy can also be detected in Stoker's attitude to the Catholic church. Unlike in many other sensational novels of the nineteenth century, the Catholic church is presented as a positive influence, and not a cause of the diabolical, as it was in the work of Matthew Lewis and Charles Maturin. On St George's day when 'all the evil things in the world ... have full sway' (pp. 4–5), the old lady at his inn in Bistritz offers Jonathan a crucifix, presumably a rosary:

> I did not know what to do, for, as an English Churchman, I have been taught to regard such things as in some measure idolatrous, and yet it seemed so ungracious to refuse an old lady meaning so well and in such a state of mind. She saw, I suppose, the doubt in my face, for she put the rosary round my neck, and said, 'For your mother's sake,' and went out of the room. (p. 5)

As we see later, crucifixes are an essential protection against vampires, but Stoker chooses to relate them pointedly to Catholicism and highlight the fact that the Church of England does not provide such paraphernalia. While this could be read as a coded attempt to present Dracula as the Protestant landlord in Ireland, it more obviously relates to the religion of the Austro-Hungarian Empire. Stoker is drawing a line between Catholic Europe, in the form of the Austro-Hungarian Empire, which he is praising, and the world that had been occupied by the Ottomans (which was Orthodox): the area that had effectively been betrayed at the Congress of Berlin.

It may have been this desire to portray Austria as a place of order and reason that forced him to excise his development of the

Carmilla-inspired story 'Dracula's Guest' from the eventual novel, in which the travelling Englishman is originally 'saved' by Dracula from an Austrian vampire, Countess Dolingen of Gratz, Styria, and which includes the German speakers' superstition of 'Walpurgis Nacht', rather than St George's Day.[32] Nevertheless, seeing Austria as a place of order, stability and sacredness in comparison with the domain of the Szekeley Dracula, helps to underline the importance of the Eastern Question and George Stoker's opinions in the book, despite the fact that Transylvania, although virtually a Turkish possession for part of its history, was not under Ottoman rule at the time of the Treaty of Berlin and so not included in its discussions. The axis in the book deals with the two powers that had gained most from it, who were still occupying large parts of South Eastern Europe at the time, and yet were most derided by the Liberals and increasingly by Conservative politicians as well. Dracula lives under Hungarian rule within the wider Austro-Hungarian Empire and has spent his whole life fighting either Turks or Hungarians. Relocating Dracula from Wallachia to Transylvania, and making him a Szekely, allows Stoker to present, using the vampire motif, a view of those Christian nations that fell between the two as being inferior and ultimately forsaken by Christianity itself through an exemplar figure. In short, Stoker's portrayal of the Austro-Hungarian Empire, the power which currently controlled Transylvania, is more positive than one would expect from a Liberal, and presents the Middle European aggressors against the East European states as being as necessary as the earlier Ottoman aggressors, thus showing sympathy with the other conservative empire to benefit from the Treaty of Berlin, while paradoxically loading any contempt for the East upon the Near Eastern Europeans and exonerating those who had occupied them from the East.

Dracula and Britain

So Dracula is defined by his historic fight and contact with the Turks, through a manipulated Balkan history in which he and his people play a dominant part, but is also geographically Eastern. He is a hero against the Turks, a valiant fighter on the part of a Christian Europe, and yet the cross has forsaken him and he must be kept out of the West at all costs. The paradox of inventing a fictitious history which involves Dracula more firmly in wars against the Ottomans on Christendom's behalf than he in fact was in Stoker's source Wilkinson, while simultaneously portraying him as a dangerous villain who must be expunged from Christendom, would seem to suggest a need to justify the effects of the Treaty of Berlin and Disraeli's hard line on the Eastern policy. Those who have tangled with the Ottomans are portrayed as being in fact worse than them, and in need of both their restraining hand or that of Austria, which latter country is represented as a gateway to civilisation. In direct contrast to Stoker's known views on the Irish Question, the politics of *Dracula* would appear to be decidedly reactionary: pro-Hapsburg and pro-Disraeli.

Stephen D. Arata has argued that Dracula's rapacity may betray the British fear of 'reverse colonisation' by degenerate hordes. Dracula takes on the culture of his victims in order to oppress them, so that 'the Count's Occidentalism both mimics and reverses the more familiar Orientalism underwriting Western imperial practices'.[33] Jules Zanger, noting that it is an Oriental Jew, Immanuel Hildesheim ('of the Adelphi type' [p. 349]) who helps Dracula transport his belongings from Galatz back to the castle, sees anti-semitism in the novel, and understands Dracula's threat as symbolic of the threat posed by the immigration of Jews into London in the 1890s.[34] Daniel Pick notices the description of racial mixture in Eastern Europe and describes Dracula as the eugenic parasite who threatens to suborn the society from abroad.[35]

However, the fear of Eastern Europe is in fact influenced by contemporary political realities, is related to recent history and is engaged with current British foreign policy rather than with general political polarities. In *Dracula* we have a portrayal of Eastern Europe as shambolic, wild and primitive, but with a sinister, threatening edge which argues not for control so much as for exclusion. Like Polidori and Le Fanu before him, Stoker is situating a symbolic figure for moral degeneration in politically sensitive areas in the hope of justifying a recent political policy rather than a vague ideological discourse.

Dracula was completed some 19 years after the Treaty of Berlin, at a time when the Ottoman Empire continued to decline, and Germany and Austria-Hungary were rising. Nevertheless, the political order put in place by Disraeli's 'Peace with Honour' was still prevalent, having shaped a new phase in the *Pax Britannica*. It would appear, therefore, that the Irish political landscape is not as important to *Dracula* as the Eastern Question and the continued effects of that Treaty of 1878 which had marked, for Liberals, a great betrayal of South East European people. As well as being an Irish male, Stoker was also a British subject, writing for a British audience that was often ignorant of the wider world in which Britain held sway, and which was prepared to have certain prejudices massaged, or indeed certain complexes assuaged. Like Le Fanu before him, Stoker uses the Gothic figure of the vampire to mix a concealed national allegory, and thus an implied rather than an overt critique of an Eastern European country, with a realist setting. This was to camouflage an argument that would otherwise have been considered reactionary and unacceptable to his Liberal colleagues and friends: that the nations of the Near East need the restraining hand of the Ottomans or of Austrians, in order to rein in the threat of their parasitism upon Britain and the West, which unbridled freedom would allow them to put into effect.

Stoker and Sergei Stepniak

Or perhaps this is not quite the case: indeed, perhaps Stoker was in reality more politically adept than most of his Liberal friends, and had an understanding of the Balkan situation which inclined him to adopt a pro-Disraeli position for pragmatic reasons whilst not contradicting his general belief in freedom and self-determination. Although his brother's position might well have inclined him to accept a pro-Turkish attitude on emotional grounds (while still ideologically condemning the East), Stoker was no naïve ingenue when it came to the politics of the Near East or the Slavic world. One of his correspondents was the Russian nihilist and exile Sergei Stepniak, who wrote to Stoker on several occasions, not simply to reserve a box at the Lyceum (which, since Stoker was Henry Irving's manager, was the sort of subject that constituted the vast bulk of his correspondence), but to discuss Russian politics. In one letter, dated 2 August 1892, he writes:

> Dear Mr Stoker,
>
> What I send you is the paper Free Russia I am editing. Since you have read all my books and have been so kind and indulgent for them and so interested in the Russian Cause, I suppose you will be interested in the attempt to give a practical expression to English Sympathies. Unfortunately the collection of Free Russia is incomplete (NI is quite out of print) – But what you will have is quite sufficient to give you an idea of the Whole.

In one of the sections for the June edition of *Free Russia* Stepniak had printed Professor Dragomanev's article on Russian foreign policy, which argued that although the real duty of Russia was to foster independence for the Balkan nations, under the present Tsarist system it could never do so and was more a threat to the region than a help, as shown by the recent kidnapping of the Crown Prince of Bulgaria (1886). He thus argues that Britain should side with neither Turkey nor Russia, 'but with the oppressed nationalities, thus boldly achieving the work that Russia has thrown down.'[36]

However, Stoker had clearly also read 'all' of Stepniak's books. If this is the case, then he would surely have read *Russia under the Tsars* (1885) the work which gives the longest consideration of Russia's involvement with, and danger to, Europe. Being a nihilist, Stepniak rejected all authority and rule by the state, putting his faith in the power to destroy it rather than any considered programme to replace it. In this particular work he describes the Tsarist system as being the most backward and anti-democratic in the whole of Europe, mainly because it is a bad bureaucracy headed by an Autocracy, which can interfere in every area of Russian life.

Although no lover of the bourgeois capitalist regimes which were growing all around the Tsar's western borders, Stepniak acknowledged that their improvements in education and emancipation were both a threat to the Tsarist regime[37] and a potential cause of its destruction by their interference (Stepniak, II 280–2). In a passage where he addresses the British people directly and engages with 'English Sympathies' he gives reasons for why the British should involve themselves:

> Humanity is the chief, the main claim of our cause for sympathy and support. But it is not the sole one.
>
> It was a question of pure humanity when the Bulgarian horrors were spoken of. It was a question of humanity when Mr. Gladstone held up to public obloquy the King of Naples, nicknamed Rè Bomba, for his atrocious treatment of political prisoners. With Russia it is no more a question of humanity only, but of general safety and common interest. However badly administered, however ruined, it is too enormous a body not to endanger by its presence other political bodies which surround it. An army of a million soldiers, who, although dying from hunger and half clad, for courage in the field is not inferior to any other in the world. Such an enormous force left to the uncontrolled caprice of a despot or a courtier is surely a great impediment to human intercourse. ... Only the destruction of Russian autocracy can constitute Russia a guarantee of peace and free Europe from external danger. That is a consideration on which it is superfluous to insist. (II 282–3)

This is implicitly a paradoxical passage. While humanity was what engaged the English public to call for Turkish withdrawal from Bulgaria in 1876–78, humanity should also prompt the English public to call for the reform of the Russian system. However, since the Russian army is nearby, they should also be considering helping the Tsar's opponents from the point of view of self-interest. If this is to be taken to its logical conclusion, however, then in the short term there must also be a rejection of the principle of humanity which had led to Gladstone and the *Daily News* condemning Turkish rule in the Balkans, since this was in fact an encouragement of Russian influence in the region,[38] an influence which Stoker had also characterised as a 'greedy arm' (Murray, p. 37) in relation to India, while still a young man in Dublin (see note 16). Stepniak saw the presence of a Tsarist Russian army next door to the more progressive European states as a huge threat to them which he hoped would galvanise the British and other Europeans to topple the Tsarist regime (a fear which Coundouriotis also mentions [*Connotations*, 9:2 154]). Pragmatically, however, his position could also be used to justify the Disraeli-line which Bram Stoker had heard echoed by his brother for more sentimental reasons. Despite Stepniak's own belief, along with Dragomanev, that the Balkan nations should be free of Turk or Russian, his frightening warning could more easily induce the opposite effect in someone who had a pro-Turkish influence in his family. The Turks are a worthy presence in the Balkans, if only for keeping the Russians out.

To reiterate, the manipulation of history and ethnography in *Dracula* develops an unusual political point of view in relation to the Eastern Question which sanctions Turkish control while paradoxically condemning the East Europeans for being Eastern. However, while Stoker's novel may sanction the Treaty of Berlin (1878) due to his brother's reactionary influence, this may be also as a result of his genuine fear of Russian influence in the Balkan region, thanks to his further immolation in the ideas of Sergei Stepniak. Thus Balkan Christian nations, while presented as vampiric for rhetorical reasons, may mask, behind the allegory, the fear of another, encroaching imperial power.

Anthony Hope's Ruritania

As a mark of how unorthodox Stoker's position is, it is worthwhile comparing his portrayal of Austria with Anthony Hope's German-speaking Ruritania in *The Prisoner of Zenda*, a work that was more popular than his own novel at the time.[39] Vesna Goldsworthy sees it as representing a colonial fantasy as well as a self-congratulatory view of the Englishman as being capable of entering Balkan countries and taking natural control over them (Goldsworthy, p. 60). However, the fact that the country is German-speaking makes Ruritania appear less a Balkan country than a part of the Mittel Europa of Austria-Hungary or Germany, the same Mittel Europa to which Transylvania more properly belongs. Indeed if one relates Ruritania to Germany and Austria, one sees that Hope takes a very different view to these countries – two countries of the *Dreikaiserbund* – to that of Stoker. While Stoker is pragmatic and reactionary with regard to supporting Austria, Hope observes the problems of Mittel Europa in relation to its constitution and compares it to his own liberal aspirations for a nation state with universal suffrage.

In *The Prisoner of Zenda*, the idle younger brother of a British Lord, Rudolf Rassendyll, a distant cousin through an illegal affair with a previous King of Ruritania,[40] travels to that country by train on a grand tour and meets the current King and his councilors just before coronation day at his brother Prince Michael's castle of Zenda (Hope, *Zenda*, pp. 17–18). In the ensuing precoronation feast the King is drugged by his brother Black Michael, and so the two councilors, Sapt and Tarlenheim, ask Rudolf to take his place (p. 26). He travels to the capital Strelsau by train, astonishing the guilty Michael by his presence (p. 34), as well as his rascally friends, known as 'the Six'. In replacing the rightful King, Rudolf meets and falls in love with the King's betrothed, Flavia, who also falls in love with him, surprised at the change that has overcome her fiancé, for whom she had previously not cared (Michael was also in love with Flavia: another reason for his hatred of his brother [p. 133]).

Meanwhile, Black Michael has arranged for the kidnap and abduction of the King through the swashbuckling but dissolute Rupert of Hentzau. Aware that Rudolf is really an imposter, Michael and Rupert arrange his assassination at the hands of other members of the Six, but Michael's mistress Antoinette forewarns him. As they come to fire at him with their revolvers, he shields himself with a tea-table (p. 65). During this period, the abductors of the real King have built a shaft from his cell with which to dispose of his body quietly once his replacement, Rudolf, is killed (p. 98). Rudolf makes an attempt to see if he can use it to enter the castle, but aborts it. Eventually he manages to suborn Zenda with the help of Antoinette (p. 112), and sets about killing the Six on his way to the King's dungeon (pp. 121–39). In the escape Rudolf kills Michael, and, despite his great love for Flavia, slips out of his assumed persona to return to England to resume his life as an English gentleman and to allow the real King (also called Rudolf) to take over. Rupert, however, manages to flee the country.

There was a sequel novel, *Rupert of Hentzau* (1895), this time told from the perspective of the councilor Fritz von Tarlenheim. Unable quite to maintain his stoical resolve, Rudolf returns to Ruritania to see his beloved queen, only to find that a love letter has been intercepted by the banished Rupert (pp. 170–2), who wishes to discover the illicit liaison to the King. When Rupert surprises King Rudolf at Zenda, he accidentally kills him before the King can read the letter (pp. 236–8), and so the Englishman has to assume the King's identity once more, an event which the good constable Sapt accepts as being the will of God (p. 306). In the ensuing story the new King punishes the plotters, and eventually kills Rupert himself (p. 337) during a bungled assassination attempt on his own life. While resisting the pressure from the others to stay on as King, he is himself assassinated by one of Rupert's accomplices (p. 365), and is buried as the real King (p. 370 the other's body having been burnt [p. 352]), and so in death finally does change places with him.

The view of Rudolf Rassendyll as iconic English gentleman, capable of superhuman feats in other countries on account of his superior nationality – a view which Vesna Goldsworthy suggests was the central appeal of the book (p. 60) – should be tempered by a consideration of Anthony Hope's political views. Hope came from a well established Liberal family, and like Stoker was a devotee of Gladstone.[41] The year before his best-selling novel made his dull career as barrister no longer necessary to him (1893), he had stood for parliament with Gladstone's Liberals and had lost in his own borough, while the party itself had won (Mallet, pp. 63–5).

One of the major issues on which the Liberals fought this election against Salisbury was that of universal suffrage.[42] Although in theory all men over the age of 21 had the right to vote, the reality was that registration was still a major problem, since many working-class people, without property of their own and frequently on the move from different work locations or from rapacious landlords, could not satisfy the registration criterion of being domiciled in a particular residence for more than six months. On the other hand wealthier people who owned more than one residence could be registered in more than one electoral borough.[43]

At the time of writing *The Prisoner of Zenda* there had been clear abuses of the suffrage principle in both Germany and Austria-Hungary, countries in which dynastic politics still overshadowed the democratic process. Both the German Kaiser and the Austrian Emperor had been interfering to various degrees in the government of their lands. In Germany the Kaiser had just replaced Bismarck, and drafted a new bill limiting work hours that had unsettled the parliament and given scope to the Radicals and Social Democrats, unseating Liberals and giving way to a socialist threat.[44] He had also been foolish enough to declare belief in his right to 'supreme law' as king, publicly writing this in the vistors' book at

Munich Town hall in 1890 (Nichols, p. 130). After the crushing of the Hungarian uprising in 1849, Emperor Franz-Josef had quashed the autonomy and diets of his various regions and reinstituted neo-absolutism and centralisation (Dec 1851).[45] This changed after the Ausgleich in 1867, with two separate diets at Vienna and Buda-Pesth, but the major ministries of the Empire, and the army, were still controlled by Franz-Josef and not by the parties of the elected governments (Jelavich, pp. 82–3). In neither Germany nor Austria-Hungary, therefore, was suffrage universal, and in both cases the government ministers could be selected or dismissed by the ruling monarch.

Further to this, there was a popular understanding of Germany amongst the British public which made these novels topical in their portrayal of Mittel Europa, and guaranteed to catch the zeitgeist. The end of Bismarck with the coming of the new Kaiser, and the rancour which this had caused, made for some gloating articles in British newspapers, as the interference and amateurism of a headstrong young ruler made all attempts at preserving protocol something of a farce. On 6th June the *The Times* reports how some sections of the German press, nostalgic for their great man, had been putting about rumours that there was to be a rapprochement. *The Times* quotes Bismarck's own *Westdeutsche Allegemeine Zeitung* as declaring in the face of this that:

> This is reversing the truth. The emperor does not want Prince Bismarck's friendship or advice on any terms. He has no more wish to be on a footing of good fellowship with Prince Bismarck than the other has to lend himself to an insincere comedy intended to produce oblivion of the manner in which he was summarily expelled from office. (*The Times*, 6th June, 1892, p. 5)

The Times, perhaps rather patronisingly, concludes that: 'Emphatic as this denial may be in reference to the rumours of reconciliation, it is scarcely more eloquent than the icy silence preserved by the semi-official press' (p. 5). Throughout June, when the British election was approaching, *The Times* continued to report on the dispute, accusing Prince Bismarck on one occasion of 'almost hysterical violence' in the tone of another public letter (*The Times*; June 14, p. 5). Thus the attitude towards the body politic in Germany at the time contained both fear and suppressed mirth at such public portrayals of juvenility by both the Kaiser and his former Chancellor.

Hope's views on the Emperor and the Kaiser are not recorded at this point, but they can hardly have been good, knowing his affection for

Gladstone and support for the Liberal cause. His attitude to the crisis of dynastic politics in Germany and Austria would not have been positive, especially since they involved the manipulation of working-class aspirations, but for wholly reactionary ends. In the novel this may be reflected in the characters of King Rudolf (the real King) and his brother Black Michael. As Rassendyll rides through Strelsau to his coronation he mentions the riches of the outer circles, where the King is popular, and the poverty of the shabby inner city, where his treacherous brother, Black Michael, is favoured, and comments: 'The New Town was for the King; but to the Old Town Michael of Strelsau was a hope, a hero, and a darling' (Hope, *Zenda*, p. 31). In Mittel Europa dynastic politics takes the place of mass political movements and their properly appointed spokesmen. Parliament, ideology and party play no part in the political aspirations of the poor: they look to a Prince instead.

The novel can thus be seen as a flattering self-comparison for Britain in relation to the Mittel Europa of Hohenzollerns and Hapsburgs. This is achieved in the novel through the doppelgänger technique, as Rudolf is slimmer, lither (p. 19) and more abstemious than his double, who thus represents figuratively the decline of the aristocracy in a society that is simply an anachronism. Anachronism is in fact the central charm of Ruritania: that an Englishman can travel through the real France of his day, with its topical salons and aesthetes, to a country with railways and revolvers, which is still ruled as a monarchy, and which possesses all the intrigue and plotting of a medieval society (when first dreaming of meeting Flavia outside Zenda, Rudolf recalls 'To remember a train in such a spot would have been a sacrilege' [p. 17]).

Coupled with contrast of the two countries' attitude to dynastic politics there is an implicit comparison between the social mores of Modern Britain and Ruritania. The country's officer class are bound by an antiquated sense of both honour and fatalism, values conspicuous to premodern societies. As imposter King, Rudolf greatly improves the country by banning duelling 'save in the gravest cases' (p. 101), indicating that it is an honour-bound society. There is also, within this, a prevailing lack of conscience in standards of morality. The devious behaviour of individuals is taken as 'Fate', opposed to the individual will and sense of responsibility of the Englishman, indicating the medieval nature of a society in which abrogation of responsibility is taken as a matter of providence. In the novel *Rupert of Hentzau*, for example, the honest councillor Sapt takes active steps to burn the dead King's body after he is killed by one of Rupert's cronies, so that Rudolf may take his place, but understands this act as God's decision, not his own:

> 'There's a fate about it,' said the Constable. 'There's a strange fate about it. The man was born to it. We'd have done it before if Michael had throttled the king in that cellar, as I thought he would. Yes, by heavens we'd have done it ... The fate brought Rudolf here again, the fate will have him King.' (p. 306)

Providence has ordained what is in fact a necessary evil, paradoxically completely against the idea of divinely ordained rule and the law of primogeniture. Tarlenheim also condones this perverse view when he excitedly narrates that 'Fate, for once penitent, was but righting the mistake made when Rudolf was not born king' (p. 345) when it is clearly a catalogue of haphazard and frankly absurd events, including his one moral weakness (a continuing affair with Flavia, the Queen) that have actually brought him where he is.

This sense of fatalism as regards Rudolf Rassendyll's one moral weakness differs entirely from the gentlemanly honour of the Englishman himself, whose perception of his own need for moral integrity indicates an acute understanding of responsibility, and leads him to be naturally appalled when, after the deaths of the plotters, Sapt still causes news to be sent to England that a certain 'Rudolf Rassendyll' has died in a fire so that he can carry on ruling without the rest of the country knowing he is not really the King (p. 352). As Rudolf Rassendyll's sister-in-law observes in the first novel, 'Good families are generally worse than any others' (p. 3), and thus Rudolf's insistence on doing nothing back in Britain rather than following his brother Lord Burlesdon's example and pursuing a career in politics, is not necessarily sloth but the just abstention of an aristocrat living in a true democracy.

The aesthetic method through which Hope expresses his political opinions is entirely different to that of Stoker, depending upon, for the most part, the aggregation of real-life details into a mixture that has a close contemporary parallel. While the plot of Black Michael and Rupert of Hentzau to kidnap the king was probably inspired by the kidnapping of Alexander Battenburg of Bulgaria (himself a German prince) in 1886, the mythic location is otherwise entirely that of a German or Austro-Hungarian province. Strelsau, the capital, could have been inspired by a number of place names, but is probably a fusion of Stettin and Breslau (now Szczecin and Wroclaw), two Polish towns then under German jurisdiction. The main villain of both novels, Rupert of Hentzau, could have been inspired by any number of gallant Prussian officers who had graced the gaming tables of Paris, but Bismarck's wayward son-in-law, Count Rantzau, who had famously got drunk with Herbert Von Bismarck one afternoon and started shooting at the Foreign Office windows (Nichols, p. 50), does seem a possible source as well. In short, Hope creates his politically charged fantasy mainly through a process of metonymic representation.

This portrayal of Middle Europe contrasts entirely with Stoker's use of Transylvania. Hope is examining Middle Europe through the doppelgänger motif, which reflects well upon his own nation state with its rule by the people and universal suffrage: furthermore, with the exception of the doppelgänger motif itself, the political ideas are presented through metonymy using naturalistic images taken from the political life of Germany and Austria combined with elements of burlesque. Stoker, on the other hand, uses the metaphor of vampirism and symbolic values of West clashing with East, as well as surreptitious historical parallels (when inviting the comparison between the gang and the Turks of earlier time in their chase for Dracula [Stoker, *Dracula*, p. 341]), to present his political message, creating an embedded national allegory through rapacious vampirism which argues for a continuation of the restrictive status quo rather than reform, and a further justification of the earlier Treaty of Berlin.

In summation, the unveiling of the seemingly urbane aristocrat Dracula as blood-thirsty vampire and sexual deviant, and the further denigration of his warlike activity as being no more than the behaviour of a childlike criminal, are an attempt to undermine the idea of Balkan freedom. Stoker manipulates his sources in order to heighten the conflict between Dracula and the Turks on one hand, and the Austrians on the other, as a means of justifying the reactionary Treaty of Berlin (1878) and the continued Turkish presence in the Balkans, which Stoker believed in. This state of affairs was due to his brother's influence and possibly the dire warnings against the Russian regime from his friend Stepniak. As in Polidori's *The Vampyre*, the use of the vampire is to suggest a potentially unacceptable opinion.

4
Bram Stoker's *The Lady of the Shroud* and the Bosnia Crisis (1908–09)

That the politics of the Near East were of singular importance to Stoker can be demonstrated by the fact that he published a second novel on a Balkan theme in 1909, *The Lady of the Shroud*, in which he went to extraordinary lengths to create the trappings and history of an entirely fictitious Balkan nation state between Greece, Albania, Serbia and Bulgaria, in the mode of Anthony Hope's Ruritania, or even Hope's later novel, *Sophy of Kravonia* (1906). In Stoker's new novel, a young Englishman, having inherited a huge fortune and a palace in the small Balkan kingdom the 'Land of the Blue Mountains', and having married a local vampire (who is really a princess in disguise), sets about modernising the country and preparing for a wider Balkan federation. David Glover has argued that it represents an attempt to create a Utopian Kingdom in keeping with both Liberal ideas of the nation state and British imperial designs,[1] however, the novel is more directly a response to certain recent events that again betray Stoker's conservative take on the Eastern Question and desire to justify the Berlin treaty, although from the vantage point of a changed political scene during the Bosnia Crisis, when Austria-Hungary was seen as a threat to British imperial interest. Furthermore, rather than seeing the Near East as an area to be conveniently forgotten about, Stoker now sees active involvement in its affairs as the right British answer to the Eastern Question. As shall be shown, Stoker both fashioned his country carefully from particular sources, but also reacted to the furore created by the British press and the public's impatience with what they perceived as the weakness of their politicians.

The Bosnia Crisis and the British press

In October 1908 Europe was thrown into turmoil by Austria-Hungary's annexation of Bosnia.[2] Under article 25 of the Treaty of Berlin in 1878, Austria's foreign minister Andrassay had agreed to occupation of both this area and the Sandjak of Novipazar with recognition of the Sultan's titular rule (Pribram, p. 94). Although at the time of the treaty Britain had agreed in a pre-summit accord to support Austria's full rule of Bosnia, Hercegovina and the Sandjak, the attitude of King Edward VII and Sir Edward Grey, the foreign minister, was nothing less than outrage. The Austrians pointed out that Britain – the most vociferous of the critics of this action – could be accused of hypocrisy for making so much of the treaty's article 25 when they had shown little support for it at the time (p. 98). Nevertheless, the reasons for both the King and the Liberal government responding so severely are not hard to determine.

The announcement of annexation could not have been worse timed. In the remains of the Ottoman Empire the Young Turks revolt had just taken place, during which progressive and democratic officers in the Turkish army had wrested control of government from the Sultan (pp. 99–100). Whereas since the 1890s the Sultan had ceased to enjoy any popular support from either Conservatives or Liberals in Britain due to both political expediency and moral contempt, the overthrow of his brutal regime by a group of modernisers, committed to universal suffrage and the emancipation of women under their leader Ahmed Riza Bey, could not but draw support from a Liberal government in Britain, especially since they pledged to hold elections to a first parliament in November. However, the loss of any of Turkey's European possessions could also help to unseat this revolt and give sustenance to the Young Turks' foes at home. This is despite the fact that as soon as the annexation was announced the Austrians vacated the Sandjak of Novipazar in order to assuage Turkish feeling (p. 106). Prince Nicholas of Montenegro demanded that it now be divided between Serbia and Montenegro, but this was ignored, further aggravating Serbian anger.

Another complication was the Bulgarian declaration of independence and Kingship by Prince Ferdinand Saxe-Coburg-Gotha (p. 102), which incorporated both Northern and Eastern Roumelia, negating the final vestiges of Ottoman rule. Furthermore, the Bulgarian seizure of the Oriental Railway from Vienna to Baghdad over its own area just before the declaration, also made matters worse. The Bulgarian position was even more difficult for Grey since, while Austria-Hungary had never been a friend in Liberal eyes, the Bulgarians, like the Young Turks, were a force which they felt duty-bound to support and had supported from the Treaty of Berlin onwards. The Bulgarian declaration had followed a recent visit of the Crown Prince Ferdinand to Austria-Hungary, and it is presumed that he and Ferdinand signed a secret pact at this point. The British Government, nevertheless, stood by the Berlin Treaty, and refused to recognise Bulgarian independence until all parties in the Balkans were content with the status quo.[3]

Aerenthal, the Austrian foreign minister, wanted the Great Powers to agree to the annulment of article 25 of the Treaty of Berlin (Pribram, 1951, p. 103). The British demanded that in this case reparations should be paid to the Turks for the breaking of this article (pp. 106 and 122), and to Serbia and Montenegro as well, as a means not only of assuaging their sense of being wronged, but also of assuring them that Austria held goodwill towards them. While the Austrians settled their differences with the Turks, by way of a hefty land purchase on 11th January 1909 (p. 119), the Serbs still continued to manoeuvre on their border and prepare for war, something which Aerenthal believed was a result of British interference. He felt sure that the British desired to use the Bosnia crisis to draw Serbia's ally, Russia, into a conflict and cement an Anglo-Franco-Russo alliance (p. 142). However, although there were some British politicians who might have desired an alliance with France and Russia against Germany and Austria-Hungary, Grey was not one of them, and the most important politicians in the government were concerned not to allow Serbia to drag them into war. Furthermore, the Austro-Hungarians were confident that their military strength could overcome Serbia very quickly, and that Tsarist Russia was too weak to get involved (pp. 120–1).

Eventually, German pressure on Russia forced their acceptance of Austria's annexation of Bosnia (p. 137). Rocked both by lack of traditional support and by a domestic scandal, in which the Crown Prince George had been forced to abdicate after beating a servant to death in a fit of anger, Serbia had accepted the annexation by 30th March 1909, and had agreed to disarm in return for assurances that Austria-Hungary would not attack. The way had been paved to abrogate articles 25 and 29 of the Treaty of Berlin. On 6th April Montenegro accepted the annexation in return for the annulment of article 29 of the Berlin Treaty, the article which had given Austria control of Antivari (pp. 143–4). This was only achieved through Cartwright and Grey making it clear to Aerenthal, and Belgrade, that the Serbs and Montenegrins could expect no support from Britain if they refused (p. 141). They were, effectively, cornered.

It was against this somewhat inglorious background that Stoker wrote his own reaction to the crisis in the form of a book which anticipated a completely different response to Austrian bullying from his robust fictional country 'The Land of the Blue Mountains'. However, his reaction was itself a response to the views of the British press which steered public opinion at home and provided him with a guide as to how to capitalise upon peoples' feelings.

The situation between Austria-Hungary and Britain was muddied throughout the conflict by the intensely anti-Austrian attitudes of the British press, which published articles condemning the Hapsburg Empire, and sometimes even urging Serbia and Montenegro to galvanise themselves into war. The London *Evening Star* (*ES*), a popular paper, summed up the popular mood by being highly turcophile and deeply anti-Austrian. Reacting to Franz-Josef's speech in justification for the annexation, the *Star* comments:

> In bitter contrast to the severe dignity of the Turk is the unctuous hypocrisy of the Austrian. It would be difficult to find any parallel in history for the cynical cant of the speeches delivered yesterday by the Emperor and by Baron von Aerenthal. The aged and once venerated Emperor solemnly declared that in violating the Treaty of Berlin he was actuated by 'the best wishes for the consolidation and strengthening' of the Constitutional regime in Turkey. ... Could hypocrisy go further? (*ES*, 9th Oct.)

The Star also reports the bellicosity of the Serbs and Montenegrins, for whom it has qualified sympathy, declaring that 'Servia is frantically opposed to Austria for unneighbourly reasons' (*ES*, 8th Oct.), meaning its commercial rivalry in the north.

The *Illustrated London News* tended to publish articles condemning all the Balkan countries, except Turkey, in frankly equal terms. While they accused Aerenthal, the Austrian foreign minister, of tearing up the Berlin treaty, and the Emperor Franz-Josef of tricking Europe,[4] they also frequently referred to Prince George of Serbia as 'bellicose' and lamented the general attitudes of all Balkan countries as being particularly dangerous. However, a new periodical, *The Near East* (*TNE*), attacked Emperor Franz-Josef personally. An anonymous reporter writes in the November 1908 edition:

> In truth he possesses most of the qualities of a peasant. He is crafty, superstitious, bigoted, spiteful, conscientious, insincere, anything

but intellectual, almost illiterate, fussy about trifles, a gross feeder, a martinet, utterly destitute of humour, coarse, moral, peevish, mawkish, a strange medley of contrasts and inconsistencies, an inhuman document.[5]

Throughout the crisis *The Near East* published articles condemning Austrian rule in Bosnia and Hercegovina (with which it gave the former Turkish rule a favourable comparison) but also sympathised with the Serbs for the provocation they had suffered, arguing, euphemistically, that they may have no choice but to arm themselves as a counterbalance to Austria (*TNE*, 'The Servian Cause' (Dec. 1908), 304–5). In March, when talking of Serbia's reported renunciation of the Sandjak of Novipazar and thus of union with Montenegro (which it regrets), *The Near East* warns: 'The guarantee by the powers, moreover, of the independence of Servia, which is now suggested as the condition in effect upon which her renunciation is based, is calculated to be illusory, unless she contemplates a resort to arms in defence of her economic interest' ('The Provocation of Servia', *TNE* (March 1909), pp. 3–4, at p. 3).[6] During the crisis Aerenthal, the Austrian foreign minister, pointed to both *The Near East*, and the *Illustrated London News* (*ILN*), when accusing the British Press of exacerbating the crisis through their biased reporting (Pribram, 1951, p. 121), and referred in particular to the personal attack on the Emperor in the October 1908 edition of *The Near East*, and to the sketches of Franz-Josef and Ferdinand in a supplement to the 17th October 1908 edition of the *Illustrated London News* in which they are labelled 'The Sly Rulers: The Men who tricked Europe' (*ILN*, 17th Oct Suppl, p. 3).

By the end of the crisis, the British newspapers were largely unimpressed with their own government's behaviour and with the result of the protracted negotiations, feeling that the Austrians had been treated too leniently. G.K. Chesterton, writing his column for the *Illustrated London News*, was alone in praising the Austrian foreign minister: 'Throughout the long-drawn crisis', writes Chesterton, 'Baron von Aerenthal, the moving spirit of the whole affair, has held his ground with wonderful firmness and courage, and has proved himself one of the ablest diplomatists of his time' (*ILN*, 3rd April, p. 472). The *Evening Star*, London's largest evening paper, was far more skeptical about the result. Throughout the crisis it had maintained a pro-Turkish, anti-Austrian bias, praising the 'dignity' of the one and the 'hypocrisy' of the other (*ES*, 9th Oct.), and while the Serbian anger at Austria's annexation is greeted with similar cynicism, there is no delight at the end result.

Under the title 'A Dubious Peace', *The Star* declares how Britain has committed a 'first-class blunder' by being seen to take sides, and argues that 'The sooner we get back to a policy of splendid isolation – a policy of friendship for all and not for a few – the better for this country and for European peace' (*ES*, 27th March). One periodical which was decidedly mute after the resolution of the crisis was *The Near East*, the one which had been the most anti-Austrian and pro-Serbian during the crisis – its mutedness an embarassed admission of defeat.

This was the political and social context in which Stoker wrote *The Lady of the Shroud*. One can see that it was a climate in which anti-Austrian sentiment was stronger in the press and in the general population than in the minds of the embarrassed British government, whose past policies haunted them awkwardly. Although the resolution of the conflict drew praise from some quarters of the press and opposition from others, we shall see that Stoker himself appears to have taken a view more akin to that of *The Near East*, and that his work is an unashamed attempt to argue for the smaller nations. As such it is a complete about-face from the time of *Dracula*, but one still prompted by the maintenance of British self-interest. Stoker's novel can in fact be read as a corrective to the policy of the Liberal government, in which the calls from some quarters of the British press to arm Serbia and Montenegro are actually given a literal manifestation; albeit through the mask of a fictional country.

Anthony Hope's *Sophy of Kravonia* (1906)

The breaking of articles 25 and 29 of the Treaty of Berlin was not the only time in recent years that the Balkans had loomed large in British popular consciousness, and afforded the *Illustrated London News* the opportunity to print pictures of Balkan potentates. The assassination of the unpopular King and Queen of Serbia by members of their own guard in 1903 had also intrigued the British public and led to an interest in popular fiction set in the Balkans around this time. Anthony Hope published *Sophy of Kravonia* in 1906, which followed the usual Ruritanian plot of the English citizen becoming crowned monarch of an East European country.

This time the protagonist is a working-class female and an orphan, a kitchen maid called Sophy Grouch, blessed with a peculiar red spot on her cheek,[7] who travels from Essex to France, where she becomes involved in spiritualism with a charlatan called Pharos (Hope, *Sophy*, p. 63), and is renamed Sophy de Gruche (p. 71). When the Franco-Prussian War breaks out (1870), she travels to the Balkan country of Kravonia where she has friends from her time in Paris (p. 93). The country is divided between two peoples, the Slavs, who mainly inhabit the centre and west of the country, and the Volsenians, the mountain people of the east who are Italian in origin. Sophy manages to stop an assassination attempt by younger officers on the rightful heir, Prince Sergius, in the capital, Slavna (p. 129), and becomes Baroness Dobrava, his fiancée (p. 164).

The Prince is unpopular with the people of the capital, and especially his own officers, because of his disciplinarian zeal: 'the pruning knife' he explains to Sophy, 'not popular with the rotten twigs' (p. 135). Implicitly, however, he is unpopular because his mother was an outsider, being an Italian Bourbon, – or rather, by being Italian, closer to the other people of the country, the Italian Volsenians, who follow him with devotion (p. 101). The people are also used to their royalty marrying closer to home, and awarding the local wives full status:

> You see, a morganatic marriage isn't such a well-established institution here as in some other countries. Oh, it's legal enough, no doubt, if it's agreed to on that basis. But the Stefanoviches have in the past often made non-royal marriages – with their own subjects generally. Well, there was nobody else for them to marry! (p. 102)

Despite such insularity, the troops support his half German younger half-brother, Alexis, who is the product of the King's marriage to his second wife, the German Countess Ellenberg, but from a morganatic relationship, meaning that neither she nor her son have any real right to title or succession.

On the other hand Sophy, despite her lowly background, is later accepted as ruler of Kravonia by the Volsenians, despite only remaining Sergius's fiancée (p. 308). She and the Prince are away in the mountain retreat of Volseni on military exercises when Sergius's father the king dies (p. 276), and the battle for succession begins. The regular soldiers, spurred by the usurping stepmother, Countess Ellenberg, come to Volseni to defeat the heir apparent, and are themselves defeated in a battle at his mountain fortress in Volseni, but not before killing the heir (pp. 290–9). The Volsenians immediately accept Sophy as uncrowned dowager Queen. She marches at the head of the loyal Volsenians to Slavna (p. 311), where she is hailed as monarch, but promptly abdicates (p. 366) to return to Essex with some friends who happen to be in Kravonia at the time, one of whom, the Earl of Dunstanbury (from the local aristocracy in Sophy's Essex home, and of the Whig tradition [p. 43]), clearly has designs upon enobling her for a second time (p. 370).

Vesna Goldsworthy notes that the use of slavic names places the country more firmly in a realistic setting than Hope's Ruritanian novels[8] (although I would disagree wholeheartedly with the two earlier novels not being realistic – see Chapter 3), since Slavna, the capital (which means 'glorious' in most Slavic languages) is probably a derivation of Plevna in Bulgaria. She argues that the Volsenians are clearly inspired by the Montenegrins by virtue of their being mountaineers (Goldsworthy, p. 58), the rest of the population by implication probably an unspecified 'Slavic' group. One could add to this that the fact that the Volsenians are of Italian origin clearly points to their being based on the Montenegrins, since parts of Montenegro had been under Venetian rulers, who had also given the country its Italian name in the West. Some work has clearly gone into the making of the fictional country, but, given the assassination plot it is more likely to be based on Serbia than Bulgaria (although the Volsenians are to the east, not the west, as the Montenegrins are to Serbia).

That Hope should have returned to the east of Europe after an absence points to the fact that the Serbian regicide made the region once again a suitable site for stirring the popular imagination. However, one might also add that the main idea of the novel involves an understanding of the limits of the nation state and, in emerging liberal fashion, a questioning of the extent to which those states should comprise class mobility and racial heterogeneity – an issue which Glover assumes to have also troubled Bram Stoker and to have been an inspiration for *Dracula* (Glover, pp. 40–2). These two themes are loosely established early on in the work with the friendly rivalry of the two Essex gentlemen, Pikes and Pindar, who represent respectively the Whig and Tory traditions (p. 42), and the reactionary views of the local Lady Duddington, who is a staunch Tory and 'counted the country ruined in 1688', despite having married into the Whig Dunstanbury family (p. 43). Hope, himself a Liberal, and thus an inheritor of the Whig tradition, clearly did not believe that the arrival of a Dutch king, or the opening of the aristocracy to the middle class, was a bad thing, and appears, through the example of both Sophy (the servant girl made queen), and the honour of the Volsenians (a marginal people), to suggest that it is the very immobility and racial homogeneity of Balkan countries which is their downfall (symbolised most fervently by the elitist practice of morganatic marriages). He implies it would have been the same for England in 1688 if the Glorious Revolution had not taken place, reinvigorating the society with a foreign king (whose claim to rule, like Sophy's, was through consort) and with a new social order. Hope centres upon an inward-looking

Balkan nation in order to teach this political lesson in relation to his own, through an implict mirroring similar to the doppelgänger technique of his earlier novels.

The Lady of the Shroud

In *The Lady of the Shroud*, Bram Stoker follows the example of Anthony Hope by writing a novel about an Englishman inheriting the crown of a small Balkan mountain kingdom, and moving socially as a result, but one that is far more extensively researched, and far more serious in intention. Whereas Hope, in *Sophy*, was reacting to a morbid fascination at scandalous events in the Balkans – as well as to the introverted nature of Balkan societies – Stoker was reacting to a more serious political attitude amongst the British public: namely, the right response to the Bosnia crisis. Furthermore, his consideration of how the nation state may be perfected is far more detailed than in Hope's work.

Stoker's name for his fictitious country is rather prosaic for so fascinating a place. The Land of the Blue Mountains is a wild and noble country, with noble and reserved Blue Mountaineers, who practice Greek Orthodoxy, and are ruled by a council which elects a Vladika (or council chief).[9] It has a priesthood represented by an Archimandrite, and has an historic ruling house of 'the old Serb race' ([Stoker, *Lady*, p. 212] although no King) whose prince is called the Voivode. The ruling house is known as the Vissarions, the daughter of which is called the Voivodin (pp. 211–9). The capital, where the ruling house's magnificent castle is to be found, is also called Vissarion, and finds itself on a set of rocks in a bay called the 'Spear of Ivan' overlooking which are the blue mountains themselves (p. 79). Its major towns are called Spazac, Plazac and Ilsin (p. 233), where there is a round tower, built in former times in response to a massacre by the Turks (p. 238). There is no manufactured form of communication in the Land of the Blue Mountains, no telegraph cable and certainly no telephone. There are no gas lamps and no electricity.

The Land of the Blue Mountains has been under constant attack from the Turks without ever acquiescing, when Rupert Sent Leger, a seven-foot psychic researcher, inherits an estate there from his philanthropist uncle, the billionaire Roger Melton (pp. 58–9) – an event all the more surprising given that Rupert was, like Sophy, an impoverished orphan, and spurned by more aristocratic relatives who then resented his sudden rise (p. 52). Rupert sets about devising a scheme to bring fresh military support to his new country in an attempt to boost their defences against the Turks, and imports a band of Scottish Highlanders prepared by his great uncle, the former General Colin MacKelpie (p. 100), whose niece Janet also arrives.

Janet has the gift of second sight (appropriately so given her cousin's profession) and has many beneficial visions concerning Rupert's love life (pp. 200–3). This goes at a fiery pace as he begins to receive nocturnal visits from a beautiful female vampire, who is also constantly spotted sailing in her coffin off the shore of the country. Their mutual ardour flourishes until he is led to a marriage ceremony one night, and accepts his part as bridegroom despite being certain that such a union will hardly be conventional (pp. 183–98).

All is revealed at a point of crisis, when the country's Archbishop writes to Aunt Janet and explains that Rupert's new wife is none other than Teuta, the Voivodin, who has simply been pretending to be a vampire in the interests of the local people. This was to allay their suspicions should they see her out during the day, since she had recently died (or at least had appeared to), but had than come back to life from her 'trance, or catalepsy' (p. 214) while lying in state, which, although a blessing in itself, would not be acceptable to her superstitious compatriots. Thus she sleeps in the chapel on certain days for her countrymen to come and see her drugged body, and pretends to be a vampire when she has to go out (pp. 216–9).

The truth has to come out now, however, since the Turks have kidnapped Teuta with the hope of bringing her as a wife to the Sultan ([p. 218] interestingly enough they clearly never believed the vampire story). Rupert and a band of Blue Mountaineers, now enlightened as to the truth, run after her and manage to wrest her from the hands of the brigands (p. 230). All appears resolved, but celebrations are cut short when they hear that her father, the Vovoide Peter Vissarion, has also been kidnapped by a group of Turkish pirates at the Land of the Blue Mountains' own port, Ilsin, and is being held prisoner in a hijacked tower (p. 233). Rupert and Teuta take an aeroplane and rescue him, while the ship the bandits use to make their getaway in is dealt with soundly by an armoured yacht that has been imported from America by Rupert (p. 260).

The last part of the book deals with how the Blue Mountaineers, believing their present conciliar system to be outmoded, adopt a British style constitutional monarchy in the years 1907–08 (p. 298). There is the further creation of a Balkan League consisting of the Land of the Blue Mountains, Greece, Albania, Bulgaria, Montenegro and Serbia, to forge a new power to resist possibly the Turks (who appear to be improving, and so are invited along to the summit themselves), but more importantly, the rising Austria-Hungary (p. 325). A Western monarch, a masked Edward VII, visits his onetime subject Rupert to hail him as an equal, and is treated to a display of aerial and gun technology – a rather eerie conclusion, given that the Great War, which began in the Balkans, was to commence in five years time.

The book is written in the journal entry and letter form employed throughout *Dracula*, flitting between the perspectives of the characters. However, whereas *Dracula* is an example of the 'fantastic-marvellous' of Todorov, in which we move slowly from sceptical hesitation to confirmation that the supernatural can exist in today's material world, *The Lady of the Shroud* constitutes an example of the 'fantastic-uncanny', in which a psychical researcher – himself the very fusion of the scientific examiner of the supernatural promulgated by the example of Van Helsing – has every reason to suspect his superstitious environment will confirm his fears, only to discover the vampire story to be a fabulous ploy.[10] As a technologically advanced London absorbs the reality of the undead in *Dracula*, so the romantic Land of the Blue Mountains, a country medieval in everything except government, sees within the space of two years a new King bring aeroplanes and battleships into their country to mould a new world power, *Balka*.

Stoker's novel was published some months after the resolution of the Bosnia crisis, but paints a political picture far removed from the one which actually came into effect. Stoker's political attitude to the crisis seems more in keeping with the anti-Austrian sentiments set forth by *The Near East* and *Illustrated London News*, which enraged Aerenthal so much. The sensitive issue of Serbian disarmament, which had been a stumbling block in getting the Austro-Hungarians to agree not to attack their neighbour and to annul article 29 of the Treaty of Berlin, was something which the British government supported despite being initially enraged with the Austrians at the annexation of Bosnia. The creation of a Balkan federation at the end of the book which includes Montenegro, Serbia, Albania and Bulgaria, as well as a newly friendly Turkey, against Austria-Hungary, and the projection of Britain helping the new federation to arm, seems like a compensatory dream for a foreign policy which Stoker abhorred, or else a serious attempt to galvanise public support for a position which he knew was popular in Britain itself thanks to the opinions of the press.

The portrayal of the Turks is also interesting. Despite the slightly racialist stereotyping in the vagabonds who kidnap Teuta and then hold the Voivode at Ilsin (they refuse to play by proper laws of conduct), if we measure the portrayal against the contemporary situation we can see that Stoker is simply dividing between the Sultan's corrupt and rapacious rule and that of the Young Turks who, by late 1908, when the federation *Balka* has its first meeting, were in control of their country, but needed to join a new federation because they were 'dwindling down to almost ineptitude' (Stoker, p. 326). Stoker may well have been exaggerating the Turkish threat to the Land of the Blue Mountains before this time exactly because he wanted to illustrate the difference between the corrupt rule of the Sultan and the wish of the Turkish people themselves, a distinction continually made by his brother George in *With 'the Unspeakables'* (1878)[11] whose partiality towards Turkey was mainly a result of their hospitable behaviour in comparison with that of Bulgarians and Greeks.

The very fact that the vampire story proves to be a hoax also shows Stoker's shifting position on the Balkan Christians: the fearful is in fact nothing of the sort, and is unmasked to be simply a noble, but fragile, spirit. Furthermore, the inversion of the motif also acts as a repudiation of the initial allegory of the Balkans represented by *Dracula*. When he first meets the lady, Rupert notes that she must be a vampire because: 'She wore her shroud – a necessity of coming fresh from grave or tomb' (p. 121). Later, however, when they are King and Queen, she always wears the shroud as a mark of her virtue. Teuta dresses in her shroud when she publicly meets Roger's revolting cousin Ernest Melton at Vissarion, and the local people 'appreciated it being worn for such a cause' (p. 280), although she is then humiliated by him. Mordred Booth, the correspondent for the *London Messenger*, describes Teuta as dressed in her white shroud at her coronation alongside Rupert (p. 312). The ghoulish vestment is converted to a symbol of moral purity and self-sacrifice. As Rupert reports in his diary after rescuing her from the Turks, she is: 'Not a Vampire; not a poor harassed creature doomed to terrible woe, but a splendid woman, brave beyond belief, patriotic in a way which has but few peers even in the wide history of bravery' (p. 219). The antithesis to the count who cannot gaze upon a crucifix could not be more complete. Thus, if the vampire in *Dracula* is understood as a dismissive political allegory of another nation in relation to Britain, then that allegory is repudiated by the unmasking of Teuta as real, and the conversion of the deathly shroud to an image of purity. The Balkans no longer present a dubious, primitive character who must be kept out, but a pure and noble Voivodin who presides over a race of noble savages, and with whom the British should actively engage.

In fact, most of *The Lady of the Shroud* does seem an inversion of *Dracula* in one rather unformalistic way: whereas in *Dracula* the informational context acts as an essential part of the suspense and plausibility of the narrative, serving to boost the reader's anticipation and speculation, *The Lady of the Shroud* seems only to have any kind of plot or set of characters at all so that Stoker's intricate plan for a fictive Balkan country and its projected foreign policy can be illustrated. The detail with which the various letters and journals describe the people and the landscape and the techniques employed by Rupert to make the country function, not to mention the attributes of modern aerial warfare – as yet unknown in 1909 – sinks whatever suspense might possibly raise its head in so feeble a plot in the spatial imaginings of a new Balkan country, which country combines not only elements of certain of the others, but enjoys a parallel history to those of the real Balkans, which is interfused and modified.

Sources for the fiction

As in *Dracula*, Stoker appears to have done much research into geography and history; unlike *Dracula*, however, the work articulates political views far more directly, against the backdrop of a more specific and topical set of political allusions. This necessitates a slightly closer mimesis of the Near East of his day than in *Dracula*, in which he had manipulated history and geography more loosely for symbolic effect.

In *Modes of Modern Writing* David Lodge declares that the achievement of the nineteenth century realist novel was to blend the public and the private effectively and plausibly – the 'rendering of an individual's experience of a common phenomenal world, whereby we share the intimate thoughts of a single character while at the same time being aware of a reality, a history, that is larger and more complex.'[12] Being an heir of Modernism, Lodge is most interested in defining realism perspectivally, and thus he sees the real as a mixture of public and personal viewpoint. However, if we wish to see the realist novel ontologically, and thus more in keeping with classical understandings of mimesis, we may divide his distinction between the public and the private into one between the copied real, the historical and quotidian, and the fictive creation.

In this respect, the use of fictional and masked spaces plays an important role in the history of realism, especially after the rise of the regional and historical novels, allowing writers to create specific and yet generic communities which, while corresponding to the experience and expectations of readers, and being set against the backdrop of real events like the Napoleonic wars, nevertheless allow the authors to develop their own fictions around recognisable circumstances. So the locations of

George Eliot's novels are firmly rooted in particular regions and particular eras in history, take part in the actual historical processes and bear all the external and metonymic attributes of towns and villages heard of or even remembered by her readers, and yet never existed. Thus they confirm an experienced and historically known 'real', distinct from the real of 'today', without impinging too heavily on the particular histories of actual towns. Venues for invented private experiences are able to coexist easily with a publicly acknowledged set of facts.

As a romance that enjoys even less characterisation than *Dracula* (whose Van Helsing throws a dash of irony and complexity into the work, as does the more Naturalist account of Dracula's child-psychology), *The Lady of the Shroud* has little in the way of either realism or naturalism as regards character or action. However, the detail with which Stoker builds his fictive land from real Balkan features, grounds it against the lived historical events and introduces the latest modern technology, is worthy of a novelist as meticulous in preparation as Emile Zola.

Whether the fictive land should be read simply as a mask (as in the work of Hardy), an amalgamation of various nations or an entirely new country is a question that must not be avoided or approached intuitively, for in answering it we come to answer what were Stoker's political intentions in writing the novel. Noticing the fact that the royal family, the Vissarions, are frequently called 'of the old Serb race' (Stoker, *Lady*, p. 212), Victor Sage claims that the Land of the Blue Mountains is a coded Serbia, and Balka a coded Greater Serbia, which can help Britain keep the Austrians at bay.[13] From the point of view of projecting foreign policy, which dominates the last part of the book, Sage is possibly right, especially given the fact that Serbia was in the brunt of fire after the Bosnia crisis. However, if we understand the 'codedness' in terms of mimesis, it must be said that most of the features of the fictive creation which form the Land of the Blue Mountains are taken from Serbia's close neighbour Montenegro, and surrounding territories, a fact which Goldsworthy notes but does not elaborate on (Goldsworthy, p. 85).

Like Montenegro, the Land of the Blue Mountains has resisted Ottoman rule throughout its history, the only Balkan country to do so – although this had more to do with the hardy terrain of the tiny country than any superhuman prowess.[14] Like Montenegro, the Land of the Blue Mountains has rugged mountaineers who always carry rifles, a rocky natural harbour (the 'Blue Mouth') which would seem to face Italy (the Bocche di Cattaro on the actual Dalmatian Coast – 'Bocche' being Italian for 'mouths'), and a chapel built into high rocks where the royal family are entombed after death (in Mt Lovchen in the real Montenegro).[15] The name of the country, the Land of the Blue Mountains, is clearly inspired by Montenegro (Tsernogora), 'black mountain', as is the position of Vladika (prince-bishop), which Roger Melton describes as similar to that of Montenegro in his will (Stoker, *Lady*, p. 59). The name of the princely house, Vissarion, is the same as that of one of the seventeenth-century Vladikas, Visarion Baitchka, and the chapel in which the ruling house is buried, St Sava, is inspired by one of the most pious, but politically ineffective of Montenegro's Vladikas, Sava (also the name of an important Serbian saint). Like Montenegro it also has Archimandrites (ordinary Bishops). The land of the Blue Mountains does, however, have a Serbian dynasty whose title, Voivode, means commander or chieftain, and was commonly used in several Balkan countries, but particularly Serbia, to mean Warrior Aristocrat in the Middle Ages, and was resurrected by the Serbs in the nineteenth century. Its major towns of Ilsin, Spazac and Plazac are, however, probably inspired by the real Montenegrin towns of Ulcinj, Spuz and Plavnica.

A question naturally arises as to what were the sources for Stoker's *The Lady of the Shroud*. There is no doubt that some of the details in the newspapers at the time of the Bosnia Crisis probably influenced Stoker to model his country on Montenegro. While *The Times* reported from Montenegro and described the attitudes of the people, *The Near East* would have provided him with the most factual accounts of life in the tiny kingdom in its two articles on Montenegro's cause and the character of Prince Nicholas.

However, no paper or supplement at the time provides the sorts of details which Stoker clearly took from extensive research on Montenegro and its surrounding territories, meaning that he must have once again consulted book length sources. Unlike with *Dracula* we have no notebook entries listing books the author had consulted or intended to consult. All we have to direct us is a letter written by Archibald Ross Colquhoun, a famous traveller, dated 10 June 1908, suggesting that Stoker look at five books – Colquhoun's own work *The Whirlpool of Europe: Austria-Hungary and the Hapsburgs*; Chedo Mijatovic's *Servia of the Servians* and three works by the celebrated French Slavonic scholar, Louis Leger, from whom Stoker may at least have taken the name of his main protagonist (pp. 13–4).

My own researches show that none of these works offer much that impressed Stoker by the time he came to write the novel, and that he looked elsewhere. Circumstances in the Balkans had changed dramatically with the flare-up of the Bosnia crisis in the Autumn of 1908, and it was with an eye to catching topical anxieties that Stoker returned to Eastern

Europe. Since the areas most threatened by this crisis were southern Serbia, Montenegro and Albania, it is from this region that he fashioned his country. Investigation into the available books describing Montenegro and the Dalmatian coast at the time (or at least from about 1870 to 1908), shows that his probable sources were William Denton's *Montenegro* (1877), R. Wyon and G. Prance's *The Land of the Black Mountain* (1903), Mary Edith Durham's *Through the Land of the Serbs* (1904), and the strangely initialled R.H.R's *Rambles in Istria, Dalmatia and Montenegro* (1875). The first two books provided information on the history, government and names of Montenegro, many of which were transported to the Land of the Blue Mountains, while the other two contain passages of description and impression which may have shaped aspects of the novel's plot and its tiny country's landscape and architecture.[16] An investigation of them also tells us much about his political intentions in the novel.

William Denton was a priest in the Anglican church (resident vicar of St Bartholomew's, Moorfields), who took an interest in the plight of the Christian population of the Balkans at the hands of their Moslem masters. Although he visited Montenegro himself, and weaves aspects of his own journey into his depiction of the country, his work is less a travelogue than a scholarly guide to the country's main features, and he reconstructs views and vistas (like that over the Bocche di Cattaro) from the correspondences of other travellers as well. He nevertheless did visit the chapel of Mt Lovchen, where Peter II is buried, and describes it in a way which bears similarities to the small cathedral in which the ruling house of Stoker's novel is buried. The chapel at Lovchen, which is effectively 'a vaulted dome surmounting a round chapel of some twelve feet diameter', is built high up on 'a small rugged plateau' 'which resembles a gigantic pedestal' (Denton, pp. 31–3). In the novel the chapel of St Sava, which is built on top of a cliff overlooking the 'spear of Ivan', is also round, 'almost circular' (Stoker, *Lady*, p. 136). Denton describes how Montenegro was ruled for years by Prince-Bishops, 'Vladikas' (Denton, p. 210), beneath whom are the minor bishops or 'Archimandrites' (p. 163). Although other sources describe this political system (the Vladikas were already defunct by 1877), of all the sources available to Stoker, Denton gives the most comprehensive description of the prince-bishops and their history, the names of several finding their way into *The Lady of the Shroud*: Sava, the Serbian saint whose name was also that of a pious Vladika of the eighteenth century (p. 236), and Visarion Baitchka, a seventeeth-century Vladika (p. 224). While Denton describes, like other travellers, the hardiness of the Montenegrins, the fact that they always carry rifles and even names the handjar, the mention of Visarion Baitchka is the one element of his book which points clearly to Stoker consulting it, since it does not appear anywhere else in an English language work on Montenegro.

Wyon, who travelled with Prance through Montenegro after finishing a term of duty for the foreign office at Sarajevo, makes the most of his knowledge of Serbo-Croatian to explore the whole country, meeting many interesting characters, and often enjoying hair-raising encounters in the areas bordering upon Albania, or in areas where, despite the Treaty of Berlin, there were still substantial Turkish populations. Like Denton, Wyon frequently mentions the fact that Montenegrin men wear handjar, revolver and rifle as part of their daily kit (Wyon, p. 196; p. 230),[17] and describes round towers left by the Turks in Cettigne, Ostrog, Dulcigno and other towns. In one anecdote he describes the daring escape from a tower by a turncoat Albanian Achmed Uicko, whom he has the pleasure to meet – a possible source for the rescue of Peter Vissarion in the novel (p. 99). Wyon also stresses the warrior-like nature of the Montenegrin priesthood (p. 192), a feature they share with the clergy of the Blue Mountains in Rupert St Leger's description (Stoker, *Lady*, p. 210).

Crucially, however, Wyon is the only writer on Montenegro to mention the ancient history of the region, in which the third century BC queen, Teuta, was pushed back by the Romans, providing a source for Stoker's Voivodin of the same name (p. 15). He also may have inspired Stoker to portray the Blue Mountaineers as being of Danish origin, by comparing the noble Serbs who fled Kossovo field in 1389 to create this new kingdom, with the Vikings (p. 196). It is perhaps also Wyon's book which inspired the name of the land of the Blue Mountains' port, Ilsin, since he alone amongst potential sources was well-versed enough in Serbo-Croatian to call Dulcigno by its new Montenegrin name of Ulcinj ([p. 109]. He mentions the towns of Spuz [pp. 25 and 89] and Plavnica as well [p. 110]).

One source which may well have influenced Stoker with regard to his creating descriptions of scenery, architecture and the story of the lady of the shroud itself, is Mary Edith Durham's *Through the Lands of the Serb* (1904). Although she visits Belgrade, the Sandjak of Novipazar, and areas of South Eastern Serbia still under Ottoman rule (Vojvodina was not then part of Serbia), she spends a considerable part of her time visiting Montenegro and Northern Albania as well. Above all, her book is most likely to have provided Stoker with the necessary key to his fictionally altered version of Montenegro. When leaving the capital Cettinje for

Podgorica she has her first glimpse of the great lake of Skodra dividing Montenegro from Albania:

> Beyond it the blue Albanian mountains, their peaks glittering with snow even in June, show fainter and fainter, and the land of mystery and the unspeakable Turk fades into the sky – a scene so magnificent and so impressive that it is worth all the journey from England just to have looked at it.[18] (p. 15)

Both Wyon and R.H.R. describe the vista of black mountains from the Bocche di Cattaro (Wyon, p. 37; R.H.R, p. 166), but when Rupert writes to Aunt Janet that the range of mountains from which the bay juts out is 'towering over everything, a mass of sapphire mountains,' (Stoker, *Lady*, p. 79) it is likely that Stoker has taken descriptions from Denton, R.H.R. and Wyon of the sight of the black mountains from the Bocche di Cattaro, and blended them with Edith Durham's unique observation of what is in fact an Albanian scene, thus introducing a geographical feature from another country and combining it.

The story of the lady of the shroud lying in her crypt may have been inspired by two other events from her accounts of travels in Montenegro. When Mary Edith Durham goes to visit the monastery of Ostrog, where lie the remains of St Vasily (a seventeenth-century Serbian who came to build a monastery in Montenegro), she climbs to one cavern where a priest serves her spirit, and then to another natural cavern where she sees the embalmed body of the saint in a coffin opened by the priest (Durham, p. 44). Wyon, who also visited the crypt at around the same time, saw a box with his remains and an open coffin with the saint's clothes nearby (Wyon, p. 256). According to Montenegrins, in fact only his arm is left. Even though Durham's observation was false, it may still have served the purpose of inspiring the man who had already written *Dracula* to write the story of the double and secret life of Teuta when she is presumed dead.

Later, however, Durham returns to the Dalmatian coast to visit a previous acquaintance who has made a chapel out of the rocks near Antivari and Spizza. This hermit friend informs her that the chapel, in a cavern shaped like a cross (Durham, p. 55), was 'not built by hands. It was made by God. His Church among the rocks' (p. 56) and has been dedicated to the Virgin Mary, a picture of whom is painted on the far wall above the altar. There is also a bier, covered in black and gold cloth (p. 57). The chapter devoted to this curious place is called 'Our Lady among the Rocks.'

If one looks at the description of the crypt in the caverns beneath St Sava's chapel in Stoker's novel, which holds the tombs of the Vissarion family, one sees that it too is described as a 'natural' manifestation from the rocky coastline of the Land of the Blue Mountains, but 'altered to its present purpose by the hand of man' (Stoker, p. 137). It is highly likely, therefore, that the story of the lady of the shroud, who is dressed like the Madonna and sails through the rocks on a coffin-like bark, has been inspired by these descriptions of rocky chapel, Virgin Mary and bier in Edith Durham's book.

It is R.H.R, travelling some 30 years before Durham, and about four years before the Treaty of Berlin, who perhaps provided Stoker with some of the political ideas which dominate the end of the book. While R.H.R's description of how rain can pour over the coast of Dalmatia for six weeks may account for why Stoker puts a rainy season in a European country,[19] and while his very lyrical observation of the castle overlooking the Bocche di Cattaro at sunset (R.H.R, p. 166) may again have inspired Stoker to place the castle Vissarion on his own jetty-like rock formation, the 'spear of Ivan' (Stoker, p. 79), his major contribution may have been simply the idea of a Balkan federation. After describing the beautiful sunset over the Bocche di Cattaro and its fortress, R.H.R, all set for Montenegro, reflects on how sad it is that large parts of the Balkans are under the Turkish Yoke, but nevertheless expresses optimism that things will change in the future:

> The monstrous anomaly of some of the richest lands of Christian Europe being still in this nineteenth century under the misrule of barbarous Asiatic hordes, whilst millions of wretched Christian inhabitants are kept in the most abject servitude, must ere long be done away with; and all those countries Servia, Bosnia, Hercegovina, Roumelia and all lying between the Danube and the Adriatic must before very long be amalgamated under some one chief. (R.H.R., pp. 175–6)

This may well be the passage from which Stoker took the idea of a federation Balka under the lead of a new King Rupert, although the later writer's understanding of the union is as a buffer against Austria, not Turkey, reflecting the changes made by 40 years. Quite apart from his brother's political stance and possible influence, Wyon and Prance's book records accurately that the Montenegrins see Austria as their enemy and that they have made their peace with the Turks (Wyon, p. 13), although their record of conversations in which Montenegrins show their great respect for England (pp. 138 and 166) may owe something to Wyon having been a British diplomat.

Most of the land of the Blue Mountains, including its government, history and main names, appears to have been taken from Montenegro, but also from Albania and other parts of Dalmatia. It is thus closely related to Montenegro, but is also modified, and idealised, so that it cannot quite be taken as a mask, but more as an ideal Balkan state which blends the noble savagery and heroic history of Montenegro with other local features, and with modern technology. This idealised, primitive society further possesses the possibility of modernisation from an honourable but outdated, theocratic, conciliar system to a British-style constitutional monarchy. Although we cannot be sure exactly what Stoker's sources were, the actual nature of the descriptions in the four books discussed above and their close parallel to features found in *The Lady of the Shroud*, makes it appear that they, and not the books cited by Colquhuon, are his sources.

Fictional manipulation

So the Land of the Blue Mountains is a fictitious country, comprising elements taken from real ones, with features which make it both plausibly and eminently a part of the acknowledged Balkan historical experience, but in its fictitiousness permitted a particular spatio-temporal reality of its own against the real-life background of Ottoman oppression and intrigue (the real Montenegro is not masked in the novel, and mentioned on more than one occasion).

The composite nature of this country, which blends the charming and heroic history of Montenegro with the much larger 'old Serb race' (Stoker, *Lady*, p. 212) and the blue mountains of Albania, seems to make it less a fictional mask for either country, but rather a blend of features, representing the exemplar Balkan state, and thus almost an aesthetic precursor of the political union of all the Balkan countries at the end of the novel. Stoker's meticulous attention to detail belies his usual reputation for taking names from real life in a journeyman way,[20] and shows a careful construction, which is crucial given the other ramifications that his work might have.

For it does not take a too-trained eye to see that Stoker has not only created a fictional world from real historical circumstances, but has also massaged those historical circumstances in accordance with his political designs. *The Lady of the Shroud* was written just at the point when British-Austrian relations took a dramatic turn for the worse, with the

Bosnia crisis in 1908, when Austria-Hungary had annexed forcibly those regions which Andrassay had agreed merely to occupy at the Treaty of Berlin, thus breaking that Treaty and infuriating Sir Edward Grey, Britain's foreign minister in the Liberal Government. The declaration of independence from Ottoman sovereignty by the already self-ruling Bulgaria complicated the issue further, as did the protestations of fear by the Serbs and of outrage by the Russians. Whereas at the time of *Dracula* a sizeable proportion of the British population may still have desired a massaging of the conscience as regards Catholic Austria and the treatment of Balkan peoples at the Treaty of Berlin (1878), this had by now abruptly turned, as both Liberal and Conservative opinion was against Austria-Hungary from the position of both morality, and self-interest.

Stoker's description of the motives behind the creation of a new Balkan federation, Balka, shows a rather slanted interpretation of history explaining the misery of recent events. King Rupert's Diary records the reasons why the federation was necessary:

> The modern aggressions of the Dual Nation, interpreted by her past history with regard to Italy, pointed towards the necessity of such a protective measure. And now, when Servia and Bulgaria were used as blinds to cover her real movements to incorporate with herself as established the provinces, once Turkish, which had been entrusted to her temporary protection by the Treaty of Berlin; when it would seem that Montenegro was to be deprived for all time of the hope of regaining the Bocche di Cattaro, which she had a century ago won, and held at the point of the sword, until a Great Power had, under a wrong conviction, handed it over to her neighbouring Goliath. (Stoker, *Lady*, pp. 325–6)

The Austro-Hungarians are presented as breaking the occupation terms of Hercegovina from the Treaty of Berlin and further wronging Montenegro by continuing to possess the natural harbours around the port of Cattaro. The Great Power mentioned here is Russia, which persuaded Montenegro to hand back the Bocche di Cattaro in 1813[21] after a valiant military campaign in which they had captured land from Napoleonic France as far as Dubrovnik (Ragusa) whilst in alliance with Austria and Russia (Denton, pp. 259–60). However, although possession of the Bocche obviously rankled the Montenegrins (who had once possessed all of Southern Dalmatia), at the time of writing the novel there had been more anger over the Austrians' possession of Spizza, a small port five miles south of the Bocche and nearer to Antivari, which was itself a Montenegrin possession (Pribram, 1915, p. 142). Prince Nicholas of Montenegro had attempted to use the Bosnian and Serb crises to wrest the port back from the Austrians in return for cooperation against Serbia, but had enjoyed no success.[22] It is to this particular town that Stoker should have more correctly alluded if he wished to be topical, but had he done so it might not have helped his cause in presenting Britain as a friend to the Balkans, since Spizza was again one of the territory changes between the Treaties of San Stefano and Berlin that went in Austria-Hungary's favour, and with full British support.

Indeed earlier in the novel Britain is praised by the Vladika for being the only power that has helped the Land of the Blue Mountains in its history (Stoker, *Lady*, p. 81), which does not accord generally with the opinions of Orthodox Balkan states who to this day claim that the Treaty of Berlin was Disraeli's shameful doing. Britain had quite happily agreed with Andrassay that his Emperor could have full possession of Bosnia, Hercegovina and the Sandjak of Novipazar (part of which had been awarded to Montenegro at the Treaty of San Stefano, but taken from them at Berlin), and was surprised when he settled for less. Whereas the Treaty of Berlin is latent in *Dracula*, *The Lady of the Shroud* alludes to it quite directly, and appropriately so given that Grey used its terms to condemn Austria-Hungary over annexation of Bosnia. However, the reason for mentioning it here is to obfuscate British attitudes at the time, and in order to misrepresent its contents along with Stoker's new, anti-Austrian political position.

Since the Land of the Blue Mountains is fictitious, it can be claimed in Stoker's defence that he is allowed to create a fictitious history. However, due to the size of the invention, which is an entire political entity, Stoker finds himself forced to contravene the normal practices of realist novelists, and actually alter publicly acknowledged history. This means that the poetic license taken as regards the new fictional space surreptitiously alters the real circumstances within which one would expect the Land of the Blue Mountain's own destiny to be fulfilled, so that the Treaty of Berlin and Britain's past policy towards the Balkans are modified along with it.

Although Stoker's attitude towards the Balkans has changed along with his attitude to Austria-Hungary since writing *Dracula*, he is nevertheless projecting a view of the region which, as Victor Sage has noted, serves British interests in providing a ballast to the newly dangerous Hapsburgs (Sage, 1998 p. 127). As Glover has also noted, the newly transformed country nevertheless represents a Utopian ideal of a nation state midway between the technological paradise of Wells (*A Modern*

Utopia [1905]) and the earlier primitivist Utopias of the Victorians (Glover, p. 53). It also represents a projection of a liberal ideal, but 'one whose dreams of empire and whose liberalism is of a very historically specific kind': namely, a citizen-based nation state that is allied to Britain, and looks to Britain as model rather than as oppressor (Glover, p. 55).

What is most interesting in this change of heart is that, despite his liberal politics on other issues, Stoker does not appear to have pursued an entirely liberal line over the Eastern Question, and presents the Balkans in keeping with a self-interested and patriotic line in both 1897 and 1909, even though his attitudes towards Orthodox Balkan countries and the Austro-Hungarian Empire have themselves changed. Nevertheless, the Treaty of Berlin, together with a need to justify its shameful results, resonates through this novel as surely as it does through *Dracula*.

The Red Hot Crown

In order to understand the boldness of Stoker's position, it is worthwhile examining another novel reacting to the crisis published that year, *The Red Hot Crown* by Dorothea Gerard. Gerard was an Englishwoman who had spent most of her life since girlhood in Austria, making her almost a real-life Laura. Married to a wealthy Austrian officer called Legrande, in her later years she began to write novels in English. Emily Gerard had notably provided Stoker with some of his sources for *Dracula*. Her sister Dorothea was now something of a rival to his second vampire novel.

Dorothea Gerard's preface note to the book is dated '*March*, 1909', and so her book unintentionally coincided with the renunciation of Crown Prince George's right to the Serbian throne. The declaration may well have done much to make her own novel appear ridiculous, since the main hero of the novel is a fictionalised George.

The preface claims that:

> In case – as is probable – points of resemblance should be discovered between the 'plot' of this story and certain modern political events, it is as well to point out that – while unable to deny its source of inspiration – *The Red-Hot Crown* not only calls itself, but *is* a political romance, laying no claim whatever to historical exactitude or to correctness of personal portraiture.[23]

The story that ensues, while fictional, is nevertheless very closely based on recent Serbian history, and presents a thinly disguised political reading of the events surrounding the Bosnian annexation.

Bazyl Korneliowicz is a middle-aged sculptor and royal Moesian exile living in London with his teenage son Marzian, when he is informed of the assassination of his rival in the capital of Moesia, Djakowar (Gerard, p. 46). A few days later the conspirators, led by a Colonel Brankowicz, come to his home to offer him the crown (p. 65). His son, despite youthful patriotism and a conviction in his father's justness, at first urges him not to profit from the regicide (p. 69), but eventually begins to believe that the call of the country outweighs this.

The young prince takes to life as a King's son with gusto, but becomes dismayed with the fact that the conspirators all profit from their actions, and that many of those loyal to the older King are treated shabbily. Falling in love with Yella, the daughter of one of the anti-conspirators, Colonel Dessowicz, and thus 'forbidden wares' (p. 181), he intercedes on her father's behalf in order to prevent their expulsion from the country. The prime minister Lazaricz's condition for stopping the expulsion is that Marzian will woo another, more suitable bride, namely a princess (pp. 200–2). Reluctant to do this, he nevertheless agrees to be matched with the pretty but corpulent Princess Romualda of Therpissia.

All goes well, and the Princess falls madly in love with him, but the annexation of Drynia by Danubia in October of 1908 puts an end to this match (p. 260). Meanwhile the Moesian crowds go on the rampage demanding justice for the annexation (pp. 277–8). Having gained a confession from his father King Bazyl that he had in fact been complicit in the murder of the previous king (p. 267), which is why he is still tied by the conspirators of the assassination, Marzian joins his enemy Brankowicz and the others in counseling war and revenge against Danubia (p. 286). The Danubians, scornful of the Moesians' chances, attack and quickly take over most of the country. In a final battle to defend the capital, Marzian is shot at by his arch rival Brankowicz (p. 300), who is eager to settle a score against a young man who once offended his honour. Yella's father intercedes and receives the bullet himself, allowing, before his death, the union of the Crown Prince and his daughter. Marzian returns to Djakowar to rescue Yella, who rows him all the way to the mountainous country of Mlavia since his right arm is wounded (p. 313). Moesia is now dead, but the Crown Prince, in losing the red hot crown, is free to marry the woman he loves back in London (p. 319).

Moesia is very clearly a masked Serbia, surrounded by fictional countries which are also, in Hardyesque fashion, masks for other real places. Danubia is Austria, Therpissia Greece, Moscovia Russia, Sultania Turkey and so on. The events described form a parallel reality to real historical events but are even more closely based upon them than in Hope's or

Stoker's work. Marzian is based on Prince George, his father on King Peter of Serbia. The event which gives them tainted restoration is the bed-chamber assassination of Alexander and Draga, the hated King and Queen of Serbia, in 1903. The annexation of Drynia by Danubia is that of Bosnia by Austria in 1908. The term 'red-hot crown' is a turn on the popular expression 'the iron throne', used in British newspapers when describing the Serbian crown to highlight the point that being king of Serbia is really a curse.[24]

Gerard's approach is also more practical and pessimistic than Stoker's, a fact which affects the intensity of the mimesis, since she was writing a work very closely related to the actual political landscape of Near Eastern Europe in 1909, rather than the Utopian and provisional creation of Stoker. Her major purpose, apart from 'cashing in' on the topicality of a romantic story set in the Balkans, was to inject a dose of pragmatism into the furore of October 1908. Although Vesna Goldsworthy states that the book is written from an Austrian point of view, 'with a somewhat patro-nising sympathy for the small Balkan nations', (Goldsworthy, p. 65), the book nevertheless expresses nothing but contempt for the Emperor Franz-Josef's treatment of Bosnia. Describing Marzian's first ride along the river bank past Djakowar – just before he first sets eyes upon Yella – we are told how:

> This time, as he regained the river side, his eyes strayed more than once resentfully across the wide waters towards that other bank, which was no longer Moesian, since the frontier of the mightiest of Moesian neighbours – the proud Danubia – marched with the river. It was she who held in her clutches the rich province of Drynia, which, although nominally still a possession of Sultania, had been under her care for thirty years past, Europe having been naïve enough to give her a mandate of occupation. Unjust as well as naïve, since, granted that the condition of Drynia had cried for reforms, where find a more accredited reformer than Moesia, under whose sceptre, in the country's era of glory, Drynia had actually stood, whose inhabitants were brothers in blood, speakers of the same tongue and bearers of the same traditions. (Gerard, p. 114)

Although this may represent the views of Marzian, it is the only political view we are presented and seems, perspectively, to blend with that of the narrator. We are never given the Danubian perspective on the rule of Drynia, and since Dorothea Gerard was attempting to market her book in Britain, she may not have wanted to give one. Before the war begins, the narrator talks of the scornful attitude of Danubians towards their Moesian neighbours as presented in the 'Danubian comic papers', and comments:

> If, during those uproarious days, there was anybody in Danubia honest enough to acknowledge to himself that Moesia's wrongs were real and her excitement justified, fear of unpopularity moved him to keep this opinion to himself – the first duty of every true citizen during times of war being to howl with the wolves. (pp. 279–80)

Beyond the fictional mask, Gerard's narrator is relating the bias apparent in Austria's state-controlled media, but also that Serbia may have had a just cause of complaint. However, the book also relates the irresponsible behaviour of the Western press and opportunism of the Great Powers in suddenly encouraging the arming of a country whose ills had barely meant anything to them previously due to 'the advisability of never letting anything go too cheap, and the advantages of stirring up mud, with the object of fishing more conveniently in troubled waters – the preliminary condition in every case being to make as much noise as possible.' Thus 'By the majority of the European Powers Moesia was being patted on the back and encouraged to "go for" Danubia, much as sporting spectators encourage the small dog to go for the big one' (p. 252).

The natural outcome of their war is extinction, since by the end of the book the country no longer exists, but on a political level it paints a complex pattern. Although she recognises the justness of Moesia's goal, Gerard scotches the idea that a just war can be successfully prosecuted against Danubia, since the romantic delusions of the Moesians, that it is better to die with honour than give in with dishonour, have a realisation beyond the shadowy hinterland of journalistic rhetoric. Furthermore, the good protagonists of the book are soured by their complicity with the foul deed of regicide, making their effectiveness impossible due to moral compromise, for which the country itself eventually pays.

Thus, through the fictional mask of Moesia, Dorothea Gerard is showing how the present corrupt body-politic of Serbia coupled with its traditional military weakness makes it a volatile and dangerous place in the present crisis, and points her finger firmly at the alien press for encouraging designs unpragmatic even if justified. She provides a small glimmer of dissenting light in Austria against the illegal tearing up of the Berlin treaty, but does not advocate exciting war. Her book acts as a warning shot to her native country, from someone sympathetic to the Serbian cause, but cognizant of its shortcomings.

Stoker's book, however, has a more ambitious plan for the British involvement in the Balkans which involves the exact reverse of Dorothea Gerard's suggestions. In summation, Stoker's new novel represents an about-face to his previous position in *Dracula*, and argues that Britain should actively arm Balkan countries, persuade them to unite, and encourage them to forget the ills of the Turkish past, given the changes from the Young Turks' regime. In doing this he is agreeing with the anti-Austrian and sometimes pro-Serbian and pro-Montenegrin attitudes of the British press, and against the recent climbdown of his own government. He creates an exemplary fictional country loosely based on Montenegro, but comprising features from other countries in the region, to promote the idea of Balkan unity. Above all, in turning round the vampire motif to reveal that a beautiful revenant is in fact a noble princess in disguise, he divests the Balkans of all the rapaciousness and evil with which he had invested it in writing *Dracula*, so as to encourage the reformation and integration of that area in a new alliance with Great Britain. As such his mimesis is less exact than Gerard's quasi 'roman-à-clef', *The Red Hot Crown*, but this is partly because he is promoting a political ideal, which also involves the massaging of previous British foreign policy mistakes. Although he has changed his tune towards both Near Eastern Christians and the Austrians since finishing *Dracula*, his position is still patriotic and in advocation of British self-interest rather than less selfish concerns.

5
The Vampires of Illyria: Nodier, Mérimée and the French Occupation of the Dalmation Coast

One of the most vile depictions of the vampire superstition appears in Prosper Mérimée's collection of Illyrian ballads *La Guzla*. In it, the Italian scholar who acts as Mérimée's disguise recounts the time in which he was staying at the house of a Morlack, when his daughter, asleep in the next room, screamed as a result of a visitation from a vampire, to which belief her parents and other villagers readily gave credence. What follows is a truly disgusting account of the exhumation of the 'vampire' and the pining away of a girl who has clearly been bitten by an insect in the middle of a nightmare. The account, which Mérimée passed off as true, acts as a sobering contrast to the equally false 'translations' of Illyrian ballads which then ensue, which present the 'local colour' of an exciting and heroic, primitive society where vampires are, in their literary forms, romantic figures.

Mérimée's contemporary (and enemy) Charles Nodier, had first publicised and popularised vampire literature in France through his dramatisation of Polidori's *The Vampyre* and further promotion of a novel based upon it, *Lord Ruthven*. He also published a collection of fantastic stories taken from *The Arabian Nights* and from Calmet's *Treatise*. It was perhaps in reaction to this fashionable love of primitivism, the marvellous and the Fantastic, or indeed to Nodier's Romantic portrayal of the Near Eastern region from which many of these superstitions hail, that Mérimée wrote *La Guzla*.

In his earliest surviving letter, to Joseph Lingay, Mérimée identifies himself as belonging to the new 'Romantisme' rather than to Classicism (9 April 1822)[1] – however, in a much later letter to the Russian Sokholiev (1835) he specifies that his first aim in writing *La Guzla* was to 'poke fun at' the recent literary fashion popularised by the work of Byron and Scott:

> I will reply candidly to your questions. I wrote *La Guzla* for two reasons, of which the first was to poke fun at [make fun of] the local colour in which we had been immersing ourselves up until the year of grace 1827.
>
> [Je répondrai candidement à vos questions. *La Guzla* a été composée par moi pour deux motifs, dont le premier était de me moquer de la couleur locale dans laquelle nous nous jetions à plein collier vers l'an de grâce 1827.] (Mérimée *Correspondance*, I 375–6 [18th January 1835]).[2]

The full force of the words 'me moquer de' are debateable. Souriau understands this letter as indicating that Mérimée's Romanticism is: 'thus only a mask, which he quickly takes off,'[3] and understands him as satirising primitivism. However, the degree to which he was 'poking fun' could have been slighter, meaning that he was laughing at the gullibility of writers and readers rather than the heroic ideals of primitive society itself, a view taken by the Serbian critic Yovanovitch, who saw *La Guzla* as an attempt to create an ideal version of primitive society, which was completely at odds with the reality of a country Mérimée never visited,[4] but faithful to sources like Abbé Fortis's *Viaggio in Dalmazia* (1774) and Chaumette-Desfossé's *Voyage en Bosnie dans les années 1807 et 1808*.

In deciding whether he was celebrating a culture and the superstitions of a society which he knew to be false, but still presented as ideal, or whether he was in fact traducing the primitive and superstitious itself, which had so recently spawned a cult in France and launched definitively the career Charles Nodier,[5] we must look both at the area's recent history, and whether the 'Illyrian' context has any specific relevance beyond being a fashionable site for the primitive. Furthermore, we must observe the career and ideas of Charles Nodier, to whom Mérimée was both in debt and yet a rival, before analysing the response of Mérimée himself.

The idea of Illyria

In 1805, at the Treaty of Presbourg, Napoleon wrested the Austrian dominions of Dalmatia and Istria from the Hapsburg Emperor's hands, minus Trieste. A year later, his trusted General Molitor entered Dalmatia and fought the Russians at the Bocche di Cattaro, which were eventually ceded together with the adjacent Republic of Ragusa, a relic of the recent Venetian era. After the Battle of Tilsitt in 1809, the Austrians also ceded Trieste, Carniola and Carinthia (sites of modern Slovenia).[6] Napoleon unified the provinces, and appointed various governors, including Marmont from 1805–11 and Fouché from 1812 until the fall of the region in 1813. After the Treaty of Paris, in 1814, the reoccupying Austrians, with Russian support, incorporated the whole region into their own empire, even to the extent of depriving the Montenegrins the Bocche di Cattaro.

Even though the region had already been under Napoleon rule for some years, the final creation of an Illyrian republic did not take place until 1811. What made the area so special compared to other recent conquests was the fact that it was incorporated into the French Empire, rather than being made into a separate kingdom for Napoleon or one of his relatives to rule as an occupied country. Illyrians, as Pavlovic writes, were given the same rights as Frenchmen, and were eligible for conscription directly into the French armies as well as entitled to the Napoleonic education system (Pavlovic, p. 3). The reasons for this have much to do with the region's classical past and proximity to Greece. As Pavlovic rather flatteringly described the era: 'For the French of that time, the Illyrians represented the ancestors of the ancient Greeks ... and the goal of the emperor is to make Illyria the oriental vanguard of the French civilisation' (p. 3).[7] Illyria, a onetime province of the Roman Empire, and the nearest of Napoleon's possessions to Greece itself, was to enjoy a cultural renaissance under the French Emperor's dominion which would prove its links to that classical past. The claim was supported by the scholarship of Abbé Fortis, who had speculated in 1774 that the reason for the number of Greek words in their dialect of Slavic (which even he, writing during the Venetian occupation, called occasionally Illyrian), was because people of that region had previously invaded Greece in classical times.[8]

Into the newly established Republic of Illyria came the young Charles Nodier in 1812,[9] formerly secretary to Sir Herbert Croft (Henry-Rosier, pp. 135–6). He was now charged with taking care of the library at Laybach in Carniola (modern Slovenia), and with editing the *Télégraph Illyrien*, a journal which would present news as well as features on Illyrian poetry and language. From his experience of working in Laybach, which lasted a mere nine months, Nodier was to gather information which would not only allow him to write several stories set in or around the region, namely *Jean Sbogar* and *Smarra*, but would also set off a renewed interest in that area among the French.

Nodier's articles on the Illyrian language attempt to show the classical antecedents of the tongue as well as its uniformity.[10] As Yovanovitch makes clear, he was unaware that there were at least two basic forms of Slavic in the region, being Slovenian, most prevalent where he was working, and the dialects now known collectively as Serbo-Croatian to the south (Yovanovitch, p. 75). Furthermore, like Abbé Fortis, he happily considered the majority of these customs to be only those of the hill people, the Morlacks, a people whom Yovanovitch, a Serb scholar, did not believe to have existed separately from the Serbo-Croats (Yovanovitch, p. 16), but who are now accepted as having been some of the oldest inhabitants of the region: either descendants of the earlier Romans, or migratory Vlachs, whose language was by then largely the same as that of the Slavs in the region.[11] He also writes about the corre-spondence between the native tradition of the 'Guzlar', the poet who travels from place to place singing of battles and deeds of yore to the accompaniment of a one-stringed instrument, itself called a 'guzla'. Again, like his source Abbé Fortis, Nodier compares the sentiments and style of this poetry to that of classical writers. These poets are similar to the bard of 'our Swiss Alps' [nos Alpes hélvetiques], 'with the slight dif-ference that the purity of the sky, the beauty of the productions, the greatness of the memories and fortunate proximity of Greece have been able to provide the bard of the Julian Alps with a crowd of inspirations that our own has not received' (Nodier, *Statistique*, p. 40).[12] He also com-pares them to the shepherds of Horace in their spontaneity of song (p. 42). This open comparison with Horace (he who had been the model for the neoclassical eighteenth century) and association with Greece,[13] is in keeping with the contemporary attempt to see the classical past as at one with the spirit of Romanticism and primitivism rather than Enlightenment, like in the work of Shelley and Byron. It should be added that French interest in both the primitive and the supernatural was far more recent than the fashions of England and Germany, due to the continuation of Voltairian principles during Bonaparte's time.

According to Yovanovitch, Nodier knew nothing of any genuine folk tradition in the region, and was entirely dependent on the work of Fortis, who had translated a 'Morlack' (really Serbian) poem called 'Sad Ballad of the Noble Wife of Asan-Aga' ([Fortis, pp. 98–105] the lament of a woman abandoned by her husband), or Ragusan scholars who were already distant from the traditions of the people in the hills (Yovanovitch, p. 75). However, his interest in primitivism and folk poetry, like his interest in the Fantastic, was earnest, and his time in Illyria clearly fired his imagination both towards his own renewed literary success once he returned to France, and towards the emergence of Romanticism and the Fantastic as a dominant current in French literature. What is also striking is the way he used his sojourn not to support, but to attack the effects of the revolution and Napoleon's occupation of Illyria.

Jean Sbogar and Smarra

The two works which supposedly draw from his experiences of life in Illyria, are *Jean Sbogar*, a 'Byronic' romance about a disaffected brigand who roams the Dalmatian coast while occasionally posing as a Venetian aristocrat, while the other, *Smarra*, is based upon what he elsewhere calls 'The nightmare, which the Dalmations call the Smarra, ... one of the most common phenomena of sleep',[14] in which a Piedmontese youth dreams back to a former life when he was witness to his friend being overcome by a seductress and set upon by a winged stryge.[15] The latter of these was passed off as a genuine piece of 'Illyrian' literature, since he published it, together with three poems (one of which he wrote himself,) as a 'translation' of a long Illyrian story by a man called 'Maxim Odine'.[16] Whatever the attempt to mock the credulity of his readers, both works reveal in different ways his political and aesthetic theories, especially the first which, although not involving vampirism, deserves considerable attention as an indicator of Nodier's attitude to Napoleon and to politics in general.

Jean Sbogar

In *Jean Sbogar* we have the story of the wealthy Breton orphan Antonia and her sister Mme Alberti, who finds herself out on the Dalmatian coast at Casa Monteleone during the Napoleonic era.[17] The whole country is gossiping about the brigand Jean Sbogar (Nodier, *Sbogar*, p. 78), and she is herself intrigued, until one day, resting in the woods, she hears two men discussing her while she keeps her eyes shut in feigned sleep. One of them professes his love for her and that she is his 'wife before God' [mon épouse devant Dieu] (p. 90). Antonia soon moves for the party season with her sister to Venice, where she meets and falls in love with the mysterious Lothario, a philanthropist of considerable accomplishments, but rather nihilist political views (p. 150), who readily defends Jean Sbogar due to the corruption and moral relativity of the era. Were not Theseus and Romulus villains, he argues (pp. 149–50)? He refuses to marry her and runs off (pp. 165–6), leaving her a collection of highly revolutionary 'tablets' containing his political thought. On her way back to Monteleone, she and her aunt are captured and taken to Jean Sbogar's castle at Duino (p. 187), where she is well looked after, but loses her reason (p. 192). While there, she is aware of Sbogar talking over her but does not see him. French soldiers come and seize the castle together with Antonia, and Sbogar is taken to justice with his men. The authorities place the revived Antonia in the crowd for the execution so that she may identify the brigand should he be Jean Sbogar (no confession has been wrung from him). Instead she screams 'Lothario!' on his arrival, at which her beloved corrects her and reveals himself as Jean Sbogar. As she dies of shock, he simply turns and orders 'Marchons' to the others, and walks to his own death (p. 201).

The work was published in 1818, anonymously at first and to very hostile reviews, which saw in the romance a melancholy entirely dissimilar to the work of Ann Radcliffe,[18] with whom it affords an obvious comparison due to its helpless heroine and mysterious events. However, according to Maixner, news that the tale was being read by the famous occupant of St Helena soon had newspapers detailing its merits and demerits,[19] the latter of which included obvious comparisons to Byron's *The Corsair*. This charge of plagiarism was strenuously denied by Nodier, but what perhaps makes the work more interesting is the interest of Bonaparte himself, since its politics are quite complex.

For one thing, at the beginning, when in Trieste and Istria, Sbogar can be understood as opposed by Austrian, and not French oppression. Although the date for the romance is 1808 (the Napoleonic era) and Madame Alberti and Antonia's presence at Casa Monteleone would suggest French colonial rule, they are in Trieste, which, along with Carniola and Istria, did not become a French possession until 1809 (Pavlovic, p. 2). Istria, we are told, is enjoying an unprecedented period of freedom due to the abandonment by one army in favour of another that has not yet occupied (Nodier, *Sbogar*, p. 77), placing the events as being just before the establishment of French rule after Austrian defeat at Tilsitt in 1809. Nonetheless, at the end it is French soldiers who, having just entered the Venetian provinces, are determined to purge it of brigands and overcome Duino (p. 198), a reference to the Napoleonic era through which Nodier himself had just lived.

In fact, his praise for the lack of institutional rule in both Istria and Venice (p. 130) is more likely a thematic device for setting the tone for the serious discussion of politics later in the work through Lothario's controversial tablets. Nodier himself was no stranger to political controversy. His outward politics had changed continuously during his adolescence and adult life, and were to continue to do so until his death, a fact which had his critics 'reproaching him at the time of his political fluctuations which make him by turns jacobin, thermidorian, napoleonian [Bonapartist], and [for] what Sainte Beuve called his "gift for inexactitude".'[20] His father was an extreme Jacobin magistrate (i.e., the Robespierre faction) from Besançon, who had presided over the local tribunal during the reign of terror (Henry-Rosier, p. 23), and who had been reappointed to the tribunal after Napoleon's coup of 1798. The son, however, was a member of a secret society called the Philadelphes that was quasi-mystical and quasi-political, and whose aim was a return, in politics and ideas, to the simplicity of classical times (p. 49). As no more than a boy, Nodier became disenchanted with the Jacobins because of their excessive zeal and hypocrisy (p. 47), but this appears to have been cynicism towards their self-righteousness rather than a considered rejection of all that they stood for.[21] However, his natural rebelliousness got him into real hot water in 1804, when he wrote and published a ballad called *Napoléone* that criticised the first consul just as he was about to declare himself Emperor (p. 105). Imprisoned for some few weeks and then pardoned due to his father's intercession (pp. 107–8), Nodier managed to reingratiate himself with the regime by working for Croft, the friend of Lady Hamilton. In going to work at Laybach under the Duc d'Otrante, Fouché, Nodier was again continuing his rehabilitation.

After the second restoration of the Bourbon dynasty in 1815, Nodier quickly regretted having been a 'lackey' of the Empire under the dreaded Bonaparte, and published a work which, although initially unnamed, did much to help rehabilitate him.[22] In *L'Histoire des sociétés secrètes de l'armée et des conspirations militaires qui ont eu pour objet la destruction du gouvernement de Bonaparte* (1815), Nodier literally changed his reality, as Rogers demonstrates, by creating a false past (Rogers, p. 45). In it Nodier claims that his secret society, the Philadelphes, had been the motor behind the restoration and the constant opponent of Napoleon on behalf of the Bourbon dynasty.[23]

That he had once opposed Napoleon publicly, as he now reminded people through an article for the *Journal de Débats*, is certainly true (Henry-Rosier, p. 160). However, the Philadelphes had barely embraced real-politik at all except in their half-hearted mockery of the elder Jacobins of Besançon, and his criticism of Napoleon in the ballad had been as the betrayer of republican liberty rather than the usurper of the throne (it calls upon him to 'Come down from your mad vanity/ Come back amongst your warriors').[24] Nodier's public pronouncements on politics, in particular his many 'souvenirs', are rarely reliable indications of how he really felt.

A far better barometer for his opinions are in fact fictional works which deal with politics, like *Jean Sbogar*, largely thanks to the high importance he placed on the powers of fantasy to divine truth (as shall be outlined below). Despite the enthusiastic reception by Napoleon, a close examination of the work shows that Nodier is in fact keeping to his 1804 attitude towards the Emperor: for if we see the pronouncements of Jean Sbogar as having any relation to Nodier's own views, then it would appear that the author was still very much against both Bourbon and Bonaparte, and wildly Utopian.

In the romance Sbogar tells Antonia of his sojourn in Montenegro (that area of Dalmatia which resisted French rule throughout), remembering it as being the happiest and most important period of his life. As a young man he penetrated the mountain kingdom, a place uncorrupted by the politics of Europe and depicted as having no social institutions, and no greed or private property (Nodier, Sbogar, pp. 161–2): a place rigorously defended by its inhabitants against 'civilised men' [des hommes civilisés (p. 157)] or 'social man' (l'homme social [p. 158]), and where exploitation is avoided by keeping the population low (p. 161). These proto-socialist views of land rights, and proto-anarchist views of government, so in keeping with Rousseau's *Discourse on Inequality*, are not in tune with the defence of property rights inscribed in Napoleonic Law throughout la Grande Empire.

Furthermore, in the rather nihilist and anti-establishment views expressed in Lothario's tablets we see one aphorism which could well have been written for Napoleon himself:

> A man flatters the people. He promises to serve them. He has come to power. It is believed he is going to ask for the division of benefits. It isn't like that. He acquires benefits, and associates himself with Tyrants in order to effect the division of the people.
>
> [Un homme flatte le peuple. Il lui promet de le servir. Il est arrivé au pouvoir. On croit qu'il va demander le partage des biens. Ce n'est pas celà [*sic*]. Il acquiert des biens, et il s'associe avec les tyrans pour le partage du peuple.] (p. 168)

This recalls the betrayal of the republican cause with which Nodier had accused Napoleon in his ballad, *Napoléone*, but even if it is not written with the intent to indicate Napoleon specifically, we can see that the politics of *Jean Sbogar* are against organised authority and private property, rather than for the bourgeois democracy of Jacobinism or the defence of property in the Napoleonic code. Furthermore, in praising both

Jean Sbogar and Montenegro, both opposed to French rule in the Balkans, Nodier is in fact condemning the extension of the Bonapartist Empire to Dalmatia.

The comparison with Byron drawn by contemporary reviewers is just, and also points to how the form of the novel, with its use of fantasy, further embodies Nodier's anti-Bonapartist political ideas: if not from Byron's genuine point of view (he remained an ardent Bonapartist until his acceptance of the cause of Venice forced him to change his views retrospectively),[25] then at least from the way in which Nodier himself saw Byron. In his preface to Pichot's *Essay on the Genius and Character of Lord Byron* (1824), Nodier declared that Byron was not so much the creator of a new kind of poetry as was the 'state of affairs' in which Byron found himself. 'He revealed it', [il l'a revélé] rather than created it, being the witness to the end of one civilisation and the beginning of another (Pichot, pp. 6–7). As Nodier understood it, the age had been betrayed by a 'cruel philosophy', and thus poets needed to 'dare' in figuring forth new fantasies and to reject the governing ideas of the time. In Nodier's case this represents a rejection of the Enlightenment ideas of Voltaire (he who had mocked the Fantastic and scorned vampires) as well as the religion of the earlier regime and the classicism of other writers which had led to the revolution and Jacobinism: a fundamental reaction against the philosophy and order of the recent past.

Another feature which Nodier attributes to Byron and writers of this 'movement' in the essay is the return, after the death of religion, to both the primeval sense of the marvellous (Pichot, *Byron*, p. 9), and 'an unbelieveable deviation from human reason'[26] due to the break up of the old human order, which allows the poet to question and challenge truths like no poet before (p. 12). From the essay one can glean that Nodier saw a world plunged into chaos by the revolution and its failure. However, the poet could shun the moral order of his time and use his imagination to probe both reason and religion and to become reacquainted with the age before 'literature' when the 'marvellous' reigned in mens's minds, although from the modern perspective of unbelief (or 'lying'/ 'mensonge').[27] However, rather than having a determinable and cohesive ontological basis, like Shelley or Blake, Nodier's theory has no underlying set of ideas beyond a nihilist conception of the universe.

In *Jean Sbogar* the fantasy is ostensibly slight since Antonia spends little time contemplating some of the uncanny events which she is witness to (like the scene in the forest); rather, the disguise motif is used to demonstrate the extent to which the modern political order desensitises modern man from his self, causing a splitting of consciousness: the Jean Sbogar who marches away from the dying Antonia is the brigand, and not the Lorenzo who loved her. In this sense, therefore, the story does explore themes for which, according to Bryan Rogers, Nodier usually employed fantasy, namely the distinction between the dream and waking self, or the essential 'I' and the fake, everyday 'I' (Rogers, p. 15). This exploration of the depths of the psyche, which is a formal corrolary of Sbogar's desire to find a more primitive and edenic society, puts into practice the nihilist aesthetic ideas which Nodier describes elsewhere and represents a reaction against the supposed order of all the dogmas which had recently been put into effect, including the Napoleonic code, which in Nodier's view would have done far better to leave the brigands of Dalmatia alone.

Smarra

In *Smarra*, the tale told several years later and published alongside three Illyrian 'poems' (one made up, one Slovenian the other Serbo-Croatian), Nodier presented a 'translation' in prose of a long 'Illyrian' story by a man called 'Maxim Odine',[28] which contains elements of fantasy and elements of vampirism: or at least of a similar superstition, which Fortis described in detail in *Viaggio in Dalmazia* (see below). *Smarra* is a brilliantly constructed tale – unusually modern in its form – in which a young man, Lorenzo, is lying in Arona, Piedmont, beside his Greek beloved Lisidis (Nodier, *Oeuvres*, III 30). He falls asleep and becomes the young scholar, Lucius, of ancient Thessaly, on his way home to his villa at nearby Larissa (III 38–41), full of exotic slaves and Lamiae. Along with his most beautiful slave Myrthe, he holds a banquet to which comes his friend Polémon, who had formerly saved him in battle (III 54–6), and is now bewitched by a beautiful sorceress. Once assured that he is safe in Lucius's house, Polémon tells the story of how he fell under the spell of the beautiful Méroé (III 70) and followed her to her palace. There she made columns come to life (III 77), and ordered the winged Smarra to leave its '*rhombus*' and attack him, which it did: 'it attached itself to my heart, grows, lifts up its enormous head and laughs' (III 80).[29] Méroé then took him through the universes that pre-existed time (III 85) and forced him to attend her banquet. After this he fell asleep and has been bewitched by the demon ever since (III 88).

After hearing the story, Lucius begins hallucinating that he is being cursed by Polémon and Myrthe (III 93). He freezes and falls into a troop of soldiers who blame him for the two's death, and is led away to his execution. Seeing them both he calls out Myrthe's name as his head rolls off the chopping block (III 97–8), but she accuses him of not sleeping well after drink. Lucius now dies and his soul soars upward to where Polémon is on a plinth (III 10). There is a sudden light in the palace, and Smarra is with Méroé, buzzing beside Polémon and 'coming to claim the recompense promised by the queen of terors' (III 101).[30] She then raises Polemon's heart and taunts the girls of Larissa with the prospect of his blood (III 103). This scene gives way to the tent where Polémon is mortally wounded at Corinth, and the subsequent funeral cortege of officers (III 104). Lorenzo awakes and begins reproaching Lisidis.

In the Preface to the tale, Nodier assures the reader that:

> Smarra is the primitive name of the bad spirit to which the ancients attribute the doleful phenomenon of the nightmare. The same word expresses yet the same idea in most of the Slavic dialects, whose speakers, of all peoples of the earth, are most subject to this horrible illness. There are few Morlack families in which someone is not tormented by it.

> [*Smarra* est le nom primitif du mauvais esprit auquel les anciens rapportoient le triste phénomène du cauchemar. Le même mot exprime encore la même idée dans la plupart des dialectes slaves, chez les peuples de la terre qui sont le plus sujets à cette affreuse maladie. Il y a peu de familles morlaques où quelqu'un n'en soit tourmenté.] (III 24)

Elsewhere Nodier insists that Smarra is a Dalmatian superstition, and further concurs that 'It is, in my opinion, out of this psychological disposition placed in the conditions which give rise to it, that the marvellous of all countries has issued forth' (Nodier, *Contes*, p. 200).[31]

The tale *Smarra* is, however, far more an example of Nodier's understanding of the Fantastic than the marvellous, even though it is from a 'Dalmatian superstition' and thus purports to be from the work of those who still believe in the reality of the supernatural. It is not an example of popular literature, but a complex tale written around a local myth. Above all Smarra is also the name given to the stryge figure in the nightmare, and represents the symbolic victory of woman (Méroé) over man and guilt over happiness. Here Lorenzo's conscience is implied through Lucius's guilt about a dead friend: it could either be the guilt of the survivor, who has prospered to enjoy life thanks to another's sacrifice, or else the guilt of the man who has stolen his dead friend's beloved, which may or may not be the underlying reality in the relation between Lorenzo and Lisidis. Thus it constitutes an excuse for exploring the relation between the dream and the waking self rather than the realisation of an actual superstition: the Fantastic in the age of 'mensonge' rather than the genuinely marvellous.

It also more generally represents part of the attempt to reenvisage classical Greece and Illyria as a place of superstition and primitivism. The story has two sources: Abbé Fortis tells the story, in which one man, lying unconscious by the roadside, is attacked by two witches ('streghe'), while the other, a Franciscan who finds himself powerless to move, lies by watching. When they run off frightened, the observer picks up the heart and makes the victim swallow it back (Fortis, I 65). Nodier himself acknowledges the closeness of both *Smarra* and Fortis's account to Book one of *The Golden Ass* (Nodier, *Oeuvres*, III 25), in which Aristomene recounts how he saw his friend Socrates attacked by the witch Méroé and her friend while powerless to move, although ran off after Socrates could move again for fear of being accused of the crime.[32] Nodier puts this down to the fact that Apuleius must have visited Dalmatia, which allows Nodier himself to present the modern day Dalmatians as being inheritors of a classical tradition of superstition (Thessaly, at the time he wrote, cut right across Northern Greece and through Albania, since it was part of the principality of Ali-Pasha, rogue Prince in the Ottoman Empire). Not only did Nodier note the similarity between Apuleius's story – also set in Thessaly – and that of Fortis, but also labelled him 'one of the most romantic writers of ancient times' (III 25).[33]

Outside his Illyrian context, Nodier was more generally one of the first people to promote the vampire as a literary theme, and was certainly among the most successful to do so. Nodier had first presented the vampire in his stageplay of Polidori's *The Vampyre*, which was a huge success (1820), but transported the battle between 'Rutwen' and Aubray to the highlands of Scotland, in an attempt to milk the presentation of a Byronic hero within a setting made popular by Sir Walter Scott. The central elements are very similar. Aubray has promised his sister Malvina to Lord Marsden, Rutwen's brother, whom he left dying in Greece,[34] only to find that Rutwen has returned alive to claim his bride (Nodier 'Vampire', p. 21). Aubray is overjoyed, and they set off to his friend Petterson's house to celebrate the nuptials of his daughter Lovette with the young Edgar (p. 33). Rutwen assaults Lovette and is shot dead by Edgar (p. 41), and begs Aubray on the point of death not to tell his sister Malvina this for twelve hours (p. 42). Needless to say he returns to claim her, and holds Aubray to his promise. As Aubray is about to tell Malvina (the hour is striking), she faints before Rutwen can kill her. Rutwen seeks flight, but shades and the exterminating angel are envelopping him, and he screams the words 'Le néant! Le néant!' (p. 56), as though he is finally being dragged down to hell in a quite arbitrary 'Deus ex machina' ending.

Perhaps due to the success of an adaptation which was attempting to cash in on the scandalous reputation of Byron himself, Nodier proceeded to publish Cyprien Bércard's *Lord Ruthwen*, a sequel to Polidori's tale which both he and Bércard still assumed to be from Byron's own pen. In this two volume romance, Ruthwen has returned to Venice where, by tricking the young lover Leonti into what he thinks will be an elopement with his beloved Bettina, he attacks Bettina once she has been drawn out unchaperoned, leaving her to die.[35] She begs Leonti to avenge her death (Bécard, I 66), but Leonti falls into a fever. After recovering from the fever he meets a man on the banks of Venice, who is none other than the still suffering Aubrey, (I 79), and they vow to go and chase Ruthwen through Italy. Having travelled through Florence and Rovedro, they arrive at Naples where they meet Bettina (who has returned to life to warn others [I 148]), and also meet a young Arab called Nadour-Heli, who has a similar grievance against Ruthwen. The vampire, it turns out, is now passing himself off as 'Seymour', and is first minister in Naples at the behest of the local Duke (II 132). Leonti kills Ruthwen with a sword through the heart in the cathedral where the vampire was supposed to be marrying Eleonore, the Duke's daughter (II 172), who has in fact already died from Ruthwen's molestation.

The story follows on from the work of Polidori in its portrayal of the aristocratic vampire and sexual predator in glamourous, aristocratic environs, but mingles it with the structure of *The Arabian Nights* and *Manuscript found in Saragossa* by including stories within the main story. It also has no horror, only terror, and there are no descriptions of the macabre: the vampire's attacks are never presented openly, and, as in the stageplay, there is no gore, only the desperate reactions of the bereaved. Furthermore, as in the stageplay the vampire is destroyed at the end, satisfying a sense of poetic justice and closure which is lacking in the original. In his introduction, Nodier states that subjects of terror should be treated with 'a timid/cautious restraint' ['une timide sobriété'] (Bércard, I iii), meaning perhaps that we should approach them from a position of fear, but disbelief.[36]

Nodier presented a slightly more visceral version of the vampire myth in his edition of fantastic tales, *Infernaliana*, culled mainly from Calmet and *The Arabian Nights*, which was published in 1825 (again, without his name). With the exception of minor changes, the pieces were almost entirely copied from their sources, and included the story of Arnold Paul, the gruesome account of a Hungarian vampire which Mérimée was to include at length in *La Guzla*.[37] However, in keeping with his desire to present the piece as being 'fantastique', rather than 'merveilleux', or with the 'timid restraint' which he believed should temper the presentation of terror, he prefixed the whole work with an ironic preface.[38] The suppleness of corpses after burial, he assured his readers, had more to do with the terrain than the superstitions having any correspondence to fact.

So Nodier turned to Dalmatian Illyria as a region of primitive contentedness, superstition and song, as an antidote to the confusions of his own day and as a source for his own work in the practice of the Fantastic. He turned in particular to the stryge/vampire myth as a means of symbolising states of consciousness which were inaccessible to either the philosophy or the religion of his own era, and also saw in the superstitions, and the poetry which articulated them, a culture akin to that of classical times. He furthermore saw in the subjects of primitive poetry marvellous themes that could serve the Fantastic in his own more civilised, and thus more confused, Napoleonic and then post-Napoleonic society. Nodier never really engaged with Dalmatian realities at all, but his love of primitive societies was genuine, as was his belief in their reality, even if he must on occasions supplement the detail.

Prosper Mérimée's treatment of both primitive customs and beliefs was somewhat more mixed, and his attitude to Napoleonic Illyria wholly different.

La Guzla

La Guzla was Mérimée's second major work after the plays of the supposed Spanish actress 'Clara Gazul'. In *La Guzla* (an obvious anagram of Gazul), Mérimée pretended to be simply an Italian scholar who had collected and translated the work of various bards, but in particular those of a drunken Morlack, Hyancinth Maglanovich, well known for his adventurous and daring life. Most of his work was based upon two sources, Abbé Fortis' *Viaggio in Dalmazia* (1774) and Antoine Chaumette-Desfossés' *Voyage en Bosnie dans les années 1807 et 1808*, as he freely admitted in a preface to the second edition of 1840.[39] From the former he discovered the traditions of the Morlacks, a people whom Fortis conjectured lived as far north as Hungary (Fortis I, 44n), but whose customs and people in Dalmatia alone he had chosen to analyse. including their wedding customs (I 71–82). These customs included their tradition of becoming 'pobratimi' ([I 58–9] similar to blood brothers), their superstitions, including vampirism (I 63–5), and their important tradition of the Guzlar, who sings of the heroes of old and the superstitions of the culture on his one-stringed instrument. From Chaumette-Desfossées, Mérimée learned of the history of Bosnia, which information helped him to expand the repertoire of a Morlack Guzlar beyond 'Illyria', to that area where, according to Fortis, the majority of the Morlack people lived, and to include much more description of both the Turks and Islam.

Fortis gave the following account about the belief in vampires, saying that: ' When a man dies who is suspected of possibly becoming a vampire, or Vukodlak, as they say, they are accustomed to cut the backs of his knees, and prick him all over with pins, thinking that after these two operations he cannot go walking any more' (Fortis, I 64).[40] Although Mérimée includes this detail in his account, he also includes long quotations from Calmet on the stories of Arnold Paul and Milo and Stanoska (Calmet, pp. 280–4). This shows that once he had read of the superstitions in Fortis, he researched them elsewhere in his attempt to maintain the guise of scholarship.

This guise of scholarship is extremely important to Mérimée's art form in *La Guzla* since, following the genuine practice of his Friend Fauriel in *Chants de Grèce*, he is providing scholarly notes and an objective backing in order to encourage the reader to stand back and analyse the poems that he reads. Indeed, the very use of prose rather than verse in translation (which is in keeping with Nodier, although not with Fortis, who gave a verse translation of 'Asan-Aga' in Italian), acts as an alienation device: the stirring emotions of the piece are variously invoked and then made strange, in order to create an effect in which the characters' customs and concerns appear as distant from those of the reader.

The effect is akin to that described by Bakhtin in 'From the Prehistory of Novelistic Discourse', except that there Bakhtin considers how parody, the forerunner of novelistic practice, acts as a framing device which puts two voices into relation to create 'indirect discourse'.[41] Here the effect is far more subtle, since while the stilted translations of the songs themselves have an effect similar to the dialogising of discourse, the collision of two opinions is not through the travestying and parodying mode, but through emotional alienation and distancing: rather than mocking the opinion, the translator is trying to emulate the ideas and opinions of the original, but fails to do so, and thus creates a framing device which causes the images to be 'qualified' and 'externalised' (Bakhtin, p. 45) through a cultural distance which the scholar cannot but adopt due to his belonging to a superior culture, shared with the implied reader. Thus the 'dialogising' is one of unavoidable cultural value rather than individual opinion (except through the occasional disparaging note). Furthermore, there is another qualifying device: not only the 'translatese' but also the scholar's notes and direct, unequivocal anecdotes, which help to give information that undercuts the pretensions and ideas of the poems, thus presenting juxtaposition and true polyglossia between two interacting texts rather than simply the 'indirect discourse' involved in the translation technique.

The cultural and emotional distancing through the translation technique is of course variable: some poems, like *La Belle Sophie* and *Cara-Ali*, use climactic action and horror in order to incite emotional response in spite of the stilted way in which the translation objectifies the cultural medium. Both these poems offer examples of the grotesque which mix horror with delight in the Burkean form of the sublime. For example, in *La Belle Sophie* the bride is ravaged by the vampire Nicéphore, her ex-lover whom she threw over due the old Bey de Moïna's great wealth. When Sophie is missing, the Bey of Moïna cries:

> Where is she, where is she, my beloved, the beautiful Sophie? Why doesn't she come beneath my tent of felt? Slaves, run and seek her, and tell the music-maids to increase their songs. May my mother put beautiful Sophie back with the wedding kuum; I have been alone in my tent for a very long time.
>
> [Où est-elle, où est-elle, ma bien-aimée, la belle Sophie? Pourquoi ne vient-elle pas sous ma tente de feutre? Esclaves, Courez la cherchez, et dites aux musiciennes de redoubler leurs chants; je leur jetterai demain matin des noix et des pieces d'or. Que ma mère remette la belle Sophie au kuum de la noce; il y a bien longtemps que je suis seul dans ma tente.] (Mérimée, *Guzla*, p. 81)

The stylised repetition of 'où est elle, où est elle' and the elaborate structure of 'que ma mère' with the subjunctive, representing wish, hint at the elaborate diction of the original: but deprived of rhythm it becomes purposely archaic and overstylised. The actual death of Sophie in the hands of her lover is more surprising, and the emotional distance recedes at this point, as in the surprising end of *Cara-Ali*, when the vampire tricks his rival into becoming a vampire by showing a page of the Koran and takes him down into the earth with him.

Despite this tension between alienation and sublimity, in the anecdotes themselves the scholar addresses the reader as an equal in an attempt to incite our sympathy unequivocally, which helps to prioritise his own voice over the Guzlar's, especially since the events described were originally supposed (and presumed) to have actually happened.[42] The occasion when the scholar recounts his own experience of the vampire superstition is such a moment.

He begins by telling us of the typical situations of the vampire: 'In Illyria, in Poland, in Hungary, in Turkey and part of Germany, one would risk being reproached for irreligion and immorality if one denied publicly the existence of vampires' (Mérimée, *Guzla*, p. 61). He informs us of how vampires ('vukodlak' in Illyrian) are those who leave their tombs at night and suck the blood of the living, and appear to have no feelings of affection left since they trouble their own friends and parents; that the signs are the preservation of the corpse and the fluidity of blood, and that the remedy is to rub one's body with their blood mixed with the earth of their tombs. He then moves onto two long quotations from Calmet, the first being about the old man of 'Gratisch' in southern Serbia, who preyed upon his own son and killed him, before being exhumed and properly dealt with by the authorities: and then the second is about the Haiduk Arnold Paul of Medreiga, who was crushed by a haywain (p. 72) to become a vampire 30 days later, and engender another vampire, Milo, who preyed upon the young girl Stanoska. This story ends with the villagers unearthing all the recent dead and giving them the customary treatment. At the end, the reader is told:

> All the reports and actions of which we have just spoken were performed in accordance with the law, properly, and attested to by several officers who are garrisoned in the country, by the surgeon-majors of the regiments and by the most important inhabitants of the place. The statement for this was sent towards the end of last January to the imperial council of war at Vienna, which had established a military commission for examining the truth of all these happenings.' (D. Calmet, t. II.)

> [Toutes les informations et exécutions dont nous venons de parler ont été faites juridiquement, en bonne forme, et attestées par plusieurs officiers qui sont en garnison dans le pays, par les chirurgiens-majors des regiments et par les principaux habitants du lieu. Le procès-verbal en a été envoyé vers la fin de janvier dernier au conseil de guerre imperialà Vienne, qui avait établi une commission militaire pour examiner la verité de tous ces faits.] (D. Calmet, t. II) (p. 74)

The inclusion of this detail, an element of the original scholarship from Calmet himself, reinforces the empirical 'proof' of vampirism, and is in keeping with the empirical nature of the scholar's own work: ironically, since he is about to explode this scholarship with a sceptical account of his own.

He now recounts the time he spent with a rich Morlack called Vuck Poglonovich in the small village of Varboska. Refusing to take money, the host made him stay at his own hospitality, which meant putting up with his conversation and drinking bouts. One night the Franco-Italian was singing national songs to avoid drinking, when the wife came from the bedroom of the 16-year-old daughter Khava, screaming: 'A vampire! A vampire! My poor girl is dead.'[43] Khava had been bitten by a vampire called 'Wiecznany'(which in Polish would mean 'the eternal one'), who had been dead for 15 days. The scholar conjectured that the marks could have been from an insect during a nightmare, but is called a 'miscreant' by the mother. The next day they go to the grave with sticks and guns, and exhume the dead man's body. They blow the corpse's head to pieces with their rifles, and begin to hack it to bits. The young men tie it to a log and take it to the house of the Poglonovichs where they set it alight and dance around it: 'The infectious smell that was expanding soon forced me to leave them and to return to my hosts' (p. 76).[44]

The scholar stays by the girl's side for several nights as she pines away, aided and abetted by the stories of the women who surround her. He tries to convince her that he can cure her through magic, and pretends to take a piece of red agate from her neck, but she is sure that she has seen it before and is not tricked (p. 77). Khava tells him that she deserves this fate because a certain man had asked her to marry him. She had refused him at first, but had then consented if he gave her a silver chain, and thus he had left her in search of one, leaving her in her parents' house. Khava then asks her father to break the backs of her knees and cut her throat when she is dead. When all is done, the scholar recalls how: 'I left the village some hours later, heartily wishing in hell vampires, revenants and those that tell stories about them' (p. 78).[45]

The piece is designed to shock and horrify the reader, and creates a neat contrast with the way in which Nodier had treated the vampire superstition. In *Infernaliana*, Nodier had stripped Calmet's accounts of passages which related them to real historical events and court inquests, making them appear like small passages of folklore, rather than gruesome realities. However, Mérimée presents the two accounts from Calmet as a support for a real life experience of the superstition. In this account, therefore, we have a work which transcends the usual aesthetic distance essential to the Burkean sublime and Ann Radcliffe's understanding of the 'Literature of Terror'; namely, that a cause of pain may become a cause of pleasure by our experiencing fear through the safe mediation of fiction.[46] The scholar presents a 'real' account which destroys the safe distance, and which places the stories of Calmet in something nearer to their original contexts: witness statements of genuine events rather than the 'contes fantastiques' into which Nodier's editing had turned them. The story itself spares no details in the description of the obliteration of the cadavre, making the text more likely a cause of nausea rather than delight mingled with terror or horror.

Crucially, the scholar appeals to the reader as an equal in contradistinction to the alienating tenor of the narrators within the songs. He describes, for example, the way in which his host's hospitality forced him to carry on drinking with him at the table: 'Whoever has dined with a Morlack will understand the difficulty of the thing' (Mérimée, *Guzla*, p. 74).[47] This puts the reader in the position of either being able to identify (if they are one of the 'whoever', which is of course unlikely) or being forced to identify through this appeal for common sympathy, with the position of the narrator as the representative of the culture from which they come, confronting the discomforts of the one he is visiting. He calls himself later the 'only stranger in the house',[48] even though the customs he is presenting are presented as absolutely alien to us: through this device he reminds the reader that he, like the narrator, is as much an alien to this world as the Illyrians would be to our own, cementing the identification between narrator and reader. This further helps to qualify and externalise the 'local colour' of the ballads we then read which relate superstitions in a more sublime and entertaining way.

One can see this dialogical division working in the relation between the account and the vampire songs themselves. Three of the songs which relate the vampire myth, *La Belle Sophie, Le Vampire* and *Cara-Ali* include the betrayal by women, and two of these to occupying powers. Another relates the superstition to the threat of Orthodox Morlacks to Catholics. In *La Belle Sophie*, the bride is marrying a local bey because of his wealth and it is her rightful beloved who becomes a vampire and sucks her blood away, in a curiously dark turn on Byron's *The Giaour*. In *Cara-Ali*, the wealthy Turk runs off with the wife of poor Basile Kaïmis, but is shot by him. Basile forgives his wife who presents him with a copy of the Koran, telling him 'May he who carries it open the book at the sixty-sixth page; he will command all the spirits of the earth and air' (p. 101).[49] As soon as he does this the bloody spectre of Cara-Ali pierces the earth and cries 'Basile, you are now mine as you have renounced your God' (p. 102).[50] He seizes him and bites him on the neck, not leaving him until he has taken every last drop of blood. In *Le Vampire*, a short fragment of a song, the faithless woman of Stavila who married the Venetian is invoked directly to look at her husband in his grave: 'Approach, Marie, come and contemplate the one for whom you have betrayed your family and your nation! Dare to kiss these pale and bloody lips which knew so well how to lie. Living he caused many tears: dead he will cost yet more' (p. 90).[51] In *Constantin Yacoubovich* the hero allows a 'Schismatic Greek' to be buried in a Catholic cemetery, only for him to come and prey upon his child. In the note, the scholar explains that if a 'Greek' (i.e., Orthodox) is buried in a Catholic churchyard, or vice versa, they inevitably become vampires.[52]

In the first three cases vampirism represents betrayal by women, in two cases for the sake of gold, and betrayal to another nation rather than simply to a man. In two cases the vampire is inexpungeable, and thus represents the continued grasp of an occupying power (Venetians and Turks). Thus we see examples of the vampire superstition being used as an articulation of political anxiety and resentment. The vampire represents both the rapaciousness of the Turk and the Venetian and the country's betrayal to them through the frailty of women: the greed of the woman allows the cupidity of the vampire to nestle in the land. While the vampire clearly has a metaphorical meaning, the female betrayal in *Cara-Ali* and *Le Vampire* can be interpreted as the literal belief that the frailty of woman and intermarriage is allowing the invader to establish himself and ruin the country, or even that the soul of Dalmatia and Bosnia is prostituting itself (since the soul and indeed that of a nation, is usually represented as being feminine). The near-immortality of the vampire is used to represent the inirradicable nature of the occupier once he has settled, and the ceaseless degeneration of the country once it has become prostituted, while the occupation of the country is represented as being less a violent overtaking than a weakness and acquiescence on the part of the Dalmatians and Bosnians.

However, since there is a framing device presented by the scholar in his relation of the death of Khava, when understanding the political satire we must not simply observe the content of the poems as national allegory but also as superstition. In three of these vampire poems the betrayal of the man or the country is caused by the woman. In the 'true story', Khava believes that it is her greed by sending her suitor off to get her a silver chain that has caused her to suffer at the hands of 'Wiecznany'. However, in the scholar's own surmise an innocent young woman suffers as a result of the superstitions which both older women tell her, but which, more poignantly, male Guzlars sing and perpetuate. While it may be complained that Mérimée was writing when 'sexism' as we understand it now was not an issue, he nevertheless presents the Dalmatians as being a highly chauvinistic people when, in a note to *Constantin Yacoubovich* he writes that the wife of a Morlack always sleeps on the floor, adding, 'It is one of the numerous examples of the scorn with which women are treated in this country' (p. 88).[53] Thus the world-view of the poems is 'qualified' and 'externalised' by this juxtaposed voice from a superior culture.

Thanks to all the distancing and framing devices the poems do not simply act as allegories of political occupation, but also as satires on the way in which the people see them, in relating the occupations to a bloody superstition rather than a genuine force which they can understand. This would seem to be a further way in which Mérimée condemns the past occupiers, Venetians or Turks. The very backwardness of the way in which the people articulate their hatred of the occupiers, through a fearful superstition about a creature that perpetually returns, and further lay blame upon women or feminity for the usurpation, is itself a comment on the dreadful state in which these past occupiers have left Illyria. Through the notes and anecdotes Mérimée creates a moment of 'dialogical contact' (Bakhtin, p. 45), in which we are left to both sympathise with the 'representing' of Dalmatians, but also to condemn their 'represented' primitivism.

Mérimée's dialogical use of 'local colour' affords comparisons with the work of Sir Walter Scott. Scott's historical novels introduced local colour as a means of creating an historical sense which romanticised the past, as past, and as a means of reconciling readers to the reality of the present. As Lukacs has shown, Scott used the presentation of forces in history to justify the idea of progress and of the 'middle way' in which those processes are reconciled,[54] but as 'transformations of popular life' (Lukacs, p. 49): that is, from the perspective of ordinary people caught up in the process, hence the need for 'local colour' and physiognomic difference from the age in which his implied reader lived. The tension between a resolved present, and a romantic but crisis-driven past, is also encoded through narrating events 'from the distance of a present-day narrator, as individual stages in the pre-history of the present' (p. 79).

Scott's historical distancing device finds its corrolary in Mérimée's pseudo-scholarship, despite the fact that Mérimée preferred the local colour of the ironic Lord Byron to that of Scott (Souriau, p. 99). The scholar stands over songs that he recounts through his flattened translations, and his interjected stories perform a similar function to the omniscient narrator in Scott's work, framing the feelings of one set of people with the attitudes of another. The major difference is that Scott's division is between two different times, whereas Mérimée is situating the division between the enlightened and the primitive as between two different but contemporary cultures.

In this light it is interesting that Mérimée does not include a vampire poem that attacks the recent Napoleonic rule. There is one poem about Napoleon, however, called 'Les Monténégrins', which details a fictitious battle involving French soldiers who try to storm the country. In the poem, by a Montenegrin Guzlar, we have a celebration of Montenegrin bravery against Napoleon from before that time. The poem begins with Napoloeon saying: "What are these men who dare to resist me? I want them to come and throw their rifles and their ataghans adorned with earcorns at my feet' (Mérimée, *Guzla*, p. 88). He sends 'immediately' twenty thousand soldiers to the mountain. The poem then recounts how five hundred brave Montenegrins in red caps, hold off the attack. A French captain charges with his men:

'Listen to the echo of our rifles,' said the captain. But, before he had returned fire, he fell dead and so did twenty-five men with him. The others took flight, and never in their life did they dare look at another red cap.

['Ecoutez l'écho de nos fusils', a dit le capitaine. Mais, avant qu'il se fût retourne, il est tombé mort et vignt-cinq hommes avec lui. Les autres ont pris la fuite, et jamais de leur vie ils n'osèrent regarder un bonnet rouge.] (p. 110)

In the poem the Montenegrins claim that the French set out to burn their villages and to take away their wives and children, a fact which the 'scholar' claims to be simply a presumption they make due to the earlier atrocities committed by the Turks (p. 111). He also notes 'I believe that Napoleon never bothered himself much with the Montenegrins,'[55] which serves to deflate the self-agrandising sentiments of the poem, retrospectively creating a point of 'dialogical contact' with the poem's direct discourse that is extremely distant, and which represents personal opinion more than simply the distance of cultural value.

More than this, however, it indicates Mérimée's own attitude to the Napoleonic occupation of Illyria. By putting such a boastful and vengeful poem about Napoleon's 'attempted invasion' in the mouths of their neighbours the Montenegrins, he again successfully directs the implied reader to contempt for their primitivism and provincialism. This time, though, the political content points to the primitivism being perpetuated by the outsiders *failing* to occupy: a point reinforced by the fact that the scholar makes a surreptitiously favourable contrast between Napoleon and the Turks by highlighting the ignorance of this 'little people' towards a different aggressor (p. 111).

This is a major political idea in the other poems, although latent rather than expressed. We have everywhere the same division between the voice of the primitive Dalmatia and the rational West which offsets it. While *La Guzla* is certainly a mockery of 'local colour', its mockery goes beyond the target of reader gullibity: Mérimée is surreptitiously bemoaning the failure of the 'Grande Empire' to stamp its identity upon Illyria and cast the net of Voltairian reason (against which 'Romantisme' was reacting). It is politically exactly what Nodier's work is not: pro-Bonapartist.

Mérimée was not a vocal supporter of Napoleon I. He grew up in an artistic household in which there was a large portrait of the Emperor, but no great interest in politics,[56] although he certainly despised the Bourbon dynasty, referring to Louis XVIII, who was king from 1815 to 1824, as 'le gros cochon' (Autin, p. 19). One of his first works was a tragedy on a hero of his, Cromwell, now sadly lost, but apparently inspired by his admiration for Cromwell's attempt to rule through parliament. After the accession of the dictatorial Charles X, Mérimée made several visits to his beloved England and was delighted by its constitution and the distant role which the king played in it (he remained a staunch Anglophile all his life [p. 33]).

Despite hating the Bourbon dynasty, Mérimée did not write for the Bonapartist papers, and even remarks in one letter how *Le Globe* (a liberal paper which also fostered 'Romantisme'), the paper to which he did contribute most, was unpopular with Napoleon's supporters.[57] During the Restoration he was in fact a known liberal and constitutionalist, frequently meeting at the house of Aubernon, an ex-commisioner of war who ran a liberal clique, and also befriended Victor Hugo.[58] As Baschet notes, this drew favour after the Revolution of 1830, and the establishment of a constitutional democracy, (Baschet p. 66), allowing him to take up various political offices under King Louis-Phillipe (1830–48), the democratic descendant of the Orleanist dynasty.

After the fall of that regime (1848), the brief return of a republic (1848–51), and then the assumed dictatorship of Napoleon III and the rise of the Second Empire, Mérimée became an important minister and confidant of the Emperor Napoleon III (1851–70), to the dismay of more republican friends. He died as the Second Empire crumbled in 1870, never having to face the consequences of its fall. It is possible, therefore, that he had early nurtured a respect for Bonaparte from his childhood, and the enlightened project of 'La Grande Empire', or at least in preference to the Bourbon Restoration, despite his open avowal of liberalism, and consequent commitment to Romanticism. This would seem to be most evident in his reaction towards Nodier, and his use of the vampire myth set in Illyria. Ultimately it was the values of his school-days (which were irony and sarcasm [Autin, p. 16]) and the influence of his Bonapartist mentor, Stendhal, which – as Souriau argued about his work more generally – was the major influence in his treatment of Romantic and primitive themes when writing *La Guzla*.

In summation, Mérimée's uses of local colour, and of the vampire superstition, are very different to those of Nodier or Bércard. Whereas Nodier uses the superstition as part of an adherence to the Fantastic, and as a means of invoking the irrational so as to rearrange a world that has been betrayed by the Voltairean principles of Enlightenment, Mérimée seeks instead to condemn the culture that has produced them as well as the fascination with primitive superstitions in the France of the 1820s. Whereas Nodier praises the primitive culture of the Illyrians, and the propensity to superstition and the marvellous against the reforming and enlightened zeal of the Empire, Mérimée bemoans the failure of the Empire to stamp its identity upon the people of Dalmatia and free them of their superstitions, as well as mocking the supernatural element in modern literature. Thus Mérimée provides us with the only truly pro-colonial vampire narrative of the Near East in this period, and interestingly enough expresses these ideas through irony and the juxtaposition of a framing device, rather than the subversion from an embedded allegory achieved through intertext, as in the majority of this other works which we have observed. Perhaps the subversion of liberal ideas depends upon suggestion through concrete images, while this expression of colonial desires must present the opposite, the benefits of Enlightenment, through the juxtaposition of different types of discourse, the rational and the primitive, for once in keeping with the binarism of Said – although not solely in relation to an Islamic influence, but the Venetian as well.

6
Jules Verne's *Le Château des Carpathes* (1892) and the Romans of Transylvania

Jules Verne's only Gothic novel set in Eastern Europe and dealing with issues which touch upon the Near East is also deeply political: both in a general sense and in terms of a local political situation. However, whereas Stoker was to use Transylvania as a convenient site for representing the wider political ramifications of the Eastern Question, Verne instead simply centres upon a local political argument between Hungarians and Rumanians in Transylvania, an argument that was topical during the time in which he wrote it. In writing the work he tailors his sources to locate the political grievances and heroic history of all Transylvanians within the experience of the Vlach (Rumanian) community, in order to make them appear the virtuous aggrieved. Furthermore, Verne, whose political views were for many years an enigma,[1] and who espoused opinions that were variously anti-colonial and pro-colonial, libertarian and conservative, was certainly a believer in the rights of smaller nations to self-determination, and here presents a vampire story whose political overtones relate very specifically to Transylvania itself and the degeneration of libertarian ideas due to Hungarian rule and the policies of 'magyarisation'.

In *Le Château des Carpathes* we are presented with the story of the Baron de Gortz, a one-time Rumanian nationalist whose earlier defeat at the hands of the Hungarians led him first to go on the run with bandits and then to forsake the Carpathian region entirely.[2] One day a local shepherd called Frik notices that smoke is pouring from the chimney of the Baron's deserted castle (Verne, p. 15). He tells this to the local villagers, who fantasise about the stryges and chort (devil) that must reside therein. A brave forester called Nic Deck and a cowardly charlatan called Patak, both travel to the castle to see what has happened (despite a ghostly warning to Nic Deck at the inn that he will die if he goes there [pp. 52–3]). They are plagued by the sight of dragons (p. 74), and the forester is paralysed on entering the castle and rendered unconscious (p. 80). Both manage to get away thanks to a rear party of villagers and swear never to return.

Some months later Count de Telek, a young Vlach from Krajowa in free Rumania, enters the village on an excursion through Transylvania (p. 99). When he hears of the tribulations of Deck and Patak he is astounded to hear that the owner of this castle is de Gortz (p. 111). This reminds him of when, several years previously, he had fallen in love with and proposed to the Italian opera singer La Stilla, who had charmed the audiences at Naples. His only rival was de Gortz, who had sat every night, with the inventor Orfanik, in a box above the stage, terrifying the singer with his demonic presence. Despite being obsessed with La Stilla, de Gortz's interest, according to the narrator, is entirely aesthetic, since he does not wish to enjoy her body, merely her form and her singing voice, never once having tried to meet the woman for whose voice he lives (p. 117). The night before she retires with the intention of marrying de Telek, the baron appears again and so frightens her by his appearance 'with eyes ablaze'[3] and face 'terrifying in its paleness' (p. 122)[4] that La Stilla dies on the spot. The baron promptly disappears from public view but after her funeral leaves de Telek a message blaming him for the death and vowing vengeance, 'It is you who have killed her. May misfortune befall you, Count de Telek' (p. 124).[5]

De Telek vows to visit the castle with his man and on approaching sees and hears La Stilla singing on the turret (p. 148). He is sure the baron has kidnapped and imprisoned her but is rendered unconscious through drugged food once he enters the castle (p. 163) and later awakes in a dungeon. Hearing the sound of La Stilla's voice, he escapes to find the baron gazing at her image in full song. As he approaches La Stilla, de Gortz smashes the glass casing around her and she disappears (pp. 190–1). The baron runs off with the magnetophone disc which holds a recording of her voice, 'her soul' (as he calls it), but is killed in the explosions he himself has prepared around the castle (p. 192).

Rather like *Udolpho*, the story ends with a set of revelations as to the real causes of the illusions. Unlike *Udolpho* these revelations relate to things prophetic but in keeping with the technology of Verne's own time, which serves to merge the Gothic features of the novel with science fiction. La Stilla's image was a large hologram made from a magnified portrait and well placed lights (as were the dragons which plagued Nic Deck and the Doctor), and her voice was a recording the baron had made from his opera box (pp. 196–7). The sounds which haunted the inn were the result of a hidden telephone running on a line to the castle (p. 176). Electrical currents were behind the paralysis of Nic Deck and the doctor (p. 180). One phenomenon which is not explained is how La Stilla dies, although this may have been the result of another Orfanik illusion or else sparks caused by the magnetophone (otherwise, as is suggested below, this may be the one element of pure fantasy in the book).

Most criticism of the story has centred upon the opera singer and the sources which Verne used in order to create her. In a letter to his publisher Hetzel fils, Verne admitted that writing about La Stilla was the hardest literary task he had ever undertaken.[6] This may have been partly due to the personal emotional investment, since La Stilla may well recall an opera singer called Estelle with whom he is believed to have been in love (Vierne, p. 346).

Simone Vierne has shown the extent to which he drew upon several sources to create the image of the perfect woman who cannot live outside her art. She shows that Jules Verne was influenced by Boïeldieu's opera *La Dame Blanche*,[7] about a phantom spirit who presides over a castle but who is later incarnated by the heir's beloved in order to save it from being sold to an usurper. Vierne also notes the similarities with George Sand's *Consuelo* – again a novel about an opera singer whose perfection cannot translate to life – and Gerard de Nerval's 'Aurelia', of whom he wrote 'my star is dead'. Vierne argues that through her name she is related to the idea of the star – la Stella – both that in de Nerval's poem and the real life Estelle. Thus, according to Vierne, 'She was only representation, through her playing, and expression, through her voice, of the desires of dilettantis – and of enthusiasts' [amateurs] (Vierne, p. 346).[8] Vierne also sees the opera singer as representing the illusory image of woman in the lover's eyes that cannot translate to reality, or 'l'amour fou', who thus escapes them both because neither of them have loved her completely ([p. 348] for one she was a sound , the other simply an image).[9]

Vierne further shows how Verne has taken up the theme of the 'mort-vivant' of earlier writers like Charles Nodier in *Inès de las Sierras*: the beloved brought back to life (p. 349), and that he understands technology as a means of making fantasy a reality. For this reason, according to Vierne, the setting in Transylvania, a 'country still preserved from civilisation' and whose legends had already been collected for some time in France,[10] is important for creating an environment where fantasy reigns over reason. The book's ultimate irony is that science can be used to create the sorcery of Goethe's *Faust* (who also wanted his beloved, Marguerite, entirely to himself [p. 354]), so that the fantasy and hence superstition of the past, as well as 'l'amour fou' of the present, can become the reality of the future through technology (pp. 354–5).

We might compare Vierne's critique of the work to the more general conclusions of Chesneaux, who wrote the most detailed political critique of Jules Verne, arguing that he was a utopian who was interested in promoting the benefits of technology. However, if we look closely at the effects of technology in this novel, its use may be seen either equivocally, given the dual uses to which Gortz and Orfanik put their holograms (the dragons which scare Dr Patak are as much a part of fantasy as the operatic image of the beloved La Stilla), or else entirely negatively.

While much of Simone Vierne's interpretation is convincing, Jules Verne's use of a Transylvanian setting may depend as much upon political reasons as upon the need to juxtapose superstition against technology and science. He makes allusions to the history of the region and its politics and, importantly, informs us that the Baron de Gortz, in keeping with the content of the Fantastic in Nodier's *Jean Sbogar* and Byron's *The Giaour*, is an ex-political rebel against the Hungarians who has turned to the bad as a result of disillusionment (Verne, p. 21). The contention of this chapter is that his cynicism is represented symbolically by his reaction to La Stilla as surely as are the views of a free and untainted Rumania by de Telek's attitude to the same woman. Verne was writing at a time when the situation for the Rumanians of Transylvania had become intolerable, and as a citizen of the country which had championed the rights of Rumanians most vociferously, and which the Rumanians themselves had considered their greatest ally, he took an interest in their plight. However, his views are complex, if not disturbing, and hence require embedded allegory rather than overt statement.

In order to understand the full political meaning of both the novel and of La Stilla herself (who is the work's key allegorical figure), we must consider first earlier novels in France about the Hungarian vampire, the geographical sources of which Verne made use and how he shaped them, the history of Transylvanian–French relations and, finally, how various intertexts allow La Stilla to embody a complex political opinion.

Féval and Faust

Paul Féval's two novels *La Vampire* and *Le Chevalier Ténèbre* may well have been an initial inspiration for a 'Hungarian' setting. The protagonist of *La Vampire*, Addhéma, lives on an island in the river Save just before the minarets of Belgrade, in what was at the time a part of Hungary, now Voivodina in Serbia.[11] The two Chevaliers Ténèbreux, although originally

East End villains or French chevaliers who were killed fighting for Jan Hunyades – depending upon whether one accepts the uncanny or marvellous ending – also have their tombs in the plains of 'Grand-Waraden' south of Szeged (again now in northern Serbia, or Vojvodina).[12] Thus Verne had a precedent for placing his story against a 'Hungarian' backdrop in the work of an earlier French writer of popular fiction.

However, it is not so much the stories of the two novels themselves that have inspired Verne as the beginning of *La Vampire*, when the narrator, in trying to explain the revenant, invokes his own memories to determine when and where he first became acquainted with the superstition. It was, he says, a 'German tale' which 'narrated simply, almost dully, stories so savage, that my heart is still shaken by them' (Féval, *La Vampire*, p. 17).[13] This story was in three volumes, each with an engraving at the front. The narrator both describes the engravings and recounts the story that caused him so much fright.

The story, although set in southern Hungary, is none other than that of Goethe's *Faust*. In *Faust* the hero is given not only the power of science but of youth as well, which he uses to seduce the beautiful Gretchen (Margrete). Mephisto contrives to separate them, but Faust returns to save her from death after she has been placed in the condemned cell for drowning her baby. Faust and Mephisto fail to convince her to flee with them, and she is executed, but God announces her salvation to both of them at the end.

In the version of the Faust story which Féval offers the reader there is no such happiness. Indeed, in referring to his memories the narrator decides to call the vampire 'Faust' simply because: 'what is Goethe's work of art, if not the splendid fictional rendering of the eternal reality of vampirism which, since the beginning of the world, has withered and emptied the hearts of so many families' (p. 17).[14] He tells the story of how 'Faust', while dancing with Marguerite in her Hungarian costume on her wedding day, stole her away in a chariot 'half Valaque, half Tartar' to his lair, towards a part of southern Hungary, just north of Belgrade. There the cadavre – for this is his real appearance – sucks her blood and leaves her in a state of death alongside many other female 'statues', 'lying down and sleeping the eternal sleep' (p. 18).[15] The vampire 'Faust', whom the narrator also compares to Don Juan and Achilles due to his insatiability and invulnerability, is eventually killed by the wedding guests with a stake through his heart, at which point, miraculously, Marguerite wakes from death (p. 19).

As Daniel Compère declares there is no traceable source for this story,[16] the fusion being of Féval's own devising. The purpose of turning the story of Faust round in this way is probably threefold: to couch the vampire-story – and thus his literary work – in a tradition of 'respectable' literature; to make the reader aware of the vampire's 'literary' genesis, in contrast to its 'real-life' appearance in Napoleon's Paris (and thus to make the reader's hesitation between an 'uncanny' and a 'marvellous' explanation all the more wavering); and to enhance the later shock the reader feels about the countess – the irony that it is a female vampire from southern Hungary, Addhéma, not a male one, who comes to life in Paris.

Verne appears to have taken much from this story within a story. First, the idea of a Hungarian vampire who is Faust, which in Féval's version is linked to the idea of eternal youth by preying upon the young and beautiful, becomes in *Le Château des Carpathes* the idea of the vampiric baron who both draws the real life out of his object of desire and preserves it like Féval's Faust vampire does the female statues in his lair but conversely can use technology, not the supernatural, to make it seem alive (although as a fantasy). This idea of bringing the dead back to life (which Vierne draws upon), the 'mort-vivant', would have been suggested by the Szandor-Gregorian motto of 'In vita mors, in morte vitae' in *La Vampire*, although in Féval's work this had a more ironic meaning than simply the ressurection of the dead, or the 'undead': as her tricked lover Réné Kervoz points out, each hour of Addhéma's life is a result of stealing a whole year from youth, beauty and love (Féval, *La Vampire*, p. 219).

Thus Féval's subtle reinterpretation of the Faust legend at the beginning of *La Vampire* is the probable reason why Verne first decided to write a novel which mixes the idea of Faust with the legend of the vampire in Hungary (or at least its environs). He turns vampirism round, however, to make the vampiric figure a preserver through science of life and beauty (although in a dead form), rather than one who destroys it through a genuine pact with the devil. However, Féval did not describe a Vlach vampire, nor one from Transylvania: in both his earlier vampire novels the landscape is conspicuously the plains just north of Belgrade which were still a part of Hungary. Verne's major sources for both the setting and atmosphere of his book – and thus its contemporary political relevance – are quite otherwise.

Reclus and de Gerando

Unlike Stoker or Le Fanu, Jules Verne actually names his sources. One is Auguste de Gerando and the other Elisée de Reclus. The former was a young French traveller, who published a long, two-volume travelogue and descriptive history called *Transylvania and its Inhabitants* in 1845,[17] three years before the Hungarian uprising. The latter was an anarchist, personal friend of Verne himself, and one of the founders of modern geography, who was writing in 1873, six years after the Austro–Hungarian Ausgleich. The specific work to which Verne refers is Reclus's *Journey to the Mining Regions of Western Transylvania*, published as a whole in the 1874 annual of *Le Tour du Monde*, volume II. De Gerando's work is full of references to recent history, the costume of each province, the legends associated with areas as well as the geographical features of the land. De Reclus is concerned mostly with geology, botany, the conditions of the working-class and the ethnic mixture of the area – understandably given his own quite radical political views. Although Reclus himself refers to Gerando when describing the conflicts that have surrounded Thorda,[18] making it possible for Verne to have known of his work without actually reading him, the novel contains references to history and custom that Verne could only have known from reading de Gerando directly. An examination of the two sources shows that although Reclus's work was the major one by far, Verne adapted both works with the twofold aim of exaggerating the opposition between Magyars and Wallachs and of highlighting the contrast between the superstitions of the local people and their engagement with the latest modern technology.

Verne actually quotes from Reclus frequently, including when describing a flower which grows in the earth of the plateau near Vulkan and Werst: 'It was a thick thistle called "Russian thorn", whose seeds, said Elisée Reclus, were carried in the hairs of the Muscovite horses – "a gift of joyful conquest made by the Russians to the Transylvanians" ' (p. 69).[19] This is an exact presentation and quotation of Reclus's comments on the reasons for a parasitical plant growing in the plain around the Valley of the Szamos, which prevents the true germination of cereals in the rather desolate plain: in the new context it adds to the austere atmosphere of the region, like a metaphor of the oppression which the locals endure. However, the original sense of 'joyful conquest' is not ironic, despite the rather unappealing memento left behind. Reclus makes it clear that in the recent uprising of 1848, which the Russians crushed on Austria's behalf in 1849, the local Vlachs (Wallachs) were against the Hungarians (Reclus, p. 8) and that by 'Transylvanians' it is really the Rumanians he has in mind, since they are the most apparent part of the population for whom he expresses most support due to their continued oppression.[20] Just as the Hungarians wanted complete separation from Austria, which was still the dominant partner in Austria–Hungary (the 'Dual Nation' after the Ausgleich of 1867), so the Vlachs (Wallachs) of Transylvania resented Hungarian domination within the borders of the 'Hungarian' nation over which the Magyars (i.e., ethnic Hungarians) had control, a point which Reclus describes well throughout his travelogue. Although in an oversight towards the complexities of the region's recent history, Verne makes the term 'joyful conquest' seem ironic, the author of *Le Château des Carpathes* elsewhere tailors the ethnic and geographical details from Reclus's travelogue in accordance with the Swiss's own sentiments, in order to express the idea of Magyars oppressing Vlachs throughout the novel.

To begin with, Verne uses Reclus to create a very exact picture of the area. The novel starts with the shepherd Frik tending his flocks near the mountain Vulkan and overlooking the 'plateau of Orgall' (Verne, p. 4). He is a native of Werst, just to the south, in the valley of the two 'Sils', elsewhere in which valley he also happens to be now (although further north). A mountebank who comes from Hermanstadt in the south and is on his way to the regional capital Koloszvar (p. 10) gives him a telescope in an attempt to make a sale (p. 12), which provides the shepherd with an opportunity to look at the whole lie of the land, so that he sees the towns of Lizvadel, Petroszeny and Petrilla to the north (p. 14). He then moves the telescope southwards to notice the smoke coming out of the Château of the Carpathians, which is situated on an isolated part of the 'neck of Vulkan' itself, the highest part of the plateau of Orgall (p. 4). The château is next to a poplar tree that loses a branch every year, the superstition being that once the last branch has gone the château will be destroyed. Only three branches are left (p. 5).

Thus the scene of the area is set. The first chapter uses the telescope motif partly to introduce the location and geography of south western Transylvania. These geographical details are all taken from Reclus's work. Travelling south from Koloszvar through the valley of Maros, Reclus visits the mining towns of Thorda and Torotzko (Reclus, pp. 17–24), as well as the new smaller mining towns of Lizvadel, Petroszeny and Lonyay where the two valleys of the 'Wallachian Sil' and the 'Hungarian Sil' conjoin (pp. 35–7), and then proceeds to a mountain ridge on the central plain called the 'neck of Vulkan' (p. 39), before returning up through the valley of Maros (pp. 46–8). He even provides a detailed map of the region which Verne no doubt used in imagining Frik's position (Reclus, p. 7)[21] (see Map 3). Thus we can see that Verne was attempting, in keeping with his claim that the work was not fantasy (Verne, p. 2), to ground his story in a very real place, in order to create the impression of both verisimilitude and plausibility.

In the second chapter there is a long discussion of the mines in the valley of Maros, some way to the north-west of Werst and the 'plateau of

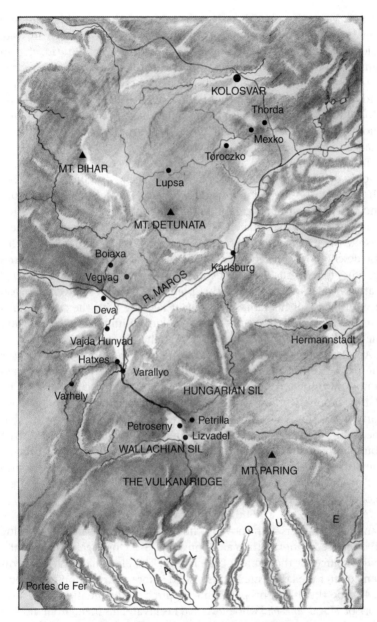

Map 3 Map of South Western Transylvania in Reclus' 'Voyage'

Orgall'. Verne describes the salt-stone mines of Thorda, which produce twenty thousand tonnes a year; the mines of Torotzko, rich in lead, galenite and mercury as well as iron; those of Vayda Hunyad, rich in minerals for steel; the coal mines in 'the district of Hatzeg, at Livadzel, at Petroseny [*sic*], a vast pocket with a capacity estimated at two hundred and fifty tonnes'[22]; and even gold mines at Offenbanya and Topanfalva. Mount Parajd (or Paring), also in the valley, has a circumference of seven kilometres at its base (Verne, p. 29). The descriptions are meant to be exact and convincing in their exactness.

These details are again all taken from Reclus's work, in particular the middle part where he describes the mines. Reclus specifically describes Thorda as possessing salt mines and Torotzko as possessing lead, mercury and coal along with its iron mines (although stresses, in a phrase which Verne clearly missed, that it is only the iron that is actually mined, despite there being other potential resources [Reclus, pp. 17–23]). Reclus also describes 'Mount Paring' as having a circumference of seven kilometres (p. 16), just as Verne does in the novel. In Verne's work these borrowed features (unacknowledged at this point) help to give a technological environment for his fantasy, so out of keeping with the superstitions already shown in Frik's panic at the smoking chimney of the castle and the superstition of the falling poplar branches.

Another theme to which Reclus also refers in relation to the mines is the oppression of the workers by the state. The local miners are paid almost nothing in comparison with their Western counterparts, he claims, despite working much harder, and the state takes the greatest part (p. 35). This is a feature which Verne recalls when he complains that the local inhabitants are exploited: 'Here is, it would appear, a district abundantly endowed by nature, and yet this abundance scarcely benefits the district's local inhabitants at all (Verne, p. 29).[23] Thus Verne has also picked up on a political detail of his source as opposed to a purely geographical one.

One can also see a political hand working in Verne's attribution of names to characters in the novel, although more with regard to suggesting an oppressed minority than an oppressed class. Once again Reclus is the major source for the names of the region. The Biro (magistrate) Koltz is named after the last castle Reclus visited before returning home (Reclus, p. 47) and the title of his position is inspired by the mention in Reclus's work of a local *falus-biró* who prevented Reclus and his friend from moving on one evening (p. 42). Nick Dec is a name inspired most probably by a mine named after Deak (p. 36), the Hungarian constitutionalist. Dr Patak is named after the stream 'Buvo-Patak', meaning 'hidden stream' (p. 26). De Telek, however, is named after an illustrious Hungarian family of the region, whose originator, Michel de Teleki, was instrumental in carving out a union with the Austrians. This name shows that Verne also used de Gerando's work (de Gerando, I 125–6), since it is not present in Reclus's account of his journey. However, the most striking feature of all these names is that they are Hungarian or German, not Rumanian in origin, signifying the extent to which Verne is taking the entire history and features of the region and reappropriating them to the Vlachs' traditions.

The story of Baron Gortz also shows the extent to which Verne manipulates his sources in order to present the Vlachs as being the oppressed. The Gortz motto '*Dâ Pe Maorte* "Give Until death" !' (Verne, p. 20) is, according to de Gerando, simply the motto of all the Vlach people of the region (de Gerando, I 334), whose heroism, he stresses, far exceeds that of their Saxon neighbours. In Verne's novel Gortz is also described as having taken part in a rebellion against the Hungarians (not the Austrians) before disappearing into two alternative myths. One myth is that:

> he had patriotically joined the famous Rosza Sandor, an ex-highwayman, of whom the war for independence had made a legendary hero. Fortunately for him, after the result of the struggle, Rodolphe de Gortz had distanced himself from the band of the dubious 'betyar' and did so wisely, since the old brigand returned to his role as a leader of thieves and ended by falling into the hands of the police, who were happy to lock him up in the prison of Szamos-Ujvar.

> [... il s'était patriotiquement joint au fameux Rosza Sandor, un ancien détrousseur de grande route, dont la guerre de l'indépendance avait fait un héros de drame. Par bonheur pour lui, après l'issue de la lutte, Rodolphe de Gortz s'était séparé de la bande du compromettant 'betyar', et il fit sagement, car l'ancien brigand, redevenu chef de voleurs, finit par tomber entre les mains de la police, qui se contenta de l'enfermer dans le prison de Szamos-Ujvar.] (Verne, p. 21)

The other myth was that he was killed in an encounter fighting alongside Sandor. The inspiration for both myths comes from the history related by Reclus about the famous bandit, Rosza Sandor, who turned his hand to rebellion in 1848, only to return to being a 'simple scoundrel' and 'the head of a band of assassins'[24] before being imprisoned (Reclus, p. 15). Verne's handling is interesting, given that Sandor was a Hungarian hero, who fought against the Austrians, and would have been an enemy to the Vlachs, who took opportunity by the 1848 uprising to throw off

Hungarian masters. It is thus hardly likely that de Gortz would have fought alongside him but would rather have been against him. Nevertheless, heroic elements of Hungarian history have again been appropriated into that of the Vlachs, stressing their experience of oppression and rebellion.[25]

Verne is keen to describe Transylvania's ethnic make-up. He depicts a region full of diverse and unconnected peoples and seems, initially, to condone the policy of magyarisation:

> ... whatever her political constitution may have been, she has remained the communal habitat of diverse races who brush up against each other without linking the Vlachs or Romanians, the Hungarians, the Gipsies, the Szecklers of Moldavian origin, as well as the Saxons that the times and circumstances will eventually magyarise to the benefit of Transylvanian unity.
>
> [... quelle qu'ait été sa constitution politique, il est resté le commun habitat de diverses races qui s'y coudoient sans se fusionner, les Valaques ou Roumains, les Hongrois, les Tsiganes, les Szeklers d'origine moldave, et aussi les Saxons que le temps et les circonstances finiront par 'magyariser' au profit de l'unité transylvaine.] (Verne, p. 4)

This idea of magyarisation being a 'benefit' (profit) again clashes with the later portrayal of the heroic history of the Gortz family, and Verne's description of how they took part in 'one of the bloody revolutions of the Rumanian peasants against Hungarian oppression'.[26] He is therefore either being ironic when talking of 'benefit' (profit) or else simply decides to show elsewhere that Transylvanian unity is not necessarily a worthy goal in itself compared with Vlach self-determination.

Again Reclus is the major source here, since he talks of how Armenians and Saxons are happy to 'magyarise' themselves when in largely Hungarian areas; however, it should be remembered that in 1873 he was writing before the Hungarian diet's policy of forced magyarisation in the 1880s, about which Verne would have known. Reclus describes the oppression of the Vlachs by the other three groups but also describes the ease with which they live alongside each other and the extent to which people adopt either Magyar or Rumanian customs, depending upon by whom they are ensconced, to the point where different ethnic groups are difficult to discern (Reclus, p. 6). Verne's treatment of the ethnography highlights instead the mixture and sense of separation between groups rather than the ability to cooperate.

The treatment of the myths and legends of the region also shows an attempt to submerge its whole history beneath the Vlach experience. We are told of how the Biro Koltz's daughter Miriota is educated in the stories and legends of the region.

> She knows the legend of Leany-Kö, the Rock of the Virgin, in which a somewhat mythical young princess escapes from the pursuit of Tartars; the legend of the grotto of the dragon, in the valley of the King's Rise; the legend of the fortress of Deva, which was built in the 'Age of the Fairies'. (Verne, p. 35)

> [Elle connait la légende de Leany-Kö, le Rocher de la Vierge, où une jeune princesse quelque peu fantastique échappe aux poursuites des Tartares; la légende de la grotte du Dragon, dans la vallée de la 'Montée du Roi'; la légende de la forteresse de Deva, qui fût construite 'au temps des Fées'] (Verne, p. 35).

All of these, and other legends, are taken from Reclus's wide travels around the region.[27] Many of the legends are in fact Hungarian in origin. We are also told that in Miriota's house there are pictures of heroes: 'Rumanian patriots, – among others, the popular hero of the XVth century, the voivode Vajda-Hunyad' (Verne, p. 34).[28] The Voivode, Jan Corvinus Hunyades, was again a Hungarian hero, not a Rumanian one. The suggestion for this detail comes from Reclus staying at a house full of lithographs of Hungarian heroes while at Torotzko – but in this case the house was actually owned by Hungarians (Reclus, pp. 22–3). Verne has again taken elements from the heroic history of the Magyars and placed them within the heroic history of Vlachs. Unlike Stoker, he has not created a political hybrid but has rather loaded the traditions of many people onto one of the ethnic groups in order to centre upon their political history.

Verne was also keen to highlight the superstitions of the region from his sources. The superstitious element of the Vlach people in Transylvania is important for two reasons. First, for suggesting an environment in which technology and fantasy can both form such a plausible contrast. The second reason is that the superstitions of the Vlachs, combined with the ease with which technology can be used to make them real, highlight the oppression of this people: they have festered in a medieval past, whose shackles are as mental as they are political, and the technology of the future can be used to keep them suppressed by making these superstitions manifest, just as the mining technology of the present is being used to exploit them today. These dual elements represent an uncharacteristically pessimistic presentation of technology as regressive rather than progressive in the furthering of political freedom, at odds with Verne's normal use of such advances in works like *20,000 Leagues under the Sea*.

While Verne drew some information about 'real-life' sorcerers from de Gerando's work (Gerando, I 316–8), Reclus has only one story involving superstition, about a girl who is visited by a vampire (Reclus, p. 27). Thus he must have used others and appears to have looked far and wide in order to create as great a plenitude of horrific creatures as possible, in order to illustrate the overburdening weight of superstitions in the minds of the local people, which include the stryge, the chort (devil), the zmei (fairies) and the hippogriff. These eclectically gathered superstitions are not only all part of the 'Wallachian mythology' but are also an instrumental part of the education provided by the local schoolmaster,[29] who teaches their veracity on the grounds of 'supporting evidence' ('preuves à l'appui' [Verne p. 22]). The continuation of a pre-Enlightenment form of education forms a further contrast with the rise of technology in the region, but another effect of all these many superstitions, of whom the chort and the stryge or vampire are the most foregrounded (Patak sees 'enormous vampires' last in the optical illusions which assail him on the way to the castle [p. 74]), is to present the possibility of the baron being either a vampire or demon and the multiple superstitions of the region which lead to the manipulability of the local population.

Thus Verne takes his sources and, while following them very accurately and carefully, adapts them to present the Vlachs as participating in all the heroic struggles of the region and as being oppressed by the Magyars or Hungarians beyond the degree stipulated in the sources themselves. He also draws the contrast between technology and superstition to suggest both the political degeneracy caused by oppression and political stagnation – represented in the official education of the local school – and the extent to which technology both can and could further be used to deprive Vlach people of their rights. The reasons why he wrote a work so evidently grounded in politics can be ascertained by observing the political attitude at that time in his own country towards the Vlachs.

France and Rumania

Rumania is one of the youngest countries of Europe. Its people were for many years divided between different principalities, rather than being members of a single sovereign state, who took their origins from the Dacians and then the settler farmers of the Italian peninsula who came during the rule of the Emperor Trajan in the second century AD.[30] Thanks to the poverty of their land and surrounding mountains, they were largely ignored during the Slavic and Byzantine invasions of the following centuries but eventually came under Bulgarian rule, until that empire in turn fell to the Ottomans in 1348. Many in Transylvania underwent Magyarisation in return for protection, during which time they effectively emerged as two separate principalities, Wallachia and Moldavia. While Wallachia became a tributary of the Sultan in 1391 (Logio, p. 14), both she and Moldavia managed to maintain the election of their own Princes for several centuries. However, the slow encroachment of Turkish aggression meant that by 1716 the election of princes in both principalities was in Turkish hands (p. 15). Since both were Orthodox principalities, and not officially a part of the Ottoman Empire, the Turks chose Greek Phanariots (from Constantinople) as leaders, who would buy the title of Prince and impose heavy taxes on the local serfs before moving on with their ill-gotten gains (p. 16).

After the Greek revolution of 1821, the Turks nominated local rulers. However, by now the Russians held more power over the area and after repeated incursions they imposed a new order upon the principalities after the Treaty of Adrianople of 1829 (p. 18). The Crimean War, and the Treaty of Paris in 1856, gave the Vlach or 'Rumanian' people of the two principalities of Wallachia and Moldavia the opportunity to become independent. Two years later, the 'United Principalities' were effectively united through Colonel Alexander Cuza, who became Prince Alexander Cuza of Moldova and Prince Alexander John I of Wallachia, with the maintenance of Russian titular rule in both (the Austrians would not countenance full unity (p. 19).[31] The two, without Transylvania, finally became a united country under one king in 1866, when Cuza was deposed and Charles Hohenzollern, a Prussian, became Prince of a single sovereign state, Rumania. At the Treaty of Berlin (1878), Rumania had to cede Bessarabia (Eastern Moldavia) to Russia in return for the Dobrudja (Dobrogea), a small part of Bulgaria to their south. Charles was now free to be crowned King and took the title in 1881 (Logio, p. 21).

Transylvania, by the late nineteenth century populated mainly by Vlachs, remained along with the rest of Hungary in the Austrian Empire until 1918 and was not included in the negotiations of the Treaty of Paris (1856).[32] Although the Ausgleich of 1867 gave assurance of language rights for all nationalities within the Hungarian kingdom, this was revoked by the Hungarian parliament from 1879 onwards, when the law to enforce the Hungarian language in elementary schools was passed,[33] and the Hungarian nationality policy of forced magyarisation began its long and ultimately counterproductive encroachment upon the other communities in the region. From 1890 new laws of magyarisation were passed further forbidding language rights, making it illegal for education to be conducted in any language except Hungarian.[34] Although in 1891 there were abortive attempts on the part of the Rumanian National Party to list grievances against this and other laws, they as yet delayed their attempt to solicit the attention of the Emperor. In January 1892, however, the month in which *Le Château des Carpathes* began to be serialised, Aurel Popovici, the young leader of the Rumanian National Party, wrote a long tract listing these grievances, which included both magyarisation and insufficient representation at the Diet, and submitted it to the Diet to be passed onto the Emperor (Haraszti, p. 119). The Hungarians returned it to him and the other leaders in May of that year without passing it on (Gaidoz, p. 5). Eventually the Rumanian leaders of Transylvania were tried for sedition, and in 1894 several tracts were published in France highlighting the plight of the Rumanians, including an article by Clemenceau for *La Justice* (Haraszti, p. 120). This was the very man who was to be so influential at Versailles 24 years later in ensuring that Transylvania became part of the new Rumania of 1919.[35]

Such strong French support should hardly be surprising, since the French connection was the most important foreign tie in the creation of modern Rumania. Quite apart from the issue of Transylvanian Rumanians, the idea of a united Rumania had always gained its most enthusiastic support in France. Indeed, it was the influence of French culture, introduced by the Phanariots, which spurred the Vlach people on to a nationalism based on a long historical trajectory to the classical world. According to George Clenton Logio:

> It is certainly owing to their saturation with French culture that the Rumanians have not been absorbed by the Russians, and for this reason the Phanariots may be pardoned for all the evils they brought in their train, since at the same time they bestowed on Rumania that which safeguarded her most precious possession, the notion of her nationhood. (Logio, p. 17)

This nationhood was supported most enthusiastically by the French Emperor Napoleon III, who argued vociferously for Wallachia and Moldavia to be united in a republic at the Congress of Paris (1856) (Iorga, p. 233) but backed down due to British pressure (pp. 236–7). In 1866, when Charles I became prince of a united Rumania, it was again Napoleon III who did most to soothe the fears of other major powers

(Logio, p. 20). Admittedly, France simply followed the British line at the Treaty of Berlin in 1878 (Iorga, p. 251) in assuaging the Russians by handing them back southern Bessarabia (Logio, p. 21), but they were still weakened by the Franco–Prussian war.

Whatever the vagaries of realpolitik, the cultural links between the two countries were always strong. Indeed, the Rumanian intelligentsia of the early to mid-nineteenth century were largely trained in Paris and took their libertarian and neoclassical ideas from the French revolution (Iorga, pp. 153–8), helping to forge the idea of a united 'Roman' Republic while on the banks of the Seine rather than the Danube.[36] French historians like Elias Regnault, in *Histoire Politique et Sociale des Principautés*, demonstrated the importance of supporting the new kingdom on the Danube (p. 206), while another writer, Taxile DeLord, openly attacked Austria for holding onto the third principality of Transylvania (1857) (p. 210). Meanwhile in Moldovia and Wallachia themselves, people from all walks of life 'remained under French influence, despite the surveillance of the restored Russian consulate' (p. 214).[37] As Iorga writes, France was seen throughout by Wallachs and Moldavians as the only power sympathetic to the idea of Rumanian unity, capable of making an impact over the Transylvanian question (pp. 247–8).

Thus due to ties of language, culture and political ideals, France and Rumania enjoyed a special relationship during the nineteenth century, which would incline a French intellectual to take their side on the Transylvanian issue.

Nevertheless, at the time when Verne was writing *Le Château des Carpathes* the Vlachs of Transylvania were still a minority issue which did not make any appearance in the pages of Verne's favourite newspaper, *Le Figaro*. Austro–Hungarian misrule of Italy, insurrections in Bulgaria and the Kaiser's attempts at rearmament, were what instead occupied the foreign section of *Le Figaro* in the early 1890s. Although much news comes from 'Pesth' concerning Bulgarian and Austrian affairs, the only long and detailed article concerning Hungarians deals with the issue of religious problems between Protestants and Catholics in Hungary (11 September 1890) and the enforcement of the law that girls must take the religion of their mother and boys that of their father. Rumania is discussed in the foreign news column on 28th August in relation to a ministerial crisis and the possible abdication of King Charles, in particular the assurance of the king that Rumania will maintain its neutrality. However, the issues concerning Vlachs in Transylvania are not once touched upon during this period, making it likely that Verne's political interest stemmed from his friendship with Reclus and was very far sighted, since rather than writing a work which corresponded to events very topical at the time, he wrote one which courted topicality once it was published: meaning that he had investigated the situation as it was simmering and released his novel while it was erupting. However, to ascertain Verne's actual position with regards to the Vlachs of Transylvania, it remains to investigate the complex allegory involving La Stilla.

The meaning of La Stilla

While most of the names in *Le Château des Carpathes* are quite arbitrary, the symbolism of La Stilla's name, the manner of her death and the part she is playing when she dies (Angelique) all indicate a very deliberate and ultimately politically oriented set of allusions in Verne's fictional weave. The relations which both de Gortz and de Telek enjoy with La Stilla in Naples and later with her re-created image in the castle point to an embedded political allegory which serves to illuminate the more realistic details of the novel and of the Transylvanians who populate it – that political allegory, however, is a highly ambivalent one, whose final interpretation is multiple or even contradictory.

Simone Vierne has already shown the debts which the forging of La Stilla bears to various women in nineteenth-century French literature. If we read the story purely naturalistically, and treat La Stilla initially as a real woman rather than simply an artistic representation of feminine perfection, then the Baron de Gortz's reaction to her indicates great character imperfections on his part, perhaps as a result of experience.[38] First, he abrogates responsibilty for her death in blaming the Count, since it is really his blazing eyes that kill her. Second, by loving simply the singing voice and acting of La Stilla, he shows that he is incapable of appreciating the physicality of the world and that in his attempt to capture its mere form he has destroyed its essence. This may have a political meaning, since in her last role, as Angelique, she represents the heroine enchained to a rock who is freed by Ruggiero and then by Orlando in Ariosto's famous romance *Orlando Furioso*. Furthermore, in French tradition Liberty is of course the half-naked Marianne, whose flowing dress is similar to that of Angelique in the Bennet illustrations to Verne's work (although a bit less modest).

However, the name 'La Stilla' may also be a reference to Ariosto's romance *Orlando Furioso*, rather than to the opera by Arconati upon which it is based (there was no such composer). While Vierne assumes that it is a twist on the Italian 'La Stella', meant to represent the real-life 'Estelle', one has to ask why Verne would change the vowel-form to make it a different word.[39] In the original romance we find the character of 'Logistilla', a beautiful fairy and daughter of Love, who presides over a heavenly kingdom where all is shining and transparent: an ideal realm. As one of the many allegorical features of the romance, she may be understood as representing the neoplatonic nous or realm of ideas, who empowers knights with reason so they may overcome tyrants. Ruggiero, Orlando's friend, discovers her shining kingdom after first being seduced and trapped by her evil sister Alcina (who represents false and fickle love and has also usurped Logistilla's rightful kingdom) and is taught there by Logistilla how to ride the hippogriff (Ariosto, pp. 111–2, ch. 10, st. 64–9): the horse crossed with a griffin, used by classical rhetoricians to represent a contradiction (and thus something illogical by Aristotle's law of excluded middle). After the hippogriff has been tamed, Ruggiero flies to where Angelique, Orlando's beloved, is chained naked to a rock waiting to be eaten by a dragon ([pp. 123–4, ch. 11, st. 37–47] one of the monsters which Patak sees on the way to the castle is also a hippogriff [Verne, p. 74] – unusual for a Gothic romance). Logistilla therefore represents both reason and pure love, of the platonic kind, as well as a force for freedom and the overcoming of tyranny.

It could be that when using the name La Stilla, Verne is in fact alluding to the original story behind the opera rather than making allusions to de Nerval or the Estelle of his own youth, in which case the allegory in the work presents all sorts of new possibilities in interpretation. Through intertext, the figure presents the possibility of there being a concealed allegorical meaning beyond the simple allegory of romantic love which is most obvious and which may or may not even contradict the surface narration.

As the Empress of reason portraying the enchained Angelique, La Stilla may signify the union of reason with liberty in the neoClassical tradition of republicanism favoured by Voltaire and Jacobin figures of the French Enlightenment. In this case, Baron de Gortz's manslaughter/murder of the actress through a contraption or device (if there is one) symbolises the suborning of both reason and freedom and a lack of faith in their potential realisation. De Telek's attempt to marry her and take her from the stage may symbolise the attempt to end her ideal or imaginary role and take her into the real and thus make reason and liberty an actuality.

Alternatively, however, the fact that La Stilla is named after another character from the original romance on which the opera in which she performs also derives may show that she is, like Lamia, simply a dream and that De Gortz, in killing her, draws attention to the illusory and fantastical nature of de Telek's love, as Vierne has argued (Vierne, pp. 345–6).

La Stilla is only a presence to us throughout: in recalling his past life with her, de Telek never remembers her words or impressions, the conversations the two had or the private image of her – only what she was like on the stage. This recalls other operatic romantic stories, not only *La Dame Blanche* and *Consuelo*, but Balzac's *Sarrasine*, in which the image of the beautiful singer Zambinella with whom Sarrasine falls in love is in real life a castrated male.

If we relate both these possibilities to the more precise political context of the novel, the magyarisation of Transylvania in 1890–91 and the reaction of the Rumanians living there, we can see two alternative views on Verne's part, encoded beneath the contradictory comments of the narrator through intertextual references, which create alternative metaphors over but including those related to the idea of romantic love. De Gortz is the Rumanian who has fought the Magyars who rule him and now roams the world stateless, whereas de Telek is the younger, fresher Rumanian who lives in a free country. The Baron represents the disillusioned Rumanian idealist who has withdrawn from society after acceding to his oppressors and who now delights in depriving others of their freedom and controlling them, while de Telek is the liberator, who exposes him and frees his fellows from the limiting superstitions which have been plaguing them. La Stilla as Angelique is both the enchained Marianne and the classical idea of reason – Enlightenment – whom de Telek tries to withdraw from the ideal into the real world and whom de Gortz, due to his degeneration and disillusionment, can only enjoy vicariously and further wishes to deprive others of enjoying.

Alternatively, rather like Zambinella in *Sarrasine*, La Stilla is an artistic mirage, incapable of existing in the reality to which de Telek wishes to take her, and who further represents the illusory nature of freedom and Enlightenment, which brutal truth the Baron realises, but which the infatuated and immature de Telek cannot as yet see, until the smashing of the glass. In this sense, Vierne is just in saying that the Baron is right to blame de Telek and not himself for the death of an opera singer who cannot live outside the realm of her art (Vierne, p. 345), although her illusory nature relates as much to political emancipation as to romantic love.

This illusory nature of La Stilla, whether in relation to love or the further embedded political allegory in the work, is symbolised through the reference to at least two more sources than those mentioned by Vierne, one from English literature, the other from the French tradition.

To state that Verne was influenced by the English tradition always has to be qualified by the fact that he spoke no English. Many of the great works of Romanticism do not appear to have been translated into French by 1891, and the work of Keats certainly belongs to this category. Nevertheless, the death of La Stilla bears such a strong resemblance to the death of Lamia in Keats's poem of the same name that it at least deserves to be mooted as a possible source, especially since the original story by Philostratus does not contain the relevant details of Keats's poem. Verne frequently used friends to investigate sources which he himself could not read and his interest in the representation of illusory love may have led him to conduct investigations outside his own language.

The death of La Stilla is uncannily similar in both form and content to Lamia's death. In Keats's poem the old sage or philosopher Apollonius destroys the 'foul dream' of the succuba by staring at her fixedly, thus proving her to be an illusion. Lycius, her lover, cries out to his wedding guests:

> Corinthians! Look upon that gray-beard wretch!
> Mark how, possess'd, his lashless eyelids stretch
> Around his demon eyes! Corinthians, see!
> My sweet bride withers at their potency.[40]

This description, of course, compares very exactly with the 'eyes ablaze' of the grey-bearded Baron de Gortz, whose gaze kills La Stilla to the despair of Count de Telek. Even though the first published translation of *Lamia* into French appears to have been by Paul Gallimard in 1910,[41] it is hard to believe that Verne did not use an assistant to research this poem along with other works on a similar theme or else that there was a translation of this poem in a piece as yet not rediscovered.

A further influence, this time within the French tradition, is Stendhal's notion of crystallisation from his famous work *De l'Amour*. Stendhal's one long work of non-fiction describes in exact detail the stages in which love for the beloved grows. These are: admiration, reflection on delight, hope, the birth of love after acceptance, first crystallisation when the imagination endows the beloved with a thousand perfections, doubt, and finally the second crystallisation.[42] The term 'crystallisation' is a metaphor taken from the practice of placing a leafless bough in the salt mines of Salzburg and removing it 24 hours later to discover that it is covered with 'an infinity' of crystals of salt (Stendhal, p. 31), magnifying and embellishing an otherwise mundane object. According to Stendhal the birth of love to the crystallisation takes as long. Stendhal also accords an important role to music in the creation of love. In two entries of

De L'Amour, he attributes music with the ability of acting as a substitute for the love feeling and states, from his experience of the opera at Naples, that 'perfect music, like perfect pantomime, makes me dream of that which currently forms the object of my dreams, and makes me attain excellent ideas' (p. 57)[43] (in this case, rather ironically, the opera was about arming the Greeks). However, he also attributes it with the power of making the lover more predisposed to loving and crystallising rather than substituting the love object (p. 58). For Stendhal, therefore, music was both a means of attenuating the love feeling but also of gratifying it and sating it as a form of substitution: making the reveries momentarily real, as though one were enjoying the presence of the love object. For him, Italian music was the most capable of inciting this feeling (he wrote a book on the life of Rossini and a guide to the Italian opera), which is all that La Stilla, herself at Naples, ever sings (Verne, p. 116).

Stendhal is therefore an obvious source for the idea of the female performing artist symbolising the stark, necessary unreality of love. Although Stendhal writes about the state of passionate love being one of the most refined and civilised conditions to which a man can aspire, a state unreachable by savages, the potential for seeing the crystallisation as what we would now call projection, narcissism or dangerous fantasy was explored long before the popularity of the works of Jung and Freud by writers. Indeed Paul Bourget, a contemporary of Verne, wrote of the process of 'de-crystallisation' in his novella *Cosmopolis*, when the illusion of crystallisation is shattered for one of the characters.[44]

In the presentation of La Stilla and her eventual end we also see such a crumbling of the imaginary object. Franz de Telek does not go through as detailed a process as that described by Stendhal since 'From the first time he saw La Stilla, Franz experienced the irresistible attractions of a first love' (Verne, p. 116).[45] However, the idea of the magnifying hologram certainly appears to acknowledge the tradition of crystallisation in the form of the beloved in the lover's mind. In this sense the form of La Stilla, love for whom has not cooled in the young count's heart over six years, decrystallises as a mirage when the baron smashes the glass: 'Suddenly, the sound of a mirror shattering is heard, and, with a thousand small pieces of glass, scattered across the room, la Stilla disappears' (p. 191).[46] The shattering of the glass into a thousand pieces represents the end of the crystallisation, broken into its component smithereens, and the image created by the lover who, in Stendhal's own terms, invests the image with perfections of his own making.

The Faustian Gortz, however, was happy simply to maintain the crystallised image and her voice, that which he calls her 'soul', without entertaining the illusion of its corresponding to reality. The idea of possessing her soul is also demonic, prompting Vierne to compare the baron as much to Mephisto as to Faust (Vierne, p. 354). However, given the role Stendhal ascribes to music in creating a crystallisation, it may represent de Gortz's understanding that her recorded words are the superior part of the love feeling, being most obviously related to the spiritual rather than the physical and the aids to crystallisation.

If we take La Stilla as Angelique to represent further not simply romantic love but Enlightenment linked to potential freedom, then this interpretation is especially pessimistic. Not only is the political ideal an illusion but one based upon irrational sentiment, which the baron, as a disillusioned idealist, is happy to entertain simply as an imaginary ideal, but which de Telek wishes to maintain as a living ideal, until he, too, is disillusioned. This implies that freedom for Transylvania is an illusion, although this is belied by the positive ending in which the baron's misrule through technology is exposed.

Whether the interpretation of La Stilla be optimistic or pessimistic, however, Verne's sympathies here are still in keeping with the view of intellectuals in France at that time who took interest in the plight of Rumanians suffering from forced magyarisation, even though this took place within the wider context of the hated Austrian Empire. Why he should have created such an equivocal and self-contradictory allegorical figure may be discerned by examining his own political views outside the text.

The politics of Verne

It was suggested by Jean Chesneaux, in *Une Lecture Politique de Jules Verne* (1971), that despite his bourgeois façade (he was a councillor in Amiens), Verne was a Utopian anarchist, with very leftist leanings, who hated colonialism and saw technology as freeing man in the further future. In this reading of Verne's politics, the exemplary hero is Nemo, a citizen of the world who sailed under the black anarchist's flag (Chesneaux, p. 87), believing in liberty for all nations and all people and an end to poverty and war, as Verne himself secretly did (pp. 125–35).

As Olivier Dumas has shown from observing Verne's more recently released family correspondence, the idea of Verne ever being a radical libertarian, socialist or anarchist is contradicted by his letters, both to his family and to the Hetzels, which portray a man who believed in order and capitalism. The most shocking of these was a letter sent to his father at the time of the Prussian occupation and restoration of the

Republic in 1870, when he wrote:

> I truly hope that they will keep the active servicemen for some time in Paris and that they will shoot the socialists like dogs. The Republic can only hold together at this price and it is the only government that has the right to show no mercy to socialism, because it is the only legitimate government.
>
> [J'espères bien que l'on gardera les mobiles quelque temps à Paris, et qu'ils fusilleront les socialistes comme des chiens. La République ne peut tenir qu'à ce prix et c'est le seul gouvernement qui ait le droit d'être sans pitié pour le socialisme, car c'est le seul gouvernement juste et légitime.][47]

Although it is possible he is trying to flatter the arch conservative views of his father by professing such reactionary measures, the fear of social- ism and desire for order are surely genuine. While he does appear to have been somewhat more cynical – certainly when younger – about Napoleon III, the French Emperor from 1852–70, who had abolished the Second Republic in favour of his own dictatorship,[48] he was by no means an unqualified supporter of the socialist and anti-bourgeois ideals which had originally swept King Louis-Phillipe from power in 1848 before Napoleon III's dictatorship. He aspired towards bourgeois republicanism rather than radical libertarianism.

He was not, however, exempt from espousing certain libertarian views within his bourgeois republicanism. His contempt for socialism and anarchy is matched by an equal contempt for the intrusions of state and bullying of the less powerful by the more powerful, as Dumas has shown (Dumas, p. 165). Another continual theme of his novels, as Chesneaux correctly expresses, is the rights of oppressed nations to take on the strong to achieve freedom. This was a definite legacy of the marvellous year of 'forty-eight', which he takes into works like *Mathias Sandorf* (about pro-Hungarian nationalism against Austria), *Little Servant* (about Irish nationalism against Britain) and *Pilot of the Danube* (about Bulgarian nationalism against the Turks). All of these address issues of national independence which were topical at the times in which they were written, betraying a desire to catch popular sentiment.

It is perhaps also with an eye for popular sentiment that in choosing a national struggle for his novel *Le Château des Carpathes*, published in 1892, Verne chose the plight of Transylvanian Vlachs. Chesneaux rightly observes that Verne's internationalist politics are full of 'occasional echoes of pro-French nationalism, anti-English and anti-German feeling'

(Chesneaux, p. 130).[49] Certainly, therefore, in terms of radical causes which could be justly supported without ruffling the feathers of France's mainstream society, the plight of Rumanians in Transylvania would have been a far safer option than the plight of Arabs in French North Africa, especially since it was a struggle that flattered France.

As has been shown throughout this work, vampire novels present political ideas through an embedded symbolism or allegory, which usually allows the author to avoid these issues at a surface level, a point hopefully already proven in the above discussions of Polidori, Le Fanu and Stoker. While not quite a fully fledged vampire novel (although with many hints throughout that it could become one), *Le Château des Carpathes* is nevertheless no exception to this rule, with its symbolic relations of the 'mort-vivant' La Stilla/Angelica to both De Gortz and de Telek, which create two alternative political allegories, one reactionary and cynical, the other revolutionary and libertarian. The pessimism represented by the decrystallisation of La Stilla perhaps shows Verne's cynicism and a very bourgeois fear of revolution and idealism. In this sense the de Gortz figure has an advantage over the de Telek figure, although his realism has led to a cynicism which is morally corrupting in itself.

I would argue, however, that neither of the allegorical meanings has precedence and that the two symbolic meanings are finally left equipoised. The intertext relating to La Stilla creates two possible and ultimately irreconcilable judgements of national freedom and enlightened society which themselves represent Verne's own equivocal and frankly self-contradictory positions towards political causes, as much as they perhaps do towards views of romantic love.

In summation, Verne sets a Gothic novel in Transylvania in order to explore both the extent to which technology may be used to intensify rather than lessen primitive superstitions as a mechanism of control and also to explore the current situation of the oppressed Vlachs of this region, and exploits his sources in order to present the Vlachs in this period as being the sole heroes and the solely oppressed in this region. This was a reaction to the rising crisis in the region as the Rumanian National party tried to object to enforced magyarisation, an issue which, due to long French support for the Rumanians, was a popular issue in France. By use of the exploration of the illusory nature of romantic love from two characters, one Transylvanian Vlach, the other free Rumanian, who have respectively pessimistic and optimistic attitudes to the possibility of physical love with the opera singer La Stilla, Verne also introduces a further political allegory by clever allusion which suggests an equivocal and self-contradictory attitude to the idea of Vlach freedom in Transylvania. His use of allegory through intertext creates a complex assessment and subtlety not seen in the work of Polidori or Mérimée, which reflects the ambivalence towards idealism and revolution which the author himself felt, a man imbued with the romantic flourishes of 'forty-eight' but naturally scared of all insurrections against the status quo.

Conclusion

It is hoped that in the previous chapters the following have been proven: first, that vampire narratives with Near Eastern or Middle European setting are reactive to events in that region of the world rather than being displaced allegories of Irish, British or French social realities; second, that although they may occasionally use cultural valences in order to condemn or condone, they can only be understood by an exact exploration of the historical context and contemporary material conditions rather than by simply relating them always to achronic binaries that transcend the particular date and time. Moreover, it has hopefully been revealed that these works do not always condemn the Ottoman influence in the Balkans in terms of realpolitik, even if, on certain occasions, there is a condemnation of the 'Oriental' (as in Stoker's work: a cultural valence from which, bizarrely, he exonerated the Turks themselves). Another important feature to be shown is that by working through embedded allegory, with its intertextual suggestion rather than overt naming, the vampire's symbolic meaning often collides with the surface expression of the work, subverting it or else, as in Verne's use of the mort-vivant, expressing ambivalent attitudes that can be located to the complex political views of the authors. In all cases there is a pretext for seeing this embedded political allegory about the Near East as an argument that is expressed surreptitiously due to the unfashionable or unacceptable nature of the opinions therein.

It should perhaps be noted that Polidori, Le Fanu and Stoker, while writing for a British public, were all marginal in their way; the one considering himself to be Italian, the other two were Irish Protestants. Polidori's view of Greece is conditioned by an Italian's resentment of philhellenism, and Le Fanu's of Hungary by its resonance with his own Anglo-Irish situation. Stoker's opinion, however, was shaped more simply by both his brother's experiences and probably by his own great interest in Russia and the Eastern Question due to a friendship with Sergei Stepniak. But in all cases, except Stoker's later work *The Lady of the Shroud*, these British writers caution against interference in the Balkans or any tampering with the status quo, in the face of Whigs or Liberals who believed that the opposite should take place. All were reacting to a world over which Britain had no colonial aspirations other than diplomatic influence and to which in all cases they responded pragmatically.

French writers, thanks to the revolution, the establishment of Napoleon's Illyrian Republic and Napoleon III's later grand scheme for aiding the establishment of free nation states in the Near East, have a different set of assumptions entirely, and whether they sanction primitivism, colonialism or the fostering of new states, nevertheless they look at the Near East in more ideal terms (as opposed to the false idealism of Polidori's Greece – a rhetorical trick to condemn Byron and philhellemnism), while British writers who use the vampire allegory are, by contrast, much more motivated by perceived self-interest.

I wish to end by relating the discoveries of this book to the present day. The vampire narrative set in the Near East is a Western, not a Balkan or Middle European, invention. In analysing it and setting it in its context we learn almost nothing about the people who really live there or their own attitudes to history or culture – merely the history of our own attitudes towards them. However, those attitudes towards them have served to condition the way they see us though our portrayal of themselves. As the European Union looks set to embark on a further stage of expansion, we in Britain might do well to keep Fortis – who was a more or less reliable and sympathetic commentator – in one hand and *Dracula* in the other, so that we may attempt to understand both the people who are joining us and the history of our own misconceptions. And then finally their own voice will start to make itself heard with a story far different to any of those analysed above.

Appendix: Translations from Mérimée's *La Guzla*

On vampirism

In Illyria, in Poland, In Hungary, in Turkey and part of Germany, one would risk being reproached for irreligion and immorality if one denied publicly the existence of vampires.

Vampire (*vukodlak* in Illyrian) is the name for a dead man who leaves his tomb, normally at night, and who torments the living. Often he sucks their necks; other times he squeezes their throats to the point of suffocating them. Those who die in such a way by the act of a vampire become vampires themselves after their deaths. It would appear that all feelings of natural affection have been destroyed within vampires; for, it has been noted that they would torment their friends and parents rather than strangers.

Some believe that a man becomes a vampire through divine punishment; others that he has been propelled towards this by a peculiar sort of fate. The most vouched-for opinion is that schismatics buried in holy ground, unable to find any rest therein, and the excommunicated are avenging themselves upon the living for the agonies which they endure.

The signs of vampirism are as follows: a corpse remaining preserved after a time when other bodies have begun to putrefy, the fluidity of blood, the suppleness of limbs etc. It is also said that vampires have their eyes open in their graves and that their nails and hair grow like those of the living. Some of them are recognisable by the noise that they make in their tombs while chewing quite about everything that surrounds them, often their very skin.

The apparitions of these phantoms cease when, after being exhumed, their heads are cut off and their bodies burnt.

The most normal remedy against a first attack by a vampire is to rub the whole of one's body, and above all the part that he has sucked, with the blood contained in his veins, mixed with the earth of his tomb. The wounds that are found on the sickly appear as a little bluish or red stain, like the little scar left by a leech.

Here follow some histories of vampires reported by dom Calmet in his *Treaty on the apparition of spirits and on vampires*, etc.

> At the beginning of september there died in the village of Kisilova, at three leagues from Gradisch, an old man aged sixty-two years, etc. Three days after being buried, he appeared in the night to his son, and demanded that he should have something to eat; once the latter had served him, he ate and then disappeared. The next day the son told his neighbours what had happened. That night the father did not appear; but the following night he turned up and demanded to eat. It is not known whether the son gave him anything or not, but the next day this son was found dead in his bed. The same day, five or six people suddenly fell ill in the village, and died one after the other in a few days.

The officer or bailiff of the place, informed of what had happened, sent a report of this to the court at Belgrade, which sent two of its officers with an executioner into the village to examine this matter. The imperial officer, from whom this account derives, went to Gradisch, in order to witness an event of which he had so often heard talk.

The tombs of all those who had been dead for six weeks were opened: when they came to that of the old man, it was found that the eyes were open, the body red and breathing naturally, although motionless like a dead man; from this it was concluded that he was evidently a vampire. The executioner plunged a stake into the heart. A pyre was made and the corpse reduced to ashes. There was no sign of vampirism found either in the corpse of the son or in those of the others.

About five years ago a certain Haiduk, an inhabitant of Medreiga named Arnold Paul, was crushed by the collapse of a haywain. Thirty days after his death four people died suddenly and in the manner by which according to the tradition of the country, those who are harassed by vampires die. It was then recalled that this Arnold Paul had often told of how he had been tormented by a Turkish vampire in the region of Cassova and on the frontiers of Turkish Serbia (because they also believe that those who have been passive vampires during their lives become active ones after their deaths, which is to say that those who have been sucked also suck in their turn); but that he had found a means of curing himself by eating the earth from the vampire's sepulchre and by rubbing himself with its blood; a precaution which did not prevent him, however, from becoming one after his death, since he was exhumed forty days after his burial, and was found to have all the signs of an archvampire upon his corpse. His body was crimson, his hair, his nails, his beard had all been growing freshly, and his veins were all replete with fluid blood and flowing from all parts of his body onto the shroud in which he was wrapped. The had-nagi or bailiff of the place, in whose presence the exhumation was done, and who was an expert in vampirism, caused there to be plunged, in accordance with custom, a very sharp stake into the heart of Arnold Paul, with which stake they crossed his body from side to side. Having accomplished this action, they cut off his head and burnt him completely. After that, the same action was performed on the corpses of the other four people who had died as a result of vampirism, lest they in their turn should cause others to die.

All these measures still could not prevent the fresh outbreak of these grievous events and deaths towards the end of last year, that is to say at the at the end of five years, with several inhabitants of the same village perishing miserably. In the space of three months, seventeen people of different sexes and different ages died of vampirism, some without being ill, and others after two or three days of languishing. Amongst others there is the account of how one named Stanoska, daughter of the Haiduk Jotuïlzo, who went to bed in perfect health, got up shaking in the middle of the night while making horrendous cries and saying that the son of Haiduk Millo, dead for nine weeks, had all but strangled her during her sleep. From this moment she began to do nothing but languish, and at the end of three days she died. What this girl had said about the son of Millo was what first got him recognised for being a vampire: he was exhumed and found to be such. The leaders of the place, the doctors, the surgeons examined how it was that vampirism had been able to be reborn after the precautions taken some years before.

It was finally discovered, after long research, that the deceased Arnold Paul had killed not only the four people of whom we have talked, but also several beasts of which the new vampires had partaken, the son of Millo being one of them. From these signs the resolution was taken to exhume all those who had been dead for a certain period, etc. From among about forty, seventeen were found with all the most evident signs of vampirism: they likewise were pierced through the heart and decapitated, and afterwards burnt with their ashes then thrown into the river.

'All the reports and actions of which we have just spoken were performed in accordance with the law, properly, and attested to by several officers who are garrisoned in the country, by the surgeon-majors of the regiments and by the most important inhabitants of the place. The statement for this was sent towards the end of last January to the imperial council of war at Vienna, which had established a military commission for examining the truth of all these happenings' (D. Calmet, t. II.).

I will finish by recounting an event of the same sort of which I myself have been witness and which I leave to my readers' contemplation.

In 1816, I had undertaken a journey by foot in the Vorgoraz, and I was lodged in the little village of Varboska. My host was a Morlack, rich by the standards of the country, a very jolly man, a bit of a drunkard, and named Vuck Poglonovich. His wife was young and still beautiful, and his sixteen year old daughter was charming. I wanted to stay some days in the house in order to draw some ancient relics in the neighbourhood, but it was impossible for me to rent a room by offer of money; I had to maintain one through his own hospitality. This made it obligatory for me to endure an insufferable acquaintanceship, in that I was constrained to keep up with my friend Poglonovich as long as it pleased him to stay at the table. Whoever has dined with a Morlack will understand the difficulty of the thing.

One evening, the two women had left us an hour before and, in order to avoid drinking, I was singing certain songs of my country to my host when we were interrupted by the ghastly screams emanating from the bedroom. There is normally only one in the house, and it serves for everybody. We ran there armed and saw a horrible spectacle inside. The mother, pale and dishevelled, was seeing to her unconscious daughter, even paler than herself and stretched out on a bale of straw which served her as a bed. The mother was crying: 'A vampire! A vampire! My poor daughter is dead!'

Our combined concerns made the poor Khava return to consciousness: she had seen, she said, the window opening, and a pale man wrapped in a shroud had thrown himself on her and had bitten her in trying to strangle her. The spectre had fled once she had forced her screams and she had fainted. However, she had thought she recognised in the vampire a local man who had died 15 days before and was called Wiecznany [literally 'the eternal one']. She had a little red mark on her neck; but I am not sure that it was not a sign of something natural or that some insect had not bitten her during her nightmare.

When I hazarded this opinion, the father pushed me back forcibly; the daughter was crying and twisting her arms, repeating endlessly: 'Alas! to die so young before being married!' And the mother poured insults on me, calling me a miscreant, and swearing that she too had seen the vampire with her two eyes and that she had recognised Wiecznany well. I decided it best to keep shut.

Soon all the amulets of the house were hung round the neck of Khava, and her father was saying while swearing that the next day he would go and unearth Wiecznany and that he would burn his body in the presence of all his elder relatives. The night passed in such a way that it was impossible to calm them down.

At daybreak all the village was in motion; the men were armed with rifles and handjars; the women carried red hot irons; the children carried sticks and stones. We went to the cemetery amid the screams and insults with which people were abusing the deceased. I had great trouble in seeing daylight in the middle of that enraged crowd and in placing myself near the ditch.

The exhumation took a long time. Since everybody wanted to take part, there was a lot of barging and jostling, and there would have even been several accidents were it not for the old men, who ordered that only two men should unearth the corpse. At the moment when the sheet which covers the vampire was lifted, a horribly piercing cry made my hair stand on end. It was from a woman next to me: 'It's a vampire! It isn't eaten with worms!' she cried out, and a hundred mouths repeated it in an instant. At the same time twenty rifle shots fired from the hip shattered the head of the corpse to pieces, and the father and older relatives of Khava struck it even harder with their long knives. Some women collected the red liquid which was coming out of the mutilated body on their linen, in order to rub the neck of the sick girl with it.

However, several young people pulled the dead man out of the hole, and, although it was riddled with blows, they still took the precaution of tying it very fast to the trunk of a fir tree; then they dragged it, with all the children following, to a small orchard opposite the house of Poglonovich where faggots meshed with straw had been prepared in advance. They set these alight and then threw the corpse on the fire and began to dance around and to vie with each other in shouting, while continually stoking the log-fire. The infectious smell wafting from it soon forced me to leave them and to return to my host.

His house was full of people: men, pipe in mouth; women speaking all at once and throwing questions at the ill one, who, still very pale, was replying to them with pain. Her neck was wrapped with these scraps coloured with the red and infected liquid which they took for blood, and which made a horrid contrast with the neck and half-naked shoulders of poor Khava.

Little by little this crowd went away, and I remained the only stranger in the house. The illness was long. Khava loathed greatly the approach of night and always wanted someone to watch over her. Since her parents, wearied by their work through the day, had difficulties staying awake, I offered my services as night-nurse, and they were accepted with appreciation. I knew that this proposition would be in no way inconvenient for Morlacks.

I shall never forget the nights that I spent with this unfortunate girl. The creaking of the floorboards, the whistling of the wind – the least noise made her shiver. When she fell asleep, she would have horrible visions, and often she would wake up with a jolt and screaming. Her imagination had been struck by a dream, and all the gossips of the country had managed to turn her mad by telling her horrifying stories. Often, feeling her eyelids closing, she would say to me: 'Do not go to sleep, I beg you. Hold your rosary with one hand and your handjar with the other; guard me well.' At other times she only wanted to go to sleep holding my arm in her two hands, and she squeezed it so forcefully that the impress of her fingers could be seen on it for a long time after.

Nothing could distract her from the melancholy thoughts that harrassed her. She had a great fear of death, and she saw herself as lost without hope, despite all the reasons for consolation of which we could remind her. In a few days she had becoming shockingly thin; her lips were totally discoloured, and her large black eyes appeared yet brighter; she was genuinely terrifying to behold.

I wanted to try to have some effect upon her imagination, by pretending to enter into her thoughts. Unfortunately, since I had at first mocked her credulity, I could no longer make pretence of her confidence. I told her that in my country I had learnt white magic, that I knew a very powerful spell against bad spirits, and that, if she wanted, I would pronounce it at my own risks and perils for love of her.

At first her natural goodness made her afraid of my getting into conflict with the heavens; but soon, the fear of death carrying her away, she begged me to try my spell. I knew by heart several French verses of Racine; I recited them loudly in front of the poor girl, who nevertheless believed she was hearing the devil's own words. Then, by rubbing her neck on several occasions, I pretended to draw from it a small piece of red agate that I had hidden between my fingers. Then I assured her in a serious tone that I had pulled it from out of her neck and that she was saved. But she looked at me sadly and told me: 'You are deceiving me; you had that stone in a little box, I saw you with it. You are not a magician.' Thus my ruse did her more harm than good. From that moment she became ever worse and worse.

The night before her death she told me: 'It is my fault if I die. A certain man (she named a boy in the village) wanted to run off with me. I didn't want to, and I asked him for a silver chain in order for me to follow him. He went to Marcaska to buy one and during that time the vampire came. In any case, she added, if I hadn't been in the house, he would have perhaps killed my mother. And so, it is for the best.' The next day she asked for her father to come and made him promise to cut her throat and knee-backs himself, so that she did not herself become a vampire, and she wished that no one but her father should commit these useless atrocities upon her body. Then she kissed her mother and begged her to go and bless a rosary at the tomb of a male saint near the village, and to bring it back to her afterwards. I admired the generosity of this peasant girl, who thought of this pretext for preventing her mother from being present at her last moments. She made me unfasten an amulet from around her neck. 'Keep it, she told me, I hope that it will be of more use to you than it was to me.' Then she received the sacraments with devotion. Two or three hours afterwards, her breathing became heavier, and her eyes fixed in a stare. All of a sudden she seized her father's arm and made an effort as if to throw herself on his breast; she had just stopped living. Her illness had lasted eleven days.

I left the village some hours later, heartily wishing in hell vampires, revenants and those that tell stories about them.

Poems

The following translations include endnotes that are part of the original text and are thus an integral part of each poem, rather than additions as a result of this study.

Beautiful Sophie[1]

Lyrical Scene

Characters

Nïcéphore
The Bey of Moïna
The hermit
The Kuum[2]
Sophie
Choir of young people
Choir of the 'Svati' (bride and bridegroom's families)[3]
Choir of young girls

I

The young people

Young people of Vrachina, saddle your black chargers, saddle your black chargers with their embroidered covers: today deck yourselves in your black costumes; today everyone must have an ataghan with a silver handle and pistols garnered with a watermark. Is it not today that the rich Bey of Moïna is marrying the beautiful Sophie?

II

Nicéphore

My mother! My mother! Is my black mare saddled. My mother! My mother! My black mare has neighed: give me the decorated pistols that I took to a bimbachi; give me my ataghan with silver handle. Listen, my mother, I have ten sequins left in a silver purse; I want to throw them to the musicians at the wedding. Is it not today that the rich Bey of Moïna is marrying the beautiful Sophie?

III

The families

Oh! Sophie, put on your red veil, the cavalcade is advancing; hear the pistol shots that they are firing in your honour.[4] Music-maids, sing the story of Jean Valathiano and the beautiful Agathe; you, old men, make your guzlas resound; you, Sophie, take a screen, throw some nuts.[5] May you have many boys! The rich Bey of Moïna is marrying the beautiful Sophie.

IV

Svati

Walk to my right, my mother; walk to my left, my sister. My elder brother, hold the horse's bridle; my younger brother, support the crupper. – What is this pale young man who is advancing on a black mare? Why doesn't he mingle with the troop of young family-members? Ah! I recognise Nicéphore; I fear that some bad luck may be coming. Nicéphore loved me before the rich Bey of Moïna.

V

Nicéphore

Sing, music-maids, sing like cicadas! I have only ten pieces of gold; I shall give five of them to the music-maids, five to the guzla players. – Oh! Bey of Moïna, why do you look at me with fear? Are you not the beloved of the beautiful Sophie? Don't you have as many sequins as you have black hairs in your beard? My pistols are not destined for you. Hoo! Hoo! My black mare, gallop to the valley of tears. This evening I shall release you from bridle and saddle, this evening you shall be free and without master.

VI

The young girls

Sophie, Sophie, may all the saints bless you! Bey of Moïna, may all the saints bless you! May you have twelve beautiful sons, all blond, hardy and courageous! The sun is setting, the bey is waiting alone under his felt roof: Sophie, hasten, say goodbye to your mother, follow the kuum: this evening you will rest on silk patches; you are the wife of the rich Bey of Moïna.

VII

The Hermit

Who dares to fire a gun shot near my cell? Who dares to kill the deers who are under the protection of Saint Chrysostome and his hermit? But it isn't a deer that this gunshot has struck, this bullet has killed a man, and there is his black mare that wanders in liberty. May God have pity on your soul, poor traveller! I am going away to dig a tomb for you in the sand around the stream.

VIII

Sophie

Oh! My lord, how icy your hands are! Oh! My lord, how damp is your hair! I tremble in your bed despite your Persian blankets. In truth, my lord, your body is icy; I am very cold, I shiver, I tremble; a cold sweat has covered all my limbs. Ah! Holy mother of God, have pity on me, but I believe I am going to die.

IX

The Bey of Moïna

Where is she, where is she, my beloved, the beautiful Sophie? Why doesn't she come beneath my tent of felt? Slaves, run and seek her, and tell the music-maids to increase their songs. May my mother put beautiful Sophie back with the wedding kuum; I have been alone in my tent for a very long time.

X

The Kuum

Noble families, may everyone refill his cup, may everyone empty his cup! The bride has taken our sequins, she has stolen our silver chains[6]; to avenge ourselves, let us not leave a pitcher of brandy in their house. The newly weds have retired; I have undone the belt of the husband, let us abandon ourselves to joy. Beautiful Sophie is marrying the rich Bey of Moïna.

XI

Sophie

My lord, what have I done to you? Why do you press my chest so? It is as though a leaden corpse were on my breast. Holy mother of God! My throat is so squeezed, that I believe I am going to suffocate. O my friends, come to my help! the Bey of Moïna wants to strangle me! O my mother! O my mother! Come to my help, for he has bitten me in the vein of my neck, and he is sucking my blood.

Notes

1. This very old piece, reframed with a dramatic form that one rarely comes across in Illyrian poems, is considered a model of style among Morlack players of the guzla. It is said that a true anecdote has provided the theme to this ballad, and there is still in the valley of the Scign an old tomb which conceals the beautiful Sophie and the Bey of Moïna.
2. The Kuum is the godfather of either the bride or bridegroom. He accompanies them to the church and follows them until they are in their bedroom, where he undoes the husband's belt, who, on that day, in accordance with an ancient superstition, cannot cut, do up, nor undo anything. The kuum even has the right to make the bride and bridegroom undress in his presence. When he judges that the marriage has been consummated, he lets off a gunshot in the air, which is immediately accompanied by shouts of joy and gunshots from by all the couples' families.
3. These are the members of the two families joined for the marriage. The chief of one of the two families is the president of the combined families and is called the *stari-svat*. Two young people, called *diveri*, accompany the bride and only leave at the moment when the kuum reunites her with her husband.
4. During the procession of the bride, the families continually shoot their pistols, an obligatory accompaniment to all celebrations, and give out appalling screams. Add to that the guzla players and music-maids, who sing wedding hymns that are frequently improvised, and you will get the idea of the horrible cacophony of a Morlack wedding.
5. The bride, on arriving at her husband's house, receives from the hands of his mother-in-law or from one of his parents (from the husband's side) a screen filled with nuts; she throws it above her head and then kisses the doorstep.

6. The wife only has her clothes and sometimes a cow for her dowry; but she has the right to demand a present from each of the family members; furthermore, all that she can steal from them is considered fairly hers. In 1812, I lost in this way a most beautiful watch; fortunately the bride was not aware of its value, and I was able to buy it back in return for two sequins.

Le Vampire[1]

I

In the swamp of Stavila, near to a source, is a corpse lying on its back. It is a scurrilous Venetian who deceived Marie and who burnt our houses. A bullet pierced his throat, an ataghan was run through his heart; but, three days after he was put in the earth, his blood is still running red and hot.

II

His blue eyes are lifeless, but observe the sky: woe to him who passes near to this corpse! Who could escape the fascination of his look? His beard is longer, his nails have grown[2]; the crows keep far from him through fright, as they cling to the brave Haiduks who are strewn over the earth around him.

III

His mouth is bloody and smiles like that of a man asleep and tormented by a hideous love. Approach, Marie, come and look at the one for whom you have betrayed your family and your nation! Dare to kiss those pale and bloody lips which knew so well how to lie. Alive he caused many tears; dead he will cause even more.

Notes

1. This fragment of a ballad recommends itself only through the beautiful description of a vampire. It seems to be referring to some little war of the Haiduks against the Venetian potentates.
2. Evident signs of vampirism.

Cara-Ali, the Vampire

I

Cara-Ali passed the yellow river[1]; he climbed towards Basile Kaïmis and took lodgings in his house.

II

Basile Kaïmis had a beautiful wife, named Jumeli; she looked at Cara-Ali, and fell in love with him.

III

Cara-Ali is covered in rich furs; he has decorated arms, and Basile is poor.

IV

Jumeli was seduced by all his riches; for what woman can resist a lot of gold?

V

Cara-Ali, having had the pleasure of this unfaithful wife, wanted to elope with her to his own country, among the unbelievers.

VI

And Jumeli said that she would follow him; wicked woman, who would prefer the harem of an infidel to a marriage bed!

VII

Cara-Ali took her by her fine waist and put her in front of him on his beautiful horse, white as the snow of November.

VIII

Where are you, Basile? Cara-Ali, whom you received in your house is eloping with your wife Jumeli whom you love so much!

IX

He ran to the edge of the yellow river and saw the two traitors who were crossing it on a white horse.

X

He took his long rifle adorned with ivory and with red tassels;[2] he fired, and immediately Cara-Ali reeled on his mount.

XI

'Jumeli! Jumeli! Your love is costing me dear. This dog of an unbeliever has killed me and will kill you too.'

XII

'Now, so that he lets you live, I am going to give you a precious talisman, with which you will buy your salvation.'

XIII

'Take this Koran in this cartridge pouch of decorated red leather[3]; whoever inquires inside it is always rich and beloved by women.'

XIV

'May he who carries this book open it at the sixty-sixth page; he will command all the spirits of the earth and water.'

XV

Then he fell into the yellow river and his body floated leaving a red cloud in the middle of the water.

XVI

Basile Kaïmis ran up and seizing the horse's bridle raised his arm to kill his wife.

XVII

'Spare me my life, Basile, and I will give you a precious talisman: he who carries it is always rich and beloved by women.'

XVIII

'May he who carries it open the book at the sixty-sixth[4] page; he will command all the spirits of the earth and water.'

XIX

Basile pardoned his unfaithful wife; he took the book that every Christian ought to throw with horror onto the fire.

XX

Night fell; a great wind whipped itself up, and the yellow river flooded over; the corpse of Cara-Ali was thrown on the bank.

XXI

Basile opened the impious book at the sixty-sixth page; suddenly the earth trembled with a frightful noise.

XXII

A bloody spectre pierced the earth; it was Cara-Ali, 'Basile you are mine now that you have renounced your God.'

XXIII

He seized the unfortunate one, biting him by the neck and not leaving him until he had emptied his veins.

XXIV

He who has made this story is Nicolas Cossiewitch, who learnt it from the grandmother of Jumeli.

Notes

1. Probably the Zamargna, which is very yellow in Autumn.
2. This ornament is frequently to be found on the rifles of Illyrians and Turks.
3. Almost all Muslims carry a Koran in a little cartridge pouch of red leather.
4. The number sixty-six is considered very powerful in spells.

The Montenegrins[1]

I

Napoleon said 'What are these men who dare to resist me? I want them to come and throw their rifles and their ataghans adorned with ear corns[2] at my feet.' Immediately he sent twenty thousand soldiers to the mountain.

II

There are dragoons, foot-soldiers, cannons and mortars. 'Come to the mountain, you will see there five hundred brave Montenegrins. For their cannons, there are precipices; for their dragoons, rocks; and for foot-soldiers, five hundred good rifles.'

III[3]

....
....

IV

They left; their arms glistened in the sunlight; they climbed so they could burn our villages; they climbed to abduct our wives and children to their own country.[4] When they arrived at the grey rock, they looked up and saw our red caps.

V

Then their captain said: 'May each man cock his rifle, may each man kill a Montenegrin.' As soon as they shot, they brought down our red caps which were mounted on pickets.[5] We, however, who were lying on our stomachs behind them, gave the French a lively fusillade.

VI

'Listen to the echo of our rifles,' said the captain. But, before he had returned fire, he fell dead and so did twenty-five men with him. The others took flight and never in their lives did they dare look at another red cap.

He who made this song was with his brothers on the grey rock; he is named Guntzar Wossieratch.

Notes

1. It is not only small peoples who imagine that the gaze of the universe is fixed upon them. Nevertheless, I believe that Napoleon was never greatly preoccupied by the Montenegrins.
2. These are the decorations chiselled on the handles of precious arms, above all on the ataghans. The carvings are filled with a beautiful bluey-black composition, the secret of whose make-up is, it is said, lost in the Levant.
3. Here a stanza is missing.
4. The custom of waging war with the Turks made the Montenegrins think that all nations enacted the same atrocities in their military excursions.
5. This trick was frequently used with success.

Notes

Introduction

1. R.H.R., *Rambles in Istria, Dalmatia and Montenegro* (London: Hurst and Blackett, 1875), p. 160.
2. Wolff, Larry, *Venice and the Slavs: The Discovery of Dalmatia in the Age of Enlightenment* (Stanford CA: Stanford University Press, 2001), p. 17.
3. Kinglake, Alexander, *Eothen* (London: George Rutledge and Sons, 1905), p. 1.
4. Woods, H. Charles, *The Danger Zone of Europe: Changes and Problems in the Near East* (London and Leipsic: T. Fisher Unwin, 1911), p. 7.
5. '[A] tottering and untoward neighbour' as the otherwise Turcophile Stratford described it just before the Treaty of Berlin (1878) – de Redcliffe, Viscount Stratford, *The Eastern Question: Being a Selection from his Writings During the Last Five Years of His Life*, with a preface by Arthur Penrhyn Stanley (London: John Murray, 1881), p. 6.
6. Todorova, Maria, *Imagining the Balkans* (Oxford and New York: Oxford University Press), p. 22.
7. Said, Edward, *Orientalism*, rev. edn (London: Penguin, 1995), p. 14.
8. In one chapter of his *The Spirit of the East*, called 'Social Intercourse with the Turks', Urquhart also argues that the Turks have gained a negative image from some European travellers because their religion forbids them from having too much intercourse with Europeans and because the majority of West Europeans they meet are quacks and charlatans. Acquaintance shows them to be a worthy people – Urquhart, David, *The Spirit of the East: A Journal of Travels through Roumali*, 2 vols (London: H. Colburn, 1838), I 362–4. He argues, at the end, that European powers should be helping and encouraging them rather than condemning them (I 369–70).
9. Linda Colley also details the accounts of travellers like Major Lowe, who registered in 1801 a great fear and respect for the Turks and the insurmountability of the Ottoman Empire – Colley, Linda, *Captives: Britain, Empire and the World 1600–1850* (London: Jonathan Cape, 2002), p. 133.
10. Canning argued through most of his life that the maintenance of Turkish rule in the Balkans was important, and as Arthur Penrhyn Stanley wrote in a preface to his works 'His policy was as simple as it was effective – to maintain the ottoman empire by reforming its abuses. The Turks listened to his rebukes because they knew that he was their friend' (de Redcliffe, *The Eastern Question*, p. ix). In the above selection, from articles written between 1874–80, Canning argued that the right response for England at the time of possible Ottoman disintegration – the crunch time in the Eastern Question – was to support Turkey, and he urged England to act to prevent an 'injurious dismemberment of Turkey' (de Redcliffe, *The Eastern Question*, p. 7).
11. Cunningham, Allan, 'Stratford Canning and the Treaty of Bucharest' in *Anglo-Ottoman Encounters in the Age of Revolution*, collected Essays, [Allan

Cunningham] ed. Edward Ingram, 2 vols (London: Frank Cass, 1995) I 144–87, at 179–80.

12. Burke, Edmund, *A Philosophical Enquiry into the Origin of our Ideas of the Sublime and Beautiful*, ed. Adam Phillips (Oxford and New York: Oxford University Press, 1990), p. 36: pt 1: Sect. VII.

13. Punter, David, *The Literature of Terror* (London: Longman, 1981), pp. 104–5.

14. Barbour, Judith, 'Dr John William Polidori, Author of the Vampire', *Imagining Romanticism: Essays on English and Australian Romanticism*, eds Peter Otto and Deirdre Coleman (West Cornwall CT: Locust Hill Press, 1992), pp. 85–110, at p. 86.

15. Twitchell, James, *The Living Dead: A Study of the Vampire in Romantic Literature* (Durham NC: Duke University Press, 1981), pp.10–12.

16. Leatherdale, Clive, *Dracula: The Novel and the Legend*, rev. edn (Brighton: Desert Island Books, 1988), pp. 173–4.

17. Pick, Daniel, *Faces of Degeneration: A European Disorder, c. 1848–c. 1918* (Cambridge: Cambridge University Press, 1989), pp. 170–3.

18. Arata, Stephen D., 'The Occidental Tourist: *Dracula* and the Anxiety of Reverse Colonisation', *Victorian Studies*, 33:4 (1990) 621–45, at 634.

19. Hughes, William, 'A Singular Invasion: Revisiting the Postcoloniality of Bram Stoker's *Dracula's Empire and the Gothic: The Politics of Genre*, eds Andrew Smith and William Hughes (Basinstoke: Palgrave Macmillan, 2003), pp. 88–102, at p. 91.

20. de Man, Paul, *Allegories of Reading: Figural Language in Rousseau, Nietzsche, Rilke and Proust* (New Haven: Yale University Press, 1979), p. 13.

21. Jameson, Fredric, 'Third-world Literature in the Era of Multinational Capitalism' (1986), *The Jameson Reader* (Oxford: Blackwell, 2000), pp. 315– 40, at p. 320.

22. Moore-Gilbert, Bart, *Postcolonial Theory: Contexts, Practices, Politics* (London and New York: Verso, 1997), pp. 129–30.

23. Féval, Paul, *La Vampire* (Castelnau-le-Lez: Bibliothèque Ombres, 2004), pp. 12–16.

24. Féval, Paul, *Le Chevalier Ténèbre, Suivi de La Ville Vampire* (Verviers: Marabout,1972, p. 118).

25. Quoted in Nodier, Charles, *Infernalia: ou Anecdotes, Petits Romans Nouvelles et Contes, sur les Révenants, les Spectres, les Démons et les Vampires*, preface by de Hubert Juin (Paris: Pierre Belfond, 1966), p. 177.

26. Féval, Paul *The Vampire Countess*, trans. and ed. Brian Stableford (Encino CA: Black Coat Press, 2003), pp. 22–3.

27. For information on the political background see the introduction to Féval, Paul, *Knightshade [Le Chevalier Ténèbre]*, trans. and ed. Brian Stableford (Mountain Ash: Sarob Press, 2001), p. xvii.

1 Polidori's *The Vampyre* and the Dangers of Philhellenism to Italian Liberation

1. Skarda, Patricia L, 'Vampirism and Plagiarism: Byron's Influence and Polidori's Practice', *Studies in Romanticism* 28:2 (Summer 1969), 249–69, at 250–1. Skarda notes that the name Aubrey is taken from that of a young antiquary of

the seventeenth century, John Aubrey (1626–97), whose work had been published in 1813, but rightly asserts that in the story he is 'in part, an image of Polidori' (Skarda, *Studies in Romanticism*, 28:2 251).

2. Skarda states that: 'Polidori harvests images and phrases and setting from Byron's *Giaour* for the Ianthe in his 'Vampyre' not merely because Byron's fields were fertile but because Polidori could not find his own' (Skarda, *Studies in Romanticism*, 28:2 255).

3. Gelder, Ken, *Reading the Vampire* (London and New York: 1994), p. 34.

4. MacCarthy, Fiona, *Byron: Life and Legend* (London: John Murray, 2002), pp. 374–5.

5. Nicolson, Harold , *The Congress of Vienna: A Study in Allied Unity: 1812–1822* , repr. (London: Cassell, 1979), p. 243.

6. Spencer, Terence, *Fair Greece, Sad Relic*, 2nd edn (Bath: Cedric Chivers, 1974), pp. 195–6.

7. Todorova, Maria, *Imagining the Balkans* (Oxford and New York: Oxford University Press, 1997), pp. 91–5.

8. In his *Osservazioni di Ludovico de Breme* (Milano: G.Pirotta, 1818), di Breme praised the work of Lord Byron for concentrating on villains like the giaour, because he felt that this allowed him to 'explore the depths of the human heart' ['trattegiare la pronfondità del cuore umano'] due to the moral complexities involved and the sheer range of feelings which it presents. 'Here romantic poetry is on its preferred province, and no-one will want to deny us that that epoch may not have arrived, in which great advances over antiquity have been made in understanding the human heart' ['Qua la poesia romantica si trova nella sua provincia prediletta, e nessuno ci vorra negare che non sia giunta quell'epoca, in cui molto si sopravvanza l'antichità in fatto di cognizione del cuore umano'] – quoted in Cotrone, Renata, *Romanticismo Italiano: Prospettive Critiche e Percorsi Intelletualli di Breme Visconti Scalvini* (Manduria-Bari-Roma: Piero Laica Editore, 1996), p. 114. Thus di Breme saw in Byron's attempts to emancipate the souls of his characters and, crucially, to raise the mind above the material, an improvement upon classical models of art, and the dawn of a new epoch.

9. In a long footnote to Book VIII of his Yemeni-based epic *Thalaba*, Southey provided the scholarly basis for the detail of Oneira, Thalaba's beloved, becoming a vampire before being speared – Southey, Robert, *Thalaba the Destroyer*, 2 vols (London: T.N. Longman and O. Rees, 1801), II 03–21. The note includes three different accounts: the story of the old man of Gradisch who killed his son, from the *Lettres Juives* in *Mercure Historique et Politique*, October 1736 (Southey, *Thalaba the Destroyer*, II104–6); the story, from the edge of 'Transilvania', of the Haiduk Arnold Paul, who became a vampire after being bruised by a cart and was staked in the heart, but not before infecting another man 'Millo' with the disease, who in turn preyed on the small girl Stanoska – from *The Gleaner*, no 18, 1732 (Southey, *Thalaba the Destroyer*, II107–11); and finally, the story of the ill-natured man of Mycone (an island in Greece) who becomes a 'Vroucolacas' (Southey, *Thalaba the Destroyer*, 114) and who, despite being exhumed and staked through the heart by the butcher, refuses to die, until the magistrate orders the body to be burnt: a story told by Tournefort – Calmet, Augustin, *Dissertation sur les Appareitions des Anges, des Démons. Et des Esprits et sur les Revenans et Vampires, De Hongrie, de Bohème, Moravie et de Silesie* (Paris: de Buré

l'aîné, 1746), pp. 278–80; 280–4; 352–61 (the first story is also originally from *Lettres Juives* but was found in a 1732 account of *Le Glaineur* by Calmet). Although it is highly likely that Southey consulted *Mercure Historique et Politique*, the initial source for all of these stories would have been Calmet, since it is there that they are all collected under one binding.

10. In a footnote recounting the superstition, Byron writes: 'The Vampire superstition is still general in the Levant. Honest Tournefort tells a long story, which Mr Southey, in the notes on Thalaba, quotes, about these 'Vroucolochas', as he calls them. The Romaic term is 'Vardoulacha'. I recollect a whole family being terrified by the scream of a child, which they imagined must proceed from such a visitation. The Greeks never mention the word without horror' – Byron, Lord George, *Complete Poetical Works*, ed. Frederick Page, rev. John Jump (Oxford, New York and London: Oxford University Press, 1970), p. 894.

11. *Goethe's Bride of Corinth*, trans. W. A. Cox (Cambridge, 1911), p. 8, st. 9.

12. *The Diary of Dr. John William Polidori (1816) Relating to Byron, Shelley etc.*, ed. William Rossetti (London: Elkin Mathews, 1911), p. 15 (2 April 1819).

13. Macdonald, David Lorne, *Poor Polidori: A Critical Biography of the Author of 'The Vampyre'* (Toronto, Buffalo and London: University of Toronto Press, 1991), p. 97.

    Polidori gives no mention of staying with other people in the Geneva set after his break-up with Byron and appears to have set off straight away for Italy, but one cannot be absolutely sure, since he was an erratic diarist.

14. Byron, Lord, 'A Fragment', in Shelley, Mary, *Frankenstein*, ed. Maurice Hindle (London: Penguin, 1991), pp. 227– 2, at p. 231.

15. Burke, Edmund, *A Philosophical Enquiry into the Origin of our Ideas of the Sublime and Beautiful*, ed. Adam Phillips (Oxford and New York: Oxford University Press, 1990), p. 36: pt 1: Sect. VII.

16. McGann, Jerome, *Byron and Romanticism*, ed. James Soderholm (Cambridge: Cambridge University Press, 2002), pp. 39–40. McGann notices how Lady Adeline, to whom Byron attributes 'mobility' in the sixteenth Canto of *Don Juan* – the 'susceptibility to immediate impressions – at the same time without *losing* the past' (Byron, *Poetry*, p. 920) – appears at first unreal to Juan but is in actual fact simply a person too given over to spontaneity and emotional fluctuation, to the point where she seems unreal due to her constant flux. McGann sees this fluctuation in the political ironies and 'ventriloquism' of Byron's poetry, not to mention its self-consciousness over what is otherwise spontaneity in poetic construction. However, it seems to me that Byron's immeditate consideration is concerned with emotional self-contradiction, since 'movement' coupled with this sense of never losing normal consciousness is similar to the Kantian sublime, except that at the moment of the imagination's free play, Kant's subject does lose all consciousness of their former self or an underlying reality, moving through a multitude of different emotions – Kant, Immanuel, *Critique of Judgement*, trans. James Creed Meredith (Oxford: Clarendon Press, 1952), Bk 2, n. 54, pp. 196–203.

17. Derrida, Jacques, *Of Grammatology*, trans. Gayatri Chakravorty Spivak (Baltimore and London: Johns Hopkins University Press, 1976), pp. 118–40.

18. Although Patricia Skarda has argued that Polidori was a 'parrot' rather than a 'critic' of his famous patient (Skarda, *Studies in Romanticism*, 28:2, 249–69, at

p. 255), she neglects to inform the reader that Polidori was supposed to be 'repeating' and 'completing' Byron's work in writing the story, which places his borrowings in an altogether different light.

19. Leask, Nigel, *British Romantic Writers and the East: Anxieties of Empire*, repr. (Cambridge: Cambridge University Press, 2004), p. 30.

20. Polidori, John, *Ximenes, the Wreath and other Poems* (London: Longman, Hurst, Rees, Orme, and Brown, Paternoster-Row, 1819), p. 11.

21. When travelling in Switzerland, Polidori describes how 'At Wyssenbach they all said grace before breakfast, and then ate out of the same dish; remarking (as I understood them) that I, not being Catholic, would laugh' (*Diary of Dr John William Polidori*, p. 155; 19 September 1816). To this the editor William Rossetti writes: 'It was a mistake to suppose that Dr Polidori was 'not a Catholic'. He was brought up as a Catholic, and never changed his religion, but may (I suppose) have been something of a sceptic' (p. 155).

22. Woolf, Stuart, *A History of Italy, 1700–1860* (London: Routledge, 1979), pp. 161–7.

23. One movement which had sporadically played a part in the pre-Napoleonic Italy and which was given sustenance by the French threat was Jacobin Unitarianism: the movement to see Italy become one country, as a guarantee of defence against external foes (Woolf, *A History of Italy*, p. 186).

24. Thayer, W. R., *The Dawn of Italian Independence*, 2 vols (Boston and New York: Houghton, Mifflin and Co., 1893), I112–3.

25. Pavlovic, Stevan K., *La France en Dalmatie: Naissance de l'Idée Illyrienne*, repr. from *Le College et le Monde* (London: 1950), p. 3.

26. Napoleon's day-to-day ruler of his Kingdom of Italy.

27. Granville, Augusto Bozzi, *L' Italico, Ossia Giornale Politico, Letterario e Miscellaneo; da una Società d'Italiani*, 3 vols (Londra: Schulze e Dean, 1813–14), I, p. 3.

28. He goes on to affirm his sense of Italianness in comparison to the English in the same letter, to his father, of December 1813 when he wrote of going to fight for Italy (Macdonald, *Poor Polidori*, p. 20).

29. Ugo Foscolo(1778–1827), nineteenth-century nationalist poet.

30. One sonnet, 'On Buonaparte entering Italy', represents this view of Napoleon the traitor to Italy admirably. Polidori remarks how 'With smiles Ausonia looks upon her child, / And spreads her richly-gifted land / Before his gaze. – With hope, see! see! she's wild, /That freedom's hers, and by his hand./ But what! what! rushes on my wilder'd sight? / Ah, Italy! no hope is thine – / Thy son against thee rushes to the fight;/ His country's spoils upon him shine – / And thou as peasant sit'st, who's viewed his corn, / By force of clouds he pray'd for, beat down, torn' (Polidori, *Ximenes*, p. 161). These anti-Napoleonic sentiments are similar to those of his sonnet 'On Entering Italy, Sept. 26, 1816', when he talks of the empire that 'bound in chains this land' (p. 160).

31. Pignotti, Lorenzo, *Storia della Toscana Sino al Principato con diversi Saggi sulle Scienze, Lettere e Arte*, 9 vols (Pisa: Co Caratteri di Didot, 1813), VIII 109–20.

32. Denton, William, *Montrenegro: Its People and their History* (London: Dalby, Isbister and Co., 1877), pp. 259–60.

33. After the Treaty of Adrinaople in 1829, Moldavia and Wallachia became Russian principalities – Logio, George Clenton, *Rumania: Its History, Politics and Economics* (Manchester: Sherratt and Hughes, 1932), p. 18.

2   J. Sheridan Le Fanu's *Carmilla* and the Austro–Hungarian *Ausgleich* (1867)

1. McCormack, W. J., *Sheridan Le Fanu and Victorian Ireland* (Oxford: Clarendon Press, 1980), p. 221. McCormack lists the small number of political articles in the *Dublin University Magazine* written between 1867 and 1869, some of which may have been written by Le Fanu, although none with any certainty. In his letters to his cousin the Marquis of Dufferin, Le Fanu details his complaint about the Tory Brewster (21 January 1868) who became Chancellor, and used Le Fanu's journalism to promote himself before dropping his friend, and was now accusing Le Fanu of having militated against him in the *Dublin Evening Mail*. At the end of the year (7 December 1868), Le Fanu is complaining to his illustrious cousin about the possibility of there being a Catholic Chancellor in Ireland, because he felt that it would prove divisive at that particular time. He never broaches foreign politics in the 12 letters to Lord Dufferin, now collected at the Public Records Office of Northern Ireland.

2. Copjec, Joan, 'Vampires, Breast-Feeding, and Anxiety', *October*, 58 (1991), pp. 25–43, at p. 36. Dolar, Mladen, ' "I shall be with you on your Wedding Night": Lacan and the Uncanny', *October*, 58 (1991), 5–23.

3. Calmet, Augustin, *The Phantom World: Or, the Philosophy of Spirits, Apparitions etc*, ed. and trans. Rev. Henry Christmas, 2 vols (London: Richard Bentley, 1850), II 6.

4. As in J. M. Rymer's *Varney, the Vampyre; Or, the Feast of Blood* (London: E. Lloyd, 1845–47), which is set in England, or Planche's *The Vampire, or the Bride of the Isles. A Romantic Melodrama in two Acts, Preceded by an Introductory Vision* (London,1820) which is set in the Orkneys.

5. Bhalla, Alok, *Politics of Atrocity and Lust*, (New Delhi: Sterling, 1989), p. 30.

6. Foster, Roy, 'Protestant Magic: W.B. Yeats and the Spell of Irish History', *Paddy and Mr Punch: Connections in Irish and English History* (London: Allen Lane, 1993), pp. 212–32, at p. 220.

7. Le Fanu, J. S., *Uncle Silas*, ed. W. J. McCormack with the assistance of Andrew Swarbrick (Oxford: Oxford University Press, 1981), pp. xviii–xix.

8. Sage, Victor, *Le Fanu's Gothic* (Basingstoke: Palgrave, 2003), p. 199. In earlier novels like *The Cock and the Anchor* (1845), Le Fanu had referred to the corrupt settlement era, as Sage successfully shows (Sage, *Le Fanu's Gothic*, pp. 31–7).

9. Leger, Louis, *A History of Austro–Hungary from the Earliest Time to the Year 1889*, trans. from the French by Mrs Birkbeck Hill (London: Rivingtons, 1889), p. 315.

10. Szabad, Emeric, *Hungary: Past and Present: Embracing its History from the Magyar Conquest to the Present Time* (Edinburgh: Adam and Charles Black, 1854), pp. 126–7.

11. Jelavich, Barbara, *Modern Austria: Empire and Republic, 1800–1986* (Cambridge: Cambridge University Press, 1987), pp. 21–3.

12. Pribram, Alfred Francis, *Austria–Hungary and Great Britain, 1908–1914*, trans. Ian F. D. Morrow (London, New York and Toronto: Oxford University Press, 1951), pp. 39–41.

13. Judd, Dennis, *Palmerston* (London: Weidenfield and Nicholas, 1975), pp. 85 and 140.

14. Le Fanu, J. S., *In a Glass Darkly*, ed. Robert Tracy (Oxford: Oxford University Press, 1993), p. 318.

15. This was reversed by Count Teleki, the adviser to the King of Transylvania who negotiated peace with the Austrians before the Treaty of Karlowicz and engaged with Tököli on the battlefield.

16. Copjec, Joan, 'Vampires, Breast-Feeding, and Anxiety', *October*, 58 (1991), pp. 25–43, at p. 36.

17. The account is from the Moravian Village of Liebava, from a priest who accompanied Canon Jeanin of Olmütz cathedral to investigate a vampire. A passing Hungarian, boasting that he could rid the town of the scourge, stole the vampire's clothes and signalled to him when he was at the top of the steeple. When the vampire came down to reclaim them, the Hungarian lopped off his head (Christmas, 'Calmet, Augustin, *The Phantom World: Or, the Philosophy of Spirits, Apparitions etc*, ed. and trans. Rev. Henry Christmas'] II 209–10). The story in Le Fanu's tale is almost exactly the same except that the vampire is (presumably) a Hungarian and the slayer a Moravian (Le Fanu, *In a Glass Darkly*, pp. 307–8). It is the same 'remarkable man' whose documents now permit the Baron Vordernberg to excavate Karnstein and who had in fact previously been Carmilla's lover (Le Fanu, *In a Glass Darkly*, p. 318).

18. Marigny, Jean, *Vampires* (London and Paris: Gallimard, 1994), p. 37.

19. Baring-Gould, Sabine, *The Book of Were-wolves* (London: Senate, 1995), p. 139.

20. Nethercott, Arthur H., 'Coleridge's "Christabel" and Le Fanu's "Carmilla" ', *Modern Philology*, 147 (1949), 32–8. See also Silvani, Giovanna, *Analisi di un Racconto Gotico: Camilla di J. S. Le Fanu*, Quaderni dell'instituto di Lingue e Letterature Germaniche no. 3, Universita degli studi di Parma (Roma: Bulzoni, 1984), p. 31.

21. Coleridge, Samuel Taylor, *Poetical Works*, ed. Ernest Hartley Coleridge (Oxford: Oxford University Press, 1909), pp. 224 and 267.

22. Piper, Horatio Walter, *The Singing of Mount Abora: Coleridge's Use of Biblical Imagery and Natural Symbolism in Poetry and Philosophy* (Rutherford, Madison and Teaneck: Fairleigh Dickinson University Press; London and Toronto: Associated University Presses, 1987), p. 77.

23. Particularly Polish, Slovak and Ukrainian.

24. Diminutives of Polish words are achieved with a /sz/ sound (pronounced /sh/) followed by a /ka/ and are used to signify affection. In Russian the word 'matka' means 'womb'. The diminutive is frequently used with women's names – for example, 'Kasia' (pronounced Kasha) becomes 'Kaszka' – 'dear little Kate'. The word 'matka' in Polish , meaning 'mother', already ends with /ka/ in its root form and is in fact made diminutive through the term 'mama', or in Slovenian something like the word 'mati'.

25. Hall, Captain Basil, *Schloss Hainfeld; or, a Winter in Lower Styria* (Edinburgh: Robert Cadell, 1836), pp. 1–3.

26. One such is J. G. Kohl's *Austria, Vienna, Prague, Hungary, Bohemia, and the Danube; Galicia, Styria, Moravia, Bukovina and the Military Frontier* (London: Chapman and Hall, 1843). This book centres, like most others, on Styria's many mines and the peasant customs rather than describing the deserted castles and dark gloomy forests which find their way into Le Fanu's work.

27. Mason, Diane, *The Secret Vice: Masturbation in Victorian Fiction and Medical Culture* (Bath Spa University College: Unpublished Doctoral Thesis, 2003), p. 127.

28. Gilman, Sander L., *Difference and Pathology: Stereotypes of Sexuality, Race, and Madness* (Ithaca and London: Cornell University Press, 1985).
29. Mauner, Georges, *Manet: Peintre-Philosophe A Study of the Painter's Themes* (University Park and London: Penn State University Press, 1975), p. 96.
30. A later critic of Manet, Theodore Bodkin, is cited as arguing that Baudelaire, with whom Manet corresponded about his painting, understood the cat to be the familiar of a witch – Bodkin, Theodore, 'Manet, Dumas, Goya, and Titian' (letter), *Burlington Magazine* 50 (1927), pp. 166–7. Cited in Mauner, *Manet*, p. 94.
31. *The Dark Blue*, ed. John C. Freund, 4 vols (London: British and Colonial Publishing Co., 1870–73), II (March–August 1872), v.
32. He had served in the Liberal government of the 1840s and attempted unsuccessfully to bring relief to the Irish peasants against the wishes of Trevelyan. Nevertheless, he still supported the continued establishment of the Church of Ireland and opposed the setting up of a Catholic university – Ziegler, Paul, *Palmerston* (Basingstoke: Palgrave, 2001), p. 125.

3 Bram Stoker's *Dracula* and the Treaty of Berlin (1878)

1. Eagleton, Terry, *Heathcliff and the Great Hunger: Studies in Irish Culture* (London: Verso, 1995), p. 57.
2. Moses, Michael, 'Dracula, Parnell and the Troubled Dreams of Nationhood', *Journal X: A Journal in Culture and Criticism*, 2:1 (Autumn 1997) 67–111, at p. 69.
3. Stewart, Bruce, 'Bram Stoker's *Dracula*: Possessed by the Spirit of the Nation?', *Irish University Review* 29:2 (1999), 238–55.
4. Foster, Roy, 'Protestant Magic: W. B. Yeats and the Spell of Irish History', *Paddy and Mr Punch: Connections in Irish and English History* (London: Allen Lane, 1993), pp. 212–32, at p. 219.
5. Backus, Margot Gayle, *The Gothic Family Romance* (Duke University Press, 1999).
6. Goldsworthy, Vesna, *Inventing Ruritania* (New Haven and London: Yale University Press, 1998), p. 84. See also Kostova, Ludmilla, 'Representing "Darkest" Eastern Europe: Bulgaria, in G. B. Shaw's *Arms and the Man* and Malcolm Bradbury's *Doctor Criminale*', *Europe: From East to West. Proceedings of the First International European Studies Conference*, eds. Martin Dangerfield, Glynn Hanbrook and Ludmilla Kostova (Bulgarian Universities: PLC Publishers, 1996), pp. 33–48.
7. Hughes, William, 'A Singular Invasion: Revisiting the Postcoloniality of Bram Stoker's *Dracula*', *Empire and the Gothic: The Politics of Genre*, ed. Andrew Smith and William Hughes (Basingstoke: Macmillan, Palgrave), pp. 88–102, at p. 92.
8. Coundouriotis, Eleni, '*Dracula* and the Idea of Europe', *Connotations*, 9:2 (Waxmann Munster, New York, 1999–2000), 143–59 at 154.
9. Watson, Robert Seton, *Disraeli, Gladstone and the Eastern Question* (London: Macmillan, 1935), p. 333.
10. Pribram, Alfred Francis, *Austria–Hungary and Great Britain, 1908–1914*, trans. Ian F. D. Morrow (London: Oxford University Press, 1951), p. 53.
11. Waterfield, Gordon, *Layard of Nineveh* (London: John Murray, 1963), p. 421.
12. Pribram, Alfred Francis, *England and the International Policy of the European Great Powers*, 1871–1914 (Oxford: Clarendon, 1931), p. 53.

13. Clayton, G.D., *Britain and the Eastern Question: Missolonghi to Galllipoli*, London History Studies, no. 8 (London: University of London Press, 1971), pp. 181–2.
14. Haining, Peter and Peter Tremayne. *The Un-Dead: The Legend of Bram Stoker and Dracula* (London: Constable, 1997), pp. 15–16.
15. Glover, David, *Vampires, Mummies and Liberals: Bram Stoker and the Politics of Popular Fiction* (Durham and London: Duke University Press, 1996), pp. 40–2 and 92–3.
16. Todorova, Maria, *Imagining the Balkans* (New York and Oxford: Oxford University Press, 1997), pp. 89–115. Paul Murray details how Stoker, as early as his Dublin years, was concerned, like Disraeli, about the threat of Russia to 'British India', and complained of how it 'stretches' its 'greedy arm' towards the area, in a presentation to the Philosophical Society of Trinity College Dublin. Murray warns, of course, that we cannot take the views expressed in a debating society of this kind as entirely indicative of how Stoker felt –Murray, Paul, *From the shadow of Dracula: a Life of Bram Stoker* (London: Jonathan Cape, 2004), pp. 36–7.
17. Leatherdale, Clive, *The Origins of Dracula* (London: William Kimber, 1987).
18. Stoker, Bram, *Dracula*, ed. Maud Ellmann (Oxford: Oxford University Press, 1996), p. 29.
19. Johnson, Major E. C, *On the Track of the Crescent* (London: Hurst and Blacket, 1885), p. 163.
20. Makkai, Laszlo, 'Transylvania's Indigenous People at the Time of the Hungarian Conquest', *History of Transylvania, Vol 1: From the Beginnings to 1606*, ed. Laszlo Makkai and Andras Mocsy, Atlantic Studies on Society and Change, no. 106 (New York: Columbia University Press, 2001), pp. 333–522, at pp. 415–6.
21. Wilkinson, William, *An Account of the Principalities of Wallachia and Moldavia: With Various Political Observations Relating to Them* (London: Hurst, 1820), pp. 17–18.
22. Leatherdale, Clive, *Dracula: The Novel and the Legend*, rev. edn (Brighton: Desert Island Books, 1985), p. 95.
23. Gerard, Emily, 'Transylvanian Superstitions', *The Nineteenth Century* (July 1885), pp. 130–50, at p. 142.
24. The battle after which John Corvinus Huniades died. Wilkinson probably got the battle name from Gibbon, although Gibbon states that Cossova field is in Bulgaria, rather than Serbia – Gibbon, Edward. *The Decline and Fall of the Roman Empire*. 6 vols (London: Everyman, 1994), II67.
25. He was really just trying to protect the right wing of the army, but is unforgiven in folklore.
26. Stoker, George, *With 'the Unspeakables'; or, Two Years Campaigning in European and Asiatic Turkey* (London: Chapman and Hall, 1878), pp. 40–5.
27. Belford, Barbara, *Bram Stoker* (London: London: Weidenfield and Nicholas, 1996), p. 128.
28. Mackenzie, Georgina and Adelina Irby, *Travels in the Slavonic Provinces of Turkey-in-Europe*, (London: Bell and Daldy, 1867).
29. See 'Introduction', note 8, for an account of Urquhart's encounters with the Turks in Urquhart, David, *The Spirit of the East: A Journal of Travels through Roumali*, 2 vols (London: H. Colburn, 1838).
30. Glover, David, *Vampires, Mummies and Liberals: Bram Stoker and the Politics of Popular Fiction* (Durham and London: Duke University Press, 1996), p. 34.

31. Stoker, Bram, *Miss Betty* (London: Constable & Co., 1898), p. 171.
32. Stoker, Bram, *The Essential Dracula: The Definitive Annotated Edition of Bram Stoker's Classic Novel*, ed. Leonard Wolf (New York, London, Victoria and Toronto: Plume, 1993), pp. 446–52, at p. 447.
33. Arata, Stephen D., 'The Occidental Tourist: *Dracula* and the Anxiety of Reverse Colonisation', *Victorian Studies*, 33 (1990), 621–45, at 634.
34. Zanger, Jules, 'A Sympathetic Vibration: Dracula and the Jews, *English Literature in Transition 1880–1920*, 34 (1991), pp. 33–44.
35. Pick, Daniel, *Faces of Degeneration: A European Disorder, c. 1848–c. 1918* (Cambridge: Cambridge University Press, 1989), pp. 170–3.
36. Dragomanav, M. P. 'Russian Policy, Home and Foreign' *Free Russia*, pp. 10–12, at p. 12.
37. Stepniak, Sergei, *Russia under the Tsars*, trans.William Westall, 2 vols (London: Ward and Downes,1885), II 277–80. See also note 16.
38. In another letter to Stoker (12 June 1894), Stepniak is organising a box for himself and two Bulgarian friends.
39. It should be taken into account that the two men actually knew each other, and that Hope was invited to dinner at least twice to the Stoker household, writing twice to regretfully decline the invitation. Hope wrote once: 'Alas, I make no way with the project! And despairing of work here, I'm off to America with the Major in the autumn' (13 June 1897). In a reference to *Dracula* a few months later, he wrote to him 'Your vampires robbed me of sleep for nights' (27 January 1898). Three years later he responds to a request for signed books, declaring: 'Of course delighted to sign the books – Any you like – I think *Zenda* & *Dolly* would probably go best' (28 May 1901). Whether these were for children or friends we can only speculate, but Stoker had probably read *The Prisoner of Zenda* before finishing *Dracula*. Otherwise, the letters (14 in all) deal with requests for theatre boxes.
40. Hope, Anthony, *The Prisoner of Zenda; Rupert of Hentzau*, ed. Gary Hoppenstand (London, Penguin, 2000), p. 5.
41. Mallet, Charles, *Anthony Hope and His Books: Being the Authorised Life of Sir Anthony Hope Hawkins* (London: Hutchinson and Co., 1935), p. 28.
42. In a speech given in Edinburgh on the eve of the General Election on 20 June 1892, Lord Rosebury of the Liberals confirmed that there were only two issues that were important for the next election, namely home rule and parliamentary reform (*The Times*, 21 June 1892, p. 7).
43. Baker, Michael, *Gladstone and Radicalism: The Reconstruction of Liberal Policy in Britain, 1885–94* (Brighton: The Harvester Press, 1975), pp. 211–2.
44. Nichols, J. Alden, *Germany after Bismarck: The Caprivi Era (1890–94)* (Cambridge, MA: Harvard University Press, 1958), pp. 76–8.
45. Jelavich, Barbara, *Modern Austria: Empire and Republic 1815–1980* (Cambridge: Cambridge University Press, 1987), p. 47.

4 Bram Stoker's *The Lady of the Shroud* and the Bosnia Crisis (1908–09)

1. Glover, David, *Vampires, Mummies and Liberals: Bram Stoker and the Politics of Popular Fiction* (Durham and London: Duke University Press, 1996), p. 53.

2. Pribram, Alfred Francis, *Austria–Hungary and Great Britain, 1908–1914*, trans. Ian D. F. Morrow (London, Toronto and New York: Oxford University Press, 1951), p. 99.
3. 'Great Britain and Bulgarian Independence', *The Times*, 25 February 1908, p. 5:

> In reply to a recent suggestion of the Bulgarian Government in favour of an immediate recognition of the independence of Bulgaria they were informed that the standpoint of his majesty's Government throughout had been that the Treaty of Berlin could not be altered without the consent of all the powers who were parties to it, and that as soon as Turkey and the other powers were willing to recognize the new state of things arising from the declaration of independence by Bulgaria, his Majesty's Government would be willing to do the same.

4. 'The Man who destroyed the Berlin Treaty' [Large Picture of Aerenthal with Tittoni]', *London Illustrated News*, 10 October 1908, p. 491 (picture page):

> It is generally accepted that Baron von Aerenthal, the Austro–Hungarian Minister of Foreign Affairs and of the Imperial and Royal House, is responsible for the destruction of the Berlin Treaty. As the 'Telegraph' puts it: 'the hand that tore the venerable document was Prince Ferdinand's, but the voice that set in motion was the voice of Baron von Aerenthal. Austria and Bulgaria now stand together as conspiring Powers, which, for their own ends, have risked, and possibly broken, the peace of Europe.

5. Anon., 'Francis Joseph', *The Near East* (November 1908), pp. 309–10, at p. 310.
6. *The Near East* also wrote two articles in the first few months of the conflict taking up the Montenegrin cause over the annexation of Spizza and Antivari at the Berlin Treaty and also wrote a piece praising the ruler of Montenegro, Crown Prince Nicholas.
7. Hope, Anthony, *Sophy of Kravonia* (Bristol: J. W. Arrowsmith; London: Simpkin, Marshall, Hamilton, Kent and Co. Ltd., 1906), p. 19.
8. Goldsworthy, Vesna, *Inventing Ruritania* (New Haven and London: Yale University Press,1998), p.50.
9. Stoker, Bram, *The Lady of the Shroud*, ed. William Hughes (Westcliffe-on-Sea: Desert Island Books, 2001), pp. 59–60.
10. Todorov, Tzvetan, *Introduction à la Littérature Fantastique* (Paris: Editions du Seuil, 1970) pp. 46–9.
11. George Stoker, *With 'the Unspeakables'; or, Two Years Campaigning in European and Asiatic Turkey* (London: Chapman and Hall, 1878), pp. 40–5.
12. Lodge, David, *Modes of Modern Writing* (London: Edward Arnold, 1977), p. 38.
13. Sage, Victor, 'Exchanging Fantasies: Sex and the Serbian Crisis', *Bram Stoker: History, Psychoanalysis and the Gothic*, ed. William Hughes and Andrew Smith (Basingstoke: Macmillan, 1998), pp. 116–33, at p. 127.
14. Montenegro in fact ceded its plain north of the river Zeta to the Sultan in the seventeenth century.
15. Denton, William, *Montenegro: Its People and their History* (London: Daldy, Istiber and Co., 1877), p. 30.
16. Another book which one might have expected Stoker to have read at the time was Major Percy E. Henderson's *A British Officer in the Balkans: The Account of a Journey through Dalmatia, Montenegro, Turkey in Austria,*

Magyarland, Bosnia and Hercegovina (London: Seeley and Co., 1909), especially since it was advertised in the press in poorly disguised plugs (e.g., *ILN* 20 February 1909, p. 278). However, my own observations show that the other books are far more likely to have influenced his novel.

17. Wyon, Reginald and Gerald Prance, *Through the Land of the Black Mountain: the Adventures of Two Englishmen in Montenegro* (London: Methuen, 1903), p. 243.

18. Durham, Mary E., *Through the Lands of the Serb* (London: Edward Arnold, 1904), p. 15.

19. After a banquet in Cattaro R.H.R. is informed by his host Pero Pejovich: 'I have known it rain here for six weeks without stopping a moment' – R.H.R, *Rambles in Istria, Dalmatia and Montenegro* (London: Hurst and Blackett, 1875).

20. Leatherdale, *The Origins of Dracula* (Brighton: Desert Island Books, 1988), p. 88.

21. 'a maze of fjords', as Mary Durham describes them (Durham, *Through the Lands of the Serb*, p.3), and as Stoker may have read about them from her.

22. Schmitt, Bernadotte E., *The Annexation of Bosnia* (Cambridge: The University Press, 1937), p. 235.

23. Gerard, Dorothea. *The Red-Hot Crown: A Semi-Historical Romance* (London: John Long, 1909), p. 7.

24. On the front page of *The Evening Star*, 19 March 1909, there is a cartoon of Alexander under the caption: 'The Iron Throne'. He is inspecting the throne, which is covered in iron spikes, and declares 'Not for me thank-you. I prefer something easier.'

5 The Vampires of Illyria: Nodier, Mérimée and the French Occupation of the Dalmation Coast

1. Letter to Joseph Lingay. Mérimée, Prosper, *Corréspondance Génerale*, établie et annotée par Maurice Parturier avec la Collaboration de Pierre Josserand et Jean Mallion, 6 vols (Paris: Le Divan, 1941), I 3. 'My romantic principles have been affirmed even more, by the society of certain provincial classics with whom I frequently break lances every evening.' ['Mes principes romantiques sont encore plus affermis, par la société de certains classiques de province avec lesquels je romps régulièrement une lance tous les soirs.']

2. The other, as he goes on to explain, was to write up the fruits of a planned expedition to Illyria for which he did not have the money, and that he had hoped to sell the account 'in advance' [d'avance] in order to then go and see whether he had been right or not! (Mérimée, *Corréspondance Génerale*, I 376–7).

3. La Romantisme de Mérimée n'est donc qu'un masque, dont il se débarrasse vite', Souriau, Maurice, *Histoire du Romantisme en France, Vol II: La Decadence du Romantisme* (Paris: Editions Spes, 1927), p. 99.

4. Yovanovitch, Voyslav M., *'La Guzla' de Prosper Mérimee: Etude d'Histoire Romantique* (Genève: Slatkine Reprints, 1973 [1910]), p. 309.

5. In the rest of the letter Mérimée complains of how he had been attacked by Nodier for 'pillaging' him, which he follows up with examples of just how bad Nodier's scholarship had been (Mérimée, *Corréspondance Génerale*, I 377).

6. Pavlovic, Stevan K., *La France en Dalmatie: Naissance de l'Idée Illyrienne*, repr. from *Le College et le Monde* (London: Frederick Printing ,1950), pp. 1–2.

7. 'Pour les Français d'alors, les Illyriens representent les ancêtres des anciens Grecs: la mode est pour l'Illyrie, pour ce mélange de classicisme mourant et de romantisme mourant et de romantisme naissant et le but de l'Empereur est de faire de l'Illyrie l'avant-garde orientale de la civilisation française' (Pavlovic, *La France en Dalmatie*, p. 3).

8. *Viaggio in Dalmazia, dell' Abate Alberto Fortis*, 2 vols (Venezia: Presso Alvise Milocco, all Apolline, 1774), I 48. I have elected to use the Italian original rather than the French translation, despite the fact that Yovanovitch used the French in *La Guzla de Prosper Mérimée*, repr. (Genève: Slatkine, 1973), because Nodier declared that the translation was unreadable and because both he and Mérimée could read Italian.

9. Henry-Rosier, Marguérite, *La Vie de Charles Nodier* (Paris: Librairie Gallimard, 1931), p. 149.

10. Nodier, Charles, 'Langue Illyrienne' [3 parts], *Statistique Illyrienne: Articles Complets du 'Telegraphe Officiel' de l'Annee 1813*, ed. France Dobrovljc (Ljubljana: Edition 'Satura', 1933), pp. 62–71. In these three articles Nodier attempts to show both the Latin and Greek antecedents of 'Illyrian' and looks, for example, at the word 'Krut', meaning cruel, having its root in the Latin word 'crudelis'(p. 67), and the word 'Pet' meaning five, having its root in the Greek word 'Pente'(p. 69).

11. Judah, Tim, *The Serbs: History, Myth and the Destruction of Yugoslavia* (New Haven and London, 1997), pp. 11–12.

12. 'à cette différence près que la pureté du ciel, la beauté des productions, la grandeur des souvenirs et l'heureux voisinage de la Grèce ont dû donner au barde des Alpes Juliennes une foule d'inspirations que le nôtre n'a pas recue' (Nodier, *Statistique Illyrienne*, p. 40).

13. See also Wolff, Larry, *Venice and the Slavs: the Discovery of Dalmatia in the Age of Enlightenment* (Stanford: Stanford university Press, 2001), pp. 181–9.

14. 'Le cauchemar, que les Dalmates appellent *Smarra*, est un des phénomènes les plus communs du sommeil' – Nodier, Charles, 'Le Pays des Reves', *Contes de la Veillée* (Paris: Charpentier, 1831), p. 200.

15. In the original, Fortis uses the term 'streghe' meaning 'witches' (Fortis, *Viaggio in Dalmazia, dell' Abate Alberto Fortis*, 2 vols (Venezia: Presso Alvise Milocco, all Apolline, 1774)] I 64). However, it is very close to the Romanian term 'strigoi' which in French is translated as 'stryge' meaning a winged, owl-like figure that attacks the heart and was the classical antecedent of the vampire – Calmet, Augustin, *Dissertation sur les Apparitions des Anges, des Demons et des Esprits et sur les Revenans et Vampires, De Hongrie, de Boheme, Moravie et de Silesie* (Paris:de Buré l'ainé, 1746), pp. 303–6. Because of this verbal similarity, it is hardly surprising that from reading the account in Fortis's Italian he should turn the attacker into a winged assailant, like the classical 'stryge', even though neither Fortis nor Apuleius mention this detail.

16. Maixner declares that the brigand on whom Nodier claimed to base Jean Sbogar actually existed, was called Repshitch, and was judged by Compte Spalatin at the court in Laybach. Furthermore, two men with the surname Sbogar were tried for the assasination of a woman in a case that was reported in Nodier's own *Télégraph Illyrien* (1813) no. 9 – Maixner, Rudolph, *Charles Nodier et L'Illyrie* (Paris: Didier, 1960), pp. 51–4.

17. Nodier, Charles, *Jean Sbogar*, ed. Jean Sgard et étudiants (Paris: Librairie Honoré Champion, 1987), pp. 72–3.

18. Yovanovitch quotes from just such a review in the *Journal de Paris*, 20 June 1818 (Yovanovitch, *'La Guzla' de Prosper Mérimee*, p. 84).

19. The article was in the 17 October 1819 edition of *La Rénommée* (Maixner, *Charles Nodier et L'Illyrie*, p. 48).

20. 'lui reprochant à la fois ses fluctuations politiques qui le font tour à tour jacobin, thermidorien, napoléonien, royaliste, et ce que Sainte-Beuve appelait son "don de l'inexactitude" ' – Delon, Michel, 'Nodier et les Mythes Révolutionnaires', *Charles Nodier: le Parrain* [Europe Revue Littéraire Mensuelle 58ème. No. 614–5] (Paris: Editions Francais Réunis, June 1980), pp. 31–42, at p. 31.

21. One night he and his friends organised a satirical performance of a meeting of the Jacobin club 'Amis de la Constitution' to which they gave the cries 'A bas les Jacobins!' (Henry-Rosier, *La Vie de Charles Nodier*, p. 65).

22. Rogers, Bryan, *Charles Nodier et la Tentation de la Folie* (Geneva: Slatkine, 1985), pp. 45–8.

23. Nodier, Charles, *Souvenirs, Portraits, Episodes de la Révolution et de l'Empire*, ed. Nouvelle, 2 vols (Paris: Charpentier, 1865), I 15.

24. 'Descends de ta pompe insensée;/ Retourne parmi tes guerriers.'

25. MacCarthy, Fiona, *Byron: Life and Legend* (London: John Murray, 2002), pp. 374–5.

26. 'incroyable deviation de la raison humaine'. Nodier, in Pichot, Amedée, *Essai sur le genie et caractère de Lord Byron, precédé d'une notice preliminaire par M. Charles Nodier* (Paris: Ladvocat, Librairire, Palais – Royal,1824), p. 12.

27. Nodier, Charles, *Du Fantastique en Literature* (1830) (Paris: Chimères – Barbe Bleue, 1989), p. 10. See also Scanu, Ada Myriam, 'Charles Nodier: Du Fantastique en Littérature', *La Naissance du Fantastique en Europe – Histoire et Théorie* (Bologna: Séminaire d'Histoire Littéraire, 2002).

28. Nodier, Charles, *Oeuvres completes*, 13 vols (Geneva: Slatline Reprints,1998), III 23.

29. 'il s'attache sur mon coeur, se développe, soulêve sa tête énorme et rit' (Nodier *Oeuvres*, III 80).

30. 'venoit reclamer la recompense promise par la reine des terreurs nocturnes' (Nodier *Oeuvres*, III 101).

31. 'C'est, selon moi, de cette disposition physiologique placée dans les conditions qui la développent, qu'est sorti le merveilleux de tous les pays' (Nodier, 'Le Pays des Reves', *Contes de la Veillée*, p. 200).

32. Apuleius, *The Golden Ass*, trans. Robert Graves (London: Penguin, 1950), p. 40.

33. 'un des écrivains les plus romantiques des temps anciens' (Nodier, *Oeuvres*, II25).

34. Nodier, Charles, *Le Vampire, Melodrame en Trois Actes, avec un Prologue* (Paris: J. N. Barba, Libraire, 1920), p. 19.

35. Bércard, Cyprien, [C.B.] *Lord Ruthwen, ou les Vampires*, publié par l'Auteur de Jean Sbogar et de Thérèse Aubert (Paris: Chez Ladvocat, Librairie, 1820), I66.

36. In *Du Fantastique en Litterature*, Nodier equates the power of the vampire superstition with the imagination of the earliest examples of the marvellous in Classical literature, citing in particular Odysseus's descent into Hades (Nodier, *Du Fantastique*, p. 14).

37. Calmet, Augustin, *Dissertation sur les Appareitions des Anges, des Démons et des Esprits et sur les Revenans et Vampires, De Hongrie, de Bohemè, Moravie et de Silesie* (Paris:de Buré l'ainé, 1746), pp. 280–4.

38. Nodier, Charles, *Infernaliana: ou Anecdotes, Petits Romans Nouvelles et Contes, sur les Révenants, les Spectres, les Démons et les Vampires*, preface by Hubert Juin (Paris: Pierre Belfond, 1966), pp. 27–8.

39. Mérimée, Prosper, *La Guzla: ou Choix de Poésies Illyriques Recueillies dans la Dalmatie, la Bosnie, La Croatie et l'Herzégowine*, introduction by Antonia Fonyi (Paris: Editions Kime, 1994), p. 19.

40. 'Allor che muore un uomo sospetto di poter divenire Vampiro, o Vukodlak, com'essi dicono, usano di tagliargli i garetti, e pungerlo tutto colle spille, pretendo che dopo queste due operazioni egli non possa piu andar girando' (Fortis, *Viaggio in Dalmazia* , II64). Fortis clearly did do some original research into the subject, since his account of the superstition is the only one of this era that is not influenced either by Calmet, or Calmet's own sources and their offshoots, namely *Lettres Juives, Le Glaineur* and De Tournefort, making Mérimée's own description in his account and poems one of the only ones which is influenced from beyond Calmet.

41. Bakhtin, M. M., 'From the Prehistory of Novelistic Discourse', *The Dialogic Imagination: Four Essays by M.M. Bakhtin*, trans. Carl Emerson and Michael Holquist, ed. Michael Holquist (Austin, TX: University of Texas Press, 1994), pp. 40–83, at p. 50.

42. Both Pushkin and Mickiewicz, the two most famous Slavic poets of the day, were taken in (Souriau, *Histoire du Romantisme en France*, p. 98).

43. 'Un vampire! un vampire! ma pauvre fille est morte' (Mérimée, *La Guzla* , p. 74).

44. 'L'odeur infecte qu'il repandait me força bientôt de les quitter et de rentrer chez mon hôte' (Mérimée, *La Guzla*, p. 76).

45. 'Je quittai quelques heures après le village, donnant au diable de bon coeur les vampires, les revenants et ceux qui en racontent des histoires' (Mérimée, *La Guzla*, p. 78)

46. Burke, Edmund, *A Philosophical Enquiry into the Origin of our Ideas of the Sublime and Beautiful*, ed. Adam Phillips (Oxford and New York: Oxford University Press, 1990), p. 36: pt 1: Sect. VII.

47. 'Quiconque a dîné avec un Morlaque sentira la difficulté de la chose' (Mérimée, *La Guzla*, p. 74).

48. 'le seul étranger dans la maison' (Mérimée, *La Guzla* , p.75).

49. 'Que celui qui le porte ouvre le livre à la soixante-sixième page; il commandera à tous les esprits de la terre et de l'eau' (Mérimée, *La Guzla* , p. 101).

50. 'Basile, tu es à moi maintenant que tu as renonce a ton Dieu' (Mérimée, *La Guzla* , p. 102).

51. 'Approche, Marie, viens contempler celui pur le quel tu as trahi la famille de ta nation! Ose baiser ces lèvres pâles et sanglantes qui savaient si bien mentir. Vivant il a causé bien de larmes; mort il en coûtera davantage' (Mérimée, *La Guzla*, p.90).

52. See also Twitchell, James, *The Living Dead: A Study of the Vampire in Romantic Literature* (Durham, NC: Duke University Press, 1981), p. 14.

53. 'C'est une des nombreuses preuves du mépris avec lequel sont traitées les femmes dans ce pays' (Mérimée, *La Guzla*, p. 88).

54. Lukacs, George, *The Historical Novel*, trans. Hannah and Stanley Mitchell (London: Merlin Press, 1989), p. 33.

55. 'Du reste, je crois que Napoléon ne s'est jamais beaucoup occupé des Monténégrins' (Mérimée, *La Guzla*, p. 111).

56. Autin, Jean, *Prosper Mérimée, écrivain, archeologue, homme politique* (Paris: Librairie Academique Perrin, 1983), p. 18.
57. To Paul-Francois Dubois, 26 July 1825, 'De toutes parts j'entends des complimens pour le Globe. Cependant les Bonapartistes le détestent bien cordialement' (Mérimée, *Corréspondance Génerale*, p. 11).
58. Baschet, Robert, *Mérimée: Du Romantisme au Second Empire* (Paris: Nouvelles Editions Latine, 1958), pp. 45–7.

6 Jules Verne's *Le Château des Carpathes* (1892) and the Romans of Transylvania

1. Until, that is, the recent publication of his letters to his family and his publisher Pierre-Jules Hetzel.
2. Verne, Jules, *Le Château des Carpathes* (Paris: Bibliothèque d'Education et de Recréation, 1892), p. 21.
3. 'aux yeux de flamme' (Verne, *Le Château des Carpathes*, p. 122).
4. 'sa figure extatique ... effrayante de pâleur' (Verne, *Le Château des Carpathes*, p.122).
5. 'C'est vous qui l'avez tuée! ... Malheur à Vous, Comte de Telek' (Verne, *Le Château des Carpathes*, p. 124).
6. In a letter dated 4 March 1892 – cited in Vierne, Simone, *Jules Verne: Une Vie, une Oeuvre, Une Epoque* (Paris: Editions Balland, 1986), p. 342.
7. Chesneaux, Jean, *Une Lecture Politique de Jules Verne* (Paris: Francois Maspero, 1971), pp. 23–40.
8. 'Elle n'était que représentation, par son jeu, et expression, par sa voix, des désirs des dilletanti – des "amateurs" ' (Vierne, *Jules Verne*, p. 346).
9. 'Mais celle qu'ils n'ont pas su aimer dans la totalité de son être leur échappe.' (Vierne, *Jules Verne*, p. 348).
10. 'un pays encore préservé de la civilisation' (Vierne, *Jules Verne*, p. 351).
11. Féval, Paul, *La Vampire* (Castelnau-le-Lez: Bibliothèque Ombres, 2004), p. 103.
12. Féval, Paul, *Le Chevalier Ténèbre suivi de la Ville Vampire* (Verviers: Bibliothèque Marabout, 1972), p. 118.
13. 'Il raccontait bonnement, presque timidement, des histoires si sauvages, que j'en ai encore le coeur serré' (Féval, *La Vampire*, p. 16).
14. 'Qu'est le chef-d'oeuvre de Goethe, sinon la splendide mise en scène de l'éternel fait de vampirisme qui, depuis le commencement du monde, à desséche et vidé le coeur de tant de familles' (Féval, *La Vampire*, p. 17).
15. 'couchées et dormant l'éternel sommeil' (Féval, *La Vampire*, p. 18).
16. Compère, Daniel, 'Paul Féval et les Vampires', *Paul Féval: Romancier Populaire: Colloque de Rennes, 1987*, eds Jean Rohou and Jacques Dugast (Rennes: Presses Universitaires de Rennes, 1987), pp. 59–66, at p. 60.
17. de Gerando, Auguste, *Transylvanie et ses Inhabitants*, 2 vols (Paris: Au Comptoir des Imprimateurs-Unis, 1845).
18. Reclus, Elisée, *Voyage aux Regions Minières de Transylvanie Occidentale – Le Tour du Monde xxviii*, 2 parts (Paris: Hachette, 1874), part I p. 16.
19. 'c'était un épais chardon appelé "épine russe", dont les graines, dit Elisée Reclus, furent apportées à leurs poils par les chevaux moscovites – "présent

de joyeuse conquête que les Russes firent aux Transylvains" ' (Verne, *Le Château des Carpathes*, p. 69).

20. On his way to Koloszvar at the beginning of his journey Reclus attests to a 'deep sympathy' for these oppressed people whose language has the same root as that of the Western Europeans and, on meeting a young Romanian, laments: 'A singular destiny is that of the Romanians in Transylvania! They populate almost the entire country, and yet they are not supposed to have a political existence'. ['Singulière destinée que celle des Roumaines de la Transylvanie! Ils peuplent le pays presque tout entier, et pourtant ils ne sont pas même censés avoir d'existence politique.'] (Reclus, *Voyage aux Regions Minières de Transylvanie Occidentale*, p. 3).

21. There is in fact no Plateau of Orgall in Reclus's account, just as there is no village called Werst, but we can judge from the map that Frik and the town of Werst are poised right at the bottom south west of Transylvania, near what was then the Rumanian border.

22. 'dans le district de Hatszeg, à Livadzel, à Petroseny, vaste poche d'une contenance estimée à deux cent cinquante millions de tonnes' (Verne, *Le Château des Carpathes*, p. 29).

23. 'Voilà, semble-t-il, un district très favorisé de la nature, et pourtant cette richesse ne profite guère au bien-être de sa population' (Verne, *Le Château des Carpathes*, p. 29).

24. 'simple scélérat, il se mit à la tête d'une bande d'assasins et de voleurs' (Reclus, *Voyage aux Regions Minières de Transylvanie Occidentale*, p. 15).

25. This is not to say that Verne does not also relate the wider history of oppression in the region, namely that of Austrians against Hungarians, for which Gerando is the most important source. Verne mentions the history of the region, including the Battle of Mohacs in 1526 (when Hungary fell to the Turks) and the annexation of Hungary in 1699. (Verne, *Le Château des Carpathes*, pp. 3–4.)

26. 'l'une des revolutions sanglantes des paysans roumains contre l'oppression hongroise' (Verne, *Le Château des Carpathes*, p. 21).

27. The legends concerning the landscape are gleaned from different parts of Reclus's journey: the story of Leany-Kö he learns when he is first entering Torotzko (Reclus, *Voyage aux Regions Minières de Transylvanie Occidentale*, p.22); and the fortress of Deva, when he enters the town of Veres-Patak – another source for the doctor's name (Reclus, *Voyage aux Regions Minières de Transylvanie Occidentale*, p. 32).

28. 'des Patriotes roumains, – entre autres le populaire heros du xve siecle, le voivode Vajda-Hunyad' (Verne, *Le Château des Carpathes*, p. 34).

29. *Ballades et Chants Populaire de la Roumanie (principautés Danubiennes)*, receuilli et traduits par V Alexandri avec une introduction par M A Ubicini (Paris: E Dentu, 1855) is full of fantastic tales about the little ewe who warns the Moldavian shepherd that he will be killed by a Hungarian for his flock, called 'Miorita' ([*Ballades et Chants Populaire de la Roumanie*, p. 45] hence the name 'Miriota' in the novel), and the further story of the hero's fight with the dragon, and the ballad of the fairies or '*Zmei*' (hence the reference to that superstition in Verne's work ([Verne, *Le Château des Carpathes*, p. 2]). There is a further note in Alexandri's translation relating to the continuation of Doric words in the Rumanian language, including the term 'frica' meaning 'terror'

(*Ballades et Chants Populaire de la Roumanie*, p. 30): an apt source for the name 'Frik', one might think, given the panic the shepherd falls into on seeing the smoke rise from the château's chimney.

30. Logio, George Clenton, *Rumania: Its History, Politics and Economics* (Manchester: Sherratt and Hughes, 1932), p. 3.

31. According to Iorga, there was nevertheless Moldavian unrest at unification which Cuza put down by force in 1859 – Iorga, Neculai, *Histoire des Relations entre La France et les Roumains* (Paris: Librairie Payot, 1918), p. 242.

32. De Reclus reported in his 'Voyage' that the Vlachs opposed the Magyars during the 1848 uprising, burning the house of the Local Hungarian ruler during the 1849 repression of the uprising (Reclus, *Voyage aux Regions Minières de Transylvanie Occidentale*, p. 8), while de Gerando reports that the Rumanian peasants rose up against Magyar landlords as early as 1784 (de Gerando, *Transylvanie et ses Inhabitants*, I 332).

33. Haraszti, Endre, *The Ethnic History of Transylvania* (Astor Park, FL: Danubian Press, 1971), p. 119.

34. Gaidoz, Henri, *Les Roumains de Hongrie: leur origine – leur histoire – leur état present*, Extrait de la revue de Paris 15 May 1894 (Paris: Imprimerie et librairie centrales des chemins de fer, 1894), p. 5. In 1891 there was even a law passed magyarising kindergartens (Haraszti, *The Ethnic History of Transylvania*, p. 120).

35. Others, which have also been referred to here, are Gaidoz's *Les Roumains: leur Origine – leur Histoire – Leur Etat Présent*, and Cantilli's 'Quelques Mots sur les Romains de Transylvanie', *Révue Orientale*, (September 1894).

36. It was in fact a Frenchman, Vaillant, who had spent much time in Wallachia, who popularised the idea of a combined country with his work *La Roumanie* (1844), which described the areas as one totality, with one language called 'roumaine' (Iorga, *Histoire des Relations entre La France et les Roumains*, p. 173). Students at Kogalniceanu, Alexandri, were enthused by the idea of the new country and the term 'Rumanian' took off in Wallachia as a result. (Iorga, *Histoire des Relations entre La France et les Roumains*, p. 174).

37. 'restaient soumis à l'influence française, malgré la surveillance du consultat russe restauré' (Iorga, *Histoire des Relations entre La France et les Roumains*, p. 241).

38. 'Logistilla' is the name of the fairy of ideas in the original Italian version. In the French version of the nineteenth century her name is translated as 'Logistille' – *Roland Furieux: Poeme Héroique*, trans. A-J du Pays, illustr. Gustave Dore (Paris: Hachette, 1879), p. 74.

39. In Italian, the word 'Stilla' means 'little drop'.

40. *The Poetical Works of John Keats*, ed. H. W. Garrod, 2nd edn (Oxford: Clarendon, 1958), p. 213, ll 287–90.

41. Keats, John, *Poemes et Poésies*, trans. Paul Gallimard (Paris: Mercure de France, 1910). In his bibliography, the earliest translations that Gallimard provides are Hugues Rebell's translation of the Odes for *L'Ermitage*, 15 September 1892; however, there may well have been an earlier translation of *Lamia*, or at least part of it, in a periodical to which Verne referred.

42. De Stendhal, *De l'Amour*, ed. V. Del Litto (Paris: Gallimard Folio, 1980), pp. 30–3.

43. 'la musique parfaite, comme la pantomime parfaite, me fait songer à ce qui forme actuellement l'objet de mes rêveries, et me fait venir des idées excellentes' (Stendhal, *De l'Amour*, p. 57).

44. Bourget, Paul, 'Cosmopolis', *Oeuvres Complètes*, 9 vols, (Paris: Librairie Plon, 1902), IV 545. The Prince Julien is talking of how his love for Fanny has begun 'décristallisation'.

45. 'Dès la première fois qu'il vit la Stilla, Franz éprouva les entraînements irrésistibles d'un premier amour' (Verne, *Le Château des Carpathes*, p. 116).

46. 'Soudain, le bruit d'une glace qui se brise se fait entendre, et, avec les mille éclats de verre, dispersés à travers la salle, disparait la Stilla' (Verne, *Le Château des Carpathes*, p. 191). The comparison with a mirror ('glace', here) is all the more poignant given the issue of narcisism involved in the critique of romantic love. In one story of W. B. Yeats's 'Stories of Red Hanrahan' (Verne, *Le Château des Carpathes*, p. 197), 'Hanrahan's Vision' (first published in *McClure's Magazine*, March 1905), Hanrahan the schoolteacher observes the Sidhe riding through the air with 'heart-shaped mirrors instead of hearts, and they were looking and ever looking on their own faces in one another's mirrors' – Yeats, W. B., *Mythologies* (London: Macmillan, 1959), p. 250.

47. Dumas, Olivier, 'La Correspondance Familiale de Jules Verne', Lettre 159 de Jules Verne a son pere, le 'lundi [novembre (?)] 1870', in *Jules Verne* (Lyons: La Manufacture, 1988), p. 454.

48. In a letter to his father, dated 15 July 1859, Verne accuses the Emperor of operating a divide-and-rule policy and of planning to provoke a war with England by fighting countries and then allying himself with them to provoke more divisions which will eventually isolate England (Dumas, 'La Correspondance Familiale de Jules Verne', p. 428).

49. 'échos occasionels du nationalisme profrançais, antianglais et antiallemand' (Chesneaux, *Une Lecture Politique de Jules Verne*, p. 130).

Short Chronology of Relevant Events

1809–10:   Napoleon takes over all Dalmation provinces except Montenegro.
1811:   Napoleon declares Illyrian Republic in Dalmatia.
1812:   Treaty of Bucharest. Peace between Turkey and Russia. Napoleon invades Russia.
1813:   Fall of Illyrian Republic: Russia and Austria in the region.
1814:   Napoleon's First Abdication. Austria invades Italy. Treaty of Paris. Serbian revolution and partial independence from Turks.
1815:   Battle of Waterloo. Napoleon abdicates. Treaty of Vienna. Bourbons return to France.
1821:   Ali Pasha of Thessalian provinces clashes with Constantinople. First Greek revolt.
1824:   Byron dies at Missolonghi.
1827:   Greek independence (excluding Thessaly, Macedonia and Crete).
1829:   Treaty of Adrianople. Russians become the new rulers of Moldova and Wallachia.
1830:   Second French revolution – Louis-Phillipe Orléans becomes new constitutional monarch.
1843:   Hungarian Diet establishes Hungarian as the main language.
1848:   Hungarian Uprising under Kossuth – Revolt in France and fall of Louis-Phillipe. Second Republic declared.
1849:   Hungarian uprising crushed by Russians. Emperor Franz-Josef assumes absolute power.
1851:   Louis-Napoleon Bonaparte becomes dictator after coup.
1852:   Louis-Napoleon becomes Emperor Napoleon III – Second Empire begins.
1854–56:   Crimean War.
1856:   Treaty of Paris.
1859:   Wallachia and Moldova freed from Russian rule under Colonel Cuza. Uprising in Italy under Garribaldi.
1860:   United Italian Republic born.
1866:   Wallachia and Moldova become a united kingdom, Rumania.
1867:   Austro–Hungarian Ausgleich. Hungary granted autonomy by Emperor Franz-Josef.
1870:   Franco–Prussian War. Napoleon III forced to flee. French third Republic born.
1875–78:   Russo–Turkish war.
1878:   Treaty of San Stefano (3 March) Treaty of Berlin (13 July).
1879:   Hungarian Diet introduces new policies of magyarisation of schools.
1880:   Disraeli voted out of power in Great Britain.
1882:   Signing of Dreikaiserbund between Austria, Russia and Germany.
1886:   Kidnapping of Alexander Battenburg of Bulgaria.

1890:   Bismarck forced out of power. Transylvanian Rumanians attempt to appeal against magyarisation.

1891:   Popovici sends appeal to Hungarian diet, but it is refused.

1892:   Gladstone returns to power in Great Britain.

1893:   Rumanian nationalist leaders in Transylvania tried for sedition.

1895:   Atrocities in Macedonia.

1897:   Greek armies in Crete defeated by Turks.

1903:   King and Queen of Serbia killed by their own guard.

1906:   Massacres of Armenians.

1908–09:   Young Turk revolt. Sultan Abdul Hamid II forced to become titular monarch. Bosnia crisis: Franz-Josef annexes Bosnia and Ferdinand declares himself King of Bulgaria.

Bibliography

Books

Alexandri, V. (trans.), *Ballades et Chants Populaire de la Roumanie (principautés Danubiennes)* receuilli et traduits par V Alexandri avec une introduction par M A Ubicini (Paris: E Dentu, 1855).

Apuleius, Lucius, *The Golden Ass*, trans. Robert Graves (London: Penguin, 1950).

Arata, Stephen D., 'The Occidental Tourist: *Dracula* and the Anxiety of Reverse Colonisation', *Victorian Studies*, 33 (1990), pp. 621–45.

Ariosto, Lodovico, *Roland Furieux: Poème Héroique*, trans. A-J du Pays, illustrator Gustave Dore (Paris: Hachette, 1879).

Autin, Jean, *Prosper Mérimée, écrivain, archéologue, homme politique* (Paris: Librairie Academique Perrin, 1983).

Baker, Michael, *Gladstone and Radicalism: The Reconstruction of Liberal Policy in Britain. 1885–94* (Brighton: The Harvester Press, 1975).

Bakhtin, M. M. *The Dialogic Imagination: Four Essays*, trans. Carl Emerson and Michael Holquist, ed. Michael Holquist (Austin TX: University of Texas Press, 1994).

Barbour, Judith, 'Dr John William Polidori, Author of the Vampire', *Imagining Romanticism: Essays on English and Australian Romanticism*, eds Peter Otto and Deirdre Coleman (West Cornwall, CT: Locust Hill Press, 1992), pp. 83–110.

Baring-Gould, Sabine, *The Book of Were-wolves* (London: Senate, 1995).

Baschet, Robert, *Mérimée: Du Romantisme au second Empire* (Paris: Nouvelles Editions Latine, 1958).

Belford, Barbara, *Bram Stoker* (London: Weidenfield and Nicholas, 1996).

Bércard, Cyprien [C.B.], *Lord Ruthwen, ou les Vampires*, publiée par l'Auteur de Jean Sbogar et de Thérèse Aubert (Paris: Chez Ladvocat, Librairie, 1820).

Bhalla, Alok, *Politics of Atrocity and Lust*, (New Delhi: Sterling, 1989).

Bourget, Paul, 'Cosmopolis', *Oeuvres Complètes*, 9 vols, (Paris: Librairie Plon, 1902), IV.

Burke, Edmund, *A Philosophical Enquiry into the Origin of Our Ideas of the Sublime and Beautiful*, ed. Adam Phillips (Oxford and New York: Oxford University Press, 1990).

Byron, Lord George, *Complete Poetical Works*, ed. Frederick Page, rev. John Jump (Oxford, New York and London: Oxford University Press, 1970).

——, 'A Fragment', in Shelley, Mary, *Frankenstein*, ed. Maurice Hindle (London: Penguin, 1991), pp. 227–32.

Calmet, Augustin, *Dissertation sur les Appareitions des Anges, des Démons et des Esprits. Et sur les Revenans et Vampires, De Hongrie, de Bohème, Moravie et de Silesie* (Paris: de Buré l'ainé, 1746).

——, *The Phantom World: Or, the Philosophy of Spirits, Apparitions etc*, ed. and trans. Rev Henry Christmas, 2 vols (London: Richard Bentley, 1850).

Chesneaux, Jean, *Une Lecture Politique de Jules Verne* (Paris: Francois Maspero, 1971).

Clayton, G. D., *Britain and the Eastern Question: Missolonghi to Galllipoli*, London History Studies, no. 8 (London: University of London Press, 1971).

Coleridge, Samuel Taylor, *Poetical Works*, ed. Ernest Hartley Coleridge (Oxford: Oxford University Press, 1909).

Colley, Linda, *Captives: Britian, Empire and the World 1600–1850* (London: Jonathan Cape, 2002).

Compère, Daniel, 'Paul Féval et les Vampires', *Paul Feval: Romancier Populaire: Colloque de Rennes, 1987*, eds Jean Rohou and Jacques Dugast (Rennes: Presses Universitaires de Rennes, 1987), pp. 59–66.

Copjec, Joan, 'Vampires, Breast-Feeding, and Anxiety', *October*, 58 (1991), pp. 25–43.

Cotrone, Renata, *Romanticismo Italiano: Prospettive Critiche e Percorsi Intelletualli di Breme Visconti Scalvini* (Manduria-Bari-Roma: Piero Laica Editore, 1996).

Coundouriotis, Eleni, '*Dracula* and the Idea of Europe', *Connotations*, 9:2 (Waxmann Munster, New York, 1999–2000), pp. 143–159.

Cunningham, Allan, 'Stratford Canning and the Treaty of Bucharest' in *Anglo–Ottoman Encounters in the Age of Revolution*, collected Essays, [Allan Cunningham] ed. Edward Ingram, 2 vols (London: Frank Cass, 1995) I, pp. 144–87.

de Gerando, Auguste, *Transylvanie et ses Inhabitants*, 2 vols (Paris: Au Comptoir des Imprimateurs-Unis, 1845).

Delon, Michel, 'Nodier et les Mythes Révolutionnaires', *Charles Nodier: le Parrain*, [Europe Revue Littéraire Mensuelle 58ème. No. 614–5] (Paris: Editions Français Réunis, Juin Juillet 1980), pp. 31–42.

de Man, Paul, *Allegories of Reading: Figural Language in Rousseau, Nietzsche, Rilke and Proust* (New Haven: Yale University Press, 1979).

de Reclus, Elisée, *Voyage aux Regions Minières de Transylvanie Occidentale – Le Tour du Monde xxviii*, (2 parts (Paris: Hachette, 1874).

Denton, William, *Montrenegro: Its People and Their History* (London: Dalby, Isbister and Co., 1877).

de Redcliffe, Viscount Stratford, *The Eastern Question: Being a Selection from His Writings Suring the Last Five Years of His Life*, preface by Arthur Penrhyn Stanley (London: John Murray, 1881).

de Stendhal, *De l'Amour*, ed. V. Del Litto (Paris: Gallimard Folio, 1980).

Dolar, Mladen, ' "I shall be with you on your Wedding Night": Lacan and the Uncanny', *October*, 58 (1991), pp. 5–23.

Dumas, Olivier, *Jules Verne* (Lyons: La Manufacture, 1988). Durham, Mary E., *Through the Lands of the Serb* (London: Edward Arnold, 1904).

Eagleton, Terry, *Heathcliff and the Great Hunger: Studies in Irish Culture* (London: Verso, 1995).

Eckhart, Ferenc, *A Short History of the Hungarian People* (London: Grant Richards, 1931).

Féval, Paul, *La Vampire* (Castelnau-le-Lez: Bibliothèque Ombres, 2004).

——, *Les Chevaliers Ténèbreux, suivi de la Ville Vampire* (Verviers: Bibliothèque Marabout, 1972).

Fortis, Abbé Alberto, *Viaggio in Dalmazia, dell' Abate Alberto Fortis*, 2 vols (Venezia: Presso Alvise Milocco, all Apolline, 1774).

Foster, Roy, *Paddy and Mr Punch: Connections in Irish and English History* (London: Allen Lane, 1993).

Freund, John C. (ed.), *The Dark Blue*, 4 Vols (1870–1873) (London: British and Colonial Publishing Co, 1872), II (March–August 1872).

Gaidoz, Henri, *Les Roumains de Hongrie: leur origine – leur histoire – leur état present*. Extrait de la revue de Paris 15 May 1894 (Paris: Imprimerie et librairie centrales des chemins de fer, 1894).

Gelder, Ken, *Reading the Vampire* (London and New York: 1994).

Gerard, Dorothea, *The Red-Hot Crown: A Semi-Historical Romance* (London: John Long, 1909).

Gerard, Emily, 'Transylvanian Superstitions', *The Nineteenth Century*, July (1885), pp. 130–50.

Gibbon, Edward, *The Decline and Fall of the Roman Empire*, 6 vols (London: Everyman, 1994).

Glover, David, *Vampires, Mummies and Liberals: Bram Stoker and the Politics of Popular Fiction* (Durham and London: Duke University Press, 1996).

Goethe, Johann Wolfgang von, *Goethe's Bride of Corinth*, trans. W.A.Cox (Cambridge, 1911).

Goldsworthy, Vesna, *Inventing Ruritania* (New Haven and London: Yale University Press, 1998).

Granville, Augusto Bozzi, *L' Italico, Ossia Giornale Politico, Letterario e Miscellaneo; da una Società d'Italiani*, 3 vols (Londra: Schulze e Dean, 1813–14).

Haining, Peter and Peter Tremayne, *The Un-Dead: The Legend of Bram Stoker and Dracula* (London: Constable, 1997).

Hall, Captain Basil, *Schloss Hainfeld; or, a Winter in Lower Styria* (Edinburgh: Robert, Cadell, 1836).

Haraszti, Endre, *The Ethnic History of Transylvania* (Astor Park, FL: Danubian Press, 1971).

Henderson, Major Percy E., *A British Officer in the Balkans: The Account of a Journey through Dalmatia, Montenegro, Turkey in Austria, Magyarland, Bosnia and Hercegovina* (London: Seeley and Co., 1909).

Henry-Rosier, Marguérite, *La Vie de Charles Nodier* (Paris: Librairie Gallimard, 1931).

Hope, Anthony, *Sophy of Kravonia* (Bristol: J. W. Arrowsmith; London: Simpkin, Marshall, Hamilton, Kent and Co. Ltd, 1906).

——, *The Prisoner of Zenda; Rupert of Hentzau*, ed. Gary Hoppenstand (London: Penguin, 2000).

Hughes, William, 'A Singular Invasion: Revisiting the Postcoloniality of Bram Stoker's *Dracula*', *Empire and the Gothic: The Politics of Genre*, eds Andrew Smith and William Hughes (Basinstoke: Palgrave Macmillan, 2003), pp. 88–102.

Iorga, Neculai, *Histoire des Relations entre La France et les Roumains* (Paris: Librairie Payot, 1918).

Jameson, Fredric, 'Third-world Literature in the Era of Multinational Capitalism' (1986), *The Jameson Reader* (Oxford: Blackwell, 2000), pp. 315–40.

Jelavich, Barbara, *Modern Austria: Empire and Republic, 1800–1986* (Cambridge: Cambridge University Press, 1987).

Johnson, Major E. C, *On the Track of the Crescent* (London: Hurst and Blacket, 1885).

Judd, Dennis, *Palmerston*, (London: Weidenfield and Nicholas, 1975).

Kant, Immanuel, *Critique of Judgement*, trans. James Creed Meredith (Oxford: Clarendon Press, 1952).

Kinglake, Alexander, *Eothen* (London: George Rutledge and Sons: 1905).

Keats, John, *Poemes et Poésies*, trans. Paul Gallimard (Paris: Mercure de France, 1910).

Kohl, J. G., *Austria. Vienna, Prague, Hungary, Bohemia, and the Danube; Galicia, Styria, Moravia, Bukovina and the Military Frontier* (London: Chapman and Hall, 1843).

Leask, Nigel, *British Romantic Writers and the East: Anxieties of Empire*, repr. (Cambridge: Cambridge University Press, 2004).

Leatherdale, Clive, *Dracula: The Novel and the Legend*, rev. edn (Brighton: Desert Island Books, 1988).

——, *The Origins of Dracula* (London: William Kimber, 1987).

Le Fanu, J. S., *In a Glass Darkly*, ed. Robert Tracy (Oxford: Oxford University Press, 1993).

——, *Uncle Silas*, ed. W.J. McCormack with the assistance of Andrew Swarbrick (Oxford: Oxford University Press, 1981).

Leger, Louis, *A History of Austro-Hungary from the Earliest Time to the Year 1889*, trans. from French by Mrs Birkbeck Hill (London: Rivingtons, 1889).

Lodge, David, *Modes of Modern Writing* (London: Edward Arnold, 1977).

Logio, George Clenton, *Rumania: Its History, Politics and Economics* (Manchester: Sherratt and Hughes, 1932).

Lukacs, George, *The Historical Novel*, trans. Hannah and Stanley Mitchell (London: Merlin Press, 1989).

MacCarthy, Fiona, *Byron: Life and Legend* (London: John Murray, 2002).

McCormack, W. J., *Sheridan Le Fanu and Victorian Ireland* (Oxford: Clarendon Press, 1980).

MacDonald, David Lorne, *Poor Polidori: A Critical Biography of the Author of 'The Vampyre'* (Toronto, Buffalo, London: University of Toronto Press, 1991).

McGann, Jerome, *Byron and Romanticism*, ed. James Soderholm (Cambridge: Cambridge University Press, 2002).

Maixner, Rudolph, *Charles Nodier et L'Illyrie* (Paris: Didier, 1960).

Makkai, Laszlo, 'Transylvania's Indigenous People at the Time of the Hungarian Conquest', *History of Transylvania, Vol 1: From the Beginnings to 1606*, ed. Laszlo Makkai and Andras Mocsy, Atlantic Studies on Society and Change, no. 106 (New York: Columbia University Press, 2001), pp. 333–522.

Mallet, Charles, *Anthony Hope and His Books: Being the Authorised Life of Sir Anthony Hope Hawkins* (London: Hutchinson and Co, 1935).

Marigny, Jean, *Vampires* (London and Paris: Gallimard, 1994).

Mason, Diane, *The Secret Vice: Masturbation in Victorian Fiction and Medical Culture* (Bath Spa University College: Unpublished Doctoral Thesis, 2003).

Mauner, Georges, *Manet: Peintre-Philosophe A study of the Painter's Themes* (University Park and London: Penn State University Press, 1975).

Mérimée, Prosper, *Correspondance Génerale*, établie et annotée par Maurice Parturier avec la Collaboration de Pierre Josserand et Jean Mallion, 6 vols (Paris: Le Divan, 1941).

——, *La Guzla: ou Choix de Poésies Illyriques Recueillies dans la Dalmatie, la Bosnie, la Croatie et l'Herzégowine*, introduction by Antonia Fonyi (Paris: Editions Kime, 1994).

Moore-Gilbert, Bart, *Postcolonial Theory: Contexts, Practices, Politics* (London and New York: Verso, 1997).

Moses, Michael, 'Dracula, Parnell and the Troubled Dreams of Nationhood', *Journal X: A Journal in Culture and Criticism*, 2:1 (Autumn 1997), pp. 67–111.

Murray, Paul, *From the Shadow of Dracula: a Life of Bram Stoker* (London: Jonathan Cape, 2004).

Nethercott, Arthur H., 'Coleridge's "Christabel" and Le Fanu's "Carmilla" ', *Modern Philology*, 147 (1949), pp. 32–8. Nichols, J. Alden, *Germany after Bismarck: The Caprivi Era (1890–1894)* (Cambridge MA: Harvard University Press, 1958).

Nicolson, Harold, *The Congress of Vienna: A Study in Allied Unity: 1812–1822*, repr. (London: Cassell, 1979).

Nodier, Charles, *Contes de la Veillée* (Paris: Charpentier,1831).

——, *Du Fantastique en Littérature* (Paris: Chimères-Barbe Bleue, 1989).

——, *Infernalia: ou Anecdotes, Petits Romans Nouvelles et Contes, sur les Révenants, les Spectres, les Démons et les Vampires*, preface by Hubert Juin (Paris: Pierre Belfond, 1966).

——, *Jean Sbogar*, ed. Jean Sgard et étudiants (Paris: LibrairieHonore Champion, 1987).

——, '*Statistique Illyrienne: Articles Complets du 'Télégraph Officiel' de l'Année 1813*, ed. France Dobrovjc (Ljubljana: Edition 'Satura', 1933).

——, [MM], *Le Vampire, Melodrame en Trois Actes, avec un Prologue* (Paris: J. N. Barba, Libraire, 1920).

——, *Oeuvres complètes*, 13 vols (Geneve: Slattine Reprints,1998).

——, *Souvenirs, Portraits, Episodes de la Révolution et de l'Empire*, ed. Nouvelle, 2 vols (Paris: Charpentier, 1865).

Pavlovic, Stevan K., *La France en Dalmatie: Naissance de l'Idée Illyrienne*, repr. from *Le College et le Monde* (London: Frederick Printing, 1950).

Pichot, Amédée, *Essai sur le genie et le caractère de Lord Byron*, précédé d'une notice préliminaire par M. Charles Nodier (Paris: Ladvocat, Librairie, Palais-Royal, 1824).

Pignotti, Lorenzo, *Storia della Toscana Sino al Principato con diversi Saggi sulle Scienze, Lettere e Arte*, 9 vols (Pisa: Co Caratteri di Didot, 1813).

Planche, J. R., *The Vampire, or the Bride of the Isles. A Romantic Melodrama in Two Acts*, preceded by an Introductory Vision (London: 1820).

Polidori, John, *The Diary of Dr John William Polidori (1816) Relating to Byron, Shelley etc.*, ed. William Rossetti (London: Elkin Mathews, 1911).

——, *The Vampyre*, 1st edn 1819, repr. (Oxford and New York: Woodstock Books, 1990).

——, *Ximenes, the Wreath and other Poems* (London: Longman, Hurst, Rees, Orme, and Brown, Paternoster-Row, 1819).

Pribram, Alfred Francis, *England and the International Policy of the European Great Powers, 1871–1914* (Oxford: Clarendon, 1931).

——, *Austria-Hungary and Great Britain, 1908–1914*, trans. Ian F.D. Morrow (London, New York and Toronto: Oxford University Press, 1951).

Punter, David, *The Literature of Terror* (London: Longman, 1981).

R.H.R., *Rambles in Istria, Dalmatia and Montenegro* (London: Hurst and Blackett, 1875).

Rogers, Bryan, *Charles Nodier et la Tentation de la Folie* (Geneva: Slatkine, 1985).

Rymer, J. M., *Varney, the Vampyre; or, the Feast of Blood* (London: E. Lloyd, 1845–47).

Sage, Victor, *Le Fanu's Gothic* (Basingstoke: Palgrave, 2003).

——, 'Exchanging Fantasies: Sex and the Serbian Crisis', *Bram Stoker: History, Psychoanalysis and the Gothic*, eds William Hughes and Andrew Smith (Basingstoke: Macmillan, 1998), pp. 116–33.

Said, Edward, *Orientalism*, rev. edn (London: Penguin, 1995).

Scott, Sir Walter, 'On the Supernatural in Fictitious Composition', *Essays on Chivalry, Romance, and the Drama* (London: Frederick Warne & Co., 1887).

Silvani, Giovanna, *Analisi di un Racconto Gotico: Camilla di J. S. Le Fanu*, Quaderni dell'instituto di Lingue e Letterature Germaniche no. 3, Universita degli studi di Parma (Roma: Bulzoni, 1984).

Skarda, Patricia L, 'Vampirism and Plagiarism: Byron's Influence and Polidori's Practice', *Studies in Romanticism* 28:2 (Summer 1969), pp. 249–69.

Souriau, Maurice, *Histoire du Romantisme en France, Vol II: La Decadence du Romantisme* (Paris: Editions Spes, 1927).

Southey, Robert, *Thalaba the Destroyer*, 2 vols (London: T. N. Longman and O. Rees, 1801).

Spencer, Terence, *Fair Greece, Sad Relic*, 2nd edn (Bath: Cedric Chivers, 1974).

Stepniak, Sergei, *Russia under the Tsars*, trans. William Westall, 2 vols (London: Ward and Downey, 1885).

Stewart, Bruce, 'Bram Stoker's *Dracula*: Possessed by the Spirit of the Nation?', *Irish University Review*, 29:2 (1999), pp. 238–55.

Stoker, Bram, *Miss Betty* (London: Constable & Co., 1898).

——, *Dracula*, ed. Maud Ellmann (Oxford: Oxford University Press, 1996).

——, *The Essential Dracula: The Definitive Annotated Edition of Bram Stoker's Classic Novel*, ed. Leonard Wolf (New York, London, Victoria and Toronto: Plume, 1993).

——, *The Lady of the Shroud*, ed. William Hughes (Westcliffe-on-Sea: Desert Island Books, 2001).

Stoker, George, *With 'the Unspeakables'; or, Two Years Campaigning in European and Asiatic Turkey* (London: Chapman and Hall, 1878).

Szabad, Emeric, *Hungary: Past and Present: Embracing its History from the Magyar Conquest to the Present Time* (Edinburgh: Adam and Charles Black, 1854).

Thayer, W. R., *The Dawn of Italian Independence*, 2 vols (Boston and New York: Houghton, Mifflin and Co., 1893).

Todorov, Tzvetan, *Introduction à la Littérature Fantastique* (Paris: Editions du Seuil, 1970).

Todorova, Maria, *Imagining the Balkans* (Oxford and New York: Oxford University Press).

Twitchell, James, *The Living Dead: A Study of the vampire in Romantic Literature* (Durham, NC: Duke University Press, 1981).

Urquhart, David, *The Spirit of the East: A Journal of Travels through Roumali*, 2 vols (London: H. Colburn, 1838).

Verne, Jules, *Le Château des Carpathes* (Paris: Bibliotheque d'Education et de Recreation, 1892).

Vierne, Simone, *Jules Verne: Une Vie, une Oeuvre, une Epoque* (Paris: Editions Balland, 1986).

Waterfield, Gordon, *Layard of Nineveh* (London: John Murray, 1963).

Watson, Robert Seton, *Disraeli, Gladstone and the Eastern Question* (London: Macmillan, 1935).

Wilkinson, William, *An Account of the Principalities of Wallachia and Moldavia: with Various Political Observations Relating to Them* (London: Hurst, 1820).

Wolff, Larry, *Venice and the Slavs: The Discovery of Dalmatia in the Age of Enlightenment* (Stanford, CA: Stanford University Press, 2001).

Woods, H. Charles, *The Danger Zone of Europe: Changes and Problems in the Near East* (London and Leipsic: T. Fisher Unwin, 1911).

Woolf, Stuart, *A History of Italy, 1700–1860* (London: Routledge 1979).

Wyon, Reginald and Gerald Prance, *Through the Land of the Black Mountain: The Adventures of Two Englishmen in Montenegro* (London: Methuen, 1903).

Yeats, W. B., *Mythologies* (London: Macmillan, 1959).

Yovanovitch, Voyslav M., *'La Guzla' de Prosper Mérimee: Etude d'Histoire Romantique* (Genève: Slatkine Reprints, 1973 [1910]).

Zanger, Jules, ' A Sympathetic Vibration: Dracula and the Jews, *'English Literature in Transition 1880–1920*, 34 (1991), pp. 33–44.

Newspapers and magazines (primary sources)

The Dublin Evening Mail

'News of this Day', 12, 14, 17 and 24 January 1867;
'Austria and Hungary', 29 January 1867;
'Baron Beust and Austria', 11 February 1867;
'News of this Day', 12 February 1867;
'Hungary', 14 February 1867;
'Hungary', 21 February 1867;
'Levy of Troops in Austria', 5 March 1867;
'Irish Rebellion', 8 March 1867.

The Evening Star

'Comment', 8 October 1908;
'Serb War Cry', 9 October 1908;
'Comment', 9 October 1908;
'A Dubious Peace', 27 March 1909;
'The Iron Throne', 27 March 1909.

Free Russia

Dragomanev, M. P., 'Russian Policy, Home and Foreign', June 1892, pp. 10–12.

The Illustrated London News

'The Man who Destroyed the Berlin Treaty', 10 October 1908, p. 491;
G. K. Chesterton's Column, 'Aerenthal', 3 April 1908, p. 472;
'The Sly Rulers: The Men who tricked Europe', 17 October 1908, suppl., p. 3.

Le Figaro

'A l'Etranger', 28 August 1890;
'A'Etranger: Querrelles Réligieuses', 11 September 1890.

The Near East

'Francis Joseph', November 1908, pp. 309–10;
'The Servian Cause', December 1908, pp. 304–5;
'The Provocation of Servia', March 1909, pp. 3–4.

The Times

'Foreign News', 6 June 1892, p. 5;
'Foreign News', 14 June 1892, p. 6;
'Lord Rosebury's Speech', 21 June 1892, p. 7;
'Great Britain and Bulgarian Independence', 25 February 1908.

Unpublished correspondence

Anthony Hope Hawkins to Bram Stoker on 13 June 1897, 27 January 1898 and 28 May 1901 (University of Leeds Library, Brotherton Collection).
J. S. Le Fanu to the Marquess of Dufferin on 21 January 1868 and 7 December 1868 (Public Record Office of Northern Ireland).
John Polidori's to Lord Byron on 11 January 1817 (John Murray Archive, 50 Albemarle Street, London).
John Polidori to Gaetano Polidori on December 1813 (University of British Columbia Library, Rare Books and Special Collections [Angeli-Dennis collection, box 31, folder 5]).
Sergei (Sergius) Stepniak, to Bram Stoker on 2 August 1892 and 12 June 1894 (University of Leeds Library, Brotherton Collection).
Jules Verne to Pierre-Hetzel fils on 4 March 1892; cited in Vierne, Simone, *Jules Verne: Une Vie, une Oeuvre, une Eopque* (Paris: Editions Balland, 1986), p. 342.

Index